"TALE'SEDRIN IS A DEAD CLAN...."

"*I* still live! And while I live, Tale'sedrin lives!"

"A Clan is more than a single individual. It is a living, growing thing," the Elder replied. "You are Sword-sworn, Tarma; you are barren seed by vow and by the Warrior's touch. How can Tele'sedrin be alive in you, when you cannot give it life? The Children of the Hawk are no more—you are vowed to the Shin'a'in, not to any single Clan. Let the banner be buried with the rest of the dead."

"No! Sooner than that I would die with them! Tale'sedrin *lives*!"

"It lives in *me*—" Kethry stepped between Tarma and the Council. "I am *she'enedra*, oathbound to the Sworn One. I have taken no vows of celibacy. Through *me* Tale'sedrin is a living, growing thing!"

"How do we know the bond is a true one? Tarma, she is a sorceress. She could have tricked even you."

"Kethry has saved my life. How *dare* you doubt my word. She is my true *she'endra* by a Goddess-blessed vow—and you will retract your damned lie or die on my blade!"

NOVELS BY MERCEDES LACKEY

Available from DAW Books:

THE HERALDS OF VALDEMAR
  ARROWS OF THE QUEEN
  ARROW'S FLIGHT
  ARROW'S FALL

VOWS AND HONOR
  THE OATHBOUND
  OATHBREAKERS (coming in winter 1989)

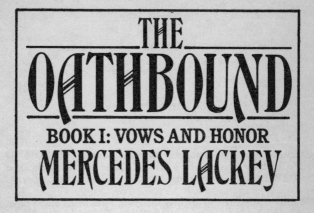

THE OATHBOUND

BOOK I: VOWS AND HONOR
MERCEDES LACKEY

DAW BOOKS, INC.
DONALD A. WOLLHEIM, PUBLISHER

1633 Broadway, New York, NY 10019

Chapter 6 appeared in slightly different form in SWORD AND
SORCERESS V, edited by Marion Zimmer Bradley, published
by DAW Books, Inc., Copyright © 1988 by Mercedes Lackey.

Chapter 8 appeared in slightly different form as an audio tape,
published by Off Centaur Publications, Copyright © 1985 by
Mercedes Lackey.

DAW Book Collectors No. 750.

First Printing, July 1988

1 2 3 4 5 6 7 8 9

PRINTED IN THE U.S.A.

Dedicated to
Lisa Waters
for wanting to see it
and my parents
for agreeing with her

Introduction

This is the tale of an unlikely partnership, that of the Shin'a'in swordswoman and celibate Kal'enedral, Tarma shena Tale'sedrin and the nobly-born sorceress Kethry, member of the White Winds school, whose devotees were sworn to wander the world using their talents for the greatest good. How these two met is told in the tale "Sword Sworn," published in Marion Zimmer Bradley's anthology SWORD AND SORCERESS III. A second of the accounts of their wandering life will be seen in the fourth volume of that series. But *this* story begins where that first tale left off, when they have recovered from their ordeal and are making their way back to the Dhorisha Plains and Tarma's home.

"I'd rather die to see them or if you've never

One

The sky was overcast, a solid gray sheet that seemed to hang just barely above the treetops, with no sign of a break in the clouds anywhere. The sun was no more than a dimly glowing spot near the western horizon, framed by a lattice of bare black branches. Snow lay at least half a foot thick everywhere in the forest, muffling sound. A bird flying high on the winter wind took dim notice that the forest below him extended nearly as far as he could see no matter which way he looked, but was neatly bisected by the Trade Road immediately below him. Had he flown a little higher (for the clouds were not as low as they looked), he might have seen the rooftops and smokes of a city at the southern end of the road, hard against the forest. Although the Trade Road had seen enough travelers of late that the snow covering it was packed hard, there were only two on it now. They had stopped in the clearing halfway through the forest that normally saw heavy use as an overnighting point. One was setting up camp under the shelter of a half-cave of rock and tree trunks piled together—partially the work of man, partially of nature. The other was a short distance away, in a growth-free pocket just off the main area, picketing their beasts.

The bird circled for a moment, swooping lower, eyeing the pair with dim speculation. Humans sometimes meant food—

But there was no food in sight, at least not that the bird recognized as such. And as he came lower still, the one with the beasts looked up at him

9

suddenly, and reached for something slung at her saddlebow.

The bird had been the target of arrows often enough to recognize a bow when he saw one. With a squawk of dismay, he veered off, flapping his wings with all his might, and tracing a twisty, convoluted course out of range. *He* wanted to be the eater, not the eaten!

Tarma sighed as the bird sped out of range, unstrung her bow, and stowed it back in the saddlequiver. She hunched her shoulder a little beneath her heavy wool coat to keep her sword from shifting on her back, and went back to her task of scraping the snow away from the grass buried beneath it with gloved hands. Somewhere off in the far distance she could hear a pair of ravens calling to each other, but otherwise the only sounds were the sough of wind in branches and the blowing of her horse and Kethry's mule. The Shin'a'in place of eternal punishment was purported to be cold; now she had an idea *why*.

She tried to ignore the ice-edged wind that seemed to cut right through the worn places in her nondescript brown clothing. This was no place for a Shin'a'in of the Plains, this frozen northern forest. She had no business being here. Her garments, more than adequate to the milder winters in the south, were just not up to the rigors of the cold season here.

Her eyes stung, and not from the icy wind. Home—Warrior Dark, she wanted to be home! Home, away from these alien forests with their unfriendly weather, away from outClansmen with no understanding and no manners . . . home. . . .

Her little mare whickered at her, and strained against her lead rope, her breath steaming and her muzzle edged with frost. *She* was no fonder of this chilled wilderness than Tarma was. Even the Shin'a'in winter pastures never got this cold, and what little snow fell on them was soon melted. The mare's sense of what was "right" was deeply offended by all this frigid white stuff.

"*Kathal, dester'edra,*" Tarma said to the ears that pricked forward at the first sound of her harsh voice. "Gently, windborn-sister. I'm nearly finished here."

Kessira snorted back at her, and Tarma's usually solemn expression lightened with an affectionate smile.

"*Li'ha'eer,* it is ice-demons that dwell in this place, and nothing else."

When she figured that she had enough of the grass cleared off to at least help to satisfy her mare's hunger, she heaped the rest of her foragings into the center of the area, topping the heap with a carefully measured portion of mixed grains and a little salt. What she'd managed to find was poor enough, and not at all what her training would have preferred—some dead seed grasses with the heads still on them, the tender tips from the branches of those trees and bushes she recognized as being nourishing, even some dormant cress and cattail roots from the stream. It was scarcely enough to keep the mare from starving, and not anywhere near enough to provide her with the energy she needed to carry Tarma on at the pace she and her partner Kethry had been making up until now.

She loosed little Kessira from her tethering and picketed her in the middle of the space she'd cleared. It showed the measure of the mare's hunger that she tore eagerly into the fodder, poor as it was. There had been a time when Kessira would have turned up her nose in disdain at being offered such inferior provender.

"Ai, we've come on strange times, haven't we, you and I," Tarma sighed. She tucked a stray lock of crow-wing-black hair back under her hood, and put her right arm over Kessira's shoulder, resting against the warm bulk of her. "Me with no Clan but one weirdling outlander, you so far from the Plains and your sibs."

11

Not that long ago they'd been just as any other youngling of the nomadic Shin'a'in and her saddle mare; Tarma learning the mastery of sword, song, and steed, Kessira running free except when the lessoning involved her. Both of them had been safe and contented in the heart of Clan Tale'sedrin—true, free Children of the Hawk.

Tarma rubbed her cheek against Kessira's furry shoulder, breathing in the familiar smell of clean horse that was so much a part of what had been home. Oh, but they'd been happy; Tarma had been the pet of the Clan, with her flute-clear voice and her perfect memory for song and tale, and Kessira had been so well-matched for her rider that she almost seemed the "four-footed sister" that Tarma frequently named her. Their lives had been so close to perfect—in all ways. The king-stallion of the herd had begun courting Kessira that spring, and Tarma had had Dharin; nothing could have spoiled what seemed to be their secure future.

Then the raiders had come upon the Clan; and all that carefree life was gone in an instant beneath their swords.

Tarma's eyes stung again. Even full revenge couldn't take away the ache of losing them, all, all—

In one candlemark all that Tarma had ever known or cared about had been wiped from the face of the earth.

"What price your blood, my people? A few pounds of silver? Goddess, the dishonor that your people were counted so *cheaply*!"

The slaughter of Tale'sedrin had been the more vicious because they'd taken the entire Clan unawares and unarmed in the midst of celebration; totally unarmed, as Shin'a'in seldom were. They had trusted to the vigilance of their sentries.

But the cleverest sentry cannot defeat foul magic that creeps upon him out of the dark and smothers the breath in his throat ere he can cry out.

The brigands had not so much as a drop of honor-

12

able blood among them; they knew had the Clan been alerted they'd have had stood the robbers off, even outnumbered as they were, so the bandit's hired mage had cloaked their approach and stifled the guards. And so the Clan had fought an unequal battle, and so they had died; adults, oldsters, children, all. . . .

"Goddess, hold them—" she whispered, as she did at least once each day. Every last member of Tale'sedrin had died; most had died horribly. Except Tarma. She *should* have died; and unaccountably been left alive.

If you could call it living to have survived with everything gone that had made life worth having. Yes, she had been left alive—and utterly, utterly alone. Left to live with a ruined voice that had once been the pride of the Clans, with a ravaged body, and most of all, a shattered heart and mind. There had been nothing left to sustain her but a driving will to wreak vengeance on those who had left her Clanless.

She pulled a brush from an inside pocket of her coat, and began needlessly grooming Kessira while the mare ate. The firm strokes across the familiar chestnut coat were soothing to both of them. She had been left Clanless, and a Shin'a'in Clanless is one without purpose in living. Clan is everything to a Shin'a'in. Only one thing kept her from seeking oblivion and death-willing herself, that burning need to revenge her people.

But vengeance and blood-feud were denied the Shin'a'in—the ordinary Shin'a'in. Else too many of the people would have gone down on the knives of their own folk, and to little purpose, for the Goddess knew Her people and knew their tempers to be short. Hence, Her law. Only those who were the Kal'enedral of the Warrior—the Sword Sworn, outClansmen called them, although the name *meant* both "Children of Her Sword" and "Her Sword-Brothers"—could cry blood-feud and take the trail of vengeance. That was because of the nature of

13

their Oath to Her—*first* to the service of the Goddess of the New Moon and South Wind, *then* to the Clans as a whole, and only after those two to their own particular Clan. Blood-feud did not serve the Clans if the feud was between Shin'a'in and Shin'a'in; keeping the privilege of calling for blood-price in the hands of those by their very nature devoted to the welfare of the Shin'a'in as a whole kept interClan strife to a minimum.

"If it had been you, what would you have chosen, hmm?" she asked the mare. "Her Oath isn't a light one." Nor was it without cost—a cost some might think far too high. Once Sworn, the Kal'enedral became weapons in Her hand, and not unlike the sexless, cold steel they wore. Hard, somewhat aloof, and totally asexual were the Sword Sworn—and this, too, ensured that their interests remained Hers and kept them from becoming involved in interClan rivalry. So it was not the kind of Oath one involved in a simple feud was likely to even consider taking.

But the slaughter of the Tale'sedrin was not a matter of private feud or Clan against Clan—this was a matter of more, even, than personal vengeance. Had the brigands been allowed to escape unpunished, would that not have told other wolf-heads that the Clans were not invulnerable—would there not have been another repetition of the slaughter? That may have been Her reasoning; Tarma had only known that she was able to find no other purpose in living, so she had offered her Oath to the Star-Eyed so that she could pledge her life to revenge her Clan. An insane plan—sprung out of a mind that might be going mad with grief.

There were those who thought she was *already* mad, who were certain She would accept no such Oath given by one whose reason was gone. But much to the amazement of nearly everyone in the Clan Liha'irden who had succored, healed, and protected her, that Oath had been accepted. Only the shamans had been unsurprised.

She had never in her wildest dreaming guessed

14

what would come of that Oath and that quest for justice.

Kessira finished the pile of provender, and moved on to tear hungrily at the lank, sere grasses. Beneath the thick coat of winter hair she had grown, her bones were beginning to show in a way that Tarma did not in the least like. She left off brushing, and stroked the warm shoulder, and the mare abandoned her feeding long enough to nuzzle her rider's arm affectionately.

"Patient one, we shall do better by you, and soon," Tarma pledged her. She left the mare to her grazing and went to check on Kethry's mule. That sturdy beast was capable of getting nourishment from much coarser material than Kessira, so Tarma had left him tethered amid a thicket of sweetbark bushes. He had stripped all within reach of last year's growth, and was straining against his halter with his tongue stretched out as far as it would reach for a tasty morsel just out of his range.

"Greedy pig," she said with a chuckle, and moved him again, giving him a bit more rope this time, and leaving his own share of grain and foraged weeds within reach. Like all his kind he was a clever beast; smarter than any horse save one Shin'a'in-bred. It was safe enough to give him plenty of lead; if he tangled himself he'd untangle himself just as readily. Nor would he eat to foundering, not that there was enough browse here to do that. A good, sturdy, gentle animal, and even-tempered, well suited to an inexperienced rider like Kethry. She'd been lucky to find him.

His tearing at the branches shook snow down on her; with a shiver she brushed it off as her thoughts turned back to the past. No, she would never have guessed at the changes wrought in her life-path by that Oath and her vow of vengeance.

"*Jel'enedra,* you think too much. It makes you melancholy."

She recognized the faintly hollow-sounding tenor at the first word; it was her chief sword-teacher.

15

This was the first time he'd come to her since the last bandit had fallen beneath her sword. She had begun to wonder if her teachers would ever come back again.

All of them were unforgiving of mistakes, and quick to chastise—this one more than all the rest put together. So though he had startled her, though she had hardly expected his appearance, she took care not to display it.

"Ah?" she replied, turning slowly to face him. Unfair that he had used his other-worldly powers to come on her unawares, but he himself would have been the first to tell her that life—as she well knew—was unfair. She would not reveal that she had not detected his presence until he spoke.

He had called her "younger sister," though, which was an indication that he was pleased with her for some reason. "Mostly you tell me I don't think enough."

Standing in a clear spot amid the bushes was a man, garbed in fighter's gear of deepest black, and veiled. The ice-blue eyes, the sable hair, and the cut of his close-wrapped clothing would have told most folk that he was, like Tarma, Shin'a'in. The color of the clothing would have told the more knowledgeable—since most Shin'a'in preferred a carnival brightness in their garments—that he, too, was Sword Sworn; Sword Sworn by custom wore only stark black or dark brown. But only one very sharp-eyed would have noticed that while he stood amid the snow, he made no imprint upon it. It seemed that he weighed hardly more than a shadow.

That was scarcely surprising since he had died long before Tarma was born.

"Thinking to plan is one case; thinking to brood is another," he replied. "You accomplish nothing but to increase your sadness. You should be devising a means of filling your bellies and those of your *jel'suthro'edrin.* You cannot reach the Plains if you do not eat."

He had used the Shin'a'in term for riding beasts

16

that meant "forever-younger-Clanschildren." Tarma was dead certain he had picked that term with utmost precision, to impress upon her that the welfare of Kessira and Kethry's mule Rodi were as important as her own—more so, since they could not fend for themselves in this inhospitable place.

"With all respect, teacher, I am ... at a loss. Once I had a purpose. Now?" She shook her head. "Now I am certain of nothing. As you once told me—"

"*Li'sa'eer!* Turn my own words against me, will you?" he chided gently. "And have you *nothing?*"

"My *she'enedra.* But she is outClan, and strange to me, for all that the Goddess blessed our oath-binding with Her own fire. I know her but little. I—only—"

"What, bright blade?"

"I wish—I wish to go home—" The longing she felt rose in her throat and made it hard to speak.

"And so? What is there to hinder you?"

"There is," she replied, willing her eyes to stop stinging, "the matter of money. Ours is nearly gone. It is a long way to the Plains."

"So? Are you not now of the mercenary calling?"

"Well, unless there be some need for blades hereabouts—the which I have seen *no* evidence for, the only way to reprovision ourselves will be if my *she'enedra* can turn her skill in magic to an honorable profit. For though I have masters of the best," she bowed her head in the little nod of homage a Shin'a'in gave to a respected elder, "sent by the Star-Eyed herself, what measure of attainment I have acquired matters not if there is no market for it."

"*Hai'she'li!* You should market that silver tongue, *jel'enedra!*" he laughed. "Well, and well. Three things I have come to tell you, which is why I arrive out-of-time and not at moonrise. First, that there will be storm tonight, and you should all shelter, mounts and riders together. Second, that because of the storm, we shall not teach you *this* night, though

17

you may expect our coming from this day on, every night that you are not within walls."

He turned as if to leave, and she called out, "And third?"

"Third?" he replied, looking back at her over his shoulder. "Third—is that everyone has a past. Ere you brood over your own, consider another's."

Before she had a chance to respond, he vanished, melting into the wind.

Wrinkling her nose over that last, cryptic remark, she went to find her *she'enedra* and partner.

Kethry was hovering over a tiny, nearly smokeless fire, skinning a pair of rabbits. Tarma almost smiled at the frown of concentration she wore; she was going at the task as if she were being rated on the results! They were a study in contrasts, she and her outClan blood-sister. Kethry was sweet-faced and curvaceous, with masses of curling amber hair and startling green eyes; she would have looked far more at home in someone's court circle as a pampered palace mage than she did here, at their primitive hearth. Or even more to the point, she would not have looked *out* of place as someone's spoiled, indulged wife or concubine; she really looked nothing at all like any mage Tarma had ever seen. Tarma, on the other hand, with her hawklike face, forbidding ice-blue eyes and nearly sexless body, was hardly the sort of person one would expect a mage *or* woman like Kethry to choose as a partner, much less as a friend. As a hireling, perhaps—in which case it should have been *Tarma* skinning the rabbits, for *she* looked to have been specifically designed to endure hardship.

Oddly enough, it was Kethry who had taken to this trip as if she were the born nomad, and Tarma who was the one suffering the most from their circumstances, although that was mainly due to the unfamiliar weather.

Well, if she had not foreseen that becoming Kal'enedral meant suddenly acquiring a bevy of long-dead instructors, this partnership had come as

18

even more of a surprise. The more so as Tarma had really not expected to survive the initial confrontation with those who had destroyed her Clan.

"Do not reject aid unlooked-for," her instructor had said the night before she set foot in the bandit's town. And unlooked-for aid had materialized, in the form of this unlikely sorceress. Kethry, too, had her interests in seeing the murderers brought low, so they had teamed together for the purpose of doing just that. Together they had accomplished what neither could have done alone—they had utterly destroyed the brigands to the last man.

And so Tarma had lost her purpose. Now—now there was only the driving need to get back to the Plains; to return before the Tale'sedrin were deemed a dead Clan. Farther than that she could not, would not think or plan.

Kethry must have sensed Tarma's brooding eyes on her, for she looked up and beckoned with her skinning knife.

"Fairly good hunting," Tarma hunched as close the fire as she could, wishing they dared build something larger.

"Yes and no. I had to use magic to attract them, poor things." Kethry shook her head regretfully as she bundled the offal in the skins and buried the remains in the snow to freeze hard. Once frozen, she'd dispose of them away from the camp, to avoid attracting scavengers. "I felt so guilty, but what else was I to do? We ate the last of the bread yesterday, and I didn't want to chance on the hunting luck of just one of us."

"You do what you have to, Keth. Well, *we're* able to live off the land, but Kessira and Rodi can't," Tarma replied. "Our grain is almost gone, and we've still a long way to go to get to the Plains. Keth, we need money."

"I know."

"And you're the one of us best suited to earning it. This land is too peaceful for the likes of me to find a job—except for something involving at least

19

a one-year contract, and that's something we can't afford to take the time for. I need to get back to the Plains as soon as I can if I'm to raise Tale'sedrin's banner again."

"I know that, too." Kethry's eyes had become shadowed, the lines around her mouth showed strain. "And I know that the only city close enough to serve us is Mornedealth."

And there was no doubt in Tarma's mind that Kethry would rather have died than set foot in that city, though she hadn't the vaguest notion why. Well, this didn't look to be the proper moment to ask—

"Storm coming; a bad one," she said, changing the subject. "I'll let the hooved ones forage for as long as I dare, but by sunset I'll have to bring them into camp. Our best bet is going to be to shelter all together because I don't think a fire is going to survive the blow."

"I wish I knew where you get your information," Kethry replied, frown smoothing into a wry half-smile. "You certainly have *me* beat at weather-witching."

"Call it Shin'a'in intuition," Tarma shrugged, wishing she knew whether it was permitted to an outland *she'enedra*—who was a magician to boot—to know of the veiled ones. Would they object? Tarma had no notion, and wasn't prepared to risk it. "Think you can get our dinner cooked before the storm gets here?"

"I may be able to do better than that, if I can remember the spells." The mage disjointed the rabbits, and spitted the carcasses on twigs over the fire. She stripped off her leather gloves, flexed her bare fingers, then held her hands over the tiny fire and began whispering under her breath. Her eyes were half-slitted with concentration and there was a faint line between her eyebrows. As Tarma watched, fascinated, the fire and their dinner were enclosed in a transparent shell of glowing gold mist.

"Very pretty; what's it good for?" Tarma asked when she took her hands away.

"Well, for one thing, I've cut off the wind; for another, the shield is concentrating the heat and the meat will cook faster now."

"And what's it costing you?" Tarma had been in Kethry's company long enough now to know that magic always had a price. And in Kethry's case, that price was usually taken out of the resources of the spell-caster.

Kethry smiled at her accusing tone. "Nowhere near so much as you might think; this clearing has been used for overnighting a great deal, and a good many of those camping here have celebrated in one way or another. There's lots of residual energy here, energy only another mage could tap. Mages don't take the Trade Road often, they take the Courier's Road when they have to travel at all."

"So?"

"So there's more than enough energy here not only to cook dinner but to give us a little more protection from the weather than our bit of canvas."

Tarma nodded, momentarily satisfied that her blood-sister wasn't exhausting herself just so they could eat a little sooner. "Well, while I was scrounging for the hooved ones, I found a bit for us, too—"

She began pulling cattail roots, mallow-pith, a few nuts, and other edibles from the outer pockets of her coat. "Not a lot there, but enough to supplement dinner, and make a bit of breakfast besides."

"Bless you! These bunnies were a bit young and small, and rather on the lean side—should this stuff be cooked?"

"They're better raw, actually."

"Good enough; want to help with the shelter, since we're expecting a blow?"

"Only if you tell me what to do. I've got no notion of what these winter storms of yours are like."

Kethry had already stretched their canvas tent across the top and open side of the enclosure of

21

rocks and logs, stuffed brush and moss into the chinks on the inside, packed snow into the chinks from the outside, and layered the floor with pine boughs to keep their own bodies off the snow. Tarma helped her lash the canvas down tighter, then weighted all the loose edges with packed-down snow and what rocks they could find.

As they worked, the promised storm began to give warning of its approach. The wind picked up noticeably, and the northern horizon began to darken. Tarma cast a wary eye at the darkening clouds. "I hope you're done cooking because it doesn't look like we have too much time left to get under cover."

"I think it's cooked through."

"And if not, it won't be the first time we've eaten raw meat on this trip. I'd better get the grazers."

Tarma got the beasts one at a time; first the mule, then her mare. She backed them right inside the shelter, coaxing them to lie down inside, one on either side of it, with their heads to the door-flap just in case something should panic them. With the two humans in the space in the middle, they should all stay as close to warm as was possible. Once again she breathed a little prayer of thankfulness for the quality of mule she'd been able to find for Kethry; with a balky beast or anything other than another Shin'a'in-bred horse this arrangement would have been impossible.

Kethry followed, grilled rabbit bundled into a piece of leather. The rich odor made Tarma's mouth water and reminded her that she hadn't eaten since this morning. While Kethry wormed her way in past her partner, Tarma lashed the door closed.

"Hold this, and find a comfortable spot," the mage told her. While Tarma snuggled up against Kessira's shoulder, Kethry knelt in the space remaining. She held her hands just at chin height, palms facing outward, her eyes completely closed and her face utterly vacant. By this Tarma knew she was attempting a much more difficult bit of magery than she had with their dinner.

She began an odd, singsong chant, swaying a little in time to it. Tarma began to see a thin streak of weak yellow light, like a watered-down sunbeam, dancing before her. In fact, that was what she probably would have taken it for—except that the sun was nearly down, not overhead.

As Kethry chanted, the light-beam increased in strength and brightness. Then, at a sharp word from her, it split into six. The six beams remained where the one had been for a moment, perhaps a little longer. Kethry began chanting again, a different rhythm this time, and the six beams leapt to the walls of their shelter, taking up positions spaced equally apart.

When they moved so suddenly, Tarma had nearly jumped out of her skin—especially since one of them had actually passed *through* her. But when she could feel no strangeness—and certainly no harm from the encounter—she relaxed again. The animals appeared to be ignoring the things, whatever they were.

Now little tendrils of light were spinning out from each of the beams, reaching out until they met in a kind of latticework. When this had spread to the canvas overhead, Tarma began to notice that the wind, which had been howling and tugging at the canvas, had been cut off, and that the shelter was noticeably warmer as a result.

Kethry sagged then, and allowed herself to half-collapse against Rodi's bulk.

"Took less than I might think, hmm?"

"Any more comments like that and I'll make *you* stay outside."

"First you'd have to fight Kessira. Have some dinner." Tarma passed her half the rabbit; it was still warm and amazingly juicy and both of them wolfed down their portions with good appetite, nibbling the bones clean, then cracking them and sucking out the last bit of marrow. With the bones licked bare, they finished with the roots of Tarma's

23

gleaning, though more than half of Tarma's share went surreptitiously to Kessira.

When they had finished, the sun was gone and the storm building to full force. Tarma peeked out the curtain of tent-canvas at the front of the shelter; the fire was already smothered. Tarma noticed then that the light-web gave off a faint illumination; not enough to read by, but enough to see by.

"What is—all this?" she asked, waving a hand at the light-lattice. "Where'd it come from?"

"It's a variation of the fire-shield I raised; it's magical energy manifesting itself in a physical fashion. Part of that energy came from me, part of it was here already and I just reshaped it. In essence, I told it I thought it was a wall, and it believed me. So now we have a 'wall' between us and the storm."

"Uh, right. You told that glowing thing you thought it was a wall, and it believed you—"

Kethry managed a tired giggle at her partner's expression. "That's why the most important tool a magician has is his will; it has to be strong in order to convince energy to be something else."

"Is that how you sorcerers work?"

"All sorcerers, or White Winds sorcerers?"

"There's more than one kind?"

"Where'd you think magicians came from anyway? Left in the reeds for their patrons to find?" Kethry giggled again.

"No, but the only 'magicians' the Clans have are the shamans, and they don't do magic, much. Healing, acting as advisors, keepers of outClan knowledge—that's mostly what they do. When we need magic, we ask Her for it."

"And She answers?" Kethry's eyes widened in fascination.

"Unless She has a damn good reason not to. She's very close to us—closer than most deities are to their people, from what I've been able to judge. But that may be because we don't ask Her for much, or very often. There's a story—" TaHrma half smiled. "—there was a hunter who'd been very lucky and

24

had come to depend on that luck. When his luck left him, his skills had gotten very rusty, and he couldn't manage to make a kill. Finally he went to the shaman, and asked him if he thought She would listen to a plea for help. The shaman looked him up and down, and finally said, 'You're not dead yet.' "

"Which means he hadn't been trying hard enough by himself?"

"Exactly. She is the very last resort—and you had damned well better be careful what you ask Her for—She'll give it to you, but in Her own way, especially if you haven't been honest with Her or with yourself. So mostly we don't ask." Tarma warmed to Kethry's interest, and continued when that interest didn't flag. This was the first chance she'd had to explain her beliefs to Kethry; before this, Kethry had either been otherwise occupied or there hadn't been enough privacy. "The easiest of Her faces to deal with are the Maiden and the Mother, they're gentler, more forgiving; the hardest are the Warrior and the Crone. Maiden and Mother don't take Oathbound to themselves, Warrior and Crone do. Crone's Oathbound—no, I won't tell you—you *guess* what they do."

"Uh," Kethry's brow furrowed in thought, and she nibbled a hangnail. "Shamans?"

"Right! And Healers and the two Elders in each Clan, who may or may not also be Healers or shamans. Those the Crone Binds are Bound, like the Kal'enedral, to the Clans as a whole, serving with their minds and talents instead of their hands. Now—you were saying about magicians?" She was as curious to know about Kethry's teaching as Keth seemed to be about her own.

"There's more than one school; mine is White Winds. Um, let me go to the very basics. Magic has three sources. The first is power from within the sorcerer himself, and you have to have the Talent to use that source—and even then it isn't fully trained by anyone I know of. I've heard that up

25

north a good ways they use *pure* mind-magic, rather than using the mind to find other sources of power."

"That would be—Valdemar, no?"

"Yes!" Kethry looked surprised at Tarma's knowledge. "Well, the second is power created by living things, rather like a fire creates light just by being a fire. You have to have the Talent to *sense* that power, but not to use it so long as you know it's there. Death releases a lot of that energy in one burst; that's why an unTalented sorcerer can turn to dark wizardry; he knows the power will be there when he kills something. The third source is from creatures that live in places that *aren't* this world, but *touch* this world—like pages in a book. Page one isn't page two, but they touch all along each other. Other Planes, we call them. There's one for each element, one for what we call 'demons,' and one for very powerful creatures that aren't quite gods, but do seem kindly inclined to humans. There may be more, but that's all anyone has ever discovered that *I* know of. The creatures of the four Elemental Planes can be bargained with—you can build up credit with them by doing them little favors, or you can promise them something they want from this Plane."

"Was that what I saw fighting beside you when you took out that wizard back in Brether's Crossroads? Other-whatsit creatures?"

"Exactly—and that fight is why my magic is so limited at the moment—I used up all the credit I had built with them in return for that help. Fortunately I *didn't* have to go into debt to them, or we'd probably be off trying to find snow-roses for the Ethereal Varirs right now. There *is* another way of dealing with them. You can coerce them with magical bindings or with your will. The creatures from the Abyssal Plane can be bought with pain-energy and death-energy—they feed off those—or coerced if your will is strong enough, although the only way you can 'bind' them magically is to hold them to this Plane; you can't force them to do anything if

26

your own will isn't stronger than theirs. The creatures of the Sixth Plane—we call it the 'Empyreal Plane'—*can't* be coerced in any way, and they'll only respond to a call if they feel like it. Any magician can contact the Other-Planar creatures, it's just a matter of knowing the spells that open the boundaries between us and them. The thing that makes schools of magic different is their ethics, really. How they feel about the different kinds of power and using them."

"So what does yours teach?" Tarma lay back with her arms stretched along Kessira's back and neck; she scratched gently behind the mare's ears while Kessira nodded her head in drowsy contentment. This was the most she'd gotten out of Kethry in the past six months.

"We don't coerce; not ever. We don't deal at all with the entities of the Abyssal Planes except to send them back—or destroy them if we can. We don't deliberately gain use of energy by killing or causing pain. We hold that our Talents have been given us for a purpose; that purpose is to use them for the greatest good. That's why we are wanderers, why we don't take up positions under permanent patrons."

"Why you're dirt-poor and why there're so few of you," Tarma interrupted genially.

" 'Fraid so," Kethry smiled. "No worldly sense, that's us. But that's probably why Need picked me."

"*She'enedra*, why don't you want to go to Mornedealth?"

"I—"

"And why haven't you ever told me about *your* home and kin?" Tarma had been letting her spirit-teacher's last remark stew in the back of her mind, and when Kethry had begun giving her the "lesson" in the ways of magic had realized she knew next to nothing about her partner's antecedents. She'd been brooding on her own sad memories, but Kethry's avoidance of the subject of the past could

27

only mean that hers were as sorry. And Tarma would be willing to bet the coin she didn't have that the mystery was tied into Mornedealth.

Kethry's mouth had tightened with an emotion Tarma recognized only too well. Pain.

"I'll have to know sooner or later, *she'enedra*. We have no choice but to pass through Mornedealth, and no choice but to try and raise money there, or we'll starve. And if it's something I can do anything about—well, I want doubly to know about it! You're my Clan, and nobody hurts my Clan and gets away with it!"

"It—it isn't anything you can deal with—"

"Let me be the judge of that, hmm?"

Kethry sighed, and visibly took herself in hand. "I—I guess it's only fair. You know next to nothing about me, but accepted me anyway."

"Not true," Tarma interrupted her, "*She* accepted you when you oathbound yourself to me as bloodsib. That's all I needed to know then. She wouldn't bind two who didn't belong together."

"But circumstances change, I know, and it isn't fair for me to keep making a big secret out of where I come from. All right." Kethry nodded, as if making up her mind to grasp the thorns. "The reason I haven't told you anything is this; I'm a fugitive. I grew up in Mornedealth; I'm a member of one of the Fifty Noble Houses. My real name is Kethryveris of House Pheregrul."

Tarma raised one eyebrow, but only said, "Do I bow, or can I get by with just kissing your hand?"

Kethry almost smiled. "It's a pretty empty title —or it was when I ran away. The House estates had dwindled to nothing more than a decaying mansion in the Old City by my father's time, and the House prerequisites to little more than an invitation to all Court functions—which we generally declined graciously—and permission to hunt the Royal Forests—which kept us fed most of the year. Father married mother for love, and it was a disaster. Her family disowned her, she became ill and

28

wouldn't tell him. It was one of those long declining things, she just faded bit by bit, so gradually that he, being absentminded at best, really didn't notice. She died three years after I was born. That left just the three of us."

"Three?"

Kethry hadn't ever mentioned any sibs before.

"Father, my brother Kavin—that's Kavinestral—and me. Kavin was eight years older than me, and from what everyone said, the very image of Father in his youth. Handsome—the word just isn't adequate to describe Kavin. He looks like a god."

"And you worshiped him." Tarma had no trouble reading *that* between the lines.

It wasn't just the dim light that was making Kethry look pale. "How could I not? Father died when I was ten, and Kavin was all I had left, and when he exerted himself he could charm the moss off the wall. We were fine until Father died; he'd had some income or other that kept the house going, well, that dried up when he was gone. That left Kavin and me with no income and nowhere to go but a falling-down monstrosity that we couldn't even sell, because it's against the law for the Fifty Families to sell the ancestral homes. We let the few servants we had go—all but one, my old nurse Tildy. She wouldn't leave me. So Tildy and I struggled to run the household and keep us all clothed and fed. Kavin hunted the Royal Forests when he got hungry enough, and spent the rest of his time being Kavin. Which, to me, meant being perfection."

"Until you got fed up and ran away?" Tarma hazarded, when Kethry's silence had gone too long. She knew it it wasn't the right answer, but she hoped it would prod Kethry back into speaking.

"Hardly." Kethry's eyes and mouth were bitter. "He had me neatly twined 'round his finger. No, things went on like that until I was twelve, and just barely pubescent. Two things happened then that I had no knowledge of. The first was that Kavin himself became fed up with life on the edge,

29

and looked around for something to make him a lot of money quickly. The second was that on one of his dips in the stews with his friends, he accidentally encountered the richest banker in Mornedealth and found out exactly what his secret vice was. Kavin may have been lazy, but he wasn't stupid. He was fully able to put facts together. He also knew that Wethes Goldmarchant, like all the other New Money moguls, wanted the one thing that all his money couldn't buy him—he wanted inside the Fifty Families. He *wanted* those Court invitations we declined; wanted them so badly it made him ache. And he'd never get them—not unless he somehow saved the realm single-handedly, which wasn't bloody likely."

Kethry's hands were clenched tightly in her lap, she stared at them as if they were the most fascinating things in the universe. "I knew nothing of all this, of course, mewed up in the house all day and daydreaming about finding a hidden cache of gold and gems and being able to pour them in Kavin's lap and make him smile at me. Then one day he *did* smile at me; he told me he had a surprise for me. I went with him, trusting as a lamb. Next thing I knew, he was handing me over to Wethes; the marriage ceremony had already taken place by proxy. You see, Wethes' secret vice was little girls—and with me, he got both his ambition *and* his lust satisfied. It was a bargain too good for either of them to resist—"

Kethry's voice broke in something like a sob; Tarma leaned forward and put one hard, long hand on the pair clenched white-knuckled in her partner's lap.

"So your brother sold you, hmm? Well, give him a little credit, *she'enedra;* he might have thought he was doing you a favor. The merchant would give you every luxury, after all; you'd be a valued and precious possession."

"I'd like to believe that, but I can't. Kavin saw some of those little girls Wethes was in the habit of despoiling. He *knew* what he was selling me into, and he didn't care, he plainly did not care. The only difference between them and me was that the chains and manacles he used on me were solid gold, and I was raped on silk sheets instead of linen. And it was rape, nothing else! I wanted to die; I prayed I would die. I didn't understand anything of what had happened to me. I only knew that the brother I worshiped had betrayed me." Her voice wavered a moment, and faded against the howl of the storm-winds outside their shelter. Tarma had to strain to hear her.

Then she seemed to recover, and her voice strengthened again. "But although I had been betrayed, I hadn't been forgotten. My old nurse managed to sneak her way into the house on the strength of the fact that she *was* my nurse; nobody thought to deny her entry. When Wethes was finished with me, she waited until he had left and went inquiring for me. When she found me, she freed me and smuggled me out."

Kethry finally brought her eyes up to meet her partner's; there was pain there, but also a hint of ironic humor. "You'd probably like her; she also stole every bit of gold and jewelry she found with me and carried them off, too."

"A practical woman; you're right, I think I *would* like her. I take it she had somewhere to hide you?"

"Her brother's farm—it's east of here. Well, I wasn't exactly in my right mind for a while, but she managed to help with that for a bit. But then—then I started having nightmares, and when I did, every movable thing in my room would go flying about. Mind you, I never broke anything—"

"Since I gather this was a 'flying about' without benefit of hands, I would think it would be rather unnerving."

"Tildy knew she hadn't any way of coping with me then, so she took me to the nearest mage-school she knew, which was White Winds. It only took one nightmare to convince them that I needed help—

and that I was going to be a pretty good mage after I got that help. That's where I got Need."

Kethry's hands unclenched, and one of them strayed to the hilt of a plain short-sword wedged in among the supplies tucked into the shelter.

"Now that's another tale you never told me."

"Not for any reason, just because there isn't much to tell. We had a guard there, an old mercenary who'd been hired on to give us a bit of protection, and to give her a kind of semiretirement. Baryl Longarm was her name. When I was ready to take the roads, she called me into her rooms."

"That must have had you puzzled."

"Since she didn't have a reputation for chasing other females, it certainly did. Thank goodness she didn't leave me wondering for long. 'You're the first wench we've had going out for a dog's age,' she said, 'and there's something I want you to have. It's time it went out again, anyway, and you'll probably have to use it before you're gone a month.' She took down this sword from the wall, unsheathed it, and laid it in my hands. And the runes appeared on the blade."

"I remember when you showed me. 'Woman's Need calls me, as Woman's Need made me. Her Need I will answer as my maker bade me.' " Tarma glanced at Kethry's hand on the hilt. "Gave me a fair turn, I can tell you. I always thought magic blades were gold-hilted and jewel-bedecked."

"Then she told me what little she knew—that the sword's name was Need, that she was indestructible so far as Baryl had been able to tell. That she only served women. And that her service was such that she only gave what you yourself did not already have. That to her, a fighter, Need gave a virtual immunity to all magic, but didn't add so much as a fillip to her fighting skills—but that for me, a mage, if I let it take control when it needed to, it would make me a master swordswoman, though it wouldn't make the least difference to any spell I

32

cast. And that it would help Heal anything short of a death-wound."

"Rather like one of Her gifts, you know?" Tarma interrupted. "Makes you do your utmost, to the best of your abilities, but bails you out when you're out of your depth."

"I never thought about it that way, but you're right. Is there any way Need could be Shin'a'in?"

"Huh-uh. We've few metal-workers, and none of them mages—and we don't go in for short-swords, anyway. Now, what's the problem with you going back to Mornedealth? Changing the subject isn't going to change my wanting to know."

"Well, you can't blame me for trying—*she'enedra*, I have angered a very powerful man, my husband—"

"Crap! He's no more your husband than I am, no matter what charade he went through."

"—and a very ruthless one, my brother. I don't know what either of them would do if they learned I was within their reach again." Kethry shuddered, and Tarma reached forward and clasped both her hands in her own.

"I have only one question, my sister and my friend," she said, so earnestly that Kethry came out of her own fear and looked deeply into the shadowed eyes that met hers. "And that is this; which way do you want them sliced—lengthwise, or widthwise?"

"Tarma!" The sober question struck Kethry as so absurd that she actually began laughing weakly.

"In all seriousness, I much doubt that either of them is going to recognize you; think about it, you're a woman grown now, not a half-starved child. But if they do, that's what I'm here for. If they try anything, I'll ask you that question again, and you'd best have a quick answer for me. Now, are you satisfied?"

"You are insane!"

"I am Shin'a'in; some say there is little difference. I am also Kal'enedral, and most say there is *no* difference. So believe me; no one is going to touch you with impunity. I am just crazed enough to cut the city apart in revenge."

"And this is supposed to make me feel better?"

"You're smiling, aren't you?"

"Well," Kethry admitted reluctantly, "I guess I am."

"When a child of the Clans falls off her horse, we make her get right back on again. *She'enedra,* don't you think it's time you remounted this one?"

"I—"

"Or do you prefer to live your life with *them* dictating that you shall not return to your own city?"

Her chin came up; a stubborn and angry light smoldered in her eyes. "No."

"Then we face this city of yours and we face it together. For now, make a mattress of Rodi, *she'enedra;* and sleep peacefully. I intend to do the same. Tomorrow we go to Mornedealth and make it deal with us on *our* terms. *Hai?*"

Kethry nodded, convinced almost against her will, and beginning to view the inevitable encounter with something a little more like confidence.

"*Hai,*" she agreed.

Two

Kethry envied her partner's ability to drop immediately into sleep under almost any circumstances. Her own thoughts were enough to keep her wakeful; add to them the snoring of her mule and the wailing of the wind outside their shelter, and Kethry had a foolproof recipe for insomnia.

She wanted to avoid Mornedealth no matter *what* the cost. Just the thought that she might encounter Wethes was enough to make her shudder almost uncontrollably. In no way was she prepared to deal with him, and she wondered now if she would ever be. . . .

And yet, Tarma was right. She would never truly be "free" unless she dealt with her fear. She would never truly be her own woman if she allowed fear and old memories to dictate where she would or would not go.

The disciplines of the Order of White Winds mandated self-knowledge and self-mastery. She had deceived herself into thinking she had achieved that mastery of self; Tarma had just shown her how wrong she was.

It's been seven years, she thought bitterly. *Seven long years—and those bastards still have power over me. And I'll never be an adept until I break that power.*

For that, after all, was the heart of the White Winds discipline; that no negative tie be permitted to bind the sorcerer in any way. Positive ties—like the oath of *she'enedran* she had sworn with Tarma, like the bond of lover to lover or parent to child— were encouraged to flourish, for the sorcerer could draw confidence and strength from them. But the negative bonds of fear, hatred, or greed must be rooted out and destroyed, for they would actually drain the magician of needed energy.

Sometimes Tarma can be so surprising, see things so clearly. And yet she has such peculiar blind spots. Or does she? Does she realize that she's driving us both to the Plains as if she was geas-bound? She's like a messenger-bird, unable to travel in any direction but the one appointed.

Kethry hadn't much cared where she wandered; this was her time of journey, she wouldn't settle in any one place until she reached the proficiency of an Adept. *Then* she would either found a school of her own, or find a place in an established White Winds enclave. So Tarma's overwhelming need to return home had suited her as well as anything else.

Until she had realized that the road they were on led directly to Mornedealth.

It all comes back to that, doesn't it? And until I face it, I'm stalemated. Dammit, Tarma's right. I'm a full sorceress, I'm a full adult, and I have one damned fine swordswoman for a partner. What in Teslat's name am I afraid of? There is nothing under the law that they can really do to me—I've been separated from Wethes for seven years, and three is enough to unmake the marriage, assuming there really was one. I'm not going in under my full name, and I've changed so much. How are they even going to recognize me?

Across the shelter Tarma stirred, and curled herself into a tighter ball. Kethry smiled and shook her head, thinking about her partner's words on the subject.

"Do you want them sliced lengthwise or widthwise"—Windborn, she is such a bundle of contradictions. We have got to start talking; we hardly know anything about one another. Up until now, we've had our hands full of bandit-extermination, then there just wasn't the privacy. But if I'd had all the world to choose a sister from, I would have picked her over any other. Goddess-

oath and all, I would have chosen her. Though that Warrior of hers certainly took the decision right out of our hands.

Kethry contemplated the sleeping face of her partner. In repose she lost a great deal of the cold harshness her expression carried when she was awake. She looked, in fact, a great deal younger than Kethry was.

When she sleeps, she's the child she was before she lost her Clan. When she's awake—I'm not sure what she is. She eats, drinks and breathes the Warrior, that's for certain, yet she hasn't made any move to convert me. I know it would please her if I did, and it wouldn't be any great change to do so; her Goddess just seems to me to be one more face of the Windborn Soulshaper. She seems like any other mercenary hire-sword—insisting on simple solutions to complicated problems, mostly involving the application of steel to offending party. Then she turns around and hits me with a sophisticated proverb, or some really esoteric knowledge—like knowing that mind-magic is used in Valdemar. And she's hiding something from me; something to do with that Goddess of hers, I think. And not because she doesn't trust me . . . maybe because I don't share her faith. Her people—nobody really knows too much about the Shin'a'in; they keep pretty much to themselves. Of course that shouldn't be too surprising; anyone who knew the Dhorisha Plains the way they do could dive into the grass and never be seen again, if that's what he wanted to do. You could hide the armies of a dozen nations out there, and they'd likely never run into each other. Assuming the Shin'a'in would let them past the Border. I suspect if Tale'sedrin had been on the Plains instead of camped on the road to the Great Horse Fair the bandits would be dead and the Hawk's Children still riding. And I would be out a sister.

Kethry shook her head. *Well, what happened, happened. Now I have to think about riding into Mornedealth tomorrow. Under a glamour?*

She considered the notion for a moment, then discarded it. *No. I'll go in wearing my own face,*

37

dammit! Besides, the first sorcerer who sees I'm wearing a glamour is likely to want to know why—and likely to try to find out. If I'm luckly, he'll come to us with his hand out. If I'm not, he'll go to Wethes or Kavin. No, a glamour would only cause trouble, not avoid it. I think Tarma's right; we'll go in as a mercenary team, no more, no less, and under her Clanname. We'll stay guiet, draw no attention to ourselves, and maybe avoid trouble altogether. The more complicated a plan is, the more likely it is to go wrong. . . .

Kethry began formulating some simple story for her putative background, but the very act of having faced and made the decision to go in had freed her of the tension that was keeping her sleepless. She had hardly begun, when her weariness claimed her.

The blizzard cleared by morning. Dawn brought cloudless skies, brilliant sun, and still, cold air that made everything look sharp-edged and brightly-painted. They cleared camp and rode off into a world that seemed completely new-made.

Tarma was taken totally by surprise by the changeling forest; she forgot her homesickness, forgot her worry over Kethry, even temporarily forgot how cold she was.

Birdcalls echoed for miles through the forest, as did the steady, muffled clop of their mounts' hooves. The storm had brought a fine, powder like snow, snow that frosted every branch and coated the underbrush, so that the whole forest reflected the sunlight and glowed so that they were surrounded by a haze of pearly light. Best of all, at least to Tarma's mind, the soft snow was easy for the beasts to move through, so they made good time. Just past midafternoon, glimpses of the buildings and walls of Mornedealth could be seen above and through the trees.

It was a city made of the wood that was its staple in trade; weathered, silver-gray wooden palisades, wooden walls, wooden buildings; only the foundations of a building were ever made of stone. The outer wall that encircled it was a monument to man's ingenuity and Mornedealth's woodworkers; it was two stories tall, and as strong as any corresponding wall of stone. Granted, it would never survive being set afire, as would inevitably happen in a siege, but the wall had never been built with sieges in mind. It was intended to keep the beasts of the forest out of the city when the hardships of winter made their fear of man less than their hunger, and to keep the comings and goings of strangers limited to specific checkpoints. If an enemy penetrated this realm so far as to threaten Mornedealth, all was lost anyway, and there would be nothing for it but surrender.

Since the only city Tarma had ever spent any length of time in was Brether's Crossroads—less than half the size of Mornedealth—the Shin'a'in confessed to Kethry that she was suitably impressed by it long before they ever entered the gates.

"But you spent more than a year hunting down Gregoth and his band. Surely you—"

"Don't remember much of that, *she'enedra*. It was a bit like being in a drug haze. I only really came awake when I was tr—" she suddenly recalled that Kethry knew nothing of her faceless trainers and what they were, and decided that discretion was in order. "When I had to. To question someone, or to read a trail. The rest of the time, I might just as well not have been there, and I surely wasn't in any kind of mood for seeing sights."

"No—you wouldn't be. I'm sorry; I wasn't thinking at all."

"Nothing to apologize for. Just tell me what I'm getting into here. You're the native; where are we going?"

Kethry reined in, a startled look on her face. "I—I've spent so much time thinking about Kavin and Wethes . . .".

"Li'sa'eer!" Tarma exclaimed in exasperation, pulling Kessira up beside her. "Well, think about it *now*, dammit!" She kneed her mare slightly; Kessira

39

obeyed the subtle signal and shouldered Rodi to one side until both of the beasts had gotten off onto the shoulder of the road, out of the way of traffic. There wasn't anybody in sight, but Tarma had had *yuthi'so'coro*—road-courtesy—hammered into her from the time she was old enough to sit a horse unaided. No Shin'a'in omitted road-courtesy while journeying, not even when among deadly enemies. And road-courtesy dictated that if you were going to sit and chat, you didn't block the progress of others while you were doing it.

"We'll have to use the Stranger's Gate," Kethry said after long thought, staring at the point where the walls of Mornedealth began paralleling the road. "That's no hardship, it's right on the Trade Road. But we'll have to register with the Gate Guard, give him our names, where we're from, where we're going, and our business here."

"Warrior's Oath! What do they want, to write a book about us?" Tarma replied with impatience.

"Look, this is as much for our sakes as theirs. Would *you* want total strangers loose in your Clan territory?"

"*Sa-hai.* You're right. Not that strangers ever get past the Border, but you're right."

"The trouble is, I daren't tell them what I really am, but I don't want to get caught in a complicated falsehood."

"Now *that's* no problem," Tarma nodded. "We just tell him a careful mixture of the truth with enough lie in it to keep your enemies off the track. Then?"

"There are specific inns for travelers; we'll have to use one of them. They won't ask us to pay straight off, we'll have three days to find work and get our reckoning taken care of. After that, they confiscate everything we own except what we're wearing."

Tarma snorted a little with contempt, which obviously surprised Kethry.

"I thought you'd throw a fit over the notion of someone taking Kessira."

"I'd rather like to see them try. You've never seen her with a stranger. She's not a battle-steed, but *nobody* lays a finger on her without my permission. Let a stranger put one hand on her rein and he'll come away with a bloody stump. And while he's opening his mouth to yell about it, she'll be off down the street, headed for the nearest gate. If I were hurt and gave her the command to run for it, she'd carry me to the closest exit she could remember without any direction from me. And if she couldn't find one, she might well *make* one. No, I've no fear of anyone confiscating her. One touch, and they wouldn't *want* her. Besides, I have something I can leave in pledge—I'd rather not lose it, but it's better than causing a scene."

Tarma took off her leather glove, reached into the bottom of her saddlebag and felt for a knobby, silk-wrapped bundle. She brought the palm-sized package out and unwrapped it carefully, uncovering to the brilliant sunlight an amber necklace. It was made of round beads alternating with carved claws or teeth; it glowed on the brown silk draped over her hand like an ornament of hardened sunbeams.

"Osberg wore that!"

"He stole it from me. I took it back off his dead body. It was the last thing Dharin gave me. Our pledge-gift. I never found the knife I gave him."

Kethry said nothing; Tarma regarded the necklace with a stony-cold expression that belied the ache in her heart, then rewrapped it and stowed it away. "As I said, I'd rather not lose it, but losing it's better than causing a riot. Now how do we find work?"

"We'd be safest going to a Hiring Hall. They charge employers a fee to find people with special talents."

"Well, that's us."

"Of course, that's money we won't see. We could get better fees if we went out looking on our own, but it would probably take longer."

"Hiring Hall; better the safe course."

"I agree, but they're sure to notice at the gate that my accent is native. Would you mind doing the talking?"

Tarma managed a quirk of the lips that approximated a half-smile. "All right, I'll do all the talking at the gate. Look stupid and sweet, and let them think you're my lover. Unless that could get us in trouble."

Kethry shook her head. "No, there's enough of that in Mornedealth. Virtually anything is allowed provided you're ready to pay for it."

"And they call this civilization! *Vai datha;* let's get on with it."

They turned their beasts once more onto the road, and within a candlemark were under scrutiny of the sentries on the walls. Tarma allowed a lazy, sardonic smile to cross her face. One thing she had to give them; these guards were well disciplined. No catcalls, no hails, no propositions to Kethry—just a steady, measuring regard that weighed them and judged them unthreatening for the moment. These "soft, city-bred" guards were quite impressive.

The Stranger's Gate was wide enough for three wagons to pass within, side by side, and had an ironwork portcullis as well as a pair of massive bleached-wood doors, all three now standing open. They clattered under the wall, through a wooden-walled tunnel about three horse-lengths deep. When they reached the other entrance, they found themselves stopped by a chain stretched across the inner side of the gate. One of the men standing sentry approached them and asked them (with short words, but courteous) to follow him to a tiny office built right into the wall. There was always a Gate Guard on duty here; the man behind the desk was, by the insignia pinned to his brown leather tunic, a captain. Kethry had told her partner as they approached the walls that those posted as Gate Guards tended to be high-ranking, and above the general cut of mercenary, because they had to be able to read and write. Their escort squeezed them inside the door, and returned to his own post. The Gate Guard was a middle-aged, lean, saturnine man who glanced up at them from behind his tiny desk, and without a word, pulled a ledger, quill and ink from underneath it.

The Gate Guard was of the same cut as the men on the walls; Tarma wondered if Kethry would be able to pass his careful scrutiny. It didn't look like he missed much. Certainly Kethry looked nothing like a Shin'a'in, so she'd have to be one damn convincing actress to get away with claiming a Shin'a'in Clanname.

Tarma stole a glance sideways at her partner and had to refrain from a hoarse chuckle. Kethry wore a bright, vapid smile, and was continuously fussing with the way her cloak draped and smoothing down her hair. She looked like a complete featherhead. No problem. The Guard would have very little doubt why the partner of a rather mannish swordswoman was claiming her Clanname!

At the Guard's brusque inquiry as to their names and business, Tarma replied as shortly, "We're Shin'a'in mercenaries. Tarma shena Tale'sedrin, Kethry shena Tale'sedrin. We're on our way back to the Dhorisha Plains; I've got inheritance coming from my Clan I need to claim. But we've run out of provisions; we're going to have to take some temporary work to restock."

"Not much call for your kind on a temporary basis, Swordlady," he replied with a certain gruff respect. "Year contract or more, sure; Shin'a'in have a helluva reputation. You'd be able to get top wage as any kind of guard, guard-captain or trainer; but not temporary. Your pretty friend's in mage-robes; that just for show, or can she light a candle?"

"Ah, Keth's all right. Good enough to earn us some coin, just no horse-sense, *he shala*? She's worth the trouble taking care of, and for more reasons than one, bless her."

"Eyah, and without you to keep the wolves away,

a pretty bit like that'd get eaten alive in a week,"
the Guard answered with a certain gleam of sympathy in his eyes. "Had a shieldmate like that in
my younger days, fancied himself a poet; didn't
have sense enough to come in out of a storm. Caught
himself a fever standing out in a blizzard, admiring
it; died of it eventually—well, that's the way of
things. You being short of coin; tell you what, one
professional to another—you go find the Broken
Sword, tell 'em Jervac sent you. And I hear tell the
Hiring Hall over by the animal market was on the
lookout for a mage on temp."

"Will do—luck on your blade, captain."

"And on yours. Ah—don't mount up; lead your
beasts, that's the law inside the gates."

As they led their mounts in the direction the
Gate Guard had indicated, Kethry whispered, "How
much of that was good advice?"

"We'll find out when we find this inn; chances
are he's getting some kickback, but he could be
doing us a good turn at the same time. Thanks for
the help with the ruse of being your protector; that
should warn off anybody that might be thinking
your services other than magery are for hire. We
couldn't have done better for a sympathizer if we'd
planned this, you know, that's why I played it a bit
thick. He had the feeling of a *she'chorne*; that bit
about a 'shieldmate' clinched it. If you're not lovers, you call your partner 'shieldbrother,' not
'shieldmate.' How are you doing?"

Kethry looked a bit strained, but it was something likely only someone who knew her would
have noticed. "Holding up; I'll manage. The more
time I spend with nobody jumping me out of the
shadows, the easier it'll get. I can handle it."

"Vai datha." If Kethry said she'd be able to handle her understandable strain, Tarma was willing
to believe her. Tarma took the chance to look around,
and was impressed in spite of herself. "Damn,
Greeneyes, you never told me this place was so
big!"

44

"I'm used to it," Kethry shrugged.

"Well, I'm not," Tarma shook her head in amazement. The street they led their beasts on was fully wide enough for two carts with plenty of space for them to pass. It was actually paved with bricks, something Tarma didn't ever remember seeing before, and had a channel down the middle and a gutter on either side for garbage and animal droppings. There were more people than she ever recalled seeing in one place in her life; she and Kethry were elbow to elbow in the crush. Kessira snorted, not liking so many strangers so close. "Why isn't anyone riding? Why'd the Guard say riding was counter the law?" Tarma asked, noticing that while there were beasts and carts in plenty, all were being led, like theirs—just as the guard had told them.

"No one but a member of one of the Fifty is allowed to ride within the walls, and for good reason. Think what would happen if somebody lost control of his beast in this crush!"

"Reasonable. Look, there's our inn—"

The sign was plain enough—the pieces of an actual blade nailed up to a shingle suspended above the road. They turned their mounts' heads into a narrow passage that led into a square courtyard. The inn itself was built entirely around this yard. It was two-storied, of the ubiquitous wood stained a dark brown; old, but in excellent repair. The courtyard itself was newly swept. The stabling was to the rear of the square, the rest of the inn forming the other three sides.

"Stay here, I want to have a look at the stabling. That will tell me everything I need to know." Tarma handed over her mare's reins to Kethry, and strode purposefully toward the stable door. She was intercepted by a gray-haired, scar-faced man in a leather apron.

"Swordlady, welcome," he said. "How may we serve you?"

"Bed, food and stabling for two—if I like what I see. And I'd like to see the stables first."

He grinned with the half of his mouth not puckered with a scar. "Shin'a'in? Thought so—this way, lady."

He himself led the way into the stables, and Tarma made up her mind then and there. It was clean and swept, there was no smell of stale dung or urine. The mangers were filled with fresh hay, the buckets with clean water, and the only beasts tied were those few whose wild or crafty eyes and laid-back ears told Tarma were that they were safer tied than loose.

"Well, I *do* like what I see. Now if you aren't going to charge us like we were gold-dripping palace fatheads, I think you've got a pair of boarders. Oh, and Jervac sent us."

The man looked pleased. "I'm Hadell; served with Jervac until a brawl got me a cut tendon and mustering-out pay. About the charges; two trade-silver a day for both of you and your beasts, if you and the mage are willing to share a bed. Room isn't big, I'll warn you, but it's private. That two pieces gets you bed and breakfast and supper; dinner you manage on your own. Food is guard-fare; it's plain, but there's plenty of it and my cook's a good one. I'll go the standard three days' grace; more, if you've got something to leave with me as a pledge. Suits?"

"Suits," Tarma replied, pleased. "I do have a pledge, but I'd rather save it until I need it. Where's your stableboy? I don't want my mare to get a mouthful of him."

"Her," Hadell corrected her. "My daughter. We're a family business here. I married the cook, my girl works the stables, my boys wait tables."

"Safer than the other way 'round, hey? Especially as she gets to the toothsome age." Tarma shared a crooked grin with him, as he gave a piercing whistle. A shaggy-haired urchin popped out of the door of what probably was the grain room, and trotted up, favoring Tarma with an utterly fearless grin.

"This is—" he cocked his head inquiringly.

46

"Tarma shena Tale'sedrin. Shin'a'in, as you said."

"She and her partner are biding here for a bit, and she wants to make sure her mount doesn't eat you."

"Laeka, Swordlady." The urchin bobbed her head. "At your service. You're Shin'a'in?" Her eyes widened and became eager. "You got a battlesteed?"

"Not yet, Laeka. If I can make it back to the Plains in one piece, though, I'll be getting one. Kessira is a saddle-mare; she fights, but she hasn't the weight or the training of a battlesteed."

"Well, Da says what the Shin'a'in keep for thesselves is ten times the worth o' what they sells us."

The innmaster cuffed the girl—gently, Tarma noticed. "Laeka! Manners!" Laeka rubbed her ear and grinned, not in the least discomfited.

Tarma laughed. "No insult taken, Keeper, it's true. We sell you outClan folk our culls. Come with me, Laeka, and I'll introduce you to what we keep."

With the child trotting at her side and the innkeeper following, Tarma strolled back to Kethry. "This's a good place, she'enedra, and they aren't altogether outrageous in what they're charging. We'll be staying. This is Laeka, she's our Keeper's daughter, and his chief stableman."

Laeka beamed at the elevation in her station Tarma granted her.

"Now, hold out your hand to Kessira, little lady; let her get your measure." She placed her own hand on Kessira's neck and spoke a single command word under her breath. That told Kessira that the child was not to be harmed, and was to be obeyed—though she would only obey *some* commands if they were given in Shin'a'in, and it wasn't likely the child knew *that* tongue. Just as well, they didn't truly need a new back door to their stabling.

The mare lowered her head with grave dignity and snuffled the child's hand once, for politeness' sake, while the girl's eyes widened in delight. Then when Tarma put the reins in Laeka's hands, Kessira

47

followed her with gentle docility, taking careful, dainty steps on the unfamiliar surface. Kethry handed her the reins to the mule as well; Rodi, of course, would follow *anyone* to food and stabling.

Hadell showed them their room; on the first floor, it was barely big enough to contain the bed. But it did have a window, and the walls were freshly whitewashed. There were plenty of blankets—again, well-worn but scrupulously clean—and a feather comforter. Tarma had stayed in far worse places, and said as much.

"So have I," Kethry replied, sitting on the edge of the bed and pulling off her riding boots with a grimace of pain. "The place where I met you, for one. I think we've gotten a bargain, personally."

"Makes me wonder, but I may get the answer when I see the rest of the guests. Well, what's next?" Tarma handed her a pair of soft leather half-boots meant for indoor wear.

"Dinner and bed. It's far too late to go to the Hiring Hall; that'll be for first thing in the morning? I wonder if we could manage a bath out of Hadell? I do *not* like smelling like a mule!"

As if to answer that question, there came a gentle rap on the door. "Lady-guests?" a boy's soprano said carefully, "Would ye wish th' use o' the steamhouse? If ye be quick, Da says ye'll have it t' yerselves fer a candlemark or so."

Tarma opened the door to him; a sturdy, dark child, he looked very like his father. "And the charge, lad?" she asked, "Though if it's in line with the rest of the bill, I'm thinking we'll be taking you up on it."

"Copper for steamhouse and bath, copper for soap and towels," he said, holding out the last. "It's at the end of the hallway."

"Done and done, and point us the way." Kethry took possession of what he carried so fast he was left gaping. "Pay the lad, Tarma; if I don't get clean soon, I'm going to rot of my own stink."

Tarma laughed, and tossed the boy four coppers.

"And here I was thinking you were more trail-hardened than me," she chuckled, following Kethry down the hall in the direction the boy pointed. "Now you turn out to be another soft sybarite."

"I didn't notice *you* saying no."

"We have a saying—"

"Not another one!"

" 'An enemy's nose is always keener than your own.' "

"When I want a proverb, I'll consult a cleric. Here we are," Kethry opened the door to the bathhouse, which had been annexed to the very end of the inn. "Oh, heaven!"

This was, beyond a doubt, a well managed place. There were actually three rooms to the bathing area; the first held buckets and shallow tubs, and hot water bubbled from a wooden pipe in the floor into a channel running through it, while against the wall were pumps. This room was evidently for actual bathing; the bather mixed hot water from the channel with cold from the pumps, then poured the dirty water down the refuse channel. The hot-water channel ran into the room beside this one, which contained one enormous tub sunk into the floor, for soaking out aches and bruises. Beyond this room was what was obviously a steamroom. Although it was empty now, there were heated rocks in a pit in the center of the floor, buckets with dippers in them to pour water on the rocks, and benches around the pit. The walls were plain, varnished wood; the windows of something white and opaque that let light in without making a mockery of privacy.

"Heaven, in very deed," Tarma was losing no time in shedding her clothing. "I think I'm finally going to be warm again!"

One candlemark later, as they were blissfully soaking in hot mineral water—"This is a hot spring," Kethry remarked after sniffing the faint tang of copper in the air. "That's why he can afford to give

49

his baths away"—a bright grin surmounted by a thatch of tousled brown hair appeared out of the steam and handed them their towels.

"Guard-shift's changin', miladies; men as stays here'll be lookin' fer their baths in a bit. You wants quiet, ye'd best come t' dinner. You wants a bit o' summat else—you jest stays here, they'll gie' ye that!"

"No doubt," Tarma said wryly, taking the towel Laeka held out to her and emerging reluctantly from the hot tub, thinking that in some ways a child being raised in an inn grew up even faster than a child of the Clans. "We'll take the quiet, thanks. What's wrong?"

The child was staring at her torso with stricken eyes. "Lady—you—how did—who did—"

Tarma glanced down at her own hard, tawny-gold body, that was liberally latticed with a network of paler scars and realized that the child had been startled and shocked by the evidence of so many old wounds on one so relatively young. She also thought about the adulation that had been in Laeka's eyes, and the concern in her father's when the man had seen it there. This might be a chance to do the man a good turn, maybe earn enough gratitude that he'd exert himself for them.

"A lot of people did that to me, child," she said quietly. "And if you've ever thought to go adventuring, think of these marks on me first. It isn't like the tales, where people go to battle one candlemark and go feast the next, with never a scratch on them. I was months healing from the last fight I had, and the best that those I fought for could give me was a mule, provisions, and a handful of coin as reward. The life of a mercenary is far from profitable most of the time."

Laeka gulped, and looked away. "I like horses," she ventured, finally. "I be good with 'em."

"Then by all means, become a horse-trainer," Tarma answered the unspoken question. "Train 'em well, and sell 'em to fools like me who earn their

50

bread with swords instead of brains. Tell you what—you decide to do that, you send word to the Clans in my name. I'll leave orders you're to get a better choice than we give most outlanders. Hmm?"

"Aye!" The girl's eyes lighted at the promise, and she relaxed a little as Tarma donned her close-fitting breeches, shirt, and wrapped Shin'a'in jacket, covering the terrible scars. "Da says t' tell you supper be stew, bread 'n' honey, an' ale."

"Sounds fine—Keth?"

"Wonderful."

"Tell him we'll be there right behind you."

The child scampered out, and Kethry lifted an eyebrow. "Rather overdoing it, weren't you?"

"Huh! You didn't see the hero-worship in the kid's eyes, earlier, or the worry in her Da's. Not too many female mercenaries ride through here, I'd guess; the kid's seen just enough to make it look glamorous. Well, now she knows better, and I'm thinking it's just as well."

"You knew better, but you took this road anyway."

"Aye, I did," Tarma laced her boots slowly, her harsh voice dropping down to a whisper. "And the only reason I left the Plains was to revenge my Clan. All Shin'a'in learn the sword, but that doesn't mean we plan to live by it. We—we don't live to fight, we fight when we have to, to live. Sometimes we don't manage the last. As for me, I had no choice in taking up the blade, in becoming a merce-nary; no more than did you."

Kethry winced, and touched Tarma's arm lightly. "Put my foot in it, didn't I? *She'enedra,* I'm sorry—I meant no offense—"

Tarma shook off her gloom with a shake of her head. "I know that. None taken. Let's get that food. I could eat this towel, I'm that hungry."

The whitewashed common room was quite empty, although the boy who brought them their supper (older than the other two children, darker, and quieter) told them it would be filling shortly. And so it proved; men of all ages and descriptions slowly trickling in to take their places at table and bench, being served promptly by Hadell's two sons. The room could easily hold at least fifty; the current crowd was less than half that number. Most of the men looked to be of early middle-age with a sprinkling of youngsters; all wore the unconsciously competent air of a good professional soldier. Tarma liked what she saw of them. None of these men would ever be officers, but the officers they did serve would be glad to have them.

The talk was muted; the men were plainly weary with the day's work. Listening without seeming to, the women soon gleaned the reason why.

As Tarma had already guessed, these men were foreign mercenaries, like themselves. This would be Hadell's lean season—one reason, perhaps, that his prices were reasonable, and that he was so glad to see them. The other reason was that he was that rare creature, an honest man, and one who chose to give the men he had served beside a decent break. Right now, only those hire-swords with contracts for a year or more—or those one or two so prosperous that they could afford to bide out the mercenary's lean season in an inn—were staying at the Broken Sword. Normally a year-contract included room and board, but these men were a special case. All of them were hired on with the City Guard, which had no barracks for them. The result was that their pay included a stipend for board, and a good many of them stayed at inns like the Broken Sword. The job was never the easy one it might appear to the unknowing to be; and today had been the occasion of a riot over bread prices. The Guard had been ordered to put down the riot; no few of these men had been of two minds about their orders. On the one hand, *they* weren't suffering; but on the other, most of them were of the same lower-classes as those that were rioting, and could remember winters when they *had* gone hungry. And the inflated grain prices, so rumor had it, had no basis for being so high. The harvest had been good, the granaries full. Rumor said that shortages were being created. Rumor said, by Wethes Goldmarchant.

Both Tarma and her partner took to their bed with more than a bellyful of good stew to digest.

"Are you certain you want to come with me, even knowing there probably won't be work for you? You deserved a chance to sleep in for a change."

Kethry, standing in the light from the window, gave her sorcerer's robe a good brushing and slipped it on over her shirt and breeches—and belted on her blade as well.

"Eyah. I want to be lurking in the background looking protective and menacing. I want to start rumors about how it's best to approach my partner with respect. You put on whatever act you think will reinforce mine. And I don't think you should be wearing *that*."

Kethry glanced down at Need and pursed her lips. "You're probably right, but I feel rather naked without her."

"We don't want to attract any attention, right? You know damn well mages don't bear steel other than eating knives and ritual daggers." Tarma lounged fully-clothed—except for her boots—on the bed, since there wasn't enough room for two people to be standing beside it at the same time.

"Right," Kethry sighed, removing the blade and stowing it under the bed with the rest of their goods. "All right, let's go."

The Hiring Hall was no more than a short stroll from the inn; an interesting walk from Tarma's point of view. Even at this early an hour the streets were full of people, from ragged beggars to well-dressed merchants, and *not* all from around here— Tarma recognized the regional dress of more than a dozen other areas, and might have spotted more had she known what to look for. This might be the lean season, but it was evident that Mornedealth always had a certain amount of trade going.

At the Hiring Hall—just that, a hall lined with

benches on both sides, and a desk at the end, all of the ubiquitous varnished wood—they gave essentially the same story they'd given the guard. Their tale differed only in that Kethry was being more of herself; it wouldn't do to look an idiot when she was trying to get work. As they had been told, the steward of the hall shook his blond head regretfully when Tarma informed him that she was only interested in short-term assignments.

"I'm sorry, Swordlady," he told her, "Very sorry. I could get you your pick of a round dozen one-to-five-year contracts. But this is the lean season, and there just isn't anything for a hire-sword but long-term. But your friend—yes."

"Oh?" Kethry contrived to look eager.

"There's a fellow from a cadet branch of one of the Fifty; he just came into a nice fat Royal grant. He's getting the revenue from Upvale wine taxes, and he's bent on showing the City how a *real* aristo does things when he gets the cash to work with. He's starting a full stable; hunters, racers, carriage beasts and pleasure beasts. He knows his horse-flesh; what he *doesn't* know is how to tell if there's been a glamour put on 'em. Doesn't trust City mages, as who could blame him. They're all in the pay of somebody, and it's hard to say who might owe whom a favor or three. So he's had me on the lookout for an independent, and strictly temporary. Does that suit your talents?"

"You couldn't have suited me better!" Kethry exclaimed with delight. "Mage-sight's one of my strongest skills."

"Right then," the steward said with satisfaction. "Here's your address; here's your contract—sign here—"

Kethry scrutinized the brief document, nodded, and made her mage-glyph where he indicated.

"—and off you go; and good luck to you."

They left together; at the door, Tarma asked, "Want me with you?"

"No, I know the client, but he won't know me.

54

He's not one of Kavin's crowd, which is all I was worried about. I'll be safe enough on my own."

"All right then; I'll get back to the inn. Maybe Hadell has a connection to something."

Hadell poured Tarma a mug of ale, sat down beside her at the bench, and shook his head with regret. "Not a thing, Swordlady. I'm—"

"Afraid this is the lean season, I know. Well look, I'm half mad with boredom, is there at least somewhere I can practice?" Her trainers would not come to her while she was within city boundaries, so it was up to her to stay in shape. If she neglected to—woe betide her the next time they *did* come to her!

"There's a practice ground with pells set up behind the stable, if you don't mind that it's outside and a simple dirt ring."

"I think I'll survive," she laughed, and went to fetch her blades.

The practice ground was easy enough to find; Tarma was pleased to find it deserted as well. There was a broom leaning against the fence to clear off the light snow; she used it to sweep the entire fenced enclosure clean. The air was crisp and still, the sun weak but bright, and close enough to the zenith that there would be no "bad" sides to face. She stood silently for a moment or two, eyes closed; shaking off the "now" and entering that timeless state that was both complete concentration and complete detachment. She began with the warmup exercises; a series of slow, deliberate movement patterns that blurred, each into the next. When she had finished with them, she did not stop, but proceeded to the next stage, drawing the sword at her back and executing another movement series, this time a little faster. With each subsequent stage her moves became more intricate, and a bit more speed was added, until her blade was a shining blur and an onlooker could almost see the invisible opponent she dueled with.

She ended exactly where she had begun, slowing her movements down again to end with the resheathing of her blade, as smooth and graceful as a leaf falling. As it went home in the scabbard with a metallic click, the applause began.

Startled, Tarma glanced in the direction of the noise; she'd been so absorbed in her exercises that she hadn't noticed her watchers. There were three of them—Hadell, and two fur-cloaked middle-aged men who had *not* been part of the Guard contingent last night.

She half-bowed (with a wry grin), and let them approach her.

"I'd heard Shin'a'in were good—Swordlady, you've just proved to me that sometimes rumor speaks truth," said the larger of the two, a weathered-looking blond with short hair and a gold clasp to his cloak. "Lady, I'm Justin Twoblade, this is my shieldbrother Ikan Dryvale."

"Tarma shena Tale'sedrin," she supplied, "And my thanks. A compliment comes sweeter from a brother in the trade."

"We'd like to offer you more than compliments, if you're willing," said the second, amber-haired, like Kethry, but with blue eyes; and homely, with a plowboy's ingenuous expression.

"Well, since I doubt it's a bid for bed-services, I'll at least hear you out."

"Lessons. We'll pay your reckoning and your partner's in return for lessons."

Tarma leaned on the top bar of the practice-enclosure and gave the notion serious thought. "Hmm, I'll admit I like the proposition," she replied, squinting into the sunlight. "Question is, why, and for how long? I'd hate to miss a chance at the only short-term job for months and then have you two vanish on me."

Hadell interceded for them. "They'll not vanish, Swordlady," he assured her. "Justin and Ikan are wintering here, waiting for the caravans to start up again in spring. They're highly valued men to

56

the Jewel Merchant's Guild—valued enough that the merchants pay for 'em to stay here idle during the lean season."

"Aye, valued and bored!" Ikan exclaimed. "That's one reason for you. Few enough are those willing to spar with either of us—fewer still with the leisure for it. And though I've seen your style before, I've never had a chance to learn it—or how to counter it. If you wouldn't mind our learning how to counter it, that is."

"Mind? Hardly. Honest guards like you won't see Clan facing your blades, and anyone else who's learned our style thinking he'll have an easy time against hirelings deserves to meet someone with the counters. Done, then; for however long it takes Keth to earn us the coin to reprovision, I'll be your teacher."

"And we'll take care of the reckoning," Justin said, with a sly grin. "We'll just add it to our charges on the Guild. Odds are they'll think we've just taken to drinking and wenching away the winter nights!"

"Justin, I think I'm going to like you two," Tarma laughed. "You think a lot like me!"

Three

Yellow lamplight made warm pools around the common room of the Broken Sword, illuminating a scene far more relaxed than that of the night before. The other residents of the inn were much more cheerful, and certainly less weary, for there had been no repetition of yesterday's riot.

The two women had taken a table to themselves at the back of the room, in the corner. It was quieter there, and easier for them to hear each other. A lamp just over the table gave plenty of light, and Kethry could see that Tarma was quite well pleased with herself.

". . . so I've got a pair of pupils. Never thought I'd care for teaching, but I'm having a rare good time of it," Tarma concluded over fish stew and fried potatoes. "Of course it helps that Ikan and Justin are good-tempered about their mistakes, and they've got the proper attitude about learning swordwork."

"Which is?" Kethry asked, cheered to see a smile on Tarma's face for a change. A real smile, one of pleasure, not of irony.

"That inside that enclosure, I'm the only authority there is."

Kethry sniffed in derision; it was quiet enough in the back-wall corner they'd chosen that Tarma heard the sniff and grinned. "Modest, aren't you?" the mage teased.

She was feeling considerably better herself. No spies of Wethes or Kavin had leapt upon her during the day, and nothing that had occurred had brought back any bad memories. In point of fact she had frequently forgotten that she was in Mornedealth at all. All her apprehension now seemed rather pointless.

"No, seriously," Tarma replied to her japing. "That's the way it is; no matter what your relationship is outside the lessons, inside the lesson the master is The Master. The Master's word is law, and don't argue about the way you learned something before." Tarma wiped her plate clean with a last bit of bread, and settled back against the wall. "A lot of hire-swords don't understand that relationship—especially if it's a woman standing in the Master's place—but Ikan and Justin have had good teaching, and got it early enough to do some good. They're able, and they're serious, and they're going to come along fast."

"What if you wanted to learn something from one of them?" Kethry asked, idly turning a ring on her finger. "Wouldn't all this Master business cause problems?"

"No, because when I become the pupil, my teacher becomes the Master—actually that's already happened. Just before we wrapped up for the day, I asked Justin to show me a desperation-counter he'd used on me earlier." Tarma sighed regretfully. "Wish you knew something of swordwork, Greeneyes—that was a clever move he showed me. If you knew enough to appreciate it, I could go on about it for a candlemark. Could get you killed if you tried it without timing it exactly right, but if you did, it could save your getting spitted in a situation I couldn't see any way out of."

Kethry shook her head. "I don't see how you keep things straight. Back at the School, we only had *one* Master for each pupil, so we didn't get mixed up in trying to learn two different styles of magery."

"But half of your weaponry as a hire-sword is flexibility. You've got to be able to learn anything from anybody," Tarma replied. "If you can't be flexible enough mentally to accept any number of

Masters, you've no business trying to make your living with a blade, and that's all there is to say. How did your day go?"

"Enlightening." Kethry wore a fairly wry smile. She raised her voice slightly so as to be heard above the hum of conversation that filled the room. "I never quite realized the extent to which polite feuding among the Fifty goes before I took this little job."

"Ah?" Tarma cocked an inquiring eyebrow and washed down the last bite of bread and butter with a long pull on her mug.

"Well, I thought that business the fellow at the Hiring Hall told us was rather an exaggeration—until I started using mage-sight on some of the animals my client had picked out as possibles. A good half of them had been beglamoured, and I recognized the feel of the kind of glamour that's generally used by House mages around here. Some of what was being covered was kind of funny, in a nasty-brat sort of way—like the pair of matched grays that turned out to be fine animals, just a particularly hideous shade of muddy yellow."

"What would that have accomplished? A horse is a horse, no matter the color."

"Well, just imagine the young man's chagrin to be driving these beasts hitched to his maroon rig; in a procession, perhaps—and then the glamour is lifted, with all eyes watching and tongues ready to flap."

Tarma chuckled. "He'd lose a bit of face over it, not that I can feel too sorry for any idiot that would drive a maroon rig."

"You're heartless, you are. Maroon and blue are his House colors, and he hasn't much choice but to display them. He'd lose more than a little face over it; he wouldn't dare show himself with his rig in public until he got something so spectacular to pull it that his embarrassment would be forgotten, and for a trick like that, he'd practically have to have hitched trained griffins to overcome his loss of pride. By the way, that's *my* client you're calling an idiot, and he's paying quite well."

"In that case, I forgive him the rig. How long do you think you'll be at this?"

"About a week, maybe two."

"Good; that will give my pupils their money's worth and get us back on the road in good time."

"I hope so," Kethry looked over her shoulder a little, feeling a stirring of her previous uneasiness. "The longer I stay here, the more likely it is I'll be found out."

"I doubt it," Tarma took another long pull at her mug. "Who'd think to look for you here?"

"She's *where?*" The incredulous voice echoed in the high vaulting and bounced from the walls of the expensively appointed, blackwood paneled office.

"At one of the foreigner's inns; the Broken Sword. It's used mostly by mercenaries," Kavin replied, leaning back in his chair and dangling his nearly-empty wineglass from careless fingers. He half-closed his gray eyes in lazy pleasure to see Wethes squirming and fretting for his heirloom carpet and fragile furniture. "She isn't using her full name, and is claiming to be foreign herself."

"What's she doing there?" Wethes ran nervous fingers through his carefully oiled black locks, then played with the gold letter opener from his desk set. "Has she any allies? I don't like the notion of going after her in an inn full of hire-swords. There could be trouble, and more than money would cover."

"She wears the robes of a sorceress, and from all I could tell, has earned the right to—"

"That's trouble enough right there," Wethes interrupted.

Kavin's eyes narrowed in barely-concealed anger at the banker's rudeness. *"That* is what you have a house mage to take care of, my gilded friend. *Use* him. Besides, I strongly doubt she could be his equal, else she'd have a patron, and be spending the winter in a cozy little mage-tower. Instead of that,

61

she's wandering about as an itinerant, doing nothing more taxing than checking horses for beglamouring. As to her allies, there's only one that matters. A Shin'a'in swordswoman."

"Shin'a'in? One of the sword-dancers? I don't like the sound of that."

"They seem," he continued, toying with a lock of his curly, pale gold hair, "to be lovers."

"I like that even less."

"Wethes, for all your bold maneuvering in the marketplace, you are a singularly cowardly man." Kavin put his imperiled glass safely on one of Wethes' highly-polished wooden tables, and smiled to himself when Wethes winced in anticipation of the ring its moist bottom would cause. He stood up and stretched lazily, consciously mirroring one of the banker's priceless marbles behind him; then smoothed his silk-velvet tunic back into its proper position. He smiled to himself again at the flash of greed in Wethes' eyes; the banker valued him as much for his decorative value as for his lineage. With Kavin as a guest, any party Wethes held was certain to attract a high number of Mornedealth's acknowledged beauties as well as the younger members of the Fifty. It was probably time again to grace one of the fat fool's parties with his presence, after all, he did owe him something. His forbearance in not negating their bargain when Kavin's brat-sister vanished deserved some reward.

Of course, their arrangement was not all one-sided. Wethes would have lost all he'd gained by the marriage and more had it become known that his child-bride had fled him before the union was a day old. And now that she'd been gone more than three years—by law, she was no longer his wife at all. That would have been infinitely worse. It had been Kavin who had suggested that they pretend that Kethry had gone to stay on Wethes' country estate. Kethry was unused to dealing with people in any numbers, and found her new position as Wethes' helpmeet somewhat overwhelming—so they told the curious. She was happier away from the city and the confusion of society. Kavin was only too pleased to represent her interests with Wethes, and play substitute for her at formal occasions. They'd kept up the fiction for so long that even Kavin was starting to half-believe in Wethes' "shy" spouse.

"The Shin'a'in will be no problem," Kavin said soothingly, "She's a stranger in this city; she doesn't know it, she has no friends. All we need do is take your wayward wife when she's out from under the swordswoman's eye, and the Shin'a'in will be helpless to find her. She wouldn't even begin to know where to look. Although why you're bothering with this is beyond me. Kethry's hardly of an age to interest you anymore. And you have the connections you want without the burden of a real wife."

"She's mine," Wethes said, and the expression in his eyes was cold and acquisitive. "What's mine, I keep. No one robs me or tricks me with impunity. I'll keep her in chains for the insult she's done me—chains of her own body. She'll do to breed a dozen heirs, and they tell me no pregnant mage can work her tricks while so burdened."

Kavin raised a sardonic eyebrow, but made no further comment except to say, "I wouldn't believe that particular peasant's tale if I were you—I've had friends thought the same and didn't live to admit they were wrong. Now, I suspect your next question was going to be whether or not the Shin'a'in might be able to get a hearing with the Council. It might be possible—but who would believe a foreigner's tale of abduction against the word of the wealthiest man in Mornedealth?"

"Put that way, I see no risk of any kind to us," Wethes put down the gold paper knife. "And certainly I wish above all to have this accomplished at no risk of exposure. There are enough stories about why I mew my wife up in the country as it is. I'd rather no one ever discovered she's never been in my possession at all. But how do we get her away from her lover?"

"Just leave that—" Kavin smiled, well aware that his slow smile was not particularly pleasant to look on, "—to me."

Kethry woke with an aching head and a vile taste in her mouth; lying on her side, tied hand and foot, in total darkness. It hurt even to think, but she forced herself to attempt to discipline her thoughts and martial them into coherency, despite their tendency to shred like spiderwebs in a high wind. What had happened to her—where was she?

Think—it was so hard to think—it was like swimming through treacle to put one thought after another. Everything was fogged, and her only real desire was to relax and pass back into oblivion.

Which meant she'd been drugged.

That made her angry; anger burned some of the befuddlement away. And the resulting temporary surge in control gave her enough to remember a cleansing ritual.

Something like a candlemark later, she was still tied hand and foot and lying in total darkness. But the rest of the drug had been purged from her body and she was at last clearheaded and ready to think—and act. Now, what had happened?

She thought back to her last clear memory—parting with her client for the day. It had been a particularly fruitless session, but he had voiced hopes for the morrow. There were supposed to be two horse tamers from the North arriving in time for beast-market day. Her client had been optimistic, particularly over the rumored forest-hunters they were said to be bringing. They had parted, she with her day's wages safely in the hidden pocket of her robe, he accompanied by his grooms.

And she'd started back to the inn by the usual route.

But—now she had it!—there'd been a tangle of carts blocking the Street of the Chandlers. The carters had been swearing and brawling, laughingly goaded on by a velvet-clad youth on his high-bred palfrey who'd probably been the cause of the accident in the first place. She'd given up on seeing the street cleared before supper, and had ducked into an alley.

Then had come the sound of running behind her. Before she could turn to see who it was, she was shoved face-first against the rough wood of the wall, and a sack was flung over her head. A dozen hands pinned her against the alley wall while a sickly-sweet smelling cloth was forced over her mouth and nose. She had no chance to glimpse the faces of her assailants, and oblivion had followed with the first breath of whatever-it-was that had saturated the cloth.

But for who had done this to her—oh, that she knew without seeing their faces. It could only be Kavin and his gang of ennobled toughs—and to pay for it all, Wethes.

As if her thought had conjured him, the door to her prison opened, and Wethes stood silhouetted against the glare of light from the torch on the wall of the hallway beyond him.

Terror overwhelmed her, terror so strong as to take the place of the drug in befuddling her. She could no longer think, only feel, and all she felt was fear. He seemed to be five hundred feet tall, and even more menacing than her nightmares painted him.

"So," he laughed, looking down at her as she tried to squirm farther away from him, "My little bride returns at last to her loving husband."

"Damn, damn, damn!" Tarma cursed, and paced the icy street outside the door of the Broken Sword; exactly twenty paces east, then twenty west, then twenty east again. It was past sunset: Kethry wasn't back yet; she'd sent no word that she'd be late, and that wasn't like her. And—

She suddenly went cold, then hot, then her head spun dizzily. She clutched the lintel for support while the street spun before her eyes. The door of the inn opened, but she dared not try and move. Her ears told her of booted feet approaching, yet she was too giddy to even turn to see who it was.

"I'd ask if you had too much wine, except that I didn't see you drink more than a mouthful or two before you left the room," Justin spoke quietly, for her ears alone, as he added his support to that of the lintel. "Something's wrong?"

"Keth—something's happened to Keth—" Tarma gasped for air.

"I know she's late, but—"

"The—bond, the *she'enedran*-oath we swore to each other—it was Goddess-blessed. So if anything happens to one of us—"

"Ah—the other knows. Ikan and I have something of the kind, but we're spell-bound and we had it done a-purpose; useful when scouting. Sit. Put your head between your knees. I'll get Ikan. He knows a bit more about leechcraft and magery than I."

Tarma let him ease her down to the ice-covered doorstep, and did as she was told. The frosted stone was very cold beneath her rump, but the cold seemed to shake some of the dizziness away, getting her head down did a bit more. Just as her head began to clear, there were returning footsteps, and two pairs of booted feet appeared beside her.

"Drink this—" Ikan hunched on his heels beside her as she cautiously raised her head; he was holding out a small wooden bottle, and his whole posture showed concern. "Just a swallow; it's only for emergencies."

She took a gingerly mouthful, and was glad she'd been cautious. The stuff burned all the way down her gullet, but left a clear head and renewed energy behind it.

"Goddess—oh, Goddess, I have to—" she started to rise, but Justin's hands on her shoulders prevented her.

"You have to stay right where you are. You want to get yourself killed?" Ikan asked soberly. "You're a professional, Shin'a'in—act like one."

"All right;" Justin said calmly, as she sank back to the stone. "Something's happened to your oath-sister. Any clue as to what—"

"—or who?" Ikan finished. "Or why? You're not rich enough to ransom, and too new in Mornedealth to have acquired enemies."

"Why and who—I've got a damn good idea," Tarma replied grimly, and told them, in brief, Kethry's history.

"Gods, how am I to get her away from them? I don't know where to look, and even if I did, what's one sword against what Wethes can hire?" she finished in despair. "Why, oh why didn't I listen to her?"

"Kavin—Kavinestral—hmm," Justin mused. "Now that sounds familiar."

"It bloody well should," Ikan replied, stoppering his precious bottle tightly and tucking it inside his tunic. "He heads the Blue faction."

"The—what?" Tarma blinked at him in bewilderment.

"There are five factions among the wilder offspring of the Fifty; Blue, Green, Red, Yellow, and Black. They started out as racing clubs, but it's gotten down to a nastier level than that within the last few years," Ikan told her. "Duels in plenty, one or two deaths. Right now only two factions are strong enough to matter; Blue and Green. Kavin heads the Blues; a fellow called Helansevrith heads Green. They've been eyeblinks away from each other's throats for years, and the only thing that has kept them from taking each other on, is that Kavin is essentially a coward. He'd rather get his followers to do his dirty work for him. He makes a big pose of being a tough, but he's never personally taken anyone out. Mostly that doesn't matter, since he's got his followers convinced."

He stood up, offering his hand to Tarma. "I can give you a quick guess who could find out where Kethry is, because I know where Wethes won't take her. He won't dare take her to his home, his ser-

67

vants would see and gossip. He won't risk that, because the tale he's given out all these years is that Kethry is very shy and has been staying in seclusion on his country estate. No, he'll take her to his private brothel; I know he has one, I just don't know where. But Justin's got a friend who could tell us."

"That she could—and be happy to. Any harm she could bring that man would make her right glad." Even in the dim light from the torch over the door Tarma could see that Justin looked grim.

"How do you know all this about Wethes and Kavin?" Tarma looked from one to the other of them.

"Because, Swordlady," Ikan's mouth stretched in something that bore very little resemblence to a smile, "my name wasn't always Dryvale."

Kethry had wedged herself back into a corner of her barren, stone-floored cell. Wethes stood over her, candle-lantern in one hand, gloating. It was the very worst of her nightmares come true.

"What's mine remains mine, dear wife," he crowed, "You won't be given a second chance to escape me. I bought you, and I intend to keep you." He was enjoying every moment, was taking pleasure in her fright, just as he had taken pleasure in her pain when he'd raped her.

Kethry was paralyzed with fear, her skin crawling at the bare presence of him in the same room with her. What would she do if he touched her? Her heart was pounding as if she'd been running for miles. And she thought wildly that if he did touch her, perhaps her heart would give out.

He bent and darted his hand forward suddenly, as if intending to catch one of her arms, and she gave a little mew of terror and involuntarily kicked out at him with her bound feet.

His startled reaction took her completely by surprise.

He jumped backward, eyes widening, hands shaking so that the candle flame wavered. Fear was a mask over *his* features—absolute and utter fear of *her*. For one long moment he stared at her, and she at him, hardly able to believe what her own eyes were telling her.

He was *afraid* of her. For all his puffing and threatening, he was *afraid* of her!

And in that moment she saw him for what he was—an aging, paunchy, greedy coward. Any sign of resistance in an *adult* woman obviously terrified *him*.

She kicked out again, experimentally, and he jumped back another pace.

Probably the only females he *could* dominate were helpless children; probably that was why he chose them for his pleasures. At this moment he was as terrified of her as she had been of him.

And the nightmare-monster of her childhood revealed itself to be a thing of old clothes stuffed with straw.

Her fear of him evaporated, like a thing spun of mist. Anger quickly replaced the fear; and while fear paralyzed her magecraft, anger *fed* her powers. That she had been held in thrall for seven long years by fear of *this!*

He saw the change from terror to rage on her face; she could see his realization that she was no longer cowed mirrored on his. He bit his lip and stepped backward another three or four paces.

With three barked words she burned through the ropes on her hands and feet. She rose swiftly to her feet, shaking the bits off her wrists as she did so, her eyes never once leaving his face.

"Kidnap me, will you?" she hissed at him, eyes narrowed. "Drug me and leave me tied up, and think you can use me as you did before—well, I've grown up, even if you haven't. I've learned how to deal with slime like you."

Wethes gulped, and backed up again.

"I'll teach *you* to mend your ways, you fat, slobbering bastard! I'll show *you* what it feels like to be a victim!"

She pointed a finger at him, and miniature lightning leapt from it to his feet.

Wethes yelped, hopping from one foot to the other. Kethry aimed her finger a bit higher.

"Let's see how *you* like being hurt."

He screeched, turned, and fled, slamming the door behind him. Kethry was at it in an eyeblink, clawing at it in frustration, for there was no handle on this side. She screamed curses at him; in her own tongue, then in Shin'a'in when that failed her, pounding on the obdurate portal with both fists.

"Come back here, you half-breed son of a pig and an ape! I'll wither your manhood like a fifty-year-old sausage! Coward! Baby-raper! If I ever get my hands on your neck, I'll wrap a rope around it and spin you like a top! I'll peel your skull like a chestnut! *Come back here!*"

Finally her bruised fists recalled her to her senses. She stopped beating senselessly on the thick wood of the door, and rested for a moment, eyes closed as she reined in her temper. Anger did feed her power, but uncontrolled anger kept her from using it. She considered the door, considered her options, then acted.

A half-dozen spells later, her magic energies were becoming exhausted; the wood of the door was blackened and splintered, and the floor before it warped, but the door remained closed. It had been warded, and by a mage who was her equal at the very least. She used the last of her power to fuel a feeble mage-light; it hovered over her head, illuminating the barren cell in a soft blue radiance. She leaned her back against the far wall and allowed herself to slide down it, wearily. Wrapping her arms around her tucked-up knees, she regarded the warded door and planned her next move.

If Wethes could have seen the expression on her face, he'd have died of fright on the spot.

Tarma had been expecting Justin's "friend" to be a whore. Certainly she lived on a street where every other door housed one or more who practiced that trade—and the other doors led to shops that catered to their needs or those of their customers. They stopped midway down the block to tap lightly at one of those portals that plainly led to a small apartment, and Tarma expected it to be opened by another of the painted, bright-eyed trollops who bestowed themselves on doorways and windows all up and down this thoroughfare. She was shivering at the sight of most of them, not from dislike, but from sympathy. *She* was half-frozen (as usual), and could not imagine for a moment how they managed to stay warm in the scarves and shreds of silk they wore for bodices and skirts.

She didn't hold them in low esteem for selling themselves to earn their bread. After all, wasn't that exactly what she and Keth were doing? It was too bad that they had no other commodity to offer, but that was what fate had dealt them.

But the dark-eyed creature who opened her door at Justin's coded knock was no whore, and was unlikely to ever be mistaken for one, no matter how murky the night or intoxicated the customer.

In some ways she was almost a caricature of Tarma herself; practically sexless. Nothing other than Justin's word showed she was female—her sable hair cut so short it was hardly more than a smooth dark cap covering her skull; the thin, half-starved-looking body of an acrobat. She wore midnight blue; the only relief of that color came from the dozens of knives she wore, gleaming in the light that streamed from the room behind her, the torches of the street, and the lantern over the door, which Tarma noticed belatedly was of blue glass, not red. Two bandoliers were strapped across her slim chest, and both housed at least eight or nine matched throwing daggers. More were in sheaths strapped to her arms and legs; two longer knives, almost short swords, resided on each hip. Her face was as hard as marble, with deeply etched lines of pain.

"Justin, it's late," she said in a soft voice, frowning a little. "I take my shift soon."

71

"Cat-child, I know," Justin replied; Tarma realized in that instant that the hard lines of the girl's face had deceived her; she couldn't have been more than fifteen or sixteen. "But we have a chance to get at Wethes Goldmarchant and—"

The girl's face blazed with an unholy light. "When? *How?* I'll have somebody else sub for me; Gesta owes me a favor—"

"Easy, girl," Ikan cautioned. "We're not sure what we're going to be doing yet, or how much we're going to be able to hurt him, if at all."

She gave Ikan a sidelong look, then fixed her attention again on Justin. "Him—who?" she asked, shortly, jerking her head at Ikan.

"My shieldbrother; you've heard me talk about him often enough," he replied, interpreting the brief query, "And this swordlady is Tarma shena Tale'sedrin, Shin'a'in mercenary. Wethes has her oathsister, a sorceress—it's rather too long a tale to go into, but we know he took her, he's got his reasons for wanting her and we know he won't be taking her to his house in the District."

"And you want to know if I know where his latest pleasure-house is. Oh, aye; I do that. But unless you swear to let me in on this, I won't tell you."

"Cat, you don't know what you're asking—"

"Let her buy in,"" Tarma interrupted, and spoke to the girl directly. "I'm guessing you're one of Wethes' discards."

"You're not wrong. I hate his littlest nail-paring. I want a piece of him—somehow, some way—preferably the piece he prizes the most."

"That's a reasonable request, and one I'm inclined to give you a chance at. Just so long as you remember that our primary goal is the rescue of my oathsister, and you don't jeopardize getting Keth out in one piece."

"Let me roust out Gesta."

The girl darted between Tarma and Justin; ran up the staircase to the second floor to knock on

72

another nondescript door. The ugliest man Tarma had ever seen in her life answered it; Cat whispered something inaudible. He grinned, pulled a savage-looking half-ax from somewhere just inside the door, and sauntered down the stairs with it, whistling tunefully. He gave all three of them a wink as he passed them, said shortly, "Good hunting," and passed out of sight around a corner. The girl returned with a thoughtful look in her eyes.

"Come on in. Let's sit and plan this over. Being too hasty to look before I acted got me *into* Wethes' hands."

"And you won't be making that mistake a second time, will you, my girl?" Justin finished for her.

They filed into the tiny room; it held a few cushions and a pallet, a small clothes chest, more knives mounted on the wall, and a lantern, nothing more.

"You say your friend's a sorceress? The old bastard probably has her under binding from his house mage," she mused as she dropped down cross-legged on the pallet, leaving them to choose cushions. "Think she could break herself free if we gave him something else to think about?"

"Probably; Keth's pretty good—"

"The mage isn't all we have to worry about. Kavinestral's crowd is bound to be hanging around," Ikan interrupted.

"Damn—there's only four of us, and that lot is nearly thirty strong." The girl swore under her breath. "Where in *sheva* are we going to get enough bodies to throw at them?"

Whatever had been in that drink Ikan had given her seemed to be making Tarma's mind work at high speed. " 'Find your enemy's enemy.' That's what my people would say."

Ikan stared at her, then began to grin.

The last explosion from the sealed room below made the whole house rattle. Wethes turned to Kavin with stark panic in his face. "What have you

73

gotten me into?" he choked hysterically, grabbing Kavin by the front of his tunic and shaking him. *"What kind of monster has she become?"*

Kavin struck the banker's hands away, a touch of panic in his own eyes. Kethry wasn't going to be any happier with him than she was with Wethes—and if she got loose— "How was I to know? Magecraft doesn't breed true in my family! Mages don't show up oftener than one in every ten births in my House! She never gave any indication she had that much power when I was watching her! Can't your mage contain her?"

"Barely—and *then* what do I do? She'll kill me if I try and let her go, and may the gods help us if Regyl has to contend with more than simply containing her."

He might have purposefully called the sounds of conflict from the yard beyond the house. Shouts and cries of pain, and the sound of steel on steel penetrated the door to the courtyard; mingled in those shouts was the rally cry of the Greens. That galvanized Kavin into action; he started for the door to the rear of the house and the only other exit, drawing his sword as he ran, obviously hoping to escape before the fracas penetrated into the building.

But he stopped dead in his tracks as the door burst inward, and narrowly missed being knocked off his feet by the force that blew it off its hinges. His blade dropped from numb fingers, clattering on the slate-paved floor. His eyes grew round, and he made a tiny sound as if he were choking. Behind him, Wethes was doing the same.

There were five people standing in the doorway; whether Wethes knew all of them, he didn't know, but Kavin recognized only two.

First in line stood Kethry. Her robes were slightly torn and scorched in one place; she was disheveled, smoke-stained, and dirty. But she was very clearly in control of the situation—and Kavin found himself completely cowed by her blazing eyes.

74

Behind her was the Shin'a'in Tarma; a sword in one hand, a dagger in the other, and the look of an angry wolf about her. Should Kethry leave anything of him, he had no doubt that his chances of surviving a single candlemark with her were nil.

Next to Tarma stood a young girl in midnight blue festooned with throwing daggers and with a long knife in either hand. She was the only one of the lot not dividing her attention between himself and Wethes. Kavin looked sideways over his shoulder at the banker, and concluded that he would rather not be in Wethes' shoes if that girl were given her way with him; Wethes looked as if he were as frightened of her as of the rest combined.

Behind those three stood a pair of men, one of whom looked vaguely familiar, although Kavin couldn't place him. They took one look at the situation, grinned at each other, sheathed their own weapons, and left, closing what remained of the door behind the three women.

Kavin backed up, feet scuffling on the floor, until he ran into Wethes.

"Surprise, kinsmen," Kethry said. "I am *so* glad to find you both at home."

The Broken Sword was the scene of general celebration; Hadell had proclaimed that the ale was on the house, in honor of the victory the five had just won. It was a double victory, for not only had they rescued Kethry, but Ikan had that very day gotten them a hearing and a highly favorable verdict from the Council. Wethes was, insofar as his ambitions went, a ruined man. Worse, he was now a laughing-stock to the entire city.

"Cat-child, I expected you at least to want him cut up into collops." Justin lounged back precariously in his chair on the hearth, balancing it on two legs. "I can't fathom why you went along with this."

"I wanted to *hurt* him," the girl replied, trimming her nails with one of her knives. "And I knew

75

after all these years of watching him that there's only two ways to hurt that bastard; to hit his pride or his moneybags. Revenge, they say, is a dish best eaten cold, and I've had three years of cooling."

"And here's to Kethry, who figured how to get both at the same time," Ikan raised his mug in a toast.

Kethry reciprocated. "And to you, who convinced the Council I was worth heeding."

Ikan smiled. "Just calling in a few old debts, that's all. You're the one who did the talking."

"Oh, really? I was under the impression that you did at least half of it."

"Some, maybe. Force of habit, I'm afraid. Too many years of listening to my father. You may know him—Jonis Revelath—"

"Gods, yes, I remember him!" Kethry exclaimed. "He's the legal counsel for half the Fifty!"

"Slightly more than half."

"That must be why you're the one who remembered it's against the law to force any female of the Fifty into *any* marriage without her consent," Kethry said admiringly. "Ikan, listening to you in there—I was truly impressed. You're clever, you're persuasive, you're a good speaker. Why aren't you . . ."

"Following in my father's footsteps? Because he's unable to fathom why I am more interested in justice than seeing that every client who hires me gets off without more than a reprimand."

"Which is why the old stick wouldn't defend Wethes for all the gold that bastard threw at him," Justin chuckled, seeing if he could balance the chair on *one* leg. "Couldn't bear to face his son with Ikan on the side of Good, Truth, and Justice. Well, shieldbrother, going to give up the sword and Fight for Right?" The irony in his voice was so strong it could have been spread on bread and eaten.

"Idiot!" Ikan grinned. "What do you think I am, a dunderhead like you? Swords are safer and usually fairer than the law courts any day!"

"Well, I think you were wonderful," Kethry began.

"I couldn't have done it without you and Cat being so calm and clear. You had an answer for everything they could throw at you."

"Enough!" Tarma growled, throwing apples at all of them. "You were all brilliant. So now Wethes is poorer by a good sum; Cat has enough to set herself up as anything she chooses, we have enough to see us to the Plains, and the entire town knows Wethes isn't potent with anything over the age of twelve. He's been the butt of three dozen jokes that I've heard so far; there are gangs of little boys chanting rude things in front of his house at this moment."

"I've heard three songs about him out on the street, too," Cat interrupted with an evil grin.

"And last of all, Keth's so-called marriage has been declared null. What's left?"

"Kavin?" Justin hazarded. "Are we likely to see any more trouble from him?"

"Well, I saw to it that he's been declared disinherited by the Council for selling his sister. Keth didn't want the name or the old hulk of a house that goes with it, so it's gone to a cadet branch of her family."

"With my blessings; they're very religious, and I think they intend to set up a monastic school in it. As for my brother, when last seen, Kavin was fleeing for his life through the stews with the leader of the Greens in hot pursuit," Kethry replied with a certain amount of satisfaction. "I saw him waiting for Kavin outside the Council door, and I was kind enough to pinpoint my brother for him with a ball of mage-light. I believe his intention was to paint Kavin a bright emerald when he caught him."

Justin burst into hearty guffaws—and his chair promptly capsized.

The rest of them collapsed into helpless laughter at the sight of him, looking surprised and indignant, amid the ruins of his chair.

"Well!" he said, crossing his arms and snorting. "There's gratitude for you! That's the last time I *ever* do any of you a fav—"

Whatever else he was going to say ended in a splutter as Ikan dumped his mug over his head.

"Still set on getting back to the Plains?" Kethry asked into the darkness.

A sigh to her right told her that Tarma wasn't asleep yet. "I have to," came the reluctant answer. "I can't help it. I have to. If you want to stay . . ."

Kethry heard the unspoken plea behind the words and answered it. "I'm your *she'enedra*, am I not?"

"But do you really understand what that means?"

"Understand—no. Beginning to understand, yes. You forget, I'm a mage; I'm used to taking internal inventory on a regular basis. I've never had a Talent for Empathy, but now I find myself knowing what you're feeling, even when you're trying to hide it. And you knew the instant I'd been taken, didn't you?"

"Yes."

"And now you're being driven home by something you really don't understand."

"Yes."

"Does it have anything to do with that Goddess of yours, do you think?"

"It might; I don't know. We Sworn Ones move mostly to Her will, and it may be She has some reason to want me home. I *know* She wants Tale'sedrin back as a living Clan."

"And She wants me as part of it."

"She must, or She wouldn't have marked the oathtaking."

Kethry stretched tired muscles, and put her hands under her head. "How much time do you have before you *have* to be back?"

"Before Tale'sedrin is declared dead? Four years, maybe five. Kethry . . ."

"It's all right, I told you, I can feel some of what you're feeling now, I understand."

"You're—you're better. I'm—I'm feeling some of what you're feeling, too."

"This whole mess was worth it," Kethry replied

slowly, only now beginning to articulate what she'd only sensed. "It really was. My ghosts have been laid to rest. And revenge—great Goddess, I couldn't have hoped for a better revenge! Kavin is terrified of me; he kept expecting me to turn him into a toad, or something. And Wethes is utterly ruined. He's still got his money, but it will never buy him back his reputation. Indirectly, you got me that, Tarma. I finally realized that I would *never* reach Adept without coming to terms with my past. You forced me into the confrontation I'd never have tried on my own. For that alone I would be indebted to you."

"*She'enedran* don't have debts."

"I rather figured that. But—I want you to know, I'm going with you because I want to, not because I think that I owe you. I didn't understand what this oath meant at first, but I do now, and I would repeat it any time you asked."

A long silence. Then, "*Gestena, she'enedra.*"

That meant "thank you," Kethry knew—thanks, and a great deal more than thanks.

"*Yai se corthu,*" she replied uncertainly. "Two are one." For she suddenly felt all Tarma's loneliness and her own as well, and in the darkness of the night it is sometimes possible to say things that are too intense and too true for daylight.

"*Yai se corthu.*" And a hand came from the darkness to take hers.

It was enough.

Four

"**T**arma, we've been riding for weeks, and I still haven't seen any sign that this country is going to turn into grass-plains," Kethry complained, shifting uncomfortably in Rodi's saddle. "Brush-hills, yes. Near-desert, certainly. Forest, ye gods! I've seen more trees than I ever want to see again!"

"What's wrong with forest, other than that you can't do a straight-line gallop or get a clear shot at anything, that is?"

Kethry gazed in all directions, and then glanced up to where branches cut off every scrap of sky overhead. Huge evergreens loomed wherever she looked; the only sunlight came from those few beams that managed to penetrate the canopy of needles. It seemed as if she'd been breathing resin forever, the smell clung to everything; clothing, hair—it even got into the food. It wasn't unpleasant; the opposite, in fact, especially after they'd first penetrated the edges of the forest after days of fighting a dusty wind. But after days of eating, drinking, and breathing the everlasting odor of pine, she was heartily tired of it.

It was chilly and damp on the forest floor, and lonely. Kethry hadn't seen a bird in days, for they were all up where the sun was. She could hear them calling, but the echoes of their far-off singing only made the empty corridors between the tree trunks seem more desolate. This forest had to be incredibly ancient, the oldest living thing she'd ever seen, perhaps. Certainly the trees were larger than any she was familiar with. They towered for yards before branching out, and in the case of a few giants she had noticed, their trunks were so large that several adults could have circled the biggest of them with their arms without touching hand to hand. The road they followed now was hardly more than a goat track; the last person they had seen had been two weeks ago, and since that time they'd only had each other's voices to listen to.

At first it had been pleasurable to ride beneath these branches, especially since they had spent weeks skirting that near-desert she had mentioned, riding through furlong after furlong of stony, brush-covered hills with never anything taller than a man growing on them. While the spring sun had nowhere near the power it would boast in a mere month, it had been more than hot enough for Kethry during the height of the day. She couldn't imagine how Tarma, dressed in her dark Sword Sworn costume, could bear it. When the hills began to grow into something a bit more impressive, and the brush gave way to real trees, it was a genuine relief to spend all day in their cool shade. But now . . .

"It's like they're—watching. I haven't sensed anything, either with mage-senses or without, so I know it must be my imagination, but . . ."

"It's not your imagination; something is watching," Tarma interrupted calmly. "Or rather, some*one*. I thought I'd not mention it unless you saw or felt something yourself, since they're harmless to *us*. Hadn't you ever wondered why I haven't taken any shots at birds since we entered the trees?"

"But—"

"Oh, the watchers themselves aren't within sensing distance, and not within the scope of your mage-senses either—just their feathered friends. Hawks, falcons, ravens and crows by day, owls and night-hawks by dark. *Tale'edras*, my people call them— the Hawkbrothers. We really don't know what they call themselves. We don't see them much, though they've been known to trade with us."

81

"Will we see any of them?"

"Why, do you want to?" Tarma asked, with a half-grin at Kethry's nod. "You mages must be curiosity incarnate, I swear! Well, I might be able to do something about that. As I said, we're in no danger from them, but if you really want to meet one—let's see if I still have my knack for identifying myself."

She reined in Kessira, threw back her head, and gave an ear-piercing cry—not like the battle shriek of a hawk, but a bit like the mating cry, or the cry that identifies mate to mate. Rodi started, and backed a few steps, fighting his bit, until Kethry got him back into control. A second cry echoed hers, and at first Kethry thought it *was* an echo, but it was followed by a winged streak of gold lightning that swooped down out of the highest branches to land on Tarma's outstretched arm.

It braked its descent with a thunder of wings, wings that seemed to Kethry to belong to something at least the size of an eagle. Talons like ivory knives bit into the leather of Tarma's vambrace; the wings fanned the air for a heartbeat more, then the bird settled on Tarma's forearm, regal and gilded.

"Well if I'd wanted a good omen, I couldn't have asked for a better," Tarma said in astonishment. "This is a vorcel-hawk; you see them more on the plains than in the forests—it's my Clan's standard."

The bird was half-again larger than any hawk Kethry had ever seen; its feathers glistened with an almost metallic gold sheen, no more than a shade darker than the bird's golden eyes. It cocked its head to one side and regarded Kethry with an intelligent air she found rather disturbing. Rodi snorted at the alien creature, but Kessira stood calmly when one wing flipped a hair's-breadth from her ear, apparently used to having huge birds swoop down at her rider from out of nowhere.

"Now, who speaks for you, winged one?" Tarma turned her attention fully to the bird on her arm, stroking his breast feathers soothingly until he settled, then running her hand down to his right leg and examining it. Kethry edged closer, cautiously; wary of the power in that beak and those sharp talons. She saw that what Tarma was examining was a wide band on its leg, a band of some shiny stuff that wasn't metal and wasn't leather.

"Moonsong k'Vala, hmm? Don't know the name. Well, let's send the invitation to talk. I really should at least pay my respects before leaving the trees, if anyone wants to take them, so . . ."

Tarma lowered her arm a little, and the hawk responded by moving up it until he perched on her shoulder. His beak was in what Kethry considered to be uncomfortably close proximity to Tarma's face, but Tarma didn't seem at all concerned. Thinking about the uncertain temperament of all the raptors *she'd* ever had anything do to with, Kethry shivered at Tarma's casualness.

When the bird was safely on her shoulder, Tarma leaned over a little and rummaged in her saddlebag, finally coming up with a cluster of three small medallions. Kethry could see that they were light copper disks, beautifully enameled with the image of the bird that sat her shoulder.

She selected one, dropped the other two back in her bag; then with great care, took a thong from a collection of them looped to a ring on her belt, passed the thong through the hole in the top of the medallion and knotted it securely. She offered the result to the bird, who looked at it with a surprising amount of intelligence before opening his beak slowly and accepting the thong. He bobbed his head twice, the medallion bouncing below his head, and Tarma raised her arm again. He sidled along it until he reached her wrist, and she launched him into the air. His huge wings beat five or six times, raising a wind that fanned their hair, then he was lost to sight among the branches.

"What was that all about?"

"Politeness, more than anything. The Hawk-brothers have known we were here from the moment we entered the forest, and they knew I was Shin'a'in Kal'enedral when they came to look at us in person—that would have been the first night we camped. Since then they've just been making sure we didn't wander off the track, or get ambushed by something we couldn't handle. We'll be leaving the forest soon."

"Soon? When?"

"Keep your breeches on, girl! Tomorrow afternoon at the latest. Anyway, you wanted to see one of the Hawkbrothers, and it's only polite for me to acknowledge the fact that they've been guarding us."

"I thought you said they were watching us."

"Since I'm Shin'a'in and we're allies, it amounts to the same thing. *Sa-hai;* I just sent my Clan token off to our current guardian, whoever it is. If he or she chooses, we'll get a response before we leave."

"Moonsong sounds like a female name to me," Kethry replied.

"Maybeso, maybeno. The Hawkbrothers are v-e-r-y different—well, you'll see if we get a visitor. Keep your eyes busy looking for a good campsite; stick to the road. As Shin'a'in I have certain privileges here, and I'm tired of dried beef. I'm going hunting."

She swung Kessira off under the trees, following the path the hawk had taken, leaving Kethry alone on the track. With a shrug, Kethry urged Rodi back into a walk and did as she'd been told.

Still homing in on the Plains; she's been easier than she was before Mornedealth, but still—home is drawing her with a power even I can feel. I wonder if it's because she hasn't a real purpose *anymore, not since she accomplished her revenge.*

Kethry kept Rodi to a walk, listening with half her attention for the sound of water. Running surface water was somewhat scarce in the forest; finding it meant they made a campsite then and there.

I don't really have a purpose either, except to learn and grow stronger in magic—but I expected that. I knew that's the way my life would be once I left the school until I could found my own. But Tarma—she needs a purpose, and this home-seeking is only a substitute for one. I wonder if she realizes that.

When Tarma caught up with her, it was a candle-mark or so before sunset, but it was already dark under the trees. Kethry had found a site that looked perfect, with a tiny, clear stream nearby and a cleared area where one of the giant trees had fallen and taken out a wide swath of seedlings with it. That had left a hole in the green canopy above where sunlight could penetrate, and there were enough grasses and plants growing that there was browse for their animals. The tree had been down for at least a season, so the wood was dry and gathering enough firewood for the evening had been the task of less than a candlemark.

Kethry discovered when she was sweeping out the area for stones to line a firepit that others had found the site just as perfect, for many of the stones bore scorch marks. Now their camp was set up, and the tiny fire burning brightly in the stone-lined pit. When they had entered this forest, Tarma had emphasized the importance of keeping their fires small and under strict control. Now that Kethry knew about the Hawkbrothers, she could guess why. This tree-filled land was theirs, and they doubtless had laws that a visitor to it had better keep, especially with winged watchers all about.

She heard Tarma approaching long before she saw her; a dark shape looming back along the trail, visible only because it was moving.

"Ho, the camp!" Tarma's hoarse voice called cheerfully.

"Ho, yourself—what was your luck?"

"Good enough. From *this* place you take no more than you need, ally or not. Got browse?"

Tarma appeared in the firelight, leading Kessira, something dangling from her hand.

"Behind me about forty paces; Rodi's already tethered there, along a downed tree. If you'll give me what you've got, I'll clean it."

"Skinning is all you need to do, I field-gutted 'em." Tarma tossed two odd creatures at Kethry's feet, the size and shape of plump rabbits, but with short, tufted ears, long claws, and bushy, flexible tails.

"I'll go take care of Rodi and my baby, and I'll be right back." Tarma disappeared into the darkness again, and sounds from behind her told Kethry that she was unsaddling her mare and grooming both the animals. She had unsaddled Rodi but had left the rest to Tarma, knowing the Shin'a'in could tend a saddlebeast in the dark and half asleep. Rodi, while well-mannered for a mule, was too ticklish about being groomed for Kethry to do it in uncertain light.

When Tarma returned, she brought with her their little copper traveling-kettle filled with water. "We'll have to stew those devils; they're tough as old boots after the winter," she said; then, so softly Kethry could hardly hear her, "I got a reply to my invitation. We'll have a visitor in a bit. Chances are he'll pop in out of nowhere; try not to look startled, or we'll lose face. I can guarantee he'll look very strange; in this case, the stranger the better—if he really looks odd it will mean he's giving us full honors."

Just at the moment the stewed meat seemed ready, their visitor appeared.

Even though she'd been forewarned, Kethry *still* nearly jumped out of her skin. One moment the opposite side of the fire was empty—the next, it was not.

He was tall; like Tarma, golden-skinned and blue-eyed. Unlike Tarma, his hair was a pure silver-white; it hung to his waist, two braids framing his face, part of the rest formed into a topknot, the remainder streaming unconfined down his back. Feathers had been woven into it—a tiny owlet nestled at the base of the topknot, a nestling Kethry thought to be a clever carving, until it moved its head and blinked.

His eyes were large and slightly slanted, his features sharp, with no trace of facial hair. His eyebrows had a slight, upward sweep to them, like wings. His clothing was green, all colors of green— Kethry thought it at first to be rags, until she saw how carefully those seeming rags were cut to resemble foliage. In a tree, except for that hair, he'd be nearly invisible, even with a wind blowing. He wore delicate jewelry of woven and braided silver wire and crystals.

He carried in his right hand a strange weapon; a spearlike thing with a wicked, curving point that seemed very like a hawk's talon at one end and a smooth, round hook at the other. In his left he carried Tarma's medallion.

Tarma rose to her feet, gracefully. "Peace, Moonsong."

"And upon you, Child of the Hawk." Both of them were speaking Shin'a'in—after months of tutoring Kethry was following their words with relative ease.

"Tarma," the Shin'a'in replied, "and Kethry. My *she'enedra.* You will share hearth and meal? It is tree-hare, taken as is the law; rejected suitors, no mates, no young, and older than this season's birthing."

"Then I share, and with thanks." He sank to the ground beside the fire with a smoothness, an ease, that Kethry envied; gracefully and soundlessly as a falling leaf. She saw then that besides the feathers he had also braided strings of tiny crystals into his hair, crystals that reflected back the firelight, as did the staring eyes of the tiny owlet. She remembered what Tarma had told her, and concluded they were being given high honor.

He accepted the bowl of stewed meat and dried vegetables with a nod of thanks, and began to eat with his fingers and a strange, crystalline knife hardly longer than his hand. When Tarma calmly began her own portion, Kethry did the same, but couldn't help glancing at their visitor under cover of eating.

He impressed her, that was certain. There was an air of great calm and patience about him, like that of an ancient tree, but she sensed he could be a formidable and implacable enemy if his anger was ever aroused. His silver hair had made her think of him as ancient, but now she wasn't so certain of his age. His face was smooth and unlined; he could have been almost any age at all, from stripling to oldster.

Then she discovered something that truly frightened her; when she looked for him with mage-sight, he wasn't there.

It wasn't a shielding, either—a shield either left an impression of a blank wall or of an absolute nothingness. No, it was as if there was no one across the fire from them at all, nothing but the plants and stones of the clearing, the woods beyond, and the owlet sitting in a young tree.

The owlet sitting in a young tree!

It was then she realized that he was somehow appearing to her mage-sight as a part of the forest, perfectly blended in with the rest. She switched back to normal vision and smiled to herself. And as if he had known all along that she had been scanning him—in fact, if he were practiced enough to pull off what he was doing, he probably *did*—he looked up from his dinner and nodded at her.

"The banner of the Hawk's Children has not been seen for seasons," he said breaking the silence. "We heard ill tales. Tales of ambush on the road to the Horse Fair; tales of death come to their very tents."

"True tales," Tarma replied, the pain in her voice

88

audible to Kethry . . . and probably to Moonsong. "I am the last."

"Ah. Then the blood-price—"

"Has been paid. I go to raise the banner again; this, my *she'enedra*, goes with me."

"Who holds herds for Tale'sedrin?"

"Liha'irden. You have knowledge of the camps this spring?

"Liha'irden . . ." he brooded a moment. "At Ka'tesik on the border of their territory and yours. So you go to them. And after?"

"I have given no thought to it." Tarma smiled suddenly, but it was with a wry twist to her mouth. "Indeed, the returning has been sufficient to hold my attention."

"You may find," he said slowly, "that the Plains are no longer the home to you that they were."

Tarma looked startled. "Has aught changed?"

"Only yourself, Lone Hawk. Only yourself. The hatched chick cannot go back to the shell, the falcon who has found the sky does not willingly sit the nest. When a task is completed, it is meet to find another task—and you may well serve the Lady by serving outlanders."

Tarma looked startled and pale, but nodded.

"OutClan Shin'a'in—" He turned his attention abruptly to Kethry. "You bear a sword—"

"Aye, Elder."

He chuckled. "Not so old as you think me, nor so young either. Three winters is age to a polekit, but fifty is youth to a tree. You bear a sword, yet you touched me with mage-sight. Strange to see a mage with steel. Stranger still to see steel with a soul."

"What?" Kethry was too startled to respond politely.

"Hear me, mate of steel and magic," he said, leaning forward so that he and the owlet transfixed her with unblinking stares. "What you bear will bind you to herself, more and more tightly with each hour you carry her. It is writ that Need is her name—you shall come to need her, as she needs

89

you, as both of you answer need. This is the price of bearing her, and some of this you knew already. I tell you that you have not yet reached the limit to which she can—and will—bind you to herself, to her goals. It is a heavy price, yet the price is worth her service; you know she can fight for you, you know she can heal you. I tell you now that her powers will extend to aid those you love, so long as they return your care. Remember this in future times—"

His blue eyes bored into hers with an intensity that would have been frightening had he not held her beyond fear with the power he now showed himself to possess. She knew then that she was face-to-face with a true Adept, though of a discipline alien to hers; that he was one such as she hardly dared dream of becoming. Finally he leaned back, and Kethry shook off the near-trance he had laid on her, coming to herself with a start.

"How did you—"

He silenced her with a wave of his hand.

"I read what is written for me to see, nothing more," he replied, rising with the same swift grace he had shown before. "Remember what I have read, both of you. As you are two-made-one, so your task will be one. First the binding, then the finding. For the hearth, for the meal, my thanks. For the future, my blessing. Lady light thy road—"

And as abruptly as he had appeared, he was gone.

Kethry started to say something, but the odd look of puzzlement on Tarma's face stopped her.

"Well," she said at last, "I have only one thing to say. I've passed through this forest twenty times, at least. In all that time, I must have met Hawkbrothers ten out of the twenty, and that was extraordinary. But this—" she shook her head. "That's more words at once from one of them than any of my people has ever reported before. Either we much impressed him—"

"Or?"

"Or," she smiled crookedly, "We are in deep trouble."

Kethry wasn't quite sure what it was that woke her; the cry of a bird, perhaps; or one of the riding beasts waking out of a dream with a snort, and so waking her in turn.

The air was full of gray mist that hung at waist height above the needle-strewn forest floor. It glowed in the dim blue light that signaled dawn, and the treetops were lost beyond thought within it. It was chill and thick in the back of her throat; she felt almost as if she were drinking it rather than breathing it.

The fire was carefully banked coals; it was Tarma's watch. Kethry sighed and prepared to go back to another hour of sleep—then stiffened. There were no sounds beyond what she and the two saddle-beasts were making. Tarma was gone.

Then, muffled by the fog, came the sound of blade on blade; unmistakable if heard once. And Kethry had heard that peculiar *shing* more times than she cared to think.

Kethry had lain down fully-clothed against the damp; now she sprang to her feet, seizing her blade as she rose. Barefooted, she followed the sound through the echoing trunks, doing her own best to make no sound.

For why, if this had been an attack, had Tarma not awakened her? An ambush then? But why hadn't Tarma called out to her? Why wasn't she calling for help now? What of the Hawkbrothers that were *supposed* to be watching out for them?

She slipped around tree trunks, the thick carpet of needles soft beneath her feet, following the noise of metal scissoring and clashing. Away from the little cup where they had camped the fog began to wisp and rise, winding around the trunks in wooly festoons, though still thick as a storm cloud an arm's length above her head. The sounds of blades came clearer now, and she began using the tree trunks to hide behind as she crept up upon the scene of conflict.

She rounded yet another tree, and shrank again behind it; the fog had deceived her, and she had almost stumbled into the midst of combat.

The fog ringed this place, moving as if alive, a thick tendril of it winding out, now and again, to interpose itself between Tarma and her foe. It glowed—it glowed with more than the predawn light. To mage-sight it glowed with power, power bright and pure, power strong, true, and—strange. It was out of her experience—and it barred her from the charmed circle where the combatants fenced.

Tarma's eyes were bright with utter concentration, her face expressionless as a sheet of polished marble. Kethry had never seen her quite like this, except when in the half-trance she induced when practicing or meditating. She was using both sword and dagger to defend herself—

Against another Shin'a'in.

This man was unmistakably of Tarma's race. The tawny gold skin of hands and what little Kethry could see of his face showed his kinship to her. So did the strands of raven hair that had been bound out of his face by an equally black headband, and ice-blue eyes that glinted above his veil.

For he *was* veiled; this was something Tarma never had worn for as long as Kethry had known her. Kethry hadn't even known till this moment that a veil could be part of a Shin'a'in costume, but the man's face was obscured by one, and it did not have the feeling of a makeshift. He was veiled *and* garbed entirely in black, the black Tarma had worn when on the trail of those who had slaughtered her Clan. Black was for blood-feud—but Tarma had sworn that there was *never* blood-feud between Shin'a'in and Shin'a'in. And black was for Kal'ene-dral—three times barred from internecine strife.

There was less in their measured counter and

riposte of battle than of dance. Kethry held her breath, transfixed by more than the power of the mist. She was caught by the deadly beauty of the weaving blades, caught and held entranced, drawn out of her hiding place to stand in the open.

Tarma did not even notice she was there—but the other did.

He stepped back, breaking the pattern, and motioned slightly with his left hand. Tarma instantly broke off her advance, and seemed to wake just as instantly from her trance, staring at Kethry with the startled eyes of a wild thing broken from hiding.

The other turned, for his back had been to Kethry. He saluted the sorceress in slow, deliberate ceremony with his own blade. Then he winked slowly and gravely over his veil, and—vanished, taking the power in the magic fog with him.

Released from her entrancement, Kethry stared at her partner, not certain whether to be frightened, angry or both.

"What—was—that—" she managed at last.

"My trainer; my guide," Tarma replied sheepishly. "One of them, anyway." She sheathed her sword and stood, to all appearances feeling awkward and at a curious loss for words. "I . . . never told you about them before, because I wasn't sure it was permitted. They train me every night we aren't within walls . . . one of them takes my watch to see you safe. I . . . I guess they decided I was taking too long to tell you about them; I suppose they figured it was time you knew about them."

"You said your people didn't *use* magic—but he—he was alive with it! Only your Goddess—"

"He's Hers. In life, was Kal'enedral; and now—" she lifted up her hand, "—as you saw. His magic *is* Hers—"

"What do you mean, 'in life'?" Kethry asked, an edge of hysteria in her voice.

"You mean—you couldn't tell?"

"Tell *what*?"

"He's a spirit. He's been dead at least a hundred years, like all the rest of my teachers."

It took Tarma the better part of an hour to calm her partner down.

They broke out of the trees, as Tarma had promised, just past midafternoon.

Kethry stared; Tarma sat easily in Kessira's saddle, and grinned happily. "Well?" she asked, finally.

Kethry sought for words, and failed to find them.

They had come out on the edge of a sheer drop-off; the mighty trees grew to the very edge of it, save for the narrow path on which they stood. Below them, furlongs, it seemed, lay the Dhorisha Plains.

Kethry had pictured acres of grassland, a sea of green, as featureless as the sea itself, and as flat.

Instead she saw beneath her a rolling country of gentle, swelling rises; like waves. Green grass there was in plenty—as many shades of green as Kethry had ever seen, and more—and golden grass, and a faint heathered purple. And flowers—it must have been flowers that splashed the green with irregular pools of bright blue and red, white and sunny yellow, orange and pink. Kethry took an experimental sniff and yes, the breeze rising up the cliff carried with it the commingled scents of growing grass and a hundred thousand spring blossoms.

There were dark masses, like clouds come to earth, running in lines along the bottoms of some of the swells. After a long moment Kethry realized that they must be trees, far-off trees, lining the water-courses.

"How—" she turned to Tarma with wonder in her eyes, "how could you ever bear to leave this?"

"It wasn't easy, she'enedra," Tarma sighed, deep and abiding hunger stirring beneath the smooth surface of the mask she habitually wore. "Ah, but you're seeing it at its best. The Plains have their hard moments, and more of them than the soft.

94

Winter—aye, that's the coldest face of all, with all you see out there sere and brown, and so barren all the life but the Clans and the herds sleeps beneath the surface in safe burrows. High summer is nearly as cruel, when the sun burns everything, when the watercourses shrink to tiny trickles, when you long for a handsbreadth of shade, and there is none to be found. But spring—oh, the Plains are lovely then, as lovely as She is when She is Maiden—and as welcoming."

Tarma gazed out at the blowing grasslands with a faint smile beginning to touch her thin lips.

"Ah, I swear I am as sentimental as an old granny with a mouthful of tales of how golden the world was when *she* was young," she laughed, finally, "and none of this gets us down to the Plains. Follow me, and keep Rodi exactly in Kessira's footsteps. It's a long way down from here if you slip."

They followed a narrow trail along the face of the drop-off, a trail that switched back and forth constantly as it dropped, so that there was never more than a length or two from one level of the trail to the next below it. This was no bad idea, since it meant that if a mount and rider *were* to slide off the trail, they would have a fighting chance of saving themselves one or two levels down. But it made for a long ride, and all of it in the full sun, with nowhere to rest and no shade anywhere. Kethry and her mule were tired and sweat-streaked by the time they reached the bottom, and she could see that Tarma and Kessira were in no better shape.

But there was immediate relief at the bottom of the cliff, in the form of a grove of alders and willows with a cool spring leaping out of the base of the escarpment right where the trail ended. They watered the animals first, then plunged their own heads and hands into the tinglingly cold water, washing themselves clean of the itch of sweat and dust.

Tarma looked at the lowering sun, slicking back wet hair. "Well," she said finally, "We have a choice. We can go on, or we can overnight here. Which would you rather?"

"You want the truth? I'd rather overnight here. I'm tired, and I ache; I'd like the chance to rinse all of me off. But I know how anxious you are to get back to your people."

"Some," Tarma admitted, "But ... well, if we quit now, then made an early start of it in the morning, we wouldn't lose too much time."

"I won't beg you, but—"

"All right, I yield!" Tarma laughed, giving in to Kethry's pleading eyes.

Camp was quickly made; Tarma went out with bow and arrow and returned with a young hare and a pair of grass-quail.

"This—this is strange country," Kethry commented sleepily over the crackle of the fire. "These grasslands shouldn't be here, and I could swear that cliff wasn't cut by nature."

"The gods alone know," Tarma replied, stirring the fire with a stick. It's possible, though. My people determined long ago that the Plains are the bowl of a huge valley that is almost perfectly circular, even though it takes weeks to ride across the diameter of it. This is the only place where the rim is that steep, though. Everywhere else it's been eroded down, though you can still see the boundaries if you know what to look for."

"Perfectly circular—that hardly seems possible."

"You're a fine one to say 'hardly possible,'" Tarma teased. "Especially since you've just crossed through the lowest reaches of the Pelagir Hills."

"I *what?*" Kethry sat bolt upright, no longer sleepy.

"The forest we just passed through—didn't you know it was called the Pelgiris Forest? Didn't the name sound awfully familiar to you?"

"I looked at it on the map—I guess I just never made the connection."

"Well, keep going north long enough and you're in the Pelagirs. My people have a suspicion that the Tale'edras are Shin'a'in originally, Shin'a'in who went a bit too far north and got themselves changed. They've never said anything, though, so we keep our suspicions to ourselves."

"The Pelagirs . . ." Kethry mused.

"And just what are you thinking of? You surely don't want to go in there, do you?"

"Maybe."

"Warrior's Oath! Are you *mad*? Do you know the kind of things that live up there? Griffins, fire-birds, colddrakes—things without names 'cause no one who's seen 'em has lived long enough to give them any name besides 'AAAARG!' "

Kethry had to laugh at that. "Oh, I know," she replied, "Better than you. But I also know how to keep us relatively safe in there—"

"What do you mean, 'us'?"

"—because one of my order came from the heart of the Pelagirs. The wizard Gervase."

"Gervase?" Tarma's jaw dropped. "The Lizard Wizard? You mean that silly song about the Wizard Lizard is true?"

"Truer than many that are taken for pure fact. Gervase was a White Winds adept, because the mage that gifted him was White Winds—and it was a good day for the order when he made that gift. Gervase, being a reptile, and being a Pelagir change-ling as well, lived three times the span of a normal sorcerer, and we are notoriously long-lived. He became the High Adept of the order, and managed to guide it into the place it holds today."

"Total obscurity," Tarma taunted.

"Oh, no—protective obscurity. Those who need us know how to find us. Those we'd rather couldn't find us can't believe anyone who holds the power a White Winds Adept holds would *ever* be found ankle-deep in mud and manure, tending his own onions. Let other mages waste their time in politics and sorcerer's duels for the sake of proving that one of them is better—or at least more devious—than the other. We save our resources for those who are in need of them. There's this, too—*we* can sleep sound of nights, knowing nobody is likely to conjure an adder into one of *our* sleeping rolls."

"Always provided he could ever find the place where you've laid that sleeping roll," Tarma laughed. "All right, you've convinced me."

"When we find your people—"

"Hmm?"

"Well, then what?"

"I'll have to go before a Council of the Elders of three Clans, and present myself. They'll give me back the Clan banner, and—" Tarma stopped, nonplussed.

"And—" Kethry prompted.

"I don't know; I hadn't thought about it. Liha'irden has been taking care of the herds; they'll get first choice of yearlings for their help. But—I don't know, *she'enedra*; the herds of an entire Clan are an awful lot for just two women to tend. My teacher told me I should turn mercenary . . . and I'm not sure now that he meant it to be temporary."

"That *is* how we've been living."

"I suppose we could let Liha'irden continue as caretakers, at least until we're ready to settle down, but—I don't want to leave yet."

"I don't blame you," Kethry teased, "After all, you just got here!"

"Well, look—if we're going to really try and become mercenaries, and not just play at it to get enough money to live on, we're both going to have to get battlesteeds—and *you* are going to have to learn how to manage one."

Kethry paled. "A battlesteed?" she faltered. "Me? I've never ridden anything livelier than a pony!"

"I don't want you at my side in a fight on anything *less* than a Shin'a'in-bred and trained battlesteed," Tarma said in a tone that brooked no argument.

Kethry swallowed, and bit her lip a little.

Tarma grinned suddenly. "Don't go lathering yourself, *she'enedra*, we may decide to stay here, after all, and you can confine yourself to ponies and mules or your own two feet if that's what you want."

"That prospect," Kethry replied, "sounds more attractive every time you mention battlesteeds!"

Kethry had no idea how she did it, but Tarma led them straight into the Liha'irden camp without a single false turning.

"Practice," she shrugged, when Kethry finally asked, "I know it looks all the same to you, but I know every copse and spring and hill of this end of the Plains. The Clans are nomadic, but we each have territories; Liha'irden's was next to Tale'sedrin's. I expected with two Clans' worth of herds they would be camped by one of the springs that divided the two, and pasturing in both territories. When the Hawkbrother told me which spring, I knew I was right."

Tarma in her costume of Kal'enedral created quite a stir—but Kethry was a wonder, especially to the children. When they first approached the camp, Tarma signaled a sentry who had then ridden in ahead of them. As they got nearer, more and more adolescents and older children came out on their saddle-beasts, forming a polite but intensely curious escort. When they entered the camp itself, the youngest came running out to see the visitors, voluble and quite audible in their surprise at the sight of Kethry.

"She has grass-eyes!"

"And sunset-hair!"

"Mata, how come she's riding a mule? She doesn't *look* old or sick!"

"Is she Sworn, too? Then why is she wearing dust-colors?" That from a tiny girl in blazing scarlet and bright blue.

"Is she staying?" "Is she outClan?" "Is she from the magic place?"

99

Tarma swung down off Kessira and took in the mob of children with a mock-stern expression. "What is this clamor? Is this the behavior of Shin'a'in?"

The babble cut off abruptly, the children keeping complete silence.

"Better. Who will take my mare and my *she'-enedra's* mule?"

One of the adolescents handed his reins to a friend and presented himself. "I will, Sworn One."

"My thanks," she said, giving him a slight bow. He returned a deeper bow, and took both animals as soon as Kethry had dismounted.

"Now, will someone bring us to the Elders?"

"No need," said a strong, vigorous voice from the rear of the crowd. "The Elders are here."

The gathering parted immediately to allow a collection of four Shin'a'in through. One was a woman of middle years, with a square (for a Shin'a'in) face, gray-threaded hair, and a look of determination about her. She wore bright harvest-gold breeches, soft, knee-high, fringed leather boots, a cream-colored shirt with embroidered sleeves, and a scarlet-and-black embroidered vest that laced closed in the front. By the headdress of two tiny antelope horns she wore, Kethry knew she was the Shaman of Liha'irden.

The second was a very old man, his face wrinkled so that his eyes twinkled from out of the depths of deep seams, his hair pure white. He wore blue felt boots, embroidered in green; dark blue breeches, a lighter blue shirt, and a bright green vest embroidered with a pattern to match the boots, but in blue. The purely ornamental riding crop he wore at his belt meant he was the Clan Chief. He was far from being feeble; he walked fully erect with never a hint of a limp or a stoop, and though his steps were slow, they were firm.

Third was a woman whose age lay somewhere between the Clan Chief and the Shaman. She wore scarlet; nothing but shades of red. That alone told

Kethry that this was the woman in whose charge lay both the duties of warleader and of instructing the young in the use of arms.

Last was a young man in muted greens, who smiled widely on seeing Tarma. Kethry knew this one from Tarma's descriptions; he was Liha'irden's Healer and the fourth Elder.

"Either news travels on the wings of the birds, or you've had scouts out I didn't see," Tarma said, giving them the greeting of respect.

"In part, it did travel with birds. The Hawk-brothers told us of your return," the Healer said. "They gave us time enough to bring together a Council."

The crowd parted a second time to let five more people through, all elderly. Tarma raised one eyebrow in surprise.

"I had not expected to be met by a full Council," she said, cautiously. "And I find myself wondering if this is honor, or something else."

"Kal'enedra, I wish you to know that this was nothing of my doing," the Clan Chief of Liha'irden replied, his voice heavy with disapproval. "Nor will my vote be cast against you."

"Cast against me? *Me?* For why?" Tarma flushed, then blanched.

"Tale'sedrin is a dead Clan," one of the other five answered her, an old woman with a stubborn set to her mouth. "It only lacks a Council's pronouncement to make history what is already fact."

"*I* still live! And while I live, Tale'sedrin lives!"

"A Clan is more than a single individual, it is a living, growing thing," she replied, "You are Kal'ene-dral; you are barren seed by vow and by the War-rior's touch. How can Tale'sedrin be alive in you, when you cannot give it life?"

"Kal'enedra, Tarma, we have no wish to take from you what is yours by right of inheritance," the Warleader of Liha'irden said placatingly. "The herds, the goods, they are still yours. But the Children of

101

the Hawk are no more; you are vowed to the Shin'a'in, not to any single Clan. Let the banner be buried with the rest of the dead."

"No!" Tarma's left hand closed convulsively on the hilt of her dagger, and her face was as white as marble. "Sooner than that I would die with them! Tale'sedrin *lives!*"

"It lives in *me.*" Kethry laid one restraining hand on Tarma's left and then stepped between her and the Council. "I am *she'enedra* to the Sworn One—does this not make me Shin'a'in also? *I* have taken no vows of celibacy; more, I am a White Winds sorceress, and by my arts I can prolong the period of my own fertility. Through *me* Tale'sedrin is a living, growing thing!"

"How do we know the bond is a true one?" One of the group of five, a wizened old man, asked querulously.

Kethry held up her right hand, palm out, and reached behind her to take Tarma's right by the wrist and display it as well. Both bore silvered, crescent-shaped scars.

"By the fact that She blessed it with Her own fire, it can be nothing but a true bond—" Tarma began, finding her tongue again.

"Sheka!" the old man spat, interrupting her. "She says openly she is a sorceress. She could have produced a seeming sign—could have tricked even you!"

"For what *purpose?*"

"To steal what outClan have always wanted; our battlesteeds!"

Tarma pulled her hand away from Kethry's and drew her sword at that venomous accusation.

"Kethry has saved my life; she has bled at my side to help me avenge Tale'sedrin," Tarma spat, holding her blade before her in both hands, taking a wide-legged, defensive stance. "How *dare* you doubt the word of Kal'enedral? She is my true *she'enedra* by a Goddess-blessed vow, and you will retract your damned lie or die on my blade!"

Whatever tragedy might have happened next was

102

forestalled by the battle scream of a hawk high in the sky above Kethry. For some reason—she never could afterward say why—she flung up her arm as Tarma had to receive the hawk in the forest.

A second scream split the air, and a golden meteor plummeted down from the sun to land on Kethry's wrist. The vorcel-hawk was even larger than Moonsong's had been, and its talons bit into Kethry's arm as it flailed the air with its wings, mantling angrily at the Council. Pain raced up her arm and blood sprang out where the talons pierced her, for she had no vambrace such as Tarma wore. Blood was dying the sleeve of her robe a deep crimson, but Kethry had endured worse in her training as a sorceress. She bit her lip to keep from crying out and kept her wrist and arm steady.

The members of the Council—with the exception of the Clan Chief, the Shaman and the Healer of Liha'irden—stepped back an involuntary pace or two, murmuring.

Tarma held out her arm, still gripping her blade in her right hand; the hawk lifted itself to the proffered perch, allowing Kethry to lower her wounded arm and clutch it to her chest in a futile effort to ease the pain. Need would not heal wounds like these; they were painful, but hardly life-threatening. She would have to heal them herself when this confrontation was over; for now, she would have to endure the agony in silence, lest showing weakness spoil Tarma's bid for the attention of the Council.

"Is *this* omen enough for you?" Tarma asked, in mingled triumph and anger. "The emblem of Tale'sedrin has come, the spirit of Tale'sedrin shows itself—and it comes to Kethry, whom you call outClan and deceiver! *To me, she'enedra!*"

Again, without pausing for second or third thoughts, Kethry reached out her wounded right hand and caught Tarma's blade-hand; the hawk screamed once more, and mantled violently. It hopped along Tarma's arm until it came to their joined hands, hands that

103

together held Tarma's blade outstretched, pointing at the members of the Council. There it settled for one moment, one foot on each wrist.

Then it screamed a final time, the sound of its voice not of battle, but of triumph, and it launched itself upward to be lost in the sun.

Kethry scarcely had time to notice that the pain of her arm was gone, before the young Healer of Liha'irden was at her side with a cry of triumph of his own.

"You doubt—you dare to doubt still?" he cried, pulling back a sleeve that was so soaked with blood that beneath it the flesh was surely pierced to the bone. "Look here, all of you—*look!*"

For beneath Kethry's sleeve her arm was smooth and unwounded, without so much as a scar.

Five

The gathering-tent was completely full; crowded with gaudily garbed Shin'a'in as it was, it would have been difficult to find space for even a small child. Tarma and Kethry had places of honor near the center and the firepit. Since the confrontation with the Council and their subsequent vindication, their credit had been very high with the Liha'irden.

"Keth—" Tarma's elbow connected gently with Kethry's ribs.

"Huh?" Kethry started; she'd been staring at the fire, more than half mesmerized by the hypnotic music three of her Liha'irden "cousins" had been playing. Except for her hair and eyes she looked as Shin'a'in as Tarma; weeks in the sun this summer had turned her skin almost the same golden color as her partner's, and she was dressed in the same costume of soft boots, breeches, vest and shirt, all brightly colored and heavily embroidered, that the Shin'a'in themselves wore. If anything, it was Tarma who stood out in her sober brown.

It had been a good time, this past spring and summer; a peaceful time. And yet, Kethry was feeling a restlessness. Part of it *had* to be Need's fault; the sword wanted her about and doing. But part of it—part of it came from within her. And Tarma was often unhappy, too. She hadn't said anything, but Kethry could feel it.

"It's your turn. What's it going to be; magic, or tale?"

The children, who had been lulled by the music, woke completely at that. Their young voices rose above the murmuring of their elders, all of them trying to have some say in the choice of entertainment. Half of them were clamoring for magic, half for a story.

These autumn gatherings were anticipated all year; in spring there were the young of the herds to guard at night, in summer night was the time of moving the herds, and in winter it was too cold and windy to put up the huge gathering-tent. Children were greatly prized among the Clans, but normally were not petted or indulged—except here. During the gatherings, they were allowed to be a little noisy; to beg shamelessly for a particular treat.

This was the first time Tarma had included her *she'enedra* in the circle of entertainment, and the Liha'irden were as curious about her as young cats.

"Does it have to be one or the other?" Kethry asked.

"Well, no . . ."

"All right then," Kethry said, raising her voice to include all of them. "In that case, I'll tell you *and* show you a tale I learned when I was an apprentice with Melania of the White Winds Adepts." She settled herself carefully and spun out some of her own internal energy into an illusion-form. She held out her hands, which began to glow, then the thin thread of the illusion-form spun up away from them like a wisp of rising smoke. The tendril rose until it was just above the heads of the watching Shin'a'in, then the end thickened and began to rotate, drawing the rest of the glow up into itself until it was a fat globe dancing weightlessly up near the centerpole.

"This is the tale as it was told me," Kethry began, just as the Shin'a'in storytellers had begun, while the children oohed and whispered and the adults tried to pretend they weren't just as fascinated as the children. "Once in a hollow tree on the top of a hill, there lived a lizard."

Within the globe the light faded and then brightened, and a scene came into focus; a stony, vetch-covered hill surmounted by a lightning-blasted tree

106

of great girth, a tree that glowed ever so faintly. As the Clansfolk watched, a green and brown scaled lizard poked his head cautiously out of a crevice at the base of it; the lizard looked around, and apparently saw nothing, for the rest of him followed. Now even the adults gasped, for this lizard walked erect, like a man, and had a head more manlike than lizardlike.

"The lizard's name was Gervase, and he was one of the *hertasi* folk that live still in the Pelagir Hills. *Hertasi* once were tree-lizards long, long ago, until magic changed them. Like humans, they can be of any nature; good or bad, kind or cruel, giving or selfish. But they all have one thing in common. All are just as intelligent as we are, and all were made that way long ago by magic wars. Now this Gervase knew a great deal about magic; it was the cause of him being the way he was, after all, and there was so much of it in the place where he lived that his very tree-home glowed at night with it. So it isn't too surprising that he should daydream about it, now, is it?"

The scene changed; the children giggled, for the lizard Gervase was playing at being a wizard, just as they had often done, with a hat of rolled-up birch bark and a "wand" of a twisted branch.

"He wanted very badly to *be* a wizard; he used to dream about how he would help those in trouble, how he would heal the sick and the wounded, how he would be so powerful he could stop wars with a single wave of his wand. You see, he had a very kind heart, and all he ever really wanted to do was to make the world a little better. But of course, he knew he couldn't; after all, he was nothing but a lizard."

The lizard grew sad-looking (odd how body-language could convey dejection when the creature's facial expressions were nil), put aside his hat and wand, and crawled up onto a branch to sit in the sun and sigh.

"Then one day while he was sunning himself, he heard a noise of hound and horse in the distance."

Now the lizard jumped to his feet, balancing himself on the branch with his tail while he craned his neck to see as far as he could.

"While he was trying to see what all the fuss was about, a man stumbled into his clearing."

A tattered and bloody human of early middle age fell through the bushes, catching himself barely in time to keep from cracking his head open on the rocks. There was a gasp from the assembled Clansfolk, for the man had plainly been tortured. Kethry had not toned the illusion-narrative down much from the one she'd been shown; firstly, the children of the Clans were used to bloodshed, secondly, it brought the fact home to all of them that this was a *true* tale.

The man in the illusion was dark-haired and bearded; bruised and beaten-looking. And if one looked very carefully, it was possible to see that the rags he wore had once been a wizard's robe.

"Gervase didn't stop to wonder about who the man was or why he was being chased; he only knew that no thinking creature should hunt another down like a rabbit with dogs and horses. He ran to the man—"

The lizard slid down the tree trunk and scampered to the fallen wizard. Now it was possible to see, as he helped the man to his feet, that he was very close to being man-sized himself, certainly the size of a young adolescent. At first the man was plainly too dazed to realize what it was that was helping him, then he came to himself and did a double take. The shock and startlement on his face made the children giggle again—and not just the children.

" 'Come, human,' Gervase said. 'You must hide in my tree, it's the only place where you can be safe. I will keep the dogs away from you.' The wizard—for that was what he was—did not waste any breath in arguing with him, for he could clearly hear the dogs baying on his track."

The lizard half-carried the man to the crevice in

108

the tree; the man crawled inside. Gervase then ran over to a rock in the sun and arranged himself on it, for all the world like an ordinary (if overly-large) lizard basking himself.

"When the dogs came over the hill, with the hunters close behind them, Gervase was ready."

As the dogs and the horses burst through the underbrush, Gervase jumped high in the air, as if startled out of his wits. He dashed back and forth on all fours for a moment, then shot into the crack in the tree. There he remained, with his head sticking out, obviously hissing at the dogs that came to bark and snap at him and the man he was protecting. When one or two got too close, Gervase bit their noses. The dogs yelped and scuttled to the rear of the pack, tails between their legs, while the entire tent roared with laughter.

"Then the man who had been hunting the wizard arrived, and he was not pleased. He had wanted the wizard to serve him; he had waited until the wizard's magics were either exhausted or nullified by his own magicians, then he had taken him prisoner and tortured him. But our wizard had pretended to be unconscious and had escaped into the Pelagirs. The lord was so angry he had escaped that he had taken every hunter and dog he had and pursued him—but thanks to Gervase, he thought now that he had lost the trail."

The plump and oily man who rode up on a sweating horse bore no small resemblance to Wethes. Tarma smiled at that, as the "lord" whipped off his hounds and laid the crop across the shoulders of his fearful huntsman, all the while turning purple with rage. At length he wrenched his horse's head around, spurring it savagely, and led the lot out of the clearing. Gervase came out of hiding; so did the wizard.

"The wizard was very grateful. 'There is a great deal of magical energy stored in your home,' he said. 'I can grant you nearly anything you want, little friend, if you'll let me use it. What way can I

109

reward you?' Gervase didn't even have to think about it. 'Make me a man like you!' he said, 'I want to be a man like you!' 'Think carefully on what you're asking,' the mage said. 'Do you want to be human, or do you want to be a magician? You have the potential within you to be a great mage, but it will take all the magic of your tree to unlock it, and even then it will take years of study before you can make use of your abilities. Or would you rather have the form of a human? That, too, will take all the magic of your tree. So think carefully, and choose.' "

The little lizard was plainly in a quandary; he twitched and paced, and looked up at the sky and down at the ground for help.

"Gervase had a terrible decision, you see? If he became a human, people would listen to him, but he wouldn't have the magic to do what he wanted to do. But if he chose to have his Gifts unlocked, where would he find someone who would teach the use of them to a lizard? But finally, he chose. 'I will be a mage,' he said, 'and somewhere I will find someone willing to teach me, someone who believes that good inside is more important than the way I look on the outside.' "

The wizard in the vision smiled and raised his hands over Gervase. The tree began to glow brightly; then the glow flowed off the tree and over the little lizard, enveloping him and sinking into him.

" 'You need look no further, little friend,' said the mage, when he'd done. 'For I myself will teach you, if you wish to be my apprentice.' "

Gervase plainly went half-mad with joy; he danced comically about for a good several minutes, then dashed into the now-dark tree and emerged again with a few belongings tied into a cloth. Together he and the mage trudged down the path and disappeared into the forest. The glowing globe went dark then, and vanished slowly, dissolving like smoke.

"And that is the tale of how Gervase became an

apprentice to Cinsley of White Winds. What happened to him after that—is another tale."

The applause Kethry received was as hearty as ever Tarma had gotten back in the days when her voice was the pride of the Clans.

"Well done," Tarma whispered, when the attentions of those gathered had turned to the next to entertain.

"I was wondering if my doing magic would offend anyone—" Kethry began, then looked up, suddenly apprehensive, seeing one of the Clansfolk approaching them.

And not just any Shin'a'in, but the Shaman.

The grave and imposing woman was dressed in earthy yellows this evening; she smiled as she approached them, as if she sensed Kethry's apprehension. "Peace, *jel'enedra*," she said quietly, voice barely audible to the pair of them over the noise of the musicians behind her. "That was well done."

She seated herself on the carpeted floor beside them. "Then—you didn't mind my working magic?" Kethry replied, tension leaving her.

"Mind? *Li'sa'eer!* Anything but! Our people seldom see outClan magic. It's well to remind them that it can be benign—"

"As well as being used to aid the slaughter of an entire Clan?" Tarma finished. "It's well to remind them that it exists, period. It was that forgetfulness that lost Tale'sedrin."

"*Hai*, you have the right of it. *Jel'enedra*, I sense a restlessness in you. More, I sense an unhappiness in both you and your oathkin."

"Is it that obvious?" Kethry asked wryly. "I'm sorry if it is."

"Do not apologize; as I said, I sense it in your *she'enedra* as well."

"Tarma?" Kethry's eyebrows rose in surprise.

"Look, I don't think this is where we should be discussing this," Tarma said uncomfortably.

"Will you come to my tent, then, Kal'enedra; you and your oathsister?" The request was more than

111

half command, and they felt almost compelled to follow her out of the tent, picking their way carefully among the crowded Clansfolk.

Tarma was curious to see what the Shaman's dome-shaped tent looked like within; she was vaguely disappointed to see that it differed very little from her own inside. There was the usual sleeping pad of sheepskins and closely-woven woolen blankets, the mule-boxes containing personal belongings and clothing, two oil-lamps, and bright rugs and hangings in profusion. It was only when Tarma took a closer look at the hangings that she realized that they were something out of the ordinary.

They seemed to be figured in random patterns, yet there was a sense of rhythm in the pattern—like writing.

The Shaman seemed uncannily aware of what Tarma was thinking. "*Hai,* they *are* a written history of our people; written in a language all their own. It is a language so concise that one hundred years of history can be contained in a single hanging."

Tarma looked around the tent, and realized that there must be close to fifty of these hangings, layered one upon the other. But—that meant *five thousand years!*

Again the Shaman seemed to sense Tarma's thoughts. "Not so many years as you may think. Some of these deal with the history of peoples other than our own, peoples whose lives impinge upon ours. But we are not here to speak of that," the Shaman seated herself on her pallet, allowing Kethry and Tarma to find places for themselves on her floor. "I think the Plains grow too small for both of you, *he shala?*"

"There's just no real need for me here," Kethry replied. "My order—well, we just can't stay where there's nothing for us to do. If some of the Clansfolk had magic gifts, or wanted to learn the magics that don't require a Gift, it would be different; I'd gladly teach them here. But no one seems interested, and

112

frankly, I'm bored. Actually, it's a bit worse than being bored. I'm not *learning* anything. I'll never reach Adept status if I stay here."

"I . . . don't fit here," Tarma sighed, "And I never thought I'd say that. Like Keth, I'd be happy to teach the children swordwork, but that would be usurping Shelana's position. I thought I could keep busy working with *her,* but—"

"I venture to guess you found her scarcely more challenging than her pupils? Don't look so surprised, my child; I of all people should know what your Oath entails. Liha'irden has not had Kal'enedral in its midst for a generation, but I know what your skill is likely to be—and how it was acquired."

There was silence for a moment, then Tarma said wryly, "Well, I wish you'd told *me!* The first time one of Them showed up, it was enough to stop my heart!"

"We were a trifle short of time to be telling you anything, even had you been in condition to hear it. So—tell me more of your troubles."

"I love my people, I love the Plains, but I have no *purpose* here. I am totally useless. I'd be of more use raising income for Tale'sedrin than I am now."

"Ah—you have seen the problem with raising the banner?"

"We're only two; we can't tend the herds ourselves. We could bring in orphans and third and fourth children from Clans with far too many to feed, but we have no income yet to feed them ourselves. And frankly, we have no Name. We aren't likely to attract the kind of young men and women that would be my first choice without a Name."

"Would you mind telling me what you two are talking about?" Kethry demanded, bewilderment written plainly on her face.

"Goddess—I'm sorry, Keth. You've fallen in with us so well, I forget you aren't one of us."

"Allow me," the Shaman interrupted gently. "*Jel'enedra,* when you pledged yourself to providing children for Tale'sedrin, you actually pledged only to provide the Clan core—unless you know some magic to cause you to litter like a grass-runner!" The Shaman's smile was warm, and invited Tarma as well as Kethry to share the joke. "So; what will be, is that when you do find a mate and raise up your children, they must spend six months of the year here, shifting by one season each year so that they see our life in harsh times as well as easy. When they come of age, they will choose—to be Shin'a'in always, or to take up a life off of the Plains. Meanwhile, we will be sending out the call, and unmated *jel'asadra* of both sexes are free to come to your banner to make it their own. Orphans, also. Until you and your *she'enedra* declare the Clan closed. Do you see?"

"I think so. Now what was the business about a Name?"

"The caliber of youngling you will attract will depend on the reputation you and Tarma have among the Clans. And right now—to be frank, you will only attract those with little to lose. Not the kind of youngling I would hope to rebuild a Clan with, if *I* were rebuilding Tale'sedrin."

"The part about income was clear enough," Kethry said after a long moment of brooding. "We—we'd either have to sell some of the herd at a loss, or starve."

"Are you in condition to hear advice, the pair of you?"

"I think so," said Tarma.

"Leave the Clans; leave the Plains. There is nothing for you here, you are wasting your abilities and you are wasting away of boredom. I think there is something that both of you wish to do—and I also think that neither of you has broached the subject for fear of hurting the other's feelings."

"I . . ." Kethry faltered. "Well, there's two things, really. Since I've vowed myself to rebuilding Tale's-edrin—that needs a man, I'm afraid. I'll grant you that I could just go about taking lovers but . . . I want something more than that, I want to care for

114

the father of any children I might have. And frankly, most of the men here are terribly alien to me."

"Understandable," the Shaman nodded. "Laudable, in fact. The Clan law holds that you, your *she'enedra*, and your children would comprise a true Clan-seed, but I think everyone would be happier if you chose a man as a long-term partner-mate, and one with whom you have more in common than one of us. And the other?"

"If I ever manage to get myself to the stage of Adept, it's more-or-less expected of a White Winds sorceress that she start a branch of the school. But to do that, to attract pupils, I'd need two things. A reputation, and money."

"So again, we come to those two things, as important to you as to the Clan."

"Well that's odd, that you've been thinking of starting a school, because I've been playing with the same notion," Tarma said in surprise. "I've been thinking I enjoyed teaching Justin and Ikan so much that it would be no bad thing to have a school of my own, one that teaches something besides swordwork."

"Teach the heart as well as the mind and body?" the Shaman smiled. "Those are praiseworthy goals, children, and not incompatible with rebuilding Tale'sedrin. Let me make you this proposition; for a fee, Liha'irden will continue to raise and tend your herds—I think a tithe of the yearlings would be sufficient. Do you go out before the snows close us in and see if you cannot raise both the reputation and the gold to build your schools and your Clan. If you do not succeed, you may always return here, and we will rebuild the harder way, but if you do, well, the Clan is where the people are; there is no reason why Tale'sedrin should not first ride in outClan lands until the children are old enough to come raise the banner themselves. Will that satisfy your hungers?"

"Aye, and then some!" Tarma spoke for both of them, while Kethry nodded, more excitement in her eyes than had been there for weeks.

Kessira and Rodi remained behind with the herds when they left two weeks later. Now that they were to pursue their avocation of mercenary in earnest, they rode a matched pair of the famed Shin'a'in battlesteeds; horses they had picked out and had been training with since spring.

Battlesteeds were the result of a breeding program that had been going on for as long as the Shin'a'in had existed as nomadic horsebreeders. Unlike most horsebreeding programs, the Shin'a'in had not been interested in looks, speed, or conformation. They had bred for intelligence, above all else—and after intelligence, agility, strength, and endurance. The battlesteeds were the highly successful result.

Both horses they now rode were mottled gray; they had thick necks and huge, ugly heads with broad foreheads. They looked like unpolished statues of rough granite, and were nearly as tough. They could live very handily on forage even a mule would reject; they could travel sunrise to sunset at a ground-devouring lope that was something like a wolf's tireless tracking-pace. They could be trusted with an infant, but would kill on signal *or* on a perceived threat. They were more intelligent than any horse Kethry had ever seen—more intelligent than a mule, even. In their ability to obey and to reason they more resembled a highly trained dog than a horse, for they could actually work out a simple problem on their own.

This was why Shin'a'in battlesteeds were so famed—and why the Clansfolk guarded them with their very lives. Between their intelligence and the training they received, battlesteeds were nearly the equal partners of those who rode them in a fight. It was in no small part due to the battlesteeds that the Shin'a'in had remained free and the Dhorisha Plains unconquered.

But they were rare; a mare would drop no more than four or five foals in a lifetime. So no matter how tempting the price offered, no battlesteed would ever be found in the hands of anyone but a Shin'a'in —or one who was pledged blood-sib to a Shin'a'in.

These horses had been undergoing a strenuous course of training for the past four years, and had just been ready this spring to accept permanent riders. They were trained to fight either on their own or with a rider—something Kethry was grateful for, since she was *nothing* like the kind of rider Tarma was. Tarma could stick to Hellsbane's back like a burr on a sheep; Kethry usually lost her seat within the first few minutes of a fight. But no matter; Ironheart would defend her quite as readily on the ground—and on the ground Kethry could work her magics without distraction.

Both battlesteeds were mares; mares could be depended on to keep their heads no matter what the provocation, and besides, it was a peculiarity of battlesteeds that they tended to throw ten or fifteen fillies to every colt. That meant colts were never gelded—and never left the Plains.

This time when Tarma left the Liha'irden encampment, it was with every living soul in it outside to bid her farewell. The weather was perfect; crisp and cool without being too cold. The sky was cloudless, and there was a light frost on the ground.

"No regrets?" Kethry said in an undertone as she tightened Ironheart's girth.

"Not many," Tarma replied, squinting into the thin sunlight, then mounting with an absentminded ease Kethry envied. "Certainly not enough to worry about."

Kethry scrambled into her own saddle—Ironheart was nearly sixteen hands high, the tallest beast she'd ever ridden—and settled her robes about herself.

"You have some, though?" she persisted.

"I just wish I knew this was the right course we're taking ... I guess," Tarma laughed at herself, "I guess I'm looking for another omen."

"Lady Bright, haven't you had *enough*—" Kethry was interrupted by a scream from overhead.

117

The Shin'a'in about them murmured in excitement and pointed—for there, overhead, was a vorcelhawk. It might have been the same one that had landed on Kethry's arm when Tarma had been challenged; it was certainly big enough. This time, however, it showed no inclination to land. Instead, it circled the encampment overhead, three times. Then it sailed majestically away northward, the very direction they had been intending to take.

As it vanished into the ice-blue sky, Kethry tugged her partner's sleeve to get her attention.

"Do me a favor, hmm?" she said in a voice that shook a trifle. "*Stop asking for bloody omens!*"

"Why I ever let you talk me into this—" Tarma stared about them uneasily. "This place is even weirder than they claim!"

They were deep into the Pelagir Hills—the *true* Pelagirs. There was a track they were following; dry-paved, it rang under their mares' hooves, and it led ever deeper into the thickly forested hills and was arrow-flight straight. To either side of them lay the landscape of dreams . . . or maybe nightmare.

The grass was the wrong color for fall. It should have been frost-seared and browning; instead it was a lush and juicy green. The air was warm; this was fall, it should have been cool, but it felt like summer, it smelled like summer. There were even flowers. Tarma disliked and distrusted this false, magic-born summer. It just wasn't *right*.

The other plants besides the grass—well, some were normal (or at least they seemed normal), but others were not. Tarma had seen plants whose leaves had snapped shut on unwary insects, flowers whose blooms glowed when the moon rose, and thorny vines whose thorns dripped some unnamable liquid. She didn't know if they were hazardous, but she wasn't about to take a chance; not after she saw the bones and skulls of small animals littering the ground beneath a dead tree laden with such vines.

The trees didn't bear thinking about, much. The

least odd of them were as twisted and deformed as if they'd grown in a place of constant heavy winds. The others . . .

Well, there was the grove they'd passed of lacy things that sang softly to themselves in childlike voices. And the ones that pulled away from them as they passed, or worse, actually reached out to touch them, feeling them like blind and curious old women. And the sapling that had torn up its roots and shuffled away last night when Tarma thought about how nice a fire would feel . . .

And by no means least, the ones like they'd spent the night in (though only after Kethry repeatedly assured her nervous partner that it was perfectly harmless). It had been hut-sized and hut-shaped, with only a thatch of green on the "roof"—and hollow. And inside had been odd protrusions that resembled stools, a table, and bed-platforms to a degree that was positively frightening. A lovely little trap it would have made—Tarma slept restlessly that night, dreaming about the "door" growing closed and trapping them inside, like those poor bugs the flowers had trapped.

"I'm at the stage where I could use a familiar," Kethry replied, "I've explained all this before. Besides, a familiar will be able to take some of the burden of night-watch off both of us, particularly if I can manage to call a *kyree*."

Tarma sighed.

"It's only fair. I came with you to the Plains. I took a battlesteed at your insistence."

"Agreed. But I don't have to like this place. Are you sure there's anything here you can call? We haven't seen so much as a mouse or a sparrow since things started looking weird."

"That's because they don't want you to see them. Relax, we're going to stop soon; we're almost where I wanted to go."

"How can you tell, if you've never been here?"

"You'll see."

Sure enough, Tarma *did* see. The paved road came

119

to a dead end; at the end it widened out into a flat, featureless circle some fifty paces in diameter.

The paved area was surrounded by yet another kind of tree, some sort of evergreen with thin, tangled branches that started a bit less than knee-high and continued straight up so that the trees were like green columns reaching to the sky. They had grown so closely together that it would have been nearly impossible for anything to force its way between them. That meant there was only one way for anything to get into the circle—via the road.

"Now what?"

"Find someplace comfortable and make yourself a camp wherever you feel safest—although I can guarantee that as long as you stay inside the trees you'll be perfectly safe."

"Myself? What about you?"

"Oh, I'll be here, but I'll be busy. The process of calling a familiar is rather involved and takes a long time." Kethry dismounted in the exact center of the pavement and began unloading her saddlebags from Ironheart's back.

"How long is 'a long time'?" The paved area really took up only about half of the circular clearing. The rest was grass and scattered boulders, a green and lumpy rim surrounding the smooth gray pavement. There was plenty of windfall lying around the grassy area, most of it probably good and dry, dry enough to make a fire. And there was a nice little nook at the back of the circle, a cluster of boulders that would make a good firepit. Somehow Tarma didn't want even the slightest chance of fire escaping from her. Not here. Not after that walking sapling; no telling what its mother might think about fire, or the makers of fire.

"Until sunset tomorrow night."

"*What?*"

"I told you, it's very complicated. Surely you can find something to do with yourself . . ."

"Well, I'm going to have to, aren't I? I'm certainly not going to leave you alone out here."

Kethry didn't bother to reply with anything more than an amused smile, and began setting up her spell-casting equipment. Tarma, grumbling, took both mares over to the side of the paved area and gave them the command to stay on the grass, unsaddled and unharnessed them, and began grooming them to within an inch of their lives.

When she slipped a look over at her partner, Kethry was already seated within a sketched-in circle, a tiny brazier emitting a spicy-scented smoke beside her. Her eyes were closed and from the way her lips were moving she was chanting. Tarma sighed with resignation, and hauled the tack over to the area where she intended to camp.

It had lacked about a candlemark to sunset when they'd reached this place; by the time Tarma finished setting up camp to her liking, the sun was down and she was heartily glad of the fire she'd lit. It wasn't that it was cold ...

No, it was the things outside that circle of trees that made her glad of the warm glow of the flames. The warm *earthly* glow of the flames. There were noises out there, sounds like she'd never heard before. The mares moved over to the fireside of their own volition, and were not really interested in the handfuls of grain Tarma offered them. They stood, one on either side of her, in defensive posture, ears twitching nervously.

It sounded like *things* were gathering just on the other side of the trees. There was a murmuring that was very like something speaking, except that no human throat ever made burbling and trilling sounds quite like those Tarma heard. There were soft little whoops, and watery chuckles. Every now and then, a chorus of whistlers exchanged responses. And as if that weren't enough—

Through the branches Tarma could see amorphous patches of glow, patches that moved about. As the moon rose above the trees, she unsheathed her sword and dagger, and held them across her lap.

121

"Child—"

Tarma screeched and jumped nearly out of her skin.

She was on her feet without even thinking about rising, and whipped around to face—

Her instructor, who had come with the first moonlight.

"You—you—*sadist!*" she gasped, trying to get her heart down out of her throat. "You nearly frightened me to death!"

"There is nothing for you to fear. What is outside the trees is curious, no more."

"And I'm the Queen of Valdemar."

"I tell you truly. This is a place where no evil can bear to tread; look about you—and look to your *she'enedra.*"

Tarma looked again, and saw that the mares had settled, their heads down, nosing out the last of the grain she'd given them. She saw that the area of the pavement was glowing—that what she'd mistaken for a soft silver reflection of the moonlight was in fact coming from within the paving material. Nor was that all—the radiance was brighter where Kethry sat oblivious within her circle, and blended from the silver of the pavement into a pale blue that surrounded her like an aura. And the trees themselves were glowing—something she hadn't noticed, being intent on the lights on the other side—a healthy, verdant green. All three colors she knew from Kethry's chance-made comments were associated with life-magic, positive magic.

And now the strange sounds from outside their enclosure no longer seemed so sinister, but rather like the giggling and murmuring of a crowd of curious small children.

Tarma relaxed, and shrugged. "Well, I still don't exactly like this place . . ."

"But you can see it is not holding a threat, *hai?*"

"*Hai.*" she placed the point of her blade on the pavement and cocked her head at him. "Well, I haven't much to do, and since you're here . . ."

"You are sadly in need of practice," he mocked.

"*Shesti!*" she scoffed back, bringing her sword up into guard position, "I'm not *that* badly off!"

By day the circle of trees no longer seemed quite so sinister, especially after Tarma's instructor had worked her into sweat-dripping exhaustion. When dawn came—and he left—she was ready to drop where she stood and sleep on the hard pavement itself.

But the mares needed more than browse and grain, they needed water. There was no water here save what they'd brought with them. And Tarma dared not truly sleep while Kethry remained enwrapped in spell-casting.

So when the first hint of the sun reddened the sky, she took Hellsbane with her and cautiously poked her nose out of the sheltered area, looking for a hint of water.

There was nothing stirring outside the circle of trees; the eerie landscape remained quiet. But when Tarma looked at the dirt at the foot of the trees she saw tracks, many tracks, and few of them were even remotely identifiable.

"*Kulath etaven,*" she said softly to her mare, "Find water."

Hellsbane raised her head and sniffed; then took two or three paces to the right. Tarma placed one hand on the mare's shoulder; Hellsbane snorted, rubbed her nose briefly against Tarma's arm, then proceeded forward with more confidence.

She headed for a tangle of vines—none of which moved, or had bones beneath them—and high, rank bushes, all of which showed the familiar summery verdancy. As the pair forced their way in past the tangle, breaking twigs and bruising leaves, Tarma found herself breathing in an astringent, mossy scent with a great deal of pleasure. The mare seemed to enjoy the odor too, though she made no move to nibble the leaves.

There was a tiny spring at the heart of the tan-

123

gle, and Tarma doubted she'd have been able to locate it without the mare's help. It was hardly more than a trickle, welling up from a cup of moss-covered stone, and running a few feet, only to vanish again into the thirsty soil. The mare slurped up the entire contents of the cup in a few swallows, and had to wait for it to fill again several times before she'd satisfied her thirst.

It was while she was awaiting Hellsbane's satiation that Tarma noticed the decided scarcity of insects within this patch of growth. Flies and the like had plagued them since they entered the Pelagirs; as a horsewoman, Tarma generally took them for granted.

There were no flies in here. Nor any other insects. Curious . . .

When the mare was finished, Tarma guided her out backward, there being no room to turn her around; it seemed almost as if the bushes and vines were willing to let them inflict a limited amount of damage in order to reach the water, but resisted any more than that. And as soon as they were clear of the scent of the crushed vegetation, the flies descended on Hellsbane again.

An idea occurred to her; she backtracked to the bushes, and got a handful of the trampled leaves and rubbed them on the back of her hand. She waited for some sort of reaction; rash, burning, itching—nothing happened. Satisfied that the vegetation at least wasn't harmful, she rubbed it into the mare's shaggy hide. It turned her a rather odd shade of gray-green, but the flies wouldn't even land on her.

Very pleased with herself, Tarma watered Ironheart and repeated the process on her. By the time she'd finished, the sun was well up, and she was having a hard time keeping her eyes open. She was going to have to get *some* rest, at least.

But that was another advantage of having battlesteeds.

She loosed Hellsbane and took her to the entrance of the circle. "Guard," she said, shortly. The mare immediately went into sentry-mode—and it would take a determined attacker indeed to get past those iron-shod hooves and wicked teeth. Now all she needed to keep alert for was attack from above.

She propped herself up with their packs and saddles, and allowed herself to fall into a half-doze. It wasn't as restful as real sleep, but it would do.

When hunger finally made further rest impossible, it was getting on to sunset—and Kethry was showing signs of breaking out of trance.

She'd carefully briefed Tarma on what she'd need to do; Tarma shook herself into full alertness, and rummaged in Kethry's pack for high-energy rations. Taking those and her waterskin, she sat on her heels just outside of the inscribed circle, and waited.

She didn't have to wait long; Kethry's eyes opened almost immediately, and she sagged forward with exhaustion, scarcely able to make the little dismissing motion that broke the magic shield about her. Tarma was across the circle the instant she'd done so, and supported her with one arm while she drank. Kethry looked totally exhausted; mentally as well as physically. She was pale as new milk, and scarcely had the energy to drink, much less speak. Tarma helped her to her feet, then half-carried her to the tiny campsite and her bedroll.

Kethry had no more than touched her head to her blankets than she was asleep. She slept for several hours, well past moonrise, then awoke again with the first appearance of the lights and noises that had so disturbed Tarma the night before.

"They seem to be harmless," Tarma began.

"They are. That's not what woke me," Kethry croaked from a raw throat. "It's coming—what I called—"

"What *did* you call, anyway?"

After a swallow or two of water, Kethry was better able to speak. "A *kyree*—they're a little like wolves, only bigger; they also have some of the

125

physical characteristics of the big grass-cats, retractile claws, that sort of thing. They're also like Gervase's folk; they're human-smart and have some gift for magic. They'd probably do quite well for themselves if they had hands instead of paws—well, that's one reason why some of them are willing to become mage-familiars. Another is gender. Or lack of."

"*Get'ke?*"

"*Kyree* throw three kinds of cubs—male, female, and neuter. The neuters really don't have much to do in pack-life, so they're more inclined to wander off and see the world."

Kethry broke off, staring over Tarma's shoulder. Tarma turned.

In the opening of the tree-circle where the road turned into the paved "court" was—something. It looked lupine—it had a wolf-type head, anyway. But it was so damn *big!*

Kethry pulled herself to her feet and half-stumbled to the entrance. "If you come in the Name of the Powers of Light, enter freely," she croaked, "If not, be you gone."

The thing bowed its head gravely, and padded into the circle. There it stood, looking first at Kethry, then at Tarma; deliberately, measuringly.

I bond to you, said a deep voice in the back of Tarma's head.

Once again she nearly jumped out of her skin.

"*Li'sa'eer!*" she choked, backing a few paces away from the thing. "What?"

I bond to you, warrior. We are alike, we two; both warriors for the Light, both—celibate— The voice in her head had a feeling of amusement about the choice of the last word. *It is fit we be soul-bonded. Besides, Lady of Power*—he turned to look at Kethry, *—you do not need me. You have the spirit-sword. But you*—he turned his huge eyes back to Tarma,—*YOU need me.*

"*She'enedra,*" Tarma said tightly, keeping a firm grip on her nerves, "What in hell am I supposed to do? He says he wants *me!*"

126

"Oh, my Lady Bright—what a bloody mess! It could only happen to me! Give in," Kethry staggered to her bedroll and half-collapsed into it, laughing weakly. "A day and a night of spell-casting, and what happens? My familiar decides he'd rather bond to my partner! Lady Bright—if it weren't so damned funny I think I'd kill you both!"

"But what am I supposed to *do?*"

You could try talking to me.

Tarma gulped, and approached the beast cautiously. It sat at its ease, tongue lolling out in a kind of grin. She could sense his amusement at her apprehension in the back of her mind. Curiously, that seemed to make her fear vanish.

"Well," she said at last, after several long moments of trying to think of something appropriate. "I'm Tarma."

And I—am Warrl. The creature lay down on the pavement, and cocked its head to one side. Its—no, his; it might have been a "neuter" but there was a distinctly masculine feeling to him—his eyes caught the moonlight and reflected greenishly.

"I'm not quite sure what I should do about you," she confessed. "I mean I'm no mage—what's the next move?"

You might start by offering me something to eat, Warrl said, *I've come a long way, and I'm hungry. Do I smell meat-bars?* There was something in his mental sending that was so like a child begging for a sweet that Tarma had to laugh.

"You do, my friend," she replied, rising to get one for him. "And if you like them as much as I *dislike* them, I have the feeling we're going to suit each other very well indeed!"

Six

They were fortunate; almost as soon as they emerged from the Pelagirs, they were able to find a short-term job as escorts. A scrawny, middle-aged man sought them at their inn within hours of when they had posted themselves at the Mercenaries' Guild and paid their fees.

"You'll be providing protection for my new bride," their employer, an hereditary knight who didn't look capable of lifting his ancestral blade, much less using it, told Tarma. "I will be remaining here for a month or more to consolidate my interests with Darthela's father, but I wish her to make the journey to Fromish now, before winter weather sets in."

"Are we to be the only guards?" Tarma asked, a little doubtfully. She shifted on the wooden bench uncomfortably, and wished Kethry was here instead of visiting the tiny White Winds enclave she'd ferreted out. She could have used the sorceress' quick wits right now.

"I'm afraid so," he replied with a sheepish smile. "To be brutally frank, Swordlady, my house is in rather impoverished condition at the moment. I couldn't afford to take any of my servants away from the harvesting to serve as guards for her, and I can't afford to hire more than the two of you. And before you ask, my bride's retinue is confined to one handmaiden. Her dower is to be in things less tangible, but ultimately more profitable, than immediate cash."

Tarma decided that she liked him. The smile had

been genuine, and his frankness with a pair of hirelings rather touching.

Of course, she thought wryly, *that could just be to convince us that the fair Darthela won't have much with her worth stealing.*

"I'll tell you what we can do to narrow the odds against us a bit," Tarma offered. "I can arrange to set out a little later than you asked us, so that we're about half a day behind that spice-trader. Anybody looking for booty is likely to go for him and miss us."

"But what about wild beasts?" he asked, looking concerned. "Won't they have been attracted to the campsites by the trader's leavings?"

Tarma's estimation of him rose a notch. She *had* been picturing him as so likely to have his nose in a book all the time that he had little notion of the realities of the road.

"Wild beasts are the one problem we *won't* have," she replied. "You're getting a bargain, you know—you aren't actually getting two guards, you're getting three."

At her unspoken call, Warrl inched out from under the bar where he'd been drowsing, stretched lazily, and opened enormous jaws in a yawn big enough to take in a whole melon. Sir Skolte regarded the *kyree* with astonishment and a little alarm.

"Bright Lord of Hosts!" he exclaimed, inching away a little. "What *is* that?"

"My partner calls him a *kyree*, and his name is Warrl."

"A Pelagir Hills *kyree*? No wonder you aren't worried about beasts!" The knight rubbed a hand across his balding pate, and looked relieved. "I am favored by your acquaintance, Sirrah Warrl. And grateful for your services."

Warrl nodded graciously and returned to his resting place beneath the bar. This close to the Hills, the innmaster and his help were fairly familiar with the *kyree* kind—and when Warrl had helped to break up a bar-fight within moments of the trio's arrival, he had earned their gratitude and a place of honor. And no few spiced sausages while he rested there.

Tarma was pleased with the knight's ready acceptance of her companion, and finalized the transaction with him then and there. By the time Kethry returned, she had already taken care of supplies for the next day.

They appeared at the house of the bride's father precisely at noon the next day, ready to go. Sir Skolte met them at the gate—which was something of a surprise to Kethry.

"I—rather expected you would send a servant to wait for us," Kethry told him, covering her confusion quickly, but not so quickly that Tarma didn't spot it.

"Darthela has been insisting that I 'properly introduce' you," he replied, a rather wry smile on his thin lips. "That isn't the sort of thing one leaves to a servant. I confess that she has been *most* eager to meet you."

Tarma caught her partner's quizzical glance and shrugged.

The odd comment was explained when they finally met the fair young bride; she entered the room all flutters and coquettishness, which affectations she dropped as soon as she saw that her escorts were female. She made no effort to hide her disappointment, and left "to pack" within moments.

"Now I see why you hired us instead of that pair of Barengians," Tarma couldn't help but say, stifling laughter.

Sir Skolte shrugged eloquently. "I won't deny I'm a bit of a disappointment for her," he replied cynically. "But beggars can't be choosers. She's the sixth in a set of seven daughters, and her father was so pleased at being able to make trade bargains with me in lieu of dower that he almost threw her at me. Fortunately, my servants are all uglier than I am."

The look in his eye told Tarma that Darthela was

going to have to be a great deal cleverer than she appeared to be if she intended to cuckold *this* fellow.

But then again . . .

"Tell me, are folk around here acquainted with the tale of 'Bloody Carthar's Fourteen Wives?' Or 'Meralis and the Werebeast?' "

He shook his head. "I would say I know most of the tales we hear in these parts by heart, and those don't sound familiar."

"Then we'll see if we can't incline Darthela's mind a bit more in an appropriate direction," Kethry said, taking her cue from the two stories Tarma had mentioned. "We'll be a week in traveling, and stories around the campfire are always welcome, no?"

"What—oh, I see!" Sir Skolte began to laugh heartily. "Now, more than ever, I am *very* glad to have met you! Ladies, if you are ever looking for work again, I shall give you the *highest* recommendations—especially to aging men with pretty young wives!'

That took them from Lythecare to Fromish, on the eastbound roads. In Fromish they ran into old friends—Ikan and Justin.

"Hey-la! Look who we have here!" Tarma would have known that voice in a mob; in the half-empty tavern it was as welcome as a word from the tents

She leapt up from her seat to catch Justin's fore arm in a welcoming clasp. And not more than a pace behind *him* came Ikan.

They got themselves sorted out, and the two new-comers gave their orders to the serving boy before settling at Tarma's table.

"Well, what brings you ladies to these benighted parts?" Ikan asked, shaking hair out of his guileless eyes. "Last we saw, you were headed south."

"Looking for work," Tarma replied shortly. "We *did* get home but . . . well, we decided, what with one thing and another, to go professional. Even got our Guild tags." She pulled the thong holding the little copper medal out of her tunic to display it for them.

"I thought you two didn't work in winter," Kethry said in puzzlement.

"It isn't winter *yet,* at least not according to our employers. Last caravan of the season. Say—we might be able to do each other a favor, though." Justin eyed the two women with speculation. "You say you're Guild members now? Lord and Lady, the Luck is with us, for certain!"

"Why?"

"We've got two guards down with flux—and it does not look good. *We* want out of here before the snows close in, but we daren't go shorthanded and *I* don't trust the scum that's been turning up, hoping to get hired on in their places. But you two—"

"Three," Tarma corrected, as Warrl shambled out of the kitchen where he'd been enjoying meat scraps and the antics of the innkeeper's two children.

"Hey-la! A *kyree!*" Ikan exclaimed in delight. "Even better!"

"Shieldbrother," Justin lounged back in his chair with an air of complete satisfaction, "I will never doubt your conjuring of the Luck again. And tonight the drink's on me!"

The nervous jewel merchants were only too pleased to find replacements that could be vouched for by their most trusted guard-chiefs. They were even happier when they learned that one of the two was Shin'a'in and the other a mage. Kethry more than earned her pay on that trip, preventing a thief-mage from substituting bespelled glass for the rubies and sapphires they had just traded for.

They left the merchants before they returned to Mornedealth, Kethry not particularly wanting to revisit quite yet. Ikan and Justin did their best to persuade them otherwise, but to no avail.

"You could stay at the Broken Sword. Tarma could keep drilling us like she did last year," Justin coaxed. "And Cat would dearly love to see you. She's set herself up as a weapons merchant."

"No . . . I want things to cool down a little more," Kethry said. "And frankly, we need to earn ourselves a reputation and a pretty good stake, and we won't do that sitting around in Mornedealth all winter."

"You," Ikan put in, a speculative gleam in his eyes, "have got more in mind than earning the kind of cozy docket we have. Am I right, or no?"

"You're right," Tarma admitted.

"So? What've you got in mind?"

"Schools—or rather *a* school, with both of us teaching what we're best at."

"You'll need more than a good stake and a rep—you'll need property. Some kind of big building, stables, maybe a real indoor training area—and a good library, warded research areas, and neighbors who aren't too fussy about what you conjure."

"Gods, I hadn't thought that far, but you're right," Tarma said with chagrin. "Sounds as if what we want is on the order of a manor house."

"Which means you'd better start thinking in terms of working for a noble with property to grant once you get that rep. A crowned head would be best." Justin looked at both of them soberly. "That's not as unlikely as you might think; a combination like you two is rare even among men; sword and magic in concert are worth any ten straight swordsmen, however good. Add to it that you're female—think about it. Say you've got a monarch needing bodyguards; who'd check out his doxy and her servant? There's a lot of ways you could parlay yourself into becoming landed, and Keth's already ennobled."

"But for now . . ." Kethry said.

"For now you've got to *earn* that rep. Just bear in mind that what you're going after is far from impossible."

"Can we—ask you for advice now and again?" Kethry asked. "Justin, you sound to me as if you've figured some of this out for yourselves."

"He did," his partner grinned. "Or rather, *we* did. But we decided that it was too big a field for the two of us to hope to plow. So we settled for making ourselves indispensable to the Jewel Merchant's Guild. Fact is, we've also been keeping our eyes out for somebody like you two. We aren't going to be young forever, and we figured on talking somebody into taking us on at their new school as instructors before we got so old our bones creaked every time we lunged." He winked at Kethry.

Tarma stared. "You really think we have a chance of pulling this off?"

"More than a chance, nomad—I'd lay money on it. I'm sure enough that I haven't even *tried* luring your lovely little partner into my bed—I don't make love to prospective employers."

"Well!" Tarma was plainly startled. "I will be damned . . ."

"I hope not," Justin chuckled, "or I'll have to find another set of prospects!"

They got a commission with another caravan to act as guards—courtesy of their friends. On their way they detoured briefly when Need called them to rid a town of a monster, a singularly fruitless effort, for the monster was slain by a would-be "hero" the very day they arrived.

After that they skirmished with banditti and a half-trained magician's ex-apprentice who thought robbing caravans was an easier task than memorizing spells. Kethry "slapped his hands," as she put it, and left him with a geas to build walls for the temple of Sun-Lord Resoden until he should learn better.

When the caravan was safely gotten home, they found an elderly mage of the Blue Mountains school who wanted some physical protection as he returned to his patron, and was delighted with the bonus of having a sorceress of a different discipline to converse with.

During these journeys Tarma and Warrl were

learning to integrate themselves as a fighting team; somewhat to Tarma's amazement, her other-worldly teachers were inclined to include him whenever he chose. After her initial shock—and, to some extent, dismay—she had discovered that they *did* have a great deal in common, especially in attitudes. He was, perhaps, a bit more cynical than she was, but he was also older. He never would admit exactly how old he was; when Tarma persisted, he seized one of her hands in his powerful jaws and mind-sent, *My years are enough, mindmate, to suffice.* She never asked again.

But now they had fallen on dry times; they had wound up on the estate of Viscount Hathkel, with no one needing their particular talents and no cities nearby. The money they had earned must now be at least partially spent in provisioning them to someplace where they were likelier to find work.

That was the plan, anyway—until Need woke from her apparent slumbers with a vengeance.

Tarma goaded her gray Shin'a'in warsteed into another burst of speed, urging her on with hand and voice (though not spur—*never* spur; that would have been an insult the battlesteed would not tolerate) as if she were pursued by the Jackels of Darkness. It had been more than long enough since she had first become Kal'enedral for her hair to have regrown—now her long, ebony braids streamed behind her; close enough to catch one of them rode Kethry. Kethry's own mare was a scant half a length after her herd-sister.

Need had left Kethry almost completely alone save for that one prod almost from the time they'd left the Liha'irden camp. Both of them had nearly forgotten just what bearing her could mean. They had been reminded this morning, when Need had woken Kethry almost before the sun rose, and had been driving the sorceress (and so her blood-oath sister as well) in this direction all day. At first it had been a simple pull, as she had often felt before.

135

Tarma had teased, and Kethry had grumbled; then they had packed up their camp and headed for the source. Kethry had even had time enough to summon a creature of the Ethereal Plane to scout and serve as a set of clairvoyant "eyes" for them. But the call had grown more urgent as the hours passed, not less so—increasing to the point where by mid-afternoon it was actually causing Kethry severe mental pain, pain that even Tarma was subject to, through the oath-bond. That was when they got Warrl up onto the special carry-pad they'd rigged for him behind Tarma's saddle, and prepared to make some speed. They urged their horses first into a fast walk, then a trot, then as sunset neared, into a full gallop. By then Kethry was near-blind with mental anguish, and no longer capable of even directing their Ethereal ally, much less questioning it.

Need *would* not be denied in this; Moonsong k'Vala, the Hawkbrother Adept they had met, had told them nothing less than the truth. Kethry was soul-bonded to the sword, just as surely as Tarma was bonded to her Goddess or Warrl to Tarma. Kethry was recalling now with some misgiving that Moonsong had also said that she had not yet found the limit to which it would bind itself to her—and if this experience was any indication of the future, she wasn't sure she *wanted* to.

All that was of any importance at the moment was that there was a woman within Need's sensing range in grave peril—peril of her life, by the way the blade was driving Kethry. And they had no choice but to answer the call.

Tarma continued to urge Hellsbane on; they were coming to a cultivated area, and surely their goal couldn't be far. Ahead of them on the road they were following loomed a walled village; part and parcel of a manor-keep, a common arrangement in these parts. The gates were open; the fields around empty of workers. That was odd—very odd. It was high summer, and there should have been folk out in the fields, weeding and tending the irrigation ditches. There was no immediate sign of trouble, but as they neared the gates, it was plain just who the woman they sought was—

Bound to a scaffold high enough to be visible through the open gates, they could see a young, dark-haired woman dressed in white, almost like a sacrificial victim. The last rays of the setting sun touched her with color—touched also the heaped wood beneath the platform on which she stood, making it seem as if her pyre already blazed up. Lining the mud-plastered walls of the keep and crowding the square inside the gate were scores of folk of every class and station, all silent, all waiting.

Tarma really didn't give a fat damn about what they were waiting for, though it was a good bet that they were there for the show of the burning. She coaxed a final burst of speed out of her tired mount, sending her shooting ahead of Kethry's as they passed the gates, and bringing her close in to the platform. Once there, she swung Hellsbane around in a tight circle and drew her sword, placing herself between the woman on the scaffold and the men with the torches to set it alight.

She knew she was an imposing sight, even covered with sweat and the dust of the road; hawk-faced, intimidating, ice-blue eyes glaring. Her clothing alone should tell them she was nothing to fool with—it was obviously that of a fighting mercenary; plain brown leathers and brigandine armor. Her sword reflected the dying sunlight so that she might have been holding a living flame in her hand. She said nothing; her pose said it all for her.

Nevertheless, one of the men started forward, torch in hand.

"I wouldn't," Kethry was framed in the arch of the gate, silhouetted against the fiery sky; her mount rock-still, her hands glowing with sorcerous energy. "If Tarma doesn't get you, *I* will."

"Peace," a tired, gray-haired man in plain, dusty-black robes stepped forward from the crowd, holding his arms out placatingly, and motioned the torch-bearer to give way. "Istan, go back to your place. Strangers, what brings you here at this time of all times?"

Kethry pointed—a thin strand of glow shot from her finger and touched the ropes binding the captive on the platform. The bindings loosed and fell from her, sliding down her body to lie in a heap at her feet. The woman swayed and nearly fell, catching herself at the last moment with one hand on the stake she had been bound to. A small segment of the crowd—mostly women—stepped forward as if to help, but fell back again as Tarma swiveled to face them.

"I know not what crime you accuse this woman of, but she is innocent of it," Kethry said to him, ignoring the presence of anyone else. "*That* is what brings us here."

A collective sigh rose from the crowd at her words. Tarma watched warily to either side, but it appeared to be a sigh of relief rather than a gasp of arousal. She relaxed the white-knuckled grip she had on her sword-hilt by the merest trifle.

"The Lady Myria is accused of the slaying of her lord," the robed man said quietly. "She called upon her ancient right to summon a champion to her defense when the evidence against her became overwhelming. I, who am priest of Felwether, do ask you—strangers, will you champion the Lady and defend her in trial-by-combat?"

Kethry began to answer in the affirmative, but the priest shook his head negatively. "No, lady-mage, by ancient law *you* are bound from the field; neither sorcery nor sorcerous weapons such as I see you bear may be permitted in trial-by-combat."

"Then—"

"He wants to know if I'll do it, *she'enedra*," Tarma croaked, taking a fiendish pleasure in the start the priest gave at the sound of her harsh voice. "I know your laws, priest, I've passed this way before. I ask

138

you in my turn—if my partner, by her skills, can prove to you the lady's innocence, will you set her free and call off the combat, no matter how far it has gotten?"

"I so pledge, by the Names and the Powers," the priest nodded—almost eagerly.

"Then I will champion this lady."

About half the spectators cheered and rushed forward. Three older women edged past Tarma to bear the fainting woman back into the keep. The rest, except for the priest, moved off slowly and reluctantly, casting thoughtful and measuring looks back at Tarma. Some of them seemed friendly; most did not.

"What—"

"Was that all about?" That was as far as Tarma got before the priest interposed himself between the partners.

"Your pardon, mage-lady, but you may not speak with the champion from this moment forward. Any message you may have must pass through me."

"Oh, no, not yet, priest." Tarma urged Hellsbane forward and passed his outstretched hand. "I told you I know your laws—and the ban starts at sundown—Greeneyes, pay attention, I have to talk fast. You're going to have to figure out just who the real culprit is, the best I can possibly do is buy you time. This business is combat to the death for the champion. I can choose just to defeat my challengers, but they *have* to kill me. And the longer you take, the more likely that is."

"Tarma, you're better than anybody here!"

"But not better than any twenty—or thirty." Tarma smiled crookedly. "The rules of the game, *she'enedra*, are that I keep fighting until nobody is willing to challenge me. Sooner or later they'll wear me out and I'll go down."

"*What?*"

"Shush, I knew what I was getting into. You're as good at your craft as I am at mine—I've just given you a bit of incentive. Take Warrl." The tall, lupine

139

creature jumped to the ground from behind Tarma where he'd been clinging to the special pad with his retractile claws. "He might well be of some use. Do your best, *veshta'cha*; there're two lives depending on you."

The priest interposed himself again. "Sunset, champion," he said firmly, putting his hand on her reins.

Tarma bowed her head, and allowed him to lead her and her horse away, Kethry staring dumbfounded after them.

"All right, let's take this from the very beginning."

Kethry was in the Lady Myria's bower, a soft and colorful little corner of an otherwise drab fortress. There were no windows—no drafts stirred the bright tapestries on the walls, or caused the flames of the beeswax candles to flicker. The walls were thick stone covered with plaster, warm by winter, cool by summer. The furnishings were of light yellow wood, padded with plump feather cushions. In one corner stood a cradle, watched over broodingly by the lady herself. The air was pleasantly scented with herbs and flowers. Kethry wondered how so pampered a creature could have gotten herself into such a pass.

"It was two days ago. I came here to lie down in the afternoon. I—was tired; I tire easily since Syrtin was born. I fell asleep."

Close up, the Lady proved to be several years Kethry's junior; scarcely past her midteens. Her dark hair was lank and without luster, her skin pale. Kethry frowned at that, and wove a tiny spell with a gesture and two whispered words while Myria was speaking. The creature of the Ethereal Plane who'd agreed to serve as their scout was still with her—it would have taken a far wilder ride than they had made to lose it. And now that they were doing something about the lady's plight, Need was quiescent; leaving Kethry able to think and work again.

The answer to her question came quickly as a thin voice breathed whispered words into her ear.

Kethry grimaced angrily. "Lady's eyes, child, I shouldn't wonder that you tire—you're still torn up from the birthing! What kind of a miserable excuse for a Healer have you got here, anyway?"

"We have *no* Healer, lady," one of the three older women who had borne Myria back into the keep rose from her seat behind Kethry and stood between them, challenge written in her stance. She had a kind, but careworn face; her gray and buff gown was of good stuff, but old-fashioned in cut. Kethry guessed that she must be Myria's companion, an older relative, perhaps. "The Healer died before my dove came to childbed and her lord did not see fit to replace him. We had no use for a Healer, or so he claimed. After all, he kept no great number of men-at-arms; he warred with no one. He felt that birthing was a perfectly normal procedure and surely didn't require the expensive services of a Healer."

"Now, Katran—"

"It is no more than the truth! He cared more for his horses than for you! He replaced the farrier quickly enough when *he* left!"

"His horses were of more use to him," the girl said bitterly, then bit her lip. "There, you see, *that* is what brought me to this pass—one too many careless remarks let fall among the wrong ears."

Kethry nodded, liking the girl; the child was *not* the pampered pretty she had first thought. No windows to this chamber, only the one entrance; a good bit more like a cell than a bower, it occurred to her. A comfortable cell, but a cell still. She stood, smoothed her buff-colored robe with an unconscious gesture, and unsheathed the sword that seldom left her side.

"Lady, what—" Katran stood, startled by the gesture.

"Peace; I mean no ill. Here," Kethry said, bending over Myria and placing the blade in the startled girl's hands, "hold this for a bit."

Myria took the blade, eyes wide, a puzzled expression bringing a bit more life to her face. "But—"

"Women's magic, child. For all that blades are a man's weapon, Need here is strong in the magic of women. She serves women only—it was her power that called me here to aid you—and given an hour of your holding her, she'll Heal you. Now, go on. You fell asleep."

Myria accepted the blade gingerly, then settled the sword somewhat awkwardly across her knees and took a deep breath. "Something woke me, a sound of something falling, I think. You can see that this room connects with my Lord's chamber, that in fact the only way in or out is through his chamber. I saw a candle burning, so I rose to see if he needed anything. He—he was slumped over his desk. I thought perhaps he had fallen asleep."

"You thought he was drunk, you mean," the older woman said wryly.

"Does it *matter* what I thought? I didn't see anything out of the ordinary, because he wore dark colors always. I reached out my hand to shake him— and it came away bloody!"

"And she screamed fit to rouse the household," Katran finished.

"And when we came, she had to unlock the door for us," said the second woman, silent till now. "Both doors into that chamber were locked—hallside with the lord's key, seneschal's side barred from within this room. And the bloody dagger that had killed him was under her bed."

"Whose was it?"

"Mine, of course," Myria answered. "And before you ask, there was only one key to the hallside door; it could only be opened with the key, and the key was under his hand. It's an ensorcelled lock; even if you made a copy of the key the copy would never unlock the door."

"Warrl?" The huge beast rose from the shadows

142

where he'd been lying and padded to Kethry's side. Myria and her women shrank away a little at the sight of him.

"You can detect what I'd need a spell for. See if the bar was bespelled into place on the other door, would you? Then see if the spell on the lock's been tampered with."

The dark gray, nearly black beast trotted out of the room on silent paws, and Myria shivered.

"I can see where the evidence against you is overwhelming, even without misheard remarks."

"I had no choice in this wedding," Myria replied, her chin rising defiantly, "but I have been a true and loyal wife to my lord."

"Loyal past his deserts, if you ask me," Katran grumbled. "Well, that's the problem, lady-mage. My Lady came to this marriage reluctant, and it's well known. It's well known that he didn't much value her. And there's been more than a few heard to say they thought Myria reckoned to set herself up as Keep-ruler with the Lord gone."

Warrl padded back into the room, and flopped down at Kethry's feet.

"Well, fur-brother?"

He shook his head negatively, and the women stared at this evidence of like-human intelligence.

"Not the bar nor the lock, hmm? And how do you get into a locked room without a key? Still ... Lady, is all as it was in the other room?"

"Yes, the priest was one of the first in the door, and would not let anyone change so much as a dust mote. He only let them take the body away."

"Thank the Goddess!" Kethry gave the exclamation something of a prayerful cast. She started to rise herself, then stared curiously at the girl. "Lady, *why* did you choose to prove yourself as you did?"

"Lady-mage—"

Kethry was surprised at the true expression of guilt and sorrow the child wore.

"If I had guessed strangers would be caught in this web I never would have. I—I thought that my

143

kin would come to my defense. I came to this marriage of their will, I thought at least one of them might—at least try. I don't think anyone here would dare the family's anger by killing one of the sons, even if the daughter is thought worthless by most of them." A slow tear slid down one cheek, and she whispered her last words. "My youngest brother, I thought at least was fond of me. . . ."

The spell Kethry had set in motion was still active; she whispered another question to the tiny air-entity she had summoned. This time the answer made her smile, albeit sadly.

"Your youngest brother, child, is making his way here afoot, having ridden his horse into foundering trying to reach you in time. He is swearing by every god that if you have been harmed he will not leave stone on stone here."

Myria gave a tiny cry and buried her face in her hands; Katran moved to comfort her as her shoulders shook with silent sobs. Kethry stood, and made her way into the other room. Need's magic was such that the girl would hold the blade until she no longer required its power. While it gave Kethry an expertise in swordwork a master would envy, it would do nothing to augment her magical abilities, so it was fine where it was. Right now there was a mystery to solve, and two lives hung in the balance until Kethry could puzzle it out.

As she surveyed the outer room, she wondered how Tarma was faring.

Tarma sat quietly beneath the window of a tiny, bare, rock-walled cell. In a few moments the light of the rising moon would penetrate it, first through the eastern window, then the skylight overhead. For now, the only light in the room was that of the oil-fed flame burning on the low table before her. There was something else on that table—the long, coarse braids of Tarma's hair.

She had shorn those braids off herself at shoulder-length, then tied a silky black headband around her

144

forehead to confine what remained. That had been the final touch to the costume she'd donned with an air of robing herself for some ceremony—clothing that had long stayed untouched, carefully folded in the bottom of her pack. Black clothing; from low, soft boots to chainmail shirt, from headband to hose—the stark, unrelieved black of a Shin'a'in Sword Sworn about to engage in ritual combat or on the trail of blood-feud.

Now she waited, patiently, seated cross-legged before the makeshift altar, to see if her preparations received an answer.

The moon rose behind her, the square of dim white light creeping slowly down the blank stone wall opposite her, until, at last, it touched the flame on the altar.

And without warning, without fanfare, *She* was there, standing between Tarma and the altar-place. Shin'a'in by Her golden skin and sharp features, clad identically to Tarma, only Her eyes revealed Her as something not human. Those eyes—the spangled darkness of the sky at midnight, without white, iris or pupil—could belong to only one being; the Shin'a'in Goddess of the South Wind, known only as the Star-Eyed, or the Warrior.

"Child, I answer." Her voice was melodious.

"Lady." Tarma bowed her head in homage.

"You have questions, child? No requests?"

"No requests, Star-Eyed. My fate—does not interest me. I will live or die by my own skills. But Kethry's fate—*that* I would know."

"The future is not easy to map, child, not even for a goddess. I must tell you that tomorrow might bring your life *or* your death; both are equally likely."

Tarma sighed. "Then what of my *she'enedra* should it be the second path?"

The Warrior smiled, Tarma felt the smile like a caress. "You are worthy, child; hear, then. If you fall tomorrow, your *she'enedra*, who is perhaps a bit more pragmatic than you, will work a spell that lifts both herself and the Lady Myria to a place

145

leagues distant from here, while Warrl releases Hellsbane and Ironheart and drives them out the gates. I fear she allows you this combat only because she knows you regard it as touching your honor to hold by these outClan customs. If the choice were in her hands, you would all be far from here by now; you, she, the lady and her child and all—well; she will abide by your choices. For the rest, when Kethry recovers from that spell they shall go to our people, to the Liha'irden; Lady Myria will find a mate to her liking there. Then, with some orphans of other Clans, they shall go forth and Tale'sedrin will ride the plains again, as Kethry promised you. The blade will release her, and pass to another's hands."

Tarma sighed, and nodded. "Then, Lady, I am content, whatever my fate tomorrow. I thank you."

The Warrior smiled again; then between one heartbeat and the next, was gone.

Tarma left the flame to burn itself out, lay down upon the pallet that was the room's only other furnishing, and slept.

Sleep was the last thing on Kethry's mind.

She surveyed the room that had been Lord Corbie's; plain stone walls, three entrances, no windows. One of the entrances still had the bar across the door, the other two led to Myria's bower and to the hall outside. Plain stone floor, no hidden entrances there. She knew the blank wall held nothing either; the other side was the courtyard of the manor. Furnishings; one table, one chair, one ornate bedstead against the blank wall, one bookcase, half filled, four lamps. A few bright rugs. Her mind felt as blank as the walls.

Start at the beginning—she told herself. *Follow what happened. The girl came in here alone, the man followed after she was asleep, then what?*

He was found at his desk, said a voice in her mind, startling her. *He probably walked straight in and sat*

146

down. What's on the desk that he might have been doing?

Every time Warrl spoke to her mind-to-mind it surprised her. She still couldn't imagine how he managed to make himself heard when she hadn't a scrap of that particular Gift. Tarma seemed to accept it unquestioningly; how she'd ever gotten used to it, the sorceress couldn't imagine.

Tarma—time was wasting.

On the desk stood a wineglass with a sticky residue in the bottom, an inkwell and quill, and several stacked ledgers. The top two looked disturbed.

Kethry picked them up, and began leafing through the last few pages, whispering a command to the invisible presence at her shoulder. The answer was prompt. The ink on the last three pages of both ledgers was fresh enough to still be giving off fumes detectable only by a creature of the air. The figures were written no more than two days ago.

She leafed back several pages worth, noting that the handwriting changed from time to time.

"Who else kept the accounts besides your lord?" she called into the next room.

"The seneschal; that was why his room has an entrance on this one," the woman Katran replied, entering the lord's room herself. "I can't imagine why the door was barred. Lord Corbie almost never left it that way."

"That's a lot of trust to place in a hireling."

"Oh, the seneschal isn't a hireling, he's Lord Corbie's bastard brother. He's been the lord's right hand since he inherited the lordship of Felwether."

The sun rose; Tarma was awake long before.

If the priest was surprised to see her change of outfit, he didn't show it. He had brought a simple meal of bread and cheese, and watered wine; he waited patiently while she ate and drank, then indicated she should follow him.

Tarma checked all her weapons. She secured all the fastenings of her clothing (how many had died

147

because they had forgotten to tie something tightly enough?), and stepped into place behind him, as silent as his shadow.

He conducted her to a small tent that had been erected in one corner of the keep's practice ground, against the keep walls. The walls of the keep formed two sides, the outer wall the third; the fourth side was open. The practice ground was of hard-packed clay, and relatively free of dust. A groundskeeper was sprinkling water over the dirt to settle it.

Once they were in front of the little pavilion, the priest finally spoke.

"The first challenger will be here within a few minutes; between fights you may retire here to rest for as long as it takes for the next to ready himself, or one candlemark, whichever is longer. You will be brought food at noon and again at sunset." His expression plainly said that he did not think she would be needing the latter, "and there will be fresh water within the tent at all times. I will be staying with you."

Now his expression was apologetic.

"To keep my partner from slipping me any magical aid?" Tarma asked wryly. "Hellfire, priest, *you* know what I am, even if these dirt-grubbers here don't!"

"I know, Sword Sworn. This is for your protection as well. There are those here who would not hesitate to tip the hand of the gods somewhat."

Tarma's eyes hardened. "Priest, I'll spare who I can, but it's only fair to tell you that if I catch anyone trying an underhanded trick, I won't hesitate to kill him."

"I would not ask you to do otherwise."

She looked at him askance. "There's more going on here than meets the eye, isn't there?"

He shook his head, and indicated that she should take her seat in the champion's chair beside the tent-flap. There was a bustling on the opposite side of the practice ground, and a dark, heavily bearded man followed by several boys carrying arms and armor appeared only to vanish within another, identical tent on that side. Spectators began gathering along the open side and the tops of the walls.

"I fear I can tell you nothing, Sword Sworn. I have only speculations, nothing more. But I pray your little partner is wiser than I."

"Or I'm going to be cold meat by nightfall," Tarma finished for him, watching as her first opponent emerged from the challenger's pavilion.

The priest winced at her choice of words, but did not contradict her.

Circles within circles. . . .

Kethry had not been idle.

The sticky residue in the wineglass had been more than just the dregs of drink; there had been a powerful narcotic in it. Unfortunately, this just pointed back to Myria; she'd been using just such a potion to help her sleep since the birth of her son. Still, it wouldn't have been all that difficult to obtain, and Kethry had a trick up her sleeve, one the average mage wouldn't have known; one she would use *if* they could find the other bottle of potion.

More encouraging was what she had found perusing the ledgers. The seneschal had been siphoning off revenues; never much at a time, but steadily. By now it must amount to a tidy sum. What if he suspected Lord Corbie was likely to catch him at it?

Or even more—what if Lady Myria *was* found guilty and executed? The estate would go to her infant son, and who would be the child's most likely guardian but his half-uncle, the seneschal?

And children die so very easily, and from so many natural causes.

Now that she had a likely suspect, Kethry decided it was time to begin investigating him.

The first place she checked was the barred door. And on the bar itself she found an odd little scratch, obvious in the paint. It looked new, her air-spirit confirmed that it was. She lifted the bar after examining it even more carefully, finding no other marks on it but those worn places where it rubbed against the brackets that held it.

She opened the door, and began examining every inch of the door and frame. And found, near the top, a tiny piece of hemp that looked as if it might have come from a piece of twine, caught in the wood of the door itself.

Further examination of the door yielded nothing, so she turned her attention to the room beyond.

It looked a great deal like the lord's room, with more books and a less ostentatious bedstead—and a wooden floor, rather than one of stone. She called Warrl in and sent him sniffing about for any trace of magic. That potion required a tiny bit of magicking to have full potency, and if there were another bottle of it anywhere about, Warrl would find it.

She turned her own attention to the desk.

Tarma's first opponent had been good, and an honest fighter. It was with a great deal of relief—especially after she'd seen an anxious-faced woman with three small children clinging to her skirt watching every move he made—that she was able to disarm him and knock him flat on his rump without seriously injuring him.

The second had been a mere boy; he had no business being out here at all. Tarma had the shrewd notion he'd been talked into it just so she'd have one more live body to wear her out. Instead of exerting herself in any way, she lazed about, letting him wear *himself* into exhaustion, before giving him a little tap on the skull with the pommel of her knife that stretched him flat on his back, seeing stars.

The third opponent was another creature altogether. He was slim and sleek, and Tarma smelled "assassin" on him as plainly as if she'd had Warrl's clever nose. When he closed with her, his first few moves confirmed her guess. His fighting style was all feint and rush, never getting in too close. This was a real problem. If she stood her ground, she'd open herself to the poisoned dart or whatever other tricks he had secreted on his person. If she let him drive her all over the bloody practice ground he'd wear her down. Either way, she lost.

Of course, she might be able to outfox him—

So far she'd played an entirely defensive game, both with him and her first two opponents. If she took the offense when he least expected it, she might be able to catch him off his guard.

She let him begin to drive her, and saw at once that he was trying to work her around so that the sun was in her eyes. She snarled inwardly, let him think he was having his way, then turned the tables on him.

She came at him in a two-handed pattern-dance, one that took her back to her days on the Plains and her first instructor; an old man she'd never *dreamed* could have moved as fast as he did. She hadn't learned that pattern then; hadn't learned it until the old man and her Clan were two years dead and she'd been Kethry's partner for more than a year. She'd learned it from one of Her Kal'enedral, a woman who'd died a hundred years before Tarma had ever been born.

It took her opponent off-balance; he back-pedaled furiously to get out the the way of the shining circles of steel, great and lesser, that were her sword and dagger. And when he stopped running, he found *himself* facing into the sun.

Tarma saw him make a slight movement with his left hand; when he came in with his sword in an over-and-under cut, she paid his sword-hand only scant attention. It was the other she was watching for.

Under the cover of his overt attack he made a strike for her upper arm with his gloved left. She avoided it barely in time; a circumstance that made her sweat when she thought about it later, and executed a spin-and-cut that took his hand off at

151

the wrist at the end of the move. While he stared in shock at the spurting stump, she carried her blade back along the arc to take his head as well.

The onlookers were motionless, silent with shock. What they'd seen from her up until now had not prepared them for this swift slaughter. While they remained still, she stalked to where the gloved hand lay and picked it up with great care. Embedded in the fingertips of the gloves, retracted or released by a bit of pressure to the center of the palm, were four deadly little needles. Poisoned, no doubt.

She decided to make a grandstand move out of this. She stalked to the challenger's pavilion, where more of her would-be opponents had gathered, and cast the hand down at their feet.

"Assassin's tricks, 'noble lords'?" she spat, oozing contempt. "Is this the honor of Felwether? I'd rather fight jackals. At least they're honest in their treachery! Have you no trust in the judgment of the gods—and their champion?"

That should put a little doubt in the minds of the honest ones—and a little fear in the hearts of the ones that weren't.

Tarma stalked stiff-legged back to her own pavilion, where she threw herself down on the little cot inside it, and hoped *she'd* get her wind back before *they* got their courage up.

In the very back of one of the drawers Kethry found a very curious contrivance. It was a coil of hempen twine, two cords, really, at the end of which was tied a barbless, heavy fishhook, the kind sea-fishers used to take shark and the great sea-salmon. But the coast was weeks from here. What on earth could the seneschal have possibly wanted with such a curious souvenir?

Just then Warrl barked sharply; Kethry turned to see his tail sticking out from under the bedstead.

There's a hidden compartment under the boards here, he said eagerly in her mind. *I smell gold, and magic— and fresh blood.*

She tried to move the bed aside, but it was far too heavy, something the seneschal probably counted on. So she squeezed in beside Warrl, who pawed at the place on the board floor where he smelled strangeness.

Sneezing several times from the dust beneath the bed, she felt along the boards—carefully, carefully; it could be booby-trapped. She found the catch, and a whole section of the board floor lifted away. And inside . . .

Gold, yes; packed carefully into the bottom of it—but on top, a wadded-up tunic, and an empty bottle.

She left the gold, but brought out the other things. The tunic was bloodstained; the bottle, by the smell, had held the narcotic potion she was seeking.

"Hey-la," she whispered in satisfaction.

Now if she just had some notion how he could have gotten into a locked room without the proper key. There was no hint or residue of any kind of magic. And no key to the door with the bar across it.

How *could* you get into a locked room?

Go before the door is locked, Warrl said in her mind.

And suddenly she realized what the fishhook was for.

Kethry wriggled out from under the bed, replacing tunic and bottle and leaving the gold in the hidden compartment untouched.

"Katran!" she called. A moment later Myria's companion appeared; quite nonplussed to see the sorceress covered with dust beside the seneschal's bed.

"Get the priest," Kethry told her, before she had a chance to ask any question. "I know who the murderer is—and I know how he did it, and why."

Tarma was facing her first real opponent of the day; a lean, saturnine fellow who used twin swords like extensions of himself. He was just as fast on his feet as she was—and he was fresher. The priest had vanished just before the beginning of this bout, and Tarma was fervently hoping this meant Kethry had found something. Otherwise, this fight bid fair to be her last.

Thank the Goddess this one was an honest warrior; if she went down, it would be to an honorable opponent. Not too bad, really, if it came to it. Not even many Sword Sworn could boast to having defeated twelve opponents in a single morning.

Even if some of them had been mere babes.

She had a stitch in her side that she was doing her best to ignore, and her breath was coming in harsh pants. The sun was punishing-hard on someone wearing head-to-toe black; sweat was trickling down her back and sides. She danced aside, avoiding a blur of sword, only to find she was moving right into the path of his second blade.

Damn!

At the last second she managed to drop and roll, and came up to find him practically on top of her again. She managed to get to one knee and trap his first blade between dagger and sword—but the second was coming in—

From the side of the field, came a voice like a trumpet call.

"Hold!"

And miracle of miracles, the blade stopped mere inches from her unprotected neck.

The priest strode onto the field, robes flapping. "The sorceress has found the true murderer of our lord and proved it to my satisfaction," he announced to the waiting crowd. "She wishes to prove it to yours."

Then he began naming off interested parties as Tarma sagged to her knees in the dirt, limp with relief, and just about ready to pass out with exhaustion. Her opponent dropped both his blades in the dust at her side, and ran off to his side of the field, returning in a moment with a cup of water.

154

And before handing it to her, he smiled sardonically, saluted her with it and took a tiny sip himself.

She shook sweat-sodden hair out of her eyes, and accepted the cup with a nod of thanks. She downed the lukewarm water, and sagged back onto her heels with a sigh.

"Sword Sworn, shall I find someone to take you to your pavilion?"

The priest was bending over her in concern. Tarma managed to find one tiny bit of unexpended energy.

"Not on your life, priest. I want to see this myself!"

There were perhaps a dozen nobles in the group that the priest escorted to the lord's chamber. Foremost among them was the seneschal; the priest most attentive on him. Tarma was too tired to wonder about that; she saved what little energy she had to get her into the room and safely leaning up against the wall within.

"I trust you all will forgive me if I am a bit dramatic, but I wanted you all to see exactly how this deed was done."

Kethry was standing behind the chair that was placed next to the desk; in that chair was an older woman in buff and gray. "Katran has kindly agreed to play the part of Lord Corbie; I am the murderer. The lord has just come into this chamber; in the next is his lady. She has taken a potion to relieve pain, and the accustomed sound of his footstep is not likely to awaken her."

She held up a wineglass. "Some of that same potion was mixed in with the wine that was in this glass, but it did not come from the batch Lady Myria was using. Here is Myria's bottle," she placed the wineglass on the desk, and Myria brought a bottle to stand beside it. "Here," she produced a second bottle, "is the bottle I found. The priest knows where, and can vouch for the fact that until

155

he came, no hand but the owner's and mine touched it."

The priest nodded. Tarma noticed with a preternatural sensitivity that made it seem as if her every nerve was on the alert that the seneschal was beginning to sweat.

"The spell I am going to cast now—as your priest can vouch, since he is no mean student of magic himself—will cause the wineglass and the bottle that contained the potion that was poured into it glow."

Kethry dusted something over the glass and the two bottles. As they watched, the residue in the glass and the fraction of potion in Kethry's bottle began to glow with an odd, greenish light.

"Is this a true casting, priest?" Tarma heard one of the nobles ask in an undertone.

He nodded. "As true as ever I've seen."

"Huh," the man replied, frowning with thoughts he kept to himself.

"Now—Lord Corbie has just come in; he is working on the ledgers. I give him a glass of wine," Kethry handed the glass to Katran. "He is grateful; he thinks nothing of the courtesy, I am an old and trusted friend. He drinks it, I leave the room, presently he is asleep."

Katran allowed her head to sag down on her arms.

"I take the key from beneath his hand, and quietly lock the door to the hall. I replace the key. I know he will not stir, not even cry out, because of the strength of the potion. I take Lady Myria's dagger, which I obtained earlier. I stab him." Kethry mimed the murder; Katran did not move, though Tarma could see she was smiling sardonically. "I take the dagger and plant it beneath Lady Myria's bed—and I know that because of the potion *she* has been taking—and which I recommended, since we have no Healer—she will not wake either."

Kethry went into Myria's chamber, and returned empty-handed.

"I've been careless—got some blood on my tunic, I've never killed a man before and I didn't know that the wound would spurt. No matter, I will hide it where I plan to hide the bottle. By the way, the priest has that bloody tunic, and he knows that his hands alone removed it from its hiding place, just like the bottle. Now comes the important part—"

She took an enormous fishhook on a double length of twine out of her beltpouch.

"The priest knows where I found this—rest assured that it was *not* in Myria's possession. Now, on the top of this door, caught on a rough place in the wood, is another scrap of hemp. I am going to get it now. Then I shall cast another spell—and if that bit of hemp came from this twine, it shall return to the place it came from."

She went to the door and jerked loose a bit of fiber, taking it back to the desk. Once again she dusted something over the twine on the hook and the scrap, this time she also chanted as well. A golden glow drifted down from her hands to touch first the twine, then the scrap.

And the bit of fiber shot across to the twine like an arrow loosed from a bow.

"Now you will see the key to entering a locked room, now that I have proved that this was the mechanism by which the trick was accomplished."

She went over to the door to the seneschal's chamber. She wedged the hook under the bar on the door, and lowered the bar so that it was only held in place by the hook; the hook was kept where it was by the length of twine going over the door itself. The other length of twine Kethry threaded *under* the door. Then she closed the door.

The second piece of twine jerked; the hook came free, and the bar thudded into place. And the whole contrivance was pulled up over the door and through the upper crack by the first piece.

All eyes turned toward the seneschal—whose white face was confession enough.

* * *

"Lady Myria was certainly grateful enough."

"If we'd let her, she'd have stripped the treasury bare," Kethry replied, waving at the distant figures on the keep wall. "I'm glad you talked her out of it."

"Greeneyes, they don't have it to spare, and we both know it. As it is, she'll have to spend most of the seneschal's hoard in making up for the shortfalls among the hirelings that his skimmings caused in the first place."

"Will she be all right, do you think?"

"Now that her brother's here I don't think she has a thing to worry about. She's gotten back all the loyalty of her lord's people and more besides. All she needed was a strong right arm to beat off unwelcome suitors, and she's got that now! Warrior's Oath, I'm glad *that* young monster wasn't one of the challengers. I'd never have lasted past the first round!"

"Tarma—"

The swordswoman raised an eyebrow at Kethry's unwontedly serious tone.

"If you—did all that because you think you owe me—"

"I 'did all that' because we're *she'enedran*," she replied, a slight smile warming her otherwise forbidding expression. "No other reason is needed."

"But—"

"No 'buts,' Greeneyes." Tarma looked back at the waving motes on the wall. "Hell, we've just accomplished something we really needed to do. This little job is going to give us a real boost on our reputation. Besides, you know I'd do whatever I needed to do to keep you safe."

Kethry did not reply to that last; not that she wasn't dead certain that it was true. That was the problem.

Tarma had been stepping between Kethry and possible danger on a regular basis, often when such intercession wasn't needed. At all other times, she treated Kethry as a strict equal, but when danger threatened—

She tried to keep the sorceress wrapped in a protective cocoon spun of herself and her blades.

She probably doesn't even realize she's doing it—but she's keeping me so safe, she's putting herself in more risk than she needs to. She knows I can take care of myself—

Then the answer occurred to her.

Without me, there will never be a Tale'sedrin. She's protecting, not just me, but her hopes for a new Clan! But she's stifling me—and she's going to get herself killed!

She glanced over at Tarma, at the distant, brooding expression she wore.

I can't tell her. She might not believe me. Or worse, she might believe, and choke when she needs to act. I wonder if Warrl has figured out what she's doing? I hope so—

She glanced again at her partner.

—or she's going to end up killing all three of us. Or driving me mad.

Seven

The sorcerer was young, thin, and sweating nervously, despite the cold of the musty cellar chamber that served as his living area and workroom. His secondhand robe was clammy with chill and soaked through with his own perspiration.

He had every reason to be nervous. This was the first time he and his apprentice (who was now huddled out of the way in the corner) had ever attempted to bind an imp to his service. The summoning of a spirit from the Abyssal Planes is no small task, even if the spirit one hopes to summon is of the very least and lowliest of the demonic varietals. Demons and their ilk are always watching for a chance misstep—and some are more eager to take advantage of a mistake than others.

The torches on the walls wavered and smoked, their odor of hot pitch nearly overwhelming the acrid tang of the incense he was burning. Mice squeaked and scuttled along the rafters overhead. Perhaps they were the cause of his distraction, for he *was* distracted for a crucial moment. And one of those that watched and waited seized the unhoped-for opportunity when the sorcerer thrice chanted, not the name "Talhkarsh"—the true-name of the imp he meant to bind—but *"Thalhkarsh."*

Incandescent ruby smoke rose and filled the interior of the diagram the mage had so carefully chalked upon the floor of his cluttered, dank, high-ceilinged stone chamber. It completely hid whatever was forming within the bespelled hexacle.

But there *was* something there; he could see shad-

160

ows moving within the veiling smoke. He waited, dry-mouthed in anticipation, for the smoke to clear, so that he could intone his second incantation, one that would coerce the imp he'd summoned into the bottle that waited within the exact center of the hexacle.

Then the smoke vanished as quickly as it had been conjured—and the young mage nearly fainted, as he looked *up* at what stood there. And looked higher. And his sallow, bearded visage assumed the same lack of color as his chalk when the occupant, head just brushing the rafters, calmly stepped across the spell-bound lines, bent slightly at the waist, and seized him none-too-gently by the throat.

Thinking quickly, he summoned everything he knew in the way of arcane protections, spending magical energy with what in other circumstances might have been reckless wastefulness. There was a brief flare of light around him, and the demon dropped him as a human would something that had unexpectedly scorched his hand. The mage cringed where he had fallen, squeezing his eyes shut.

"Oh, fool," the voice was like brazen gongs just slightly out of tune with each other, and held no trace of pity. "Look at me."

The mage opened one eye, well aware of the duplicity of demons, yet unable to resist the command. His knowledge did him little good; his face went slack-jawed with bemusement at the serpentine beauty of the creature that stood over him. It had shrunk to the size of a very tall human and its—*his*—eyes glowed from within, a rich ruby color reminiscent of wine catching sunlight. He was —wonderful.

He was the very image of everything the mage had ever dreamed of in a lover. The face was that of a fallen angel, the nude body that of a god. The ruby eyes promised and beckoned, and were filled with an overwhelming and terribly masculine power.

The magician's shields did not include those meant to ward off beglamoring. He threw every pitiful

161

protection he'd erected to the four winds in an onslaught of delirious devotion.

The demon laughed, and took him into his arms.

When he was finished amusing himself, he tore the whimpering creature that remained to shreds . . . slowly.

It was only then, only after he'd destroyed the mage past any hope of resurrection, and when he was sated with the emanations of the mage's torment and death, that he paused to think—and, thinking, to regret his hasty action.

There had been opportunity there, opportunity to be free forever of the Abyssal Planes, and more, a potential for an unlimited supply of those delights he'd just indulged in. If only he'd *thought* before he'd acted!

But even as he was mentally cursing his own impulsiveness, his attention was caught by a hint of movement in the far corner.

He grew to his full size, and reached out lazily with one bloodsmeared claw to pull the shivering, wretched creature that cowered there into the torchlight. It had soiled itself with fear, but by the torque around its throat and the cabalistic signs on its shabby robe, this pitiful thing must have been the departed mage's apprentice.

Thalhkarsh chuckled, and the apprentice tried to shrink into insignificance. All was not yet lost. In fact, this terror-stricken youth was an even better candidate for what he had in mind than his master would have been.

Thalhkarsh bent his will upon the boy's mind; it was easy to read. The defenses his master had placed about him were few and weak, and fading with the master's death. Satisfied by what he read there, the demon assumed his most attractive aspect and spoke.

"Boy, would you live? More, would you prosper?"

The apprentice trembled and nodded slightly, his eyes glazed with horror, a fear that was rapidly being subsumed by the power the demon was exerting on his mind.

"See you this?" the demon hefted the imp-bottle that had been in the diagram with him. Plain, reddish glass before, it now glowed from within like the demon's eyes. "Do you know what it is?"

"The—imp-bottle," the boy whispered, after two attempts to get words out that failed. "The one Leland meant to—to—"

"To confine me in—or rather, the imp he meant to call. It is a worthless bottle no more; thanks to having been within the magic confines of the diagram when I was summoned instead of the imp, it has become my focus. Did your master tell you what a demonic focus is?"

"It—" the boy stared in petrified fascination at the bottle in the demon's hand, "it lets you keep yourself here of your own will. If you have enough power."

The demon smiled. "But I want more than freedom, boy. I want more than power. I have greater ambitions. And if you want to live, you'll help me achieve them."

It was plain from the boy's eyes that he was more than willing to do just about anything to ensure his continued survival. "How—what do you want?"

Thalhkarsh laughed, and his eyes narrowed. "Never mind, child. I have plans—and if you succeed in what I set out for you, you will have a life privileged beyond anything you can now imagine. You will become great—and I, I will become—greater than your poor mind can dream. For now, child, *this* is how you can serve me. . . ."

"Here?" Tarma asked her mage-partner. "You're sure?"

The sunset bathed her in a blood-red glow as they approached the trade-gate of the city of Delton, and a warm spring breeze stirred a lock of coarse black hair that had escaped the confines of her short braids; her hair had grown almost magically the past few months, as if it had resented being shorn. The last light dyed her brown leather tunic and breeches a red that was nearly black.

Kethry's softly attractive face wore lines of strain, and there was worry in her emerald eyes. "I'm sure. It's here—and it's bad, whatever it is. This is the worst Need's ever pulled on me that I can remember. It's worse than that business with Lady Myria, even." She pushed the hood of her traveling robe back from an aching forehead and rubbed her temples a little.

"Huh. Well, I hope that damn blade of yours hasn't managed to get us knee-deep into more than we can handle. Only one way to find out, though."

The swordswoman kneed her horse into the lead, and the pair rode in through the gates after passing the cursory inspection of a somewhat nervous Gate Guard. He seemed oddly disinclined to climb down from his gatehouse post, being content to pass them through after a scant few moment's scrutiny.

Tarma's ice-blue eyes scanned the area just inside the gate for signs of trouble, and found none. Her brow puckered in puzzlement. "She'enedra, I find it hard to believe you're wrong, but this is the quietest town I've ever seen. I was expecting blood and rapine in the streets."

"I'm not mistaken," Kethry replied in a low, tense voice. "And there's something *very* wrong here—the very quiet is wrong. It's *too* quiet. There's no one at all on the streets—no beggars, no whores, no nothing."

Tarma looked about her with increased alertness. Now that Keth had mentioned it, this looked like an empty town. There were no loiterers to be seen in the vicinity of the trade gate or the inns that clustered about the square just inside it, and that was very odd indeed. No beggars, no thieves, no whores, no strollers, no street musicians—just the few stablehands and inn servants that *had* to be outside, leading in the beasts of fellow travelers, lighting lanterns and torches. And those few betook themselves back inside as quickly as was possible. The square of the trade inns was ominously deserted.

"Warrior's Oath! This is blamed *spooky!* I don't like the look of this, not one bit."

"Neither do I. Pick us an inn, *she'enedra;* pick one fast. If the locals don't want to be out-of-doors after sunset, they must have a reason, and I'd rather not be out here either."

Tarma chose an inn with the sign of a black sheep hanging above the door, and the words (for the benefit of those that could read) "The Blacke Ewe" painted on the wall beside the door. It looked to be about the right sort for the state of their purses, which were getting a bit on the lean side. They'd been riding the Trade Road north to Valdemar, once again looking for work, when Kethry's geas-forged blade Need had drawn them eastward until they ended up here. The sword had left them pretty much alone except for a twinge or two—and the incident with the feckless priestess, that had wound up being far more complicated than it had needed to be thanks to the Imp of the Perverse and Tarma's own big mouth. Tarma was beginning to hope that it had settled down.

And then this afternoon, Kethry had nearly fainted when it "called" with all of its old urgency. They'd obeyed its summons, until it led them at last to Delton.

Tarma saw to the stabling of their beasts; Kethry to bargaining for a room. The innkeeper looked askance at a mage wearing a sword, for those who trafficked in magic seldom carried physical weaponry, but he was openly alarmed by the sight of what trotted at Tarma's heels—a huge, black, wolflike creature whose shoulders came nearly as high as the swordswoman's waist.

Kethry saw the alarm in his eyes, realized that he had never seen a *kyree* before, and decided to use his fear as a factor in her bargaining. "My familiar," she said nonchalantly, "and he knows when I'm being cheated."

The price of their room took a mysterious plunge. After installing their gear and settling Warrl in their room, they returned to the taproom for supper and information.

If the streets were deserted, the taproom was crowded far past its intended capacity.

Tarma wrinkled her nose at the effluvia of cheap perfume, unwashed bodies, stale food odors and fish-oil lanterns. Kethry appeared not to notice.

Tarma's harsh, hawklike features could be made into a veritable mask of intimidation when she chose to scowl; she did so now. Her ice-cold stare got them two stools and a tiny, round table to themselves. Her harsh voice summoned a harried servant as easily as Kethry could summon a creature of magic. A hand to her knife-hilt and the ostentatious shrugging of the sword slung on her back into a more comfortable position got her speedy service, cleaning her fingernails with her knife got them decent portions and scrubbed plates.

Kethry's frown of worry softened a bit. "Life has been ever so much easier since I teamed with you, *she'enedra*," she chuckled quietly, moving the sides of her robe out of the way so that she could sit comfortably.

"No doubt," the swordswoman replied with a lifted eyebrow and a quirk to one corner of her mouth. "Sometimes I wonder how you managed without me."

"Poorly." The green eyes winked with mischief.

Their food arrived, and they ate in silence, furtively scanning the crowded room for a likely source of information. When they'd nearly finished, Kethry nodded slightly in the direction of a grizzled mercenary sitting just underneath one of the smoking lanterns. Tarma looked him over carefully; he looked almost drunk enough to talk, but not drunk enough to make trouble, and his companions had just deserted him, leaving seats open on the bench opposite his. He wore a badge, so he was mastered, and so was less likely to pick a fight. They picked up their tankards and moved to take those vacant seats beside him.

He nodded as they sat; warily at Tarma, appreciatively at Kethry.

He wasn't much for idle chatter, though. "Evening," was all he said.

"It is that," Tarma replied, "Though 'tis a strange enough evening and more than a bit early for folk to be closing themselves indoors, especialy with the weather so pleasant."

"These are strange times," he countered, "And strange things happen in the nights around here."

"Oh?" Kethry looked flatteringly interested. "What sort of strange things? And can we take care of your thirst?"

He warmed to the admiration—and the offer.

"Folk been going missing; whores, street trash, such as won't be looked for by the watch," he told them, wiping his mouth on his sleeve, while Tarma signaled the serving wench. He took an enormous bite of the spiced sausage that was the Blacke Ewe's specialty; grease ran into his beard. He washed the bite down by draining his tankard dry. "There's rumors—" His eyes took on a certain wariness. He cast an uneasy glance around the dim, hot and odorous taproom.

"Rumors?" Tarma prompted, pouring his tankard full again, and sliding a silver piece under it. "Well, *we* little care for rumors, eh? What's rumor to a fighter but ale-talk?"

"Plague take rumors!" he agreed, but his face was strained. "What've magickers and demons got to do with us, so long as they leave our masters in peace?" He drained the vessel and pocketed the coin. "So long as he leaves a few for me, this Thalhkarsh can have his *fill* of whores!"

"Thalhkarsh? What might that be? Some great lecher, that he has need of so many lightskirts?"

Tarma filled the tankard for the third time, and kept her tone carefully casual.

"Sh!" the mercenary paled, and made a cautionary wave with his hand. " 'Tisn't wise to bandy that name about lightly—them as does often aren't to be seen again. That—one I mentioned—well, some say he's a god, some a demon summoned by a mighty powerful magicker. All I know is that he has a temple on the Row—one that sprang up overnight, seemingly, and one with statues an' such that could make me blush, were I to go view 'em. The which I won't. 'Tisn't safe to go near there—"

"So?" Tarma raised one eyebrow.

"They sent the city guard trooping in there after the first trollops went missing. There were tales spread of blood-worship, so the city council reckoned somebody'd better check. Nobody ever saw so much as a scrap of bootleather of that guard-squad ever again."

"So folk huddle behind their doors at night, and hope that they'll be left in peace, hmm?" Kethry mused aloud, taking her turn at replenishing his drink. "But are they?"

"Rumor says not—not unless they take care to stay in company at night. Odd thing though, 'cept for the city guard, most of the ones taken by night have been women. I'd watch meself, were I you twain."

He drained his tankard yet again. This proved to be one tankard too many, as he slowly slid off the bench to lie beneath the table, a bemused smile on his face.

They took the god-sent opportunity to escape to their room.

"Well," Tarma said, once the door had been bolted, "we know why, and now we know what. Bloody Hell! I wish for once that that damned sword of yours would steer us toward something that pays!"

Kethry worked a minor magic that sent the vermin sharing their accommodations skittering under the door and out the open window. Warrl surveyed

168

her handiwork, sniffed the room over carefully, then lay down at the foot of the double pallet with a heavy sigh.

"That's not quite true—we don't really know *what* we're dealing with. Is it a god, truly? If it is, I don't stand much chance of making a dent in its hide. Is it a demon, controlled by this magician, that has been set up as a god so that its master can acquire power by blood-magic? Or is it worse than either?"

"What could possible be worse?"

"A demon loose, uncontrolled—a demon with ambition," Kethry said, flopping down beside Warrl and staring up at nothing, deep in thought.

Their lantern (more fish-oil) smoked and danced, and made strange shadows on the wall and ceiling.

"Worst case would be just that: a demon that knows exactly how to achieve godhood, and one with nothing standing in the way of his intended path. If it is a god—a real god—well, all gods have their enemies; it's simply a matter of finding the sworn enemy, locating a nest of his clerics, and bringing them all together. And a demon under the control of a mage can be sent back to the Abyssal Planes by discovering the summoning spell and breaking it. But an uncontrolled demon—the *only* way to get rid of it that I know of is to find its focus-object and break it. Even that may not work if it has achieved enough power. With enough accumulated power, or enough worshipers believing in his godhood, even breaking his focus wouldn't send him back to the Abyssal Planes. If that happens—well, you *first* have to find a demon-killing weapon, *then* you have to get close enough to strike a killing blow. And you hope that he isn't strong enough to have gone beyond needing a physical form. Or you damage him enough to break the power he gets from his followers' belief—but that's even harder to do than finding a demon-killing blade."

"And, needless to say, demon-killing weapons are few and far between."

"And it isn't terribly likely that you're going to

169

get past a demon's reach to get that killing blow in, once he's taken his normal form."

Tarma pulled off her boots, and inspected the soles with a melancholy air. "How likely is that—an uncontrolled demon?"

"Not really likely," Kethry admitted. "I'm just being careful—giving you worst-case first. It's a lot more likely that he's under the control of a mage that's using him to build a power base for himself. That's the scenario I'd bet on. I've seen this trick pulled more than once before I met you. It works quite well, provided you can keep giving your congregation what they want."

"So what's next?"

"Well, I'd suggest we wait until morning, and see what I can find out among the mages while you see if you can get any more mercenaries to talk."

"Somehow I was afraid you'd say that."

They met back at the inn at noon; Tarma was empty-handed, but Kethry had met with a certain amount of success. At least she had a name, an address, and a price—a fat skin of strong wine taken with her, with a promise of more to come.

The address was in the scummiest section of the town, hard by the communal refuse heap. Both women kept their hands on the hilts of their blades while making their way down the rank and odorous alleyway; there were flickers of movement at various holes in the walls (you could hardly call them "doors" or "windows") but they were left unmolested. More than one of the piles of what seemed to be rotting refuse that dotted the alley proved to be a human, though it was difficult to tell for certain if they were living humans or corpses. Kethry again seemed blithely unaware of the stench; Tarma fought her stomach and tried to breathe as little as possible, and that little through her mouth.

At length they came to a wall that boasted a proper door; Kethry rapped on it. A mumbled voice answered her; she whispered something Tarma couldn't make out. Evidently it was the proper response, as the door swung open long enough for them to squeeze through, then shut hurriedly behind them.

Tarma blinked in surprise at what lay beyond the alleyside door. The fetid aroma of the air outside was gone. There was a faint ghost of wine, and an even fainter ghost of incense. The walls were covered with soft, colorful rugs; more rugs covered the floor. On top of the rugs were huge, plush cushions. The room was a rainbow of subtle reds and oranges and yellows. Tarma was struck with a sudden closing of the throat, and she blinked to clear misting eyes. This place reminded her forcibly of a Shin'a'in tent.

Fortunately the woman who turned from locking the door to greet them was not a Clanswoman, or Tarma might have had difficulty in ridding her eyes of that traitorous mist. She was draped head to toe with a veritable marketplace-full of veils, so that only her eyes showed. The voluminous covering, which rivaled the room for color and variety of pattern, was not, however, enough to hide the fact that she was wraith-thin. And above the veils, the black eyes were gray-ringed, bloodshot, and haggard.

"You know my price?" came a thin whisper.

Kethry let the heavy wineskin slide to her feet, and she nudged it over to the woman with one toe. "Three more follow, one every two days, from the master of the Blacke Ewe."

"What do you wish to know?"

"How comes this thing they call Thalhkarsh here—and why?"

The woman laughed crazily; Tarma loosened one of her knives in its hidden arm-sheath. What in the name of the Warrior had Kethry gotten them into?

"For that I need not even scry! Oh, no, to my sorrow, that is something I know only too well!"

The eyes leaked tears; Tarma averted her gaze, embarrassed.

171

"A curse on my own pride, and another on my curiosity! For now *he* knows my aura, knows it well—and calls me—and only the wine can stop my feet from taking me to him—" the thin voice whined to a halt, and the eyes closed, as if in a sudden spasm of pain.

For a long moment the woman stood, still as a thing made of wood, and Tarma feared they'd get nothing more out of her. Then the eyes opened again, and fixed Kethry with a stillettolike glare.

"Hear then the tale of my folly—'tis short enough. When Thalhkarsh raised his temple, all in a single night, I thought to scry it and determine what sort of creature was master of it. My soul-self was trapped by him, like a cruel child traps a mouse, and like cruel children, he and his priest tormented it—for how long, I cannot say. Then they seemed to forget me; let me go again, to crawl back to myself. But they had *not* forgotten me. I soon learned that each night he would call me back to his side. Each night I drink until I can no longer hear the call, but each night it takes more wine to close my ears. One night it will not be enough, and I shall join his other—brides."

The veils shook and trembled.

"This much only did I learn. Thalhkarsh is a demon; summoned by mistake instead of an imp. He bides here by virtue of his focus, the bottle that was meant to contain the imp. He is powerful; his priest is a mage as well, and has his own abilities augmented by the demon's. No sane person would bide in this town with them rising to prominence here."

The woman turned back to the door in a flutter of thin fabric and cracked it open again. One sticklike arm and hand pointed the way out. "That is my rede; take it if you are not fools."

Tarma was only too pleased to escape the chamber, which seemed rather too confining of a sudden. Kethry paused, concern on her face, to reach a tentative hand toward the veiled mystery. The woman made a repudiating motion. "Do not pity me!" she whispered harshly. "You cannot know! He is terrible—but he is also glorious—so—glorious—"

Her eyes glazed for a moment, then focused again, and she slammed the door shut behind them.

Kethry laced herself into the only dress she owned, a sensuous thing of forest green silk, a scowl twisting her forehead. "Why do *I* have to be the one pawed at and drooled over?"

Tarma chuckled. "You were the one who decreed against using any more magic than we had to," she pointed out.

"Well, I don't want to chance that mage detecting it and getting curious!"

"And you were the one who didn't want to chance using illusion."

"What if something should break it?"

"Then don't complain if I can't take your place. *You* happen to be the one of us that is lovely, amber-haired, and toothsome, not I. And you are the one with the manner-born. No merchant-lord or minor noble is going to open his doors to a nomad mercenary, and no decadent stripling is going to whisper secrets into the ear of one with a face like an ill-tempered hawk and a body like a sword-blade. Now hurry up, or the market will be closed and we'll have to wait until the morrow."

Kethry grumbled under her breath, but put more speed into her preparations. They sallied forth into the late afternoon, playing parts they had often taken before, Kethry assuming the manners of the rank she actually was entitled to, playing the minor noblewoman on a journey to relatives with Tarma as her bodyguard.

As was very often the case, the marketplace was also the gathering-place for the offspring of what passed for aristocracy in this borderland trade-town. Within no great span of time Kethry had garnered

173

invitations to dine with half a dozen would-be gallants. She chose the most dissipated of them, but persuaded him to make a party of the occasion, and invite his friends.

A bit miffed by the spoiling of his plans (which had not included having any competition for Kethry's assets), he agreed. As with the common folk, the well-born had taken to closing themselves behind sturdy doors at the setting of the sun, and with it already low in the west, he hastened to send a servant around to collect his chosen companions.

The young man's father was not at home, being off on a trading expedition. This had figured very largely in his plans, for he had purloined the key to his father's plushly appointed gazebo for his entertainment. The place was as well furnished as many homes: full of soft divans and wide couches, and boasting seven little alcoves off the main room, and two further rooms for intimate entertainment besides. Tarma's acting abilities were strained to the uttermost by the evening's events; she was hard-put to keep from laughing aloud at Kethry's performance and the reactions of the young men to her. To anyone who did not know her, Kethry embodied the very epitome of light-minded, light-skirted, capricious demi-nobility. No one watching her would have guessed she ever had a thought in her head besides her own pleasuring.

To the extreme displeasure of those few female companions that had been brought to the festivities, she monopolized all the male attention in the room. It wasn't long before she had sorted out which of them had actually been to one of the infamous "Rites of Dark Desires" and which had only heard rumors. Those who had not been bold enough to attend discovered themselves subtly dismissed from the inner circle, and soon repaired to the gardens or semi-private alcoves to enjoy the attentions of the females they had brought, but ignored. Kethry lured the three favored swains into one of the private rooms, motioning Tarma to remain on guard at the door. She eventually emerged; hot-eyed, contemptuous, and disheveled. Snores echoed from the room behind her.

"Let's get out of here before I lose my temper and go back to wring their necks," she snarled, while Tarma choked back a chuckle. "Puppies! They should still be in diapers, every one of them! Not anything resembling a real adult among them! I swear to you—ah, never mind. I'd just like to see them get some of the treatment they've earned. Like a good spanking and a long stint in a hermitage—preferably one in the middle of a desert, stocked with nothing but hard bread, water, and boring religious texts!"

No one followed them out into the night, which was not overly surprising, given the fears of the populace.

"I hope it was worth it," Tarma said, as casually as she could.

"It was," Kethry replied, a little cooler. "They were all very impressed with the whole ritual, and remembered everything they saw in quite lurid detail. It seems that it *is* the High Priest who is the one truly in command; from the sound of it, my guess was right about his plans. He conducts every aspect of the ritual; he calls the 'god' up, and he sends him back again. The god selects those of the females brought to him that he wants, the male followers get what's left, or share the few female followers he has. It's a rather unpleasant combination of human sacrifice and orgy. The High Priest must be the magician that summoned the demon in the first place. He's almost certainly having the demon transform himself, since the god is almost unbearably attractive, and the females he selects go to him willingly—at least at first. After his initial attentions, they're no longer in any condition to object to much of anything. Those three back there were positively obscene. They gloated over all the

175

details of what Thalhkarsh does to his 'brides,' all the while doing their best to get me out of my clothing so they could demonstrate the 'rites.' It was all I could do to keep from throwing up on them."

"You sleep-spelled them?"

"Better, I dream-spelled them, just like I did with our 'customers' when I was posing as a whore back when we first met. It's as easy as sleep-spelling them, it's a very localized magic that isn't likely to be detected, and it will keep our disguises intact. They'll have the best time their imaginations can possibly provide."

Kethry looked suddenly weary as they approached their inn. "Bespeak me a bath, would you, dearheart? I feel filthy—inside *and* out."

The next night was the night of moon-dark, the night of one of the more important of the new deity's rituals, and there was a pair of spies watching the streets that led to Temple Row with particular care. Those two pairs of eyes paid particularly close attention to two women making their cautious way through the darkened and deserted streets, muffled head-to-toe in cloaks. Though faint squeals and curses showed that neither of them could see well enough to avoid the rocks and fetid heaps of refuse that dotted the street, they seemed not to wish any kind of light to brighten their path. Gold peeked out from the hoods; the half-seen faces were old before their time; their eyelids drooped with boredom that had become habit, but their eyes revealed a kind of fearful anticipation. Their destination was the Temple of Thalhkarsh. They were intercepted a block away, by two swiftly moving figures who neatly knocked them unconscious and spirited them into a nearby alleyway.

Tarma spat out several unintelligible oaths. The dim light of a heavily shuttered dark-lantern fell on the two bodies at her feet. Beneath the cloaks, the

176

now unconscious women had worn little more than heavy jewelry and a strategically placed veil or two.

"We'll be searched, you can bet on it," she said in disgust. "And where the bloody Hell are we going to hide weapons in these outfits?"

In truth, there wasn't enough cover among the chains and medallions to have concealed even the smallest of her daggers.

"We can't," Kethry replied flatly. "So that leaves —Warrl?"

Tarma pursed her lips. "Hmm. That's a thought. Fur-face, could you carry two swords?"

The *kyree* cocked his head to one side, and experimentally mouthed Need's sheath. Kethry took the blade off and held it for him to take. He swung his head from side to side a little, then dropped the blade.

Not that way, Tarma heard in her mind. *Too clumsy. Won't balance right; couldn't run or jump— might get stuck in a tight doorway. I want to be able to bite—these teeth aren't just for decoration, you know! And anyway, I can't carry two blades at the same time in my mouth.*

"Could we strap them to you, somehow?"

If you do, I can try how it feels.

Using their belts they managed to strap the blades along his flanks, one on either side, to Warrl's satisfaction. He ran from one end of the alley to the other, then shook himself carefully without dislodging them or getting tangled by them.

It'll work, he said with satisfaction. *Let's go.*

They left their victims sleeping in a dead-end alley; they'd be rather embarrassed when they woke stark-naked in the morning. They'd come to no harm; thanks to Thalhkarsh not even criminals moved about the city by night, and the evening was warm enough that they wouldn't suffer from exposure. Whether or not they'd die of mortification remained to be seen.

The partners left their own clothing hidden in another alley farther on. Muffled in the stolen cloaks, they approached the temple, Warrl a shadow flitting behind them.

On seeing the entrance, Tarma gave a snort of disgust. It was gaudy and decadent in the extreme, with carvings and statuary depicting every vice imaginable (and some she'd never dreamed existed) encrusting the entire front face.

The single guard was a fat, homely man who moved slowly and clumsily, as if he were under the influence of a drug. He seemed little interested in the men who passed him by, other than seeing that they dropped their cloaks and giving them a cursory search for weaponry. The women were another case altogether. Between the preoccupation he was likely to have once he'd seen Kethry and the shadows cast by the carvings in the torchlight, Warrl should have no difficulty in slipping past him.

Kethry touched the swordswoman's arm slightly as they stood in line and nodded toward the guard, giving a little wiggle as she did so. Tarma knew what that meant—Kethry was going to make certain the guard's attention stayed on her. The Shin'a'in dropped her eyelids briefly in assent. When their turn came and they dropped their cloaks, Kethry posed and postured provocatively beneath the guard's searching hands. He was so busy filling his eyes—and greasy paws—with her that he paid scant attention to either Tarma or the shadow that slipped inside behind her.

When he'd delayed long enough that there was considerable grumbling from those waiting their turn behind the two women, he finally let Kethry pass with real reluctance. They slipped inside the smoke-wreathed portal and found themselves walking down a dark corridor, heavy with the scent of cloying incense. When the corridor ended, they passed through a curtain of some heavy material that moved of itself, as if it sensed their presence, and had a slippery feel and a sour smell to it. Once past that last obstruction, they found themselves blinking in the light of the temple proper.

The interior was almost austere compared with the exterior. The walls were totally bare of ornamentation; the pillars upholding the roof were simple columns and not debauched caryatids. That simplicity left the eye only one place to go—the altar, a massive black slab with manacles at each corner and what could only be blood-grooves carved into its surface.

There was no sign of any bottle.

There *were* huge lanterns suspended from the ceiling and torches in brackets on the pillars, but the walls themselves were in shadow. There were braziers sending plumes of incense into the air on either side of the door. Beneath the too-sweet odor Tarma recognized the taint of *tran*-dust. This was where and how the guard had acquired his dreamy clumsiness. She nudged Kethry and they moved hastily along the wall to a spot where a draft carried fresher air to them. *Tran*-dust was dangerous at best, and could be fatal to them, for it slowed reactions and blurred the senses. They would need both at full sharpness tonight.

There was a drumming and an odd, wild music that was almost more felt than heard. From a doorway behind the altar emerged the High Priest, at this distance, little more than a vague shape in elaborate robes of crimson and gold. Behind him came an acolyte, carrying an object that made Kethry's eyes widen with satisfaction; it was a bottle, red, that glowed dimly from within. The acolyte fitted this into a niche in the foot of the altar near the edge; the place all the blood-grooves drained into.

They worked their way closer, moving carefully along the wall. When they were close enough to make out the High Priest's features, Kethry became aware of his intensely sexual attraction. As if to underscore this, she saw eager devotion written

179

plainly on the face of a woman standing near to the altar-place. She tightened her lips; evidently this was one aspect of domination that both high priest and demon-deity shared. She warded her own mind against beglamorment. Tarma she knew she need not protect; by her very nature as Sword Sworn she would be immune to *this* kind of deception.

A gong began sounding; slowly, insistently. The music increased in tempo; built to a crescendo—a blood-red brightness behind the altar intensified, echoing the rising music. At the climax of both, when the altar was almost too bright to look at, something appeared, pulling all the light and sound into itself.

He was truly beautiful; poisonously beautiful. Compared to him, the priest's attraction was insignificant. The line of women being brought in by two more acolytes ceased their fearful trembling, sighed, and yearned toward him.

He beckoned to one, who literally ran to him, eagerly.

Tarma turned her eyes resolutely away from the spectacle being presented at the altar-place. There was nothing either of them could do to help the intended sacrifice; she was thanking her Goddess that Need was not at Kethry's hand just now. The sorceress had been known once or twice to become a berserker under the blade's influence, and she was not altogether sure how much the sword was capable of in the way of thought. It wasn't mindless —but in a situation like this it was moot whether or not it would prefer the long term goal of destroying the demon as opposed to the short term goal of ending the sacrifice's torment.

At least the rest of the devotees were so preoccupied with the victim and her suffering that they scarcely noticed the two women slowly making their way closer to the altar. Tarma looked closely into one face, and quickly looked away, nauseated. Those glazed eyes—swollen lips—the panting—it would

180

have been obvious even to a child that the man was erotically enraptured by what he was watching. Tarma caught Kethry's eyes a moment; the other nodded, lips tightly compressed. The Shin'a'in swordswoman was past hoping to end this quietly. She had begun to devoutly wish for a chance to cleave a few skulls around here, and she had a shrewd suspicion that Kethry felt the same.

The young High Priest looked up from his work, and saw the anomalous—two women, dressed as devotees, but paying no attention to the rites, and seemingly immune to the magical charisma of Thalhkarsh. They had worked their way nearly to the altar itself.

He looked sharply at them—and noted the fighter's muscles and the faint aura of the god-touched about the thin one, then the unmistakable presence of a warding-spell on the other.

His mind flared with sudden alarm.

He stepped forward once—

He was given no time to act on his suspicions. Tarma saw his alerted glance, and whistled shrilly for Warrl.

From the crowd to the left of her came shouts—then screeches, and the sound of panic. Warrl was covering the distance between himself and Tarma with huge leaps, and was slashing out with his teeth as he did so. The worshipers scrambled to get out of the way of those awful jaws, clearing the last few feet for him. He skidded to a halt beside her; with one hand she snatched Need from her sheath and tossed her to Kethry, with the other she unsheathed her own blade, turning the operation into an expert stroke that took out the two men nearest her. Warrl took his stand, guarding Tarma's back.

Need had sailed sweetly into Kethry's hand, hilt first; she turned her catch into a slash that mirrored Tarma's and cleared space for herself. Then she found herself forced to defend against two sorts

181

of attack; the physical, by the temple guards, and the magical, by the High Priest.

While the demon unaccountably watched, but *did* nothing, the priest forced Kethry back against the wall. As bolts of force crashed against the shield she'd hastily thrown up, Kethry had firsthand proof that his magics had been augmented by the demon. Even so, she was the more powerful magician—but she was being forced to divide her attentions.

Warrl solved the problem; the priest-mage was not expecting a physical attack. Warrl's charge from the side brought him down, and in moments the *kyree* had torn out his throat. That left Kethry free to erect a magical barrier between themselves and reinforcements for the guards they were cutting down. She breathed a prayer of thanks to whatever power might be listening as she did so—thanks that the past few months had required so little of her talents that her arcane armaments and energy reserves were at their height.

Tarma grinned maliciously as a wall of fire sprang up at Kethry's command, cutting them off from the rest of the temple. Now there were only two acolytes, the remaining handful of guards, and the oddly inactive demon to face.

"Hold."

The voice was quiet, yet stirred uneasiness in Tarma's stomach. She tried to move—and found that she couldn't. The guards were utterly motionless, as lifeless as statues. Only the acolytes were able to move, and all *their* attention was on the demon.

His gaze was bent on Kethry.

Tarma heard a rumbling snarl from behind the altar. Before she could try to prevent him, Warrl leaped from the body of the high priest in a suicidal attack on the demon.

Thalhkarsh did not even glance in the *kyree's* direction; he intercepted Warrl's attack with a seemingly negligent backhanded slap. The *kyree* yelped

182

as the hand caught him and sent him crashing into the wall behind Tarma, limp and silent.

"Woman, I could use you." The demon's voice was low and persuasive. "Your knowledge is great, the power you command formidable, and you have infinitely more sense than that poor fool your familiar killed. I could make you a queen among magicians. I would make you *my* consort."

Tarma fumed in impotence as the demon reached for her oathkin.

Kethry's mind bent beneath the weight of the demon's attentions. It was incredibly difficult to think clearly; all her thoughts seemed washed out in the red glare of his gaze. Her enchantments to counter beguilement seemed as thin as silk veils, and about as protective.

"You think me cruel, evil. Yet what ever have I done save to give each of these people what he wants? The women have but to see me to desire me; the men lust for what women I do not care to take—all my worshipers want power. All these things I have given in exchange for worship. Surely that is fair, is it not? It would be cruelty to withhold these things, not cruelty to bestow them."

His voice was reasoned and persuasive. Kethry found herself wavering from what she had until now thought to be the truth.

"Is it the bonds with that scrap of steel that trouble you? Fear not—it would be the work of a single thought to break them. And think of the knowledge that would be yours in the place at my side! Think of the power . . ."

His eyes glowed yet more brightly and seductively, and they filled her vision.

"Think of the pleasure . . ."

Pain lancing across her thoughts woke her from the dreams called up by those eyes. She looked down at the blood trickling along her right hand—she'd clenched it around the bare blade of her sword with enough force to cut her palm. And with the pain came the return of independent thought. Even if everything he said were true, and not the usual truth-twisting demons found so easy, she was not free to follow her own will.

There were other, older promises that bound her. There was the geas she had willingly taken with the fighting-gifts bestowed by Need, and the pledge she had made as a White Winds sorceress to use her powers for the greater good of mankind. And by no means least, there was the vow she had made before all of Liha'irden; pledging Tarma that one day she would take a mate (or mates) and raise a clutch of children to bear the banner and name of Tarma's lost Clan. Only death itself could keep her from fulfilling that vow. And it would kill Tarma should she violate it.

She stared back at the demon's inhuman eyes, defiance written in every fiber.

He flared with anger. "You are the more foolish, then!" he growled—and backhanded her into the wall as casually as he had Warrl.

She was halfway expecting such a move, and managed to relax enough to take the blow limply. It felt rather like being hit with a battering ram, but the semiconsciousness she displayed as she slid into a heap was mostly feigned.

"You will find you have ample leisure to regret your defiance later!" he snarled in the same petulant tones as a thwarted spoiled child.

Now he turned his attentions to Tarma.

"So—the nomad—"

Tarma did her best to simulate a fascination with the demon that she did not in the least feel.

"It seems that I must needs petition the swordswoman. Well enough, it may be that you are even more suitable than your foolish companion."

The heat of his gaze was easily dissipated by the cool armoring of her Goddess that sheathed Tarma's heart and soul. There simply was *nothing* there for the demon to work on; the sensual, emotional parts

184

of her nature had been subsumed into devotion to the Warrior when Tarma had Sworn Sword-Oath. But he couldn't know that—or could he?

At any rate her attempt to counterfeit the same bemused rapture his brides had shown was apparently successful.

"You are no beauty; well, then—look into my eyes, and see the face and body that might be yours as my priestess."

Tarma looked—she dared not look away. His eyes turned mirrorlike; she saw herself reflected in them, then she saw herself change.

The lovely, lithe creature that gazed back at her was still recognizably Tarma—but oh, the differences that a few simple changes made! This was a beauty that was a match for Thalhkarsh's own. For a scant second, Tarma allowed herself to be truly caught by that vision.

The demon felt her waver—and in that moment of weakness, exerted *his* power on the bond that made her Kal'enedral.

And Tarma realized at that instant that Thalhkarsh was truly on the verge of attaining godlike powers, for she felt the bond weaken—

Thalhkarsh frowned at the unexpected resistance he encountered, then turned his full attention to breaking the stubborn strength of the bond.

And that changing of the focus of his attention in turn released Tarma from her entrapment. Not much—but enough for her to act.

Tarma had resisted the demon with every ounce of stubbornness in her soul, augmenting the strength of the bond, but she wasn't blind to what was going on around her.

And to her horror she saw Kethry creeping up on the demon's back, a fierce and stubborn anger in her eyes.

Tarma knew that no blow the sorceress struck would do more than anger Thalhkarsh. She decided to yield the tiniest bit, timing her moment of weak-

185

ness with care, waiting until the instant Need was poised to strike at the demon's unprotected back.

And as Thalhkarsh's magical grip loosened, her own blade-hand snapped out, hilt foremost, to strike and break the demon's focus-bottle.

At the exact moment Tarma moved, Kethry buried Need to the hilt in the demon's back, as the sound of breaking glass echoed and re-echoed the length and breadth of the temple.

Any one of those actions, by itself, might not have been sufficient to defeat him; but combined—

Thalhkarsh screamed in pain, unanticipated, unexpected, and all the worse for that. He felt at the same moment a good half of his stored power flowing out of him like water from a broken bottle—

—a *broken bottle!*

His focus—was gone!

And pain like a red-hot iron seared through him, shaking him to the roots of his being.

He lost his carefully cultivated control.

His focus was destroyed, and with it, the power he had been using to hold his followers in thrall. And the pain—it could not destroy him, but he was not used to being the recipient of pain. It took him by surprise, and broke his concentration and cost him yet more power.

He lost mastery of his form. He took on his true demonic aspect—as horrifying as he had been beautiful.

And now his followers saw for the first time the true appearance of what they had been calling a god. Their faith had been shaken when he did nothing to save the life of his High Priest. Now it was destroyed by the panic they felt on seeing what he was.

They screamed, turned mindlessly, and attempted to flee.

His storehouse of power was gone. His other power-source was fleeing madly in fear. His focus was destroyed, and he was racked with pain, he

186

who had never felt so much as a tiny pinprick before. Every spell he had woven fell to ruins about him.

Thalkarsh gave a howling screech that rose until the sound was nearly unbearable; he again slapped Kethry into the wall. Somehow she managed to take her blade with her, but this time her limp unconsciousness as she slid down the wall was not feigned.

He howled again, burst into a tower of red and green flame, and the walls began to shift.

Tarma dodged past him and dragged Kethry under the heavy marble slab of the altar, then made a second trip to drag Warrl under its dubious shelter.

The ground shook, and the remaining devotees rushed in panic-stricken confusion from one hoped-for exit to another. The ceiling groaned with a living voice, and the air was beginning to cloud with a sulfurous fog. Then cracks appeared in the roof, and the trapped worshipers screeched hopelessly as it began to crumble and fall in on them.

Tarma crouched beneath the altar stone, protecting the bodies of Kethry and Warrl with her own—and hoped the altar was strong enough to shelter them as the temple began falling to ruins around them.

It seemed like an eternity, but it couldn't have been more than an hour or two before dawn that they crawled out from under the battered slab, pushing and digging rubble out of the way with hands that were soon cut and bleeding. Warrl did his best to help, but his claws and paws were meant for climbing and clinging, not digging; and besides that, he was suffering from more than one cracked rib. Eventually Tarma made him stop trying to help before he lamed himself.

"Feh," she said distastefully, when they emerged. The stone—or whatever it was—that the building had been made of was rotting away, and the odor was overpowering. She heaved herself wearily up onto the cleaner marble of the altar and surveyed the wreckage about them.

"Gods—to think I wanted to do this quietly! Well, is it gone, I wonder, or did we just chase it away for a while?"

Kethry crawled up beside her, wincing. "I can't tell; there's too many factors involved. I don't *think* Need is a demon-killer, but I don't know everything there is to know about her. Did we get rid of him because he lost the faith of his devotees, because you broke the focus, because of the wound I gave him, or all three? And does it matter? He won't be able to return unless he's called, and I can't imagine anyone wanting to call him, not for a long, long time." She paused, then continued. "You had me frightened, *she'enedra.*"

"Whyfor?"

"I didn't know what he was offering you in return for your services. I was afraid if he could see your heart—"

"He didn't offer me anything I really wanted, dearling. I was never in any danger. All he wanted to give me was a face and figure to match his own."

"But if he'd offered you your Clan and your voice back—" Kethry replied soberly.

"I still wouldn't have been in any danger," Tarma replied with a little more force than she intended. "My people are dead, and no demon could bring them back to life. They've gone on elsewhere and he could never touch them. And without them—" she made a tiny, tired shrug, "—without them, what use is my voice—or for that matter, the most glorious face and body, and all the power in the universe?"

"I thought he had you for a moment—"

"So did he. He was trying to break my bond with the Star-Eyed. What he didn't know was all he was arousing was my disgust. I'd die before I'd give in to something that uses people as casually as *that* thing did."

Kethry got her belt and sheath off Warrl and slung Need in her accustomed place on her hip. Tarma suppressed the urge to giggle, despite pain and weariness. Kethry, in the sorceress' robes she usually wore, and belted with a blade looked odd enough. Kethry, dressed in three spangles and a scrap of cloth and wearing the sword looked totally absurd.

Nevertheless Tarma copied her example. "Well, that damn goatsticker of yours got us into another one we won't get paid for," she said in more normal tones, fastening the buckle so that her sword hung properly on her back. "Bloody Hell! If you count in the ale we had to pour and the bribes we had to pay, we *lost* money on this one."

"Don't be so certain of that, *she'enedra*." Kethry's face was exhausted and bloodstreaked, one of her eyes was blackened and swelling shut and she had livid bruises all over her body. On top of that she was covered in dust, and filthy, sweat-lank locks of hair were straggling into her face. But despite all of that, her eyes still held a certain amusement. "In case you hadn't noticed, these little costumes of ours are real gold and gems. We happen to be wearing a small fortune in jewelry."

"Warrior's Truth!" Tarma looked a good deal more closely at her scanty attire, and discovered her partner was right. She grinned with real satisfaction. "I guess I owe that damn blade of yours an apology."

"Only," Kethry grinned back, "If we get back into our own clothing before dawn."

"Why dawn?"

"Because that's when the rightful owners of these trinkets are likely to wake up. I don't think they'd let us keep them when we're found here if they know we have them."

"Good point—but why should we want anyone to know *we're* responsible for this mess?"

189

"Because when the rest of the population scrapes up enough nerve to find out what happened, we're going to be heroines—or at least we will until they find out how many of their fathers and brothers and husbands were trapped here tonight. By then, we'll be long gone. Even if they don't reward us—and they might, for delivering the town from a demon—our reputation has just been made!"

Tarma's jaw dropped as she realized the truth of that. "Shek," she said. "Turn me into a sheep! You're right!" She threw back her head and laughed into the morning sky. "Now all we need is the fortune and a king's blessing!"

"Don't laugh, oathkin," Kethry replied with a grin. "We just might get those, and sooner than you think. After all, aren't we demon-slayers?"

Eight

Someone wrote a song about it—but that was later. Much later—when the dust and dirt were gone from the legend. When the sweat and blood were only memories, and the pain was less than that. And when the dead were all but forgotten except to their own.

> "Deep into the stony hills
> Miles from keep or hold,
> A troupe of guards comes riding
> With a lady and her gold.
> Riding in the center,
> Shrouded in her cloak of fur
> Companioned by a maiden
> And a toothless, aged cur."

"And every packtrain we've sent out for the past two months has vanished without a trace—and without survivors," the silk merchant Grumio concluded, twisting an old iron ring on one finger. "Yet the decoy trains were allowed to reach their destinations unmolested. It's uncanny—and if it goes on much longer, we'll be ruined."

In the silence that followed his words, he studied the odd pair of mercenaries before him. He knew very well that *they* knew he was doing so. Eventually there would be no secrets in this room—eventually. But he would parcel his out as if they were bits of his heart—and he knew they would do the same. It was all part of the bargaining process.

Neither of the two women seemed in any great hurry to reply to his speech. The crackle of the fire

191

behind him in this tiny private eating room sounded unnaturally loud in the absence of conversation. Equally loud were the steady whisking of a whetstone on blade-edge, and the muted murmur of voices from the common room of the inn beyond their closed door.

The whetstone was being wielded by the swordswoman, Tarma by name, who was keeping to her self-appointed task with an indifference to Grumio's words that might—or might not—be feigned. She sat across the table from him, straddling her bench in a position that left him mostly with a view of her back and the back of her head. What little he might have been able to see of her face was screened by her unruly shock of coarse black hair. He was just as glad of that; there was something about her cold, expressionless, hawklike face with its wintry blue eyes that sent shivers up his spine. "The eyes of a killer," whispered one part of him. "Or a fanatic."

The other partner cleared her throat and he gratefully turned his attention to her. Now *there* was a face a man could easily rest his eyes on! She faced him squarely, this sorceress called Kethry, leaning slightly forward on her folded arms, placing her weight on the table between them. The light from the fire and the oil lamp on their table fell fully on her. A less canny man than Grumio might be tempted to dismiss her as being very much the weaker, the less intelligent of the two; she was always soft of speech, her demeanor refined and gentle. She was very attractive; sweet-faced and quite conventionally pretty, with hair like the finest amber and eyes of beryl-green. It would have been very easy to assume that she was no more than the swordswoman's vapid tagalong. A lover perhaps—maybe one with the right to those magerobes she wore, but surely of no account in the decision-making.

That would have been the assessment of most men. But as he'd spoken, Grumio had now and then caught a disquieting glimmer in those calm green eyes. She had been listening quite carefully, and analyzing what she heard. He had not missed the fact that she, too, bore a sword. And not for the show of it, either—that blade had a well-worn scabbard that spoke of frequent use. More than that, what he could see of the blade showed that it was well-cared-for.

The presence of that blade in itself was an anomaly; most sorcerers never wore more than an eating knife. They simply hadn't the time—or the inclination—to attempt studying the arts of the swordsman. To Grumio's eyes the sword looked very odd and quite out-of-place, slung over the plain, buff-colored, calf-length robe of a wandering sorceress.

A puzzlement; altogether a puzzlement.

"I presume," Kethry said when he turned to face her, "that the road patrols have been unable to find your bandits."

She had in turn been studying the merchant; he interested her. In his own way he was as much of an anomaly as she and Tarma were. There was muscle beneath the fat of good living, and old sword-calluses on his hands. This was no born-and-bred merchant, not when he looked to be as much retired mercenary as trader. And unless she was wildly mistaken, there was also a sharp mind beneath that balding skull. He knew they didn't come cheaply; since the demon-god affair their reputation had spread, and their fees had become quite respectable. They were even able—like Ikan and Justin—to pick and choose to some extent. On the surface this business appeared far too simple a task—one would simply gather a short-term army and clean these brigands out. *On the surface,* this was no job for a specialized team like theirs—and Grumio surely knew that. It followed then that there was something more to this tale of banditry than he was telling.

Kethry studied him further. Certain signs seemed to confirm this surmise; he looked as though he had not slept well of late, and there seemed to be a shadow of deeper sorrow upon him than the loss of mere goods would account for.

She wondered how much he really knew of them, and she paid close attention to what his answer to her question would be.

Grumio snorted his contempt for the road patrols. "They rode up and down for a few days, never venturing off the Trade Road, and naturally found nothing. Over-dressed, over-paid, underworked arrogant idiots!"

Kethry toyed with a fruit left from their supper, and glanced up at the hound-faced merchant through long lashes that veiled her eyes and her thoughts. The next move would be Tarma's.

Tarma heard her cue, and made her move. "Then guard your packtrains, merchant, if guards keep these vermin hidden."

He started; her voice was as harsh as a raven's, and startled those not used to hearing it. One corner of Tarma's mouth twitched slightly at his reaction. She took a perverse pleasure in using that harshness as a kind of weapon. A Shin'a'in learned to fight with many weapons, words among them. Kal'enedral learned the finer use of those weapons.

Grumio saw at once the negotiating ploy these two had evidently planned to use with him. The swordswoman was to be the antagonizer, the sorceress the sympathizer. His respect for them rose another notch. Most freelance mercenaries hadn't the brains to count their pay, much less use subtle bargaining tricks. Their reputation was plainly well-founded. He just wished he knew more of them than their reputation; he was woefully short a full hand in this game. Why, he didn't even know where the sorceress hailed from, or what her School was!

Be that as it may, once he saw the trick, he had no intention of falling for it.

"Swordlady," he said patiently, as though to a child, "to hire sufficient force requires we raise

194

the price of goods above what people are willing to pay."

As he studied them further, he noticed something else about them that was distinctly odd. There was a current of communication and understanding running between these two that had him thoroughly puzzled. He dismissed without a second thought the notion that they might be lovers, the signals between them were all wrong for that. No, it was something else, something more complicated than that. Something that you wouldn't expect between a Shin'a'in swordswoman and an outClansman— something perhaps, that only someone like he was, with experience in dealing with Shin'a'in, would notice in the first place.

Tarma shook her head impatiently at his reply. "Then cease your inter-house rivalries, *kadessa*, and send all your trains together under a single large force."

A new ploy—now she was trying to anger him a little—to get him off-guard by insulting him. She had called him a *kadessa*, a little grasslands beast that only the Shin'a'in ever saw, a rodent so notoriously greedy that it would, given food enough, eat itself to death; and one that was known for hoarding anything and everything it came across in its nest-tunnels.

Well it wasn't going to work. He refused to allow the insult to distract him. There was too much at stake here. "Respect, Swordlady," he replied with a hint of reproachfulness, "but we tried that, too. The beasts of the train were driven off in the night, and the guards and traders were forced to return afoot. This is desert country, most of it, and all they dared burden themselves with was food and drink."

"Leaving the goods behind to be scavenged. Huh. Your bandits are clever, merchant," the swordswoman replied thoughtfully. Grumio thought he could sense her indifference lifting.

"You mentioned decoy trains?" Kethry interjected.

195

"Yes, lady." Grumio's mind was still worrying away at the puzzle these two presented. "Only I and the men in the train knew which were the decoys and which were not, yet the bandits were never deceived, not once. We had taken extra care that all the men in the train were known to us, too."

A glint of gold on the smallest finger of Kethry's left hand finally gave him the clue he needed, and the crescent scar on the palm of that hand confirmed his surmise. He knew without looking that that swordswoman would have an identical scar and ring. These two had sword Shin'a'in blood-oath, the oath of *she'enedran*; the strongest bond known to that notoriously kin-conscious race. The blood-oath made them closer than sisters, closer than lovers—so close they sometimes would think as one. In fact, the word *she'enedran* was sometimes translated as "two-made-one."

"So who was it that passed judgment on your estimable guards?" Tarma's voice was heavy with sarcasm.

"I did, or my fellow merchants, or our own personal guards. No one was allowed on the trains but those who had served us in the past or were known to those who had."

He waited in silence for them to make reply.

Tarma held her blade up to catch the firelight and examined her work with a critical eye. Evidently satisfied, she drove it home in the scabbard slung across her back with a fluid, unthinking grace, then swung one leg back over the bench to face him as her partner did. Grumio found the unflinching chill of her eyes disconcertingly hard to meet for long.

In an effort to find something else to look at, he found his gaze caught by the pendant she wore, a thin silver crescent surrounding a tiny amber flame. That gave him the last bit of information he needed to make everything fall into place—although now he realized that her plain brown clothing should have tipped him off as well, since most Shin'a'in favored wildly-colored garments heavy with bright embroideries. Tarma was a Sworn One, Kal'enedral, pledged to the service of the Shin'a'in Warrior, the Goddess of the New Moon and the South Wind. Only three things were of any import to her at all—her Goddess, her people, and her Clan (which, of course, would include her "sister" by blood-oath). The Sword Sworn were just as sexless and deadly as the weapons they wore.

"So why come to us?" Tarma's expression indicated she thought their time was being wasted. "What makes you think that we can solve your bandit problem?"

"You—have a certain reputation," he replied guardedly.

A single bark of contemptuous laughter was Tarma's only reply.

"If you know our reputation, then you also know that we only take those assignments that—shall we say—interest us," Kethry said, looking wide-eyed and innocent. "What is there about your problem that could possibly be of any interest to *us*?"

Good—they were intrigued, at least a little. Now, for the sake of poor little Lena, was the time to hook them and bring them in. His eyes stung a little with tears he would not shed—not now—not in front of them. Not until she was avenged.

"We have a custom, we small merchant houses. Our sons must remain with their fathers to learn the trade, and since there are seldom more than two or three houses in any town, there is little in the way of choice for them when it comes time for marriage. For that reason, we are given to exchanging daughters of the proper age with our trade allies in other towns, so that our young people can hopefully find mates to their liking." His voice almost broke at the memory of watching Lena waving good-bye from the back of her little mare, but he regained control quickly. It was a poor merchant that could not school his emotions. "There were no

197

less than a dozen sheltered, gently-reared maidens in the very first packtrain they took. One of them was my niece. My only heir, and all that was left of my brother's family after the plague six years ago." He could continue no further.

Kethry's breath hissed softly, and Tarma swallowed an oath.

"Your knowledge of what interests us is very accurate, merchant," Tarma said after a long pause. "I congratulate you."

"You—you accept?" Discipline could not keep hope out of his voice.

"I pray you are not expecting us to rescue your lost ones," Kethry said as gently as she could. "Even supposing that the bandits were more interested in slaves to be sold than their own pleasure—which in my experience is *not* likely—there is very, very little chance that any of them still live. The sheltered, the gentle, well, they do not survive—shock —successfully."

"When we knew that the packtrain had been taken, we sent agents to comb the slave markets. They returned empty-handed," he replied with as much stoicism as he could muster. "We will not ask the impossible of you; we knew when we sent for you there was no hope for them. No, we ask only that you wipe out this viper's den, to insure that this can *never* happen to us again—that you make such an example of them that no one dares try this again—and that you grant us revenge for what they have done to us!" There—that was his full hand. Would it be enough?

His words—and more, the tight control of his voice—struck echoes from Tarma's own heart. And she did not need to see her partner to know *her* feelings in the matter.

"You will have that, merchant-lord," she grated, giving him the title of respect. "We accept your job—but there are conditions."

"Swordlady, any conditions you would set, I would

gladly meet. Who am I to contest the judgment of those who destroyed Tha—"

"Hush!" Kethry interrupted him swiftly, and cast a wary glance over her shoulder. "The less that is said on *that* subject, the better. I am still not altogether certain that what you were about to name was truly destroyed. It may have been merely banished, and perhaps for no great span of time. It is hardly wise if the second case is true to call attention to oneself by speaking Its name."

"Our conditions, merchant, are simple," Tarma continued, outwardly unperturbed. Inwardly she had uneasy feelings about Thalkarsh, feelings that had her ready to throw herself between Kethry and anything that even *looked* like a demon. "We will, to all appearances, leave on the morrow. You will tell all, including your fellow merchants, that you could not convince us to remain. Tomorrow night, you—and you *alone*, mind—will bring us, at a meeting place of your choosing, a cart and horse. . . ."

Now she raised an inquiring eyebrow at Kethry.

"And the kind of clothing and gear a lady of wealth and blood would be likely to have when traveling. The clothing should fit me. I will be weaving some complicated illusions, and anything I do not have to counterfeit will be of aid to me and make the rest stronger. You might include lots of empty bags and boxes," Kethry finished thoughtfully.

Tarma continued; "The following morning a fine lady will ride in and order you to include her with your next packtrain. You, naturally, will do your best to dissuade her, as loudly and publicly as possible. Now your next scheduled trip was—?"

"Coincidentally enough, for the day after tomorrow." Grumio was plainly impressed. It looked as though he'd decided that Tarma and her partner were even cleverer than he'd thought.

"Good. The less time we lose, the better off we are. Remember, only *you* are to be aware that the lady and the packtrain are not exactly what they seem to be. If you say one word otherwise to anyone—"

The merchant suddenly found himself staring at the tip of a very sharp dagger held a scant inch away from his nose.

"—I will *personally* remove enough of your hide to make both of us slippers." The dagger disappeared from Tarma's hand as mysteriously as it had appeared.

Grumio had been startled, but had not been particularly intimidated; Tarma gave him high marks for that.

"I do not instruct the weaver in her trade," he replied with a certain dignity, "nor do I dictate the setting of a horseshoe to a smith. There is no reason why I should presume to instruct you in your trade either."

"Then you are a rare beast indeed, merchant," Tarma graced him with one of her infrequent smiles. "Most men—oh, not fellow mercenaries, they know better; but most men we deal with—seem to think they know our business better than we simply by virtue of their sex."

The smile softened her harsh expression, and made it less intimidating, and the merchant found himself smiling back. "You are not the only female hire-swords I have dealt with." he replied. "Many of my trade allies have them as personal retainers. It has often seemed to me that many of those I met have had to be twice as skilled as their male counterparts to receive half the credit."

"A hit, merchant-lord," Kethry acknowledged with open amusement. "And a shrewd one at that. Now, where are we to meet you tomorrow night?"

Grumio paused to think. "I have a farmstead. It's deserted now that the harvest is in. It's just outside of town, at the first lane past the crossroad at the South Trade Road. No one would think it odd for me to pay a visit to it, and the barn is a good place to hide horses and gear."

"Well enough," Tarma replied.

All three rose as one, and Grumio caught the

faint clink of brigandine mail from Tarma's direction, though there was no outward sign that she wore any such thing beneath her worn leather tunic, brown shirt and darker breeches.

"Merchant—" Tarma said, suddenly.

He paused halfway through the door.

"I, too, have known loss. You *will* have your revenge."

He shivered at the look in her eyes, and left.

"Well?" Tarma asked, shutting the door behind him and leaning her back up against it.

"Magic's afoot here. It's the only answer to what's been going on. I don't think it's easy to deceive this merchant—he caught on to our 'divide and conquer' trick right away. He's no soft money-counter, either."

"I saw the sword-calluses." Tarma balanced herself on one foot, set the other against the door, and folded her arms. "Did he tell us all he knew?"

"I think so. I don't think he held anything back after he played his high card."

"The niece? He also didn't want us to know how much he valued her. Damn. This is a bad piece of business. Poor bastard."

"He'd rather we thought the loss of goods and trade meant more to him," Kethry replied. "They're a secretive lot in many ways, these traders."

"Almost as secretive as sorceresses, no?" One corner of Tarma's thin lips quirked up in a half-smile. The smile vanished as she thought of something else.

"Is there any chance that any of the women survived?"

"Not to put too fine a point upon it, no. *This*—" Kethry patted the hilt of her sword "—would have told me if any of them had. The pull is there, but without the urgency there'd be if there was anyone needing rescue. Still, we need more information, so I might as well add that to the set of questions I intend to ask."

Concern flickered briefly in Tarma's eyes. "An unprepared summoning? Are you sure you want to risk it? If nothing else, it will wear you down, and you have all those illusions to cast."

"I think it's worth it. There aren't that many hostile entities to guard against in this area, and I'll have all night to rest afterward—most of tomorrow as well, once we reach that farmstead. And my 'arsenal' is full, my nonpersonal energies are completely charged, and my other-Planar alliances doing well. It won't be any problem."

"You're the magic-worker," Tarma sighed. "Since we've hired this room for the whole evening, want to make use of it for your magicking? It's bigger than our sleeping room."

At Kethry's nod, Tarma pushed the table into a corner, stacking the benches on top of it, while Kethry set the oil lamp on the mantlepiece. Most of the floorspace was now cleared.

"I'll keep watch on the door." Tarma sat on the floor with her back firmly braced against it. Since it opened inward, the entrance was now solidly guarded against all but the most stubborn of intruders.

Kethry inscribed a circle on the floor with powders from her belt-pouch, chanting under her breath. She used no dramatic or spectacular ceremonies for she had learned her art in a gentler school than the other sorcerers Tarma had seen. Her powers came from the voluntary cooperation of other-Planar entities and she never coerced them into doing her bidding.

There were advantages and disadvantages to this. She need not safeguard herself against the deceptions and treacheries of these creatures, but the cost to her in terms of her own energies expended was correspondingly higher. This was particularly true at times when she had no chance to prepare herself for a summoning. It took a great deal of power to attract a being of benign intent—particularly one that did not have a previous alliance with her—and more to convince it that her intent was good. Hence, the circle—meant not to protect her, but to protect what she would call, so that it would know itself unthreatened.

As she seated herself within the circle, Tarma shifted her own position until she, too, was quite comfortable, removed one of her hidden daggers, and began honing it with her sharpening-stone.

After some time, there was a stirring in the circle Kethry had inscribed, and Tarma pulled her attention away from her task. Something was beginning to form mistily in front of the seated sorceress.

The mist began to revolve into a miniature whirlpool, coalescing into a figure as it did so. As it solidified, Tarma could see what seemed to be a jewel-bright desert lizard, but one that stood erect, like a man. It was as tall as a man's arm is long, and had a cranium far larger than any lizard Tarma had ever seen—except perhaps the image of Gervase that Kethry had used to entertain Liha'irden. Firelight winked from its scales in bands of shining colors, topaz and ruby predominating. It was regarding Kethry with intelligence and wary curiousity.

"Sa-asartha, n'hellan?" it said, tilting its head to one side and fidgeting from one foot to the other. Its voice was shrill, like that of a very young child.

"Vede, sa-asarth," Kethry replied in the same tongue—whatever the tongue was.

The little creature relaxed, and stopped fretting. It appeared to be quite eager to answer all of Kethry's questions. Now that the initial effort of calling it was done with, she had no trouble in obtaining all the information she wanted. Finally she gave the little creature the fruit she'd been toying with after supper. It snatched the gift greedily, trilled what Tarma presumed to be thanks, and vanished into mist again.

When it was completely gone, Kethry rose stiffly and began to scuff the circle into random piles of dirt with the toe of her boot. "It's about what I expected," she said. "Someone—someone with 'a smell of magic about him' according to the *khamsin*—

203

has organized what used to be several small bands of marauders into one large one of rather formidable proportions. They have no set camp, so we can't arrange for their base to be attacked while they're ambushing us, I'm sorry to say. They have no favored ambush point, so we won't know when to expect them. And none of the women—girls, really—survived for more than a day."

"Oh, hell." Tarma's eyes were shadowed. "Well, we didn't really expect anything different."

"No, but you know damn well we both hoped," Kethry's voice was rough with weariness. "It's up to you now, *she'enedra*. You're the tactician."

"Then as the tactician, I counsel rest for you." Tarma caught Kethry's shoulders to steady her as she stumbled a little from fatigue. The reaction to spell-casting was setting in fast, now. Kethry had once described summoning as being "like balancing on a rooftree while screaming an epic poem in a foreign language at the top of your lungs." Small wonder she was exhausted afterward.

The sorceress leaned on Tarma's supporting shoulder with silent gratitude as her partner guided her up the stairs to their rented sleeping room.

"It's us, Warrl," Tarma called softly at the door. A muted growl answered her, and they could hear the sound of the bolt being shoved back. Tarma pushed the door open with one foot, and picked up one of the unlit tallow candles that waited on a shelf just inside with her free hand. She lit it at the one in the bracket outside their door, and the light from it fell on Warrl's head and shoulders. He stood, tongue lolling out in a lupine grin, just inside the room. He sniffed inquisitively at them, making a questioning whine deep in his throat.

"Yes, we took the job—that's our employer you smell, so don't mangle him when he shows up tomorrow night. And Kethry's been summoning, of course, so as usual she's half dead. Close the door behind us while I put her to bed."

By now Kethry was nearly asleep on her feet;

after some summonings Tarma had seen her pass into unconsciousness while still walking. Tarma undressed her with the gentle and practiced hands of a nursemaid, and got her safely into bed before she had the chance to fall over. The *kyree,* meanwhile, had butted the door shut with his head and pushed the bolt home with his nose.

"Any trouble?" Tarma asked him.

He snorted with derision.

"Well, I didn't really expect any, either. This is the *quietest* inn I've been in for a long time. The job is bandits, hairy one, and we're all going to have to go disguised. That includes you."

He whined in protest, ears down.

"I know you don't like it, but there's no choice. There isn't enough cover along the road to hide a bird, and I want you close at hand, within a few feet of us at all times, not wandering out in the desert somewhere."

The *kyree* sighed heavily, padded over to her, and laid his heavy head in her lap to be scratched.

"I know. I know," she said, obliging him. "I don't like it any more than you do. Just be grateful that all we'll be wearing is illusions, even if they do make the backs of our eyes itch. Poor Kethry's going to have to ride muffled head-to-toe like a fine lady."

Warrl obviously didn't care about poor Kethry.

"You're being very unfair to her, you know. And you're *supposed* to have been her familiar, not mine. You're a magic beast; born out of magic. You belong with a spell-caster, not some clod with a sword."

Warrl was not impressed with Tarma's logic.

She doesn't need me, he spoke mind-to-mind with the swordswoman. *She has the spirit-sword. You need me, I've told you that before.* And that, so far as Warrl was concerned, was that.

"Well, I'm not going to argue with you. I never argue with anyone with as many sharp teeth as you've got. Maybe being Kal'enedral counts as being magic."

She pushed Warrl's head off her lap and went to open the shutters to the room's one window. Moonlight flooded the room; she seated herself on the floor where it would fall on her, just as she did every night when there was a moon and she wasn't ill or injured. Since they were within the walls of a town and not camped, she would not train this night, but the Moonpaths were there, as always, waiting to be walked. She closed her eyes and found them. Walking them was, as she'd often told Kethry, impossible to describe.

When she returned to her body, Warrl was lying patiently at her back, waiting for her. She ruffled his fur with a grin, stood, stretched stiffened muscles, then stripped to a shift and climbed in beside Kethry. Warrl sighed with gratitude and took his usual spot at her feet.

> "Three things see no end—
> A flower blighted ere it bloomed,
> A message that was wasted
> And a journey that was doomed."

The two mercenaries rode out of town in the morning, obviously eager to be gone. Grumio watched them leave, gazing sadly at the cloud of dust they raised, his houndlike face clearly displaying his disappointment. His fellow merchants were equally disappointed when he told them of his failure to persuade them; they had all hoped the women would be the solution to their problem.

After sundown Grumio took a cart and horse out to his farmstead, a saddled riding beast tied to the rear of it. After making certain that no one had followed him, he drove directly into the barn, and peered around in the hay-scented gloom. A fear crossed his mind that the women had tricked him, and had *truly* left that morning.

"Don't fret yourself, merchant," said a gravelly voice just above his head. He jumped, his heart racing. "We're here."

A vague figure swung down from the loft; when

206

it came close enough for him to make out features, he started at the sight of a buxom blonde wearing the swordswoman's clothing.

She grinned at his reaction. "Which one am I? She didn't tell me. Blonde?"

He nodded, amazed.

"Malebait again. Good choice, no one would ever think I knew what a blade was for. Or that I ever thought of anything but men and clothing, not neccessarily in that order. You don't want to see my partner." Her voice was still in Tarma's gravelly tones; Grumio assumed that *that* was only so he'd recognize her. "We don't want you to have to strain your acting ability tomorrow. Did you bring everything we asked for?"

"It's all here," he replied, still not believing what his eyes were telling him. "I weighted the boxes with sand and stones so that they won't seem empty."

"You've got a good head on you, merchant," Tarma saluted him as she unharnessed the horse. "That's something I didn't think of. Best you leave now, though, before somebody comes looking for you."

He jumped down off the wagon, taking the reins of his riding beast.

"And merchant—" she called as he rode off into the night, "—wish us luck."

He didn't have to act the next morning, when a delicate and aristocratically frail lady of obvious noble birth accosted him in his shop, and ordered him (although it was framed as a request) to include her in his packtrain. In point of fact, had he not recognized the dress and fur cloak she was wearing, he would have taken her for a *real* aristo, one who, by some impossible coincidence, had taken the same notion into her head that the swordswoman had proposed as a ruse. This sylphlike, sleepy-eyed creature with her elaborately coiffed hair of platinum silk bore no resemblance at all to the very vibrant and earthy sorceress he'd hired.

And though he was partially prepared by having seen her briefly the night before, Tarma (posing as milady's maid) still gave him a shock. He saw why she called the disguise "malebait"—this amply-endowed blonde was a walking invitation to impropriety, and nothing like the sexless Sworn One. All that remained of Tarma were the blue eyes, one of which winked cheerfully at him, to bring him out of his shock.

Grumio argued vehemently with the highborn dame for the better part of an hour, and all to no avail. Undaunted, he carried his expostulations out into the street, still trying to persuade her to change her mind even as the packtrain formed up in front of his shop. The entire town was privy to the argument by that time.

"Lady, I beg you—reconsider!" he was saying anxiously. "Wait for the King's Patrol. They have promised to return soon and in force, since the bandits have not ceased raiding us, and I'm morally certain they'll be willing to escort you."

"My thanks for your concern, merchant," she replied with a gentle and bored haughtiness, "But I fear my business cannot wait till their return. Besides, what is there about me that could possibly tempt a bandit?"

Those whose ears were stretched to catch this conversation could easily sympathize with Grumio's silent—but obvious—plea to the gods for patience, as they noted the lady's jewels, fine garments, the weight of the cart holding her possesions, and the well-bred mares she and her maid rode.

The lady turned away from him before he could continue; a clear gesture of dismissal, so he held his tongue. In stony silence he watched the train form up, with the lady and her maid in the center. Since they had no driver for the cart—though he'd offered to supply one—the lead-rein of the carthorse had been fastened to the rear packhorse's harness. Surmounting the chests and boxes in the cart was a toothless old dog, apparently supposed to be guarding her possessions and plainly incapable of guarding anything anymore. The leader of the train's six guards took his final instructions from his master, and the train lurched off down the Trade Road. As Grumio watched them disappear into the distance, he could be seen to shake his head in disapproval.

Had anyone been watching very closely—though no one was—they might have noticed the lady's fingers moving in a complicated pattern. Had there been any mages present—which wasn't the case— said mage might have recognized the pattern as belonging to the Spell of True Sight. If illusion was involved, it would not be blinding Kethry.

> "One among the guardsmen
> Has a shifting, restless eye
> And as they ride, he scans the hills
> That rise against the sky.
> He wears a sword and bracelet
> Worth more than he can afford
> And hidden in his baggage
> Is a heavy, secret hoard."

One of the guards was contemplating the lady's assets with a glee and greed that equaled his master's dismay. His expression, carefully controlled, seemed to be remote and impassive; only his rapidly shifting gaze and the nervous flicker of his tongue over dry lips gave any clue to his thoughts. Behind those remote eyes, a treacherous mind was making a careful inventory of every jewel and visible possession and calculating their probable values.

When the lady's skirt lifted briefly to display a tantalizing glimpse of white leg, his control broke enough that he bit his lip. *She* was one prize he intended to reserve for himself; he'd never been this close to a highborn woman before, and he intended to find out if certain things he'd heard about bedding them were true. The others were going to have to be content with the ample charms of the serving maid, at least until he'd tired of the mistress. At least there wouldn't be all that caterwauling and screeching there'd been with the merchant wenches. That maid looked as if she'd had a man betwixt her legs plenty of times before, and enjoyed it, too. She'd probably thank him for livening up her life when he turned her over to the men!

He had thought at first that this was going to be another trap, especially after he'd heard that old Grumio had tried to hire a pair of highly-touted mercenary women to rid him of the bandits. One look at the lady and her maid, however, had convinced him that not only was it absurd to think that they could be wary hire-swords in disguise, but that they probably didn't even know which end of a blade to hold. The wench flirted and teased each of the men in turn. Her mind was obviously on something other than ambushes and weaponry—unless those ambushes were amorous, and the weaponry of flesh. The lady herself seemed to ride in a half-aware dream, and her maid often had to break off a flirtation in order to ride forward and steady her in the saddle.

Perhaps she was a *tran*-dust sniffer, or there was *faldis*-juice mixed in with the water in the skin on her saddle-bow. That would be an unexpected bonus; she was bound to have a good supply of it among her belongings, and drugs were worth more than jewels. And it would be dstinctly interesting—his eyes glinted cruelly—to have her begging him on her knees for her drugs as withdrawal set in. Assuming, of course, that she survived that long. He passed his tongue over lips gone dry with anticipation. Tomorrow he would give the scouts trailing the packtrain the signal to attack.

> "Of three things be wary—
> Of a feather on a cat,
> The shepherd eating mutton
> And the guardsman that is fat."

The lady and her companion made camp a discreet distance from the rest of the caravan, as was only to be expected. She would hardly have a taste for sharing their rough camp, rude talk or coarse food.

Kethry's shoulders sagged with fatigue beneath the weight of her heavy cloak, and she was chilled to the bone in spite of its fur lining.

"Are you all right?" Tarma whispered sharply when she hadn't spoken for several minutes.

"Just tired. I never thought that holding up five illusions would be so *hard*. Three aren't half so difficult to keep intact." She leaned her forehead on one hand, rubbing her temples with cold fingers. "I wish it was over."

Tarma pressed a bowl into her other hand. Dutifully, she tried to eat, but the sand and dust that had plagued their progress all day had crept into the food as well. It was too dry and gritty to swallow easily, and after one attempt, Kethry felt too weary to make any further effort. She laid the bowl aside, unobtrusively—or so she hoped.

Faint hope.

"Sweeting, if you don't eat by yourself, I'm going to pry your mouth open and *pour* your dinner down your throat." Tarma's expression was cloyingly sweet, and the tone of her shifted voice dulcet. Kethry was roused enough to smile a little. When she was this wearied with the exercise of her magics, she had to be bullied into caring for herself. When she'd been on her own, she'd sometimes had to spend days recovering from the damages she'd inflicted on her body by neglecting it. Tarma had her badly worried lately with all the cosseting she'd been doing—like she was trying to keep Kethry wrapped safely in lambswool all the time—but at this moment Kethry was rather glad to have the cosseting. In fact, it was at moments like this that she valued Tarma's untiring affection and aid the most.

"What, and ruin our disguises?" she retorted with a little more life.

"There's nothing at all out of the ordinary in an

attentive maid helping her poor, sick mistress to eat. They already think there's something wrong with you. Half of them think you're ill, the other half think you're in a drug-daze," Tarma replied. "They *all* think you've got nothing between your ears but air."

Kethry capitulated, picked up her dinner, and forced it down, grit and all.

"Now," Tarma said, when they'd both finished eating. "I know *you've* spotted a suspect, I can tell by the way you're watching the guards. Tell me which one it is; I'd be very interested to see if it's the same one I've got *my* eye on."

"It's the one with the mouse-brown hair and ratty face that rode tail-guard this morning."

Tarma's eyes widened a little, but she gave no other sign of surprise. "Did you say *brown* hair? And a ratty face? Tailguard this morning had *black* hair and a pouty, babyish look to him."

Kethry revived a bit more. "Really? Are you talking about the one walking between us and their fire right now? The one with all the jewelry? And does he seem to be someone you know very vaguely?"

"Yes. One of the hired swords with the horse-traders my Clan used to deal with—I think his name was Tedric. Why?"

Kethry unbuckled a small ornamental dagger from her belt and passed it to Tarma with exaggerated care. Tarma claimed it with the same caution, caution that was quite justified, since the "dagger" was in reality Kethry's sword Need, no matter what shape it wore at the moment. Beneath the illusion, it still retained its original mass and weight.

"Now look at him."

Tarma cast a surreptitious glance at the guard again, and her lips tightened. Even when it was done by magic, she didn't like being tricked. "Mouse-brown hair and a ratty face," she said. "He changed." She returned the blade to Kethry.

"And now?" Kethry asked, when Need was safely back on her belt.

"Now *that's* odd," Tarma said thoughtfully. "If he's using an illusion, he should have gone back to the way he looked before, but he didn't. He's still mousy and ratty, but my eyes feel funny—like something's pulling at them—and he's blurred a bit around the edges. It's almost as if his face was trying to look different from what I'm seeing."

"Uh-huh. Mind-magic," Kethry said, with satisfaction. "So that's why I wasn't able to detect any spells! It's not a true illusion like I'm holding on us. They practice mind-magic a lot more up north in Valdemar—I think I must have told you about it at some time or other. I'm only marginally familiar with the way it works, since it doesn't operate quite like what I've learned. If what I've been told is true, his mind is telling your mind that you know him, and letting your memory supply an acceptable face. He could very well look like a different person to everyone in the caravan, but since he always looks familiar, any of them would be willing to vouch for him."

"Which is how he keeps sneaking into the packtrains. He looks different each time, since no one is likely to 'see' a man they know is dead. Very clever. You say this isn't a spell?"

"Mind-magic depends on inborn abilities to work; if you haven't got them, you can't learn it. It's unlike *my* magic, where it's useful to have the Gift, but not necessary. Was he the same one you were watching?"

"He is, indeed. So your True Sight spell works on this 'mind-magic' too?"

"Yes, thank the gods. I'm glad now I didn't rely on mage-sight; he would have fooled that. What tipped you off to him?"

"Nothing terribly obvious, just a lot of little things that weren't quite right for the ordinary guard he's pretending to be. His sword is a shade too expensive. His horse has been badly misused, but he's a gelding of very good lines; he's of much better breeding than a common guard should own. And lastly, he's wearing jewelry he can't afford."

213

Kethry looked puzzled. "Several of the other guards are wearing just as much. I thought most hired swords wore their savings."

"So they do. Thing is, of the others, the only ones with as much or more are either the guard-chief, or ones wearing mostly brass and glass; showy, meant to impress village tarts, but worthless. His is all real, and the quality is high. Too damned high for the likes of him."

"Now that we know who to watch, what do we do?"

"We wait," Tarma replied with a certain grim satisfaction. "He'll have to signal the rest of his troupe to attack us sooner or later, and one of us should be able to spot him at it. With luck and the Warrior on our side, we'll have enough warning to be ready for them."

"I hope it's sooner." Kethry sipped at the well-watered wine which was all she'd allow herself when holding spells in place. Her eyes were heavy, dry, and sore. "I'm not sure how much longer I can hold up my end."

"Then go to sleep, dearling," Tarma's voice held an unusual gentleness, a gentleness only Kethry, Warrl, and small children ever saw. "Fur-face and I can take turns on nightwatch; you needn't take a turn at all."

Kethry did not need further urging, but wrapped herself up in her cloak and a blanket, pillowed her head on her arm and fell asleep with the suddenness of a tired puppy. The illusions she'd woven would remain intact even while she slept. Only three things could cause them to fail. They'd break if she broke them herself, if the pressure of spells from a greater sorcerer than she were brought to bear on them, or if she died. Her training had been arduous, and quite thorough; as complete in its way as Tarma's sword training had been.

Seeing her shiver in her sleep, Tarma built up the fire with a bit more dried dung (the leavings of previous caravans were all the fuel to be found out here) and covered her with the rest of the spare blankets. The illusions were draining energy from Kethry, and she got easily chilled; Tarma didn't expect to need the other coverings. She knew *she'd* be quite comfortable with one blanket and her cloak; and if that didn't suffice, Warrl made an excellent "bedwarmer."

Warrior, guard her back, she prayed, as she had every night lately. *I can guard my own—but keep her safe.*

But the night passed uneventfully, despite Tarma's vague worries.

Morning saw them riding deeper into the stony hills that ringed the desert basin they'd spent the day before passing through. The road was considerably less dusty now, but the air held more of a chill. Both Tarma and Kethry tried to keep an eye on their suspect guard, and shortly before noon their vigilance was rewarded. Both of them saw him flashing the sunlight off his armband in what could only be a deliberate series of signals.

> "From ambush, bandits screaming
> Charge the packtrain and its prize
> And all but four within the train
> Are taken by surprise
> And all but four are cut down
> Like a woodsman fells a log
> The guardsman, and the lady,
> And the maiden and the dog.
> Three things know a secret—
> First; the lady in a dream;
> The dog that barks no warning
> And the maid that does not scream."

Even with advance warning, they hadn't much time to ready themselves.

Bandits charged the packtrain from both sides of the road, screaming at the tops of their lungs. The guards were taken completely by surprise. The three apprentice traders accompanying the train flung themselves down on their faces as their master Grumio had ordered them to do in hopes that they'd be overlooked. To the bandit master at the rear of the train, it seemed that once again all had gone completely according to plan.

Until Kethry broke her illusions.

> "Then off the lady pulls her cloak—
> In armor she is clad
> Her sword is out and ready
> And her eyes are fierce and glad
> The maiden gestures briefly
> And the dog's a cur no more.
> A wolf, sword-maid, and sorceress
> Now face the bandit corps!
> Three things never anger,
> Or you will not live for long—
> A wolf with cubs, a man with power,
> And a woman's sense of wrong."

The brigands at the forefront of the pack found themselves facing something they hadn't remotely expected. Gone were the helpless, frightened women on high-bred steeds too fearful to run. In their place sat a pair of well-armed, grim-faced mercenaries on schooled warbeasts. With them was an oversized and very hungry-looking *kyree*.

The pack of bandits milled, brought to a halt by this unexpected development.

Finally one of the bigger ones growled a challenge at Tarma, who only grinned evilly at him. Kethry saluted them with mocking gallantry—and the pair moved into action explosively.

They split up and charged the marauders, giving them no time to adjust to the altered situation. The bandits had hardly expected the fight to be carried to *them*, and reacted too late to stop them. Their momentum carried them through the pack and up onto the hillsides on either side of the road. Now *they* had the high ground.

*　　*　　*

Kethry had drawn Need, whose magic was enabling her to keep herself intact long enough to find a massive boulder to put her back against. The long odds were actually favoring the two of them for the moment, since the bandits were mostly succeeding only in getting in each other's way. Obviously they had not been trained to fight together, and had done well so far largely because of the surprise with which they'd attacked and their sheer numbers. Once Kethry had gained her chosen spot, she slid off her horse, and sent it off with a slap to its rump. The mottled, huge-headed beast was as ugly as a piece of rough granite, and twice as tough, but she was a Shin'a'in-bred and trained warsteed, and worth the weight in silver of the high-bred mare she'd been spelled to resemble. Now that Kethry was on the ground, she'd attack anything whose scent she didn't recognize—and quite probably kill it.

Warrl came to her side long enough to give her the time she needed to transfer her sword to her left hand and begin calling up her more arcane offensive weaponry.

In the meantime, Tarma was in her element, cutting a bloody swath through the bandit horde with a fiercely joyous gleam in her eyes. She clenched her mare's belly with viselike legs; only one trained in Shin'a'in-style horse-warfare from childhood could possibly have stayed with the beast. The mare was laying all about her with iron-shod hooves and enormous yellow teeth; neither animal nor man was likely to escape her once she'd targeted him. She had an uncanny sense for anyone trying to get to her rider by disabling her; once she twisted and bucked like a cat on hot metal to simultaneously crush the bandit in front of her while kicking in the teeth of the one that had thought to hamstring her from the rear. She accounted for at least as many of the bandits as Tarma did.

Tarma saw Kethry's mare rear and slash out of the corner of her eye; the saddle was empty—

She sent a brief, worried thought at Warrl.

Guard yourself, foolish child; she's doing better than you are! came the mental rebuke. Tarma grimaced, realizing she should have known better. The bond of *she'enedran* made them bound by spirit, and she'd have *known* if anything was wrong. Since the mare was fighting on her own, Kethry must have found someplace high enough to see over the heads of those around her.

As if to confirm this, things like ball-lightning began appearing and exploding, knocking bandits from their horses, clouds of red mist began to wreath the heads of others (who clutched their throats and turned interesting colors), and oddly formed creatures joined Warrl at harrying and biting at those on foot.

When *that* began, especially after one spectacular fireball left a pile of smoking ash in place of the bandit's second-in-command, it was more than the remainder of the band could stand up to. Their easy prey had turned into hellspawn, and there was *nothing* that could make them stay to face anything more. The ones that were still mounted turned their horses out of the melee and fled for their lives. Tarma and the three surviving guards took care of the rest.

As for the bandit chief, who had sat his horse in stupified amazement from the moment the fight turned against them, he suddenly realized his own peril and tried to escape with the rest. Kethry, however, had never once forgotten him. Her bolt of power—intended this time to stun, not kill—took him squarely in the back of the head.

> "The bandits growl a challenge,
> But the lady only grins.
> The sorceress bows mockingly,
> And then the fight begins
> When it ends there are but four
> Left standing from that horde—
> The witch, the wolf, the traitor,
> And the woman with the sword.
> Three things never trust in—

The maiden sworn as pure,
The vows a king has given
And the ambush that is 'sure.' "

By late afternoon the heads of the bandits had been piled in a grisly cairn by the side of the road as a mute reminder to their fellows of the eventual reward of banditry. Their bodies had been dragged off into the hills for the scavengers to quarrel over. Tarma had supervised the cleanup, the three apprentices serving as her workforce. There had been a good deal of stomach-purging on their part at first—especially after the way Tarma had casually lopped off the heads of the dead or wounded bandits—but they'd obeyed her without question. Tarma had had to hide her snickering behind her hand, for they looked at her whenever she gave them a command as though they feared that *their* heads might well adorn the cairn if they lagged or slacked.

She herself had seen to the wounds of the surviving guards, and the burial of the two dead ones.

One of the guards could still ride; the other two were loaded into the now-useless cart after the empty boxes had been thrown out of it. Tarma ordered the whole caravan back to town; she and Kethry planned to catch up with them later, after some unfinished business had been taken care of.

Part of that unfinished business was the filling and marking of the dead guards' graves.

Kethry brought her a rag to wipe her hands with when she'd finished. "Damn. I wish—oh, hellspawn; they were just honest hired swords," she said, looking at the stone cairns she'd built with remote regret. "It wasn't *their* fault we didn't have a chance to warn them. Maybe they shouldn't have let themselves be surprised like that, not with what's been happening to the packtrains lately—but still, your life's a pretty heavy price to pay for a little carelessness. . . ."

Kethry, her energy back to normal now that she was no longer being drained by her illusions, slipped a sympathetic arm around Tarma's shoulders. "Come on, *she'enedra*. I want to show you something that might make you feel a little better."

While Tarma had gone to direct the cleanup, Kethry had been engaged in stripping the bandit chief down to his skin and readying his unconscious body for some sort of involved sorcery. Tarma knew she'd had some sort of specific punishment in mind from the time she'd heard about the stolen girls, but she'd had no idea of what it was.

> "They've stripped the traitor naked
> And they've whipped him on his way
> Into the barren hillsides,
> Like the folk he used to slay.
> They take a thorough vengeance
> For the women he's cut down
> And then they mount their horses
> And they journey back to town.
> Three things trust and cherish well—
> The horse on which you ride,
> The beast that guards and watches
> And your sister at your side!"

Now before her was a bizarre sight. Tied to the back of one of the bandit's abandoned horses was— apparently—the unconscious body of the highborn lady Kethry had spelled herself to resemble. She was clad only in a few rags, and had a bruise on one temple, but otherwise looked to be unharmed.

Tarma circled the tableau slowly. There was no flaw in the illusion, if indeed it was an illusion.

"Unbelievable," she said at last. "That *is* him, isn't it?"

"Oh, yes, indeed. One of my best pieces of work."

"Will it hold without you around to maintain it?"

"It'll hold all right," Kethry replied with deep satisfaction. "That's part of the beauty and the justice of the thing. The illusion is irretrievably melded with his own mind-magic. He'll never be able to break it himself, and no reputable sorcerer

220

will break it for him. And I promise you, the only sorcerers for weeks in any direction are quite reputable."

"Why wouldn't he be able to get one to break it for him?"

"Because I've signed it." Kethry made a small gesture, and two symbols appeared for a moment above the bandit's head. One was the symbol Tarma knew to be Kethry's sigil, the other was the glyph for "Justice." "Any attempt to probe the spell will make *those* appear. I doubt that anyone will ignore the judgment sign, and even if they were inclined to, I think my reputation is good enough to make most sorcerers think twice about undoing what I've done."

"You really didn't change him, did you?" Tarma asked, a horrible thought occurring to her. "I mean, if he's *really* a woman now . . ."

"Bright Lady, what an awful paradox we'd have!" Kethry laughed, easing Tarma's mind considerably. "We punish him for what he's done to women by turning him into a woman—but as a woman, we'd now be honor-bound to protect him! No, don't worry. Under the illusion—and it's a *very* complete illusion, by the way, it extends to all senses—he's still quite male."

She gave the horse's rump a whack, breaking the light enchantment that had held it quiet, and it bucked a little, scrabbling off into the barren hills.

"The last of the band went that way," she said, pointing after the beast, "And the horse he's on will follow their scent back to where they've made their camp. Of course, none of his former followers will have any notion that he's anything other than what he appears to be."

A wicked smile crept across Tarma's face. It matched the one already curving Kethry's lips.

"I wish I could be there when he arrives," Tarma said with a note of viciousness in her harsh voice. "It's *bound* to be interesting."

"He'll certainly get *exactly* what he deserves."

Kethry watched the horse vanish over the crest of the hill. "I wonder how he'll like being on the receiving end?"

"I know somebody who *will* like this—and I can't wait to see his face when you tell him."

"Grumio?"

"Mm-hmm."

"You know," Kethry replied thoughtfully, "this was almost worth doing for free."

"She'enedra!" Tarma exclaimed in mock horror. "Your misplaced honor will have us starving yet! We're *supposed* to be mercenaries!"

"I said *almost*." Kethry joined in her partner's gravelly laughter. "Come on. We've got pay to collect. You know—this just might end up as some bard's song."

"It might at that," Tarma chuckled "And what will you bet me that he gets the tale all wrong?"

"Not only that—but given bards, I can almost guarantee that it will only get worse with age."

Nine

The aged, half-blind mage blinked confused, rheumy eyes at his visitor. The man—or was it woman?—looked as awful as the mage felt. Bloodshot and dark-circled eyes glared at him from under the concealing shelter of a moth-eaten hood and several scarves. A straggle of hair that looked first to be dirty mouse-brown, then silver-blond, then brown again, strayed into those staring eyes. Nor did the eyes stay the same from one moment to the next; they turned blue, then hazel, then back to amethyst-blue. Try as he would, the mage could not make his own eyes focus properly, and light from a lanthorn held high in one of the visitor's hands was doing nothing to alleviate his befuddlement. The mage had never seen a human that presented such a contradictory appearance. She (he?) was a shapeless bundle of filthy, lice-ridden rags; what flesh there was to be seen displayed the yellow-green of healing bruises. Yet he had clearly seen gold pass to the hands of his landlord when that particular piece of human offal had unlocked the mage's door. Gold didn't come often to this part of town—and it came far less often borne by a hand clothed in rags.

He (she?) had forced his (her?) way into the verminous garret hole that was all the mage could call home now without so much as a by-your-leave, shouldering the landlord aside and closing the door firmly afterward. So this stranger was far more interested in privacy than in having the landlord there as a possible backup in case the senile wizard proved recalcitrant. That was quite enough to bewilder the mage, but the way his visitor kept shifting from male to female and back again was bidding fair to dizzy what few wits still remained to him and was nearly leaving him too muddled to speak.

Besides that, the shapeshifting was giving him one gods-awful headache.

"Go 'way—" he groaned feelingly, shadowing his eyes both from the unsettling sight and from the too-bright glare of the lanthorn his visitor still held aloft. "—leave an old man alone! I haven't got a thing left to steal—"

He was all too aware of his pitiful state; his robe stained and frayed, his long gray beard snarled and unkempt, his eyes so bloodshot and yellowed that no one could tell their color anymore. He was housed in an equally pitiful manner; this garret room had been rejected by everyone, no matter how poor, except himself; it was scarcely better than sleeping in the street. It leaked when it rained, turned into an oven in summer and a meat-locker in winter, and the wind whistled through cracks in the walls big enough to stick a finger in. His only furnishings were a pile of rags that served as a bed, and a rickety stool. Beneath him he could feel the ramshackle building swaying in the wind, and the movement was contributing to his headache. The boards of the walls creaked and complained, each in a different key. He knew he should have been used to it by now, but he wasn't; the crying wood rasped his nerves raw and added mightily to his disorientation. The mutiple drafts made the lanthorn flame flicker, even inside its glass chimney. The resulting dancing shadows didn't help his befuddlement.

"I'm not here to *steal*, old fraud."

Even the voice of the visitor was a confusing amalgam of male and female.

"I've brought you something."

The other hand emerged from the rags, bearing an unmistakable emerald-green bottle. The hand jiggled the bottle a little, and the contents sloshed enticingly. The rags slipped, and a trifle more of his visitor's face was revealed.

But the mage was only interested now in the bottle. Lethe! He forgot his perplexity, his befogged mind, and his headache as he hunched forward on his pallet of decaying rags, reaching eagerly for the bottle of drug-wine that had been his downfall. Every cell ached for the blessed/damned touch of it—

"Oh, no." The visitor backed out of reach, and the mage felt the shame of weak tears spilling down his cheeks. "*First* you give me what I want, *then* I give you this."

The mage sagged back into his pile of rags. "I have nothing."

"It's not what you have, old fraud, it's what you *were*."

"What ... I ... was. . . ."

"You *were* a mage, and a good one—or so they claim. That was before you let *this* stuff rob you of your wits until they cast you out of the Guild to rot. But there damn well ought to be enough left of you for my purposes."

By steadfastly looking, not at the visitor, but at the bottle, the mage was managing to collect his scattering thoughts. "What purpose?"

The visitor all but screamed his answer. "*To take off this curse, old fool! Are your wits so far gone you can't even see what's in front of you?*"

A curse—of course! No wonder his visitor kept shifting and changing! It wasn't the person that was shifting, but his *own* sight, switching erratically between normal vision and mage-sight. Normal vision showed him the woman; when the rags slipped a little more, she seemed to be a battered, but still lovely little toy of a creature—amethyst-eyed and platinum-haired—

Mage-sight showed him an equally abused but far from lovely man; sallow and thin, battered, but by no means beaten—a man wearing the kind of smoldering scowl that showed he was holding in rage by the thinnest of bonds.

So the "curse" could only be illusion, but a very powerful and carefully cast illusion. There was something magic-smelling about the man-woman, too; the illusion was linked to and being fueled by that magic. The mage furrowed his brow, then tested the weave of the magic that formed the illusion. It was a more than competent piece of work; and it was complete to all senses. It was far superior to anything the mage had produced even in his best days. In his present condition—to duplicate it so that he could lay new illusion over old would be impossible; to turn it or transfer it beyond even his former level of skill. He never even considered trying to take it off. To break it was beyond the best mage in Oberdorn, much less the broken-down wreck he had become.

Eyeing the bottle with passionate longing and despair, he said as much.

To his surprise the man accepted the bad news with a nod. "That's what they told me," he said. "But they told me something else. What a human mage couldn't break, a demon might."

"A ... demon?" The mage licked his lips; the bottle of Lethe was again within his grasp. "I used to be able to summon demons. I still could, I think. But it wouldn't be easy." That was untrue; the summoning of demons had been one of his lesser skills. It was still easily within his capabilities. But it required specialized tools and ingredients he no longer had the means to procure. And it was proscribed by the Guild. . . .

He'd tried to raise a minor impling to steal him Lethe-wine when his money had run out; that was when the Guild had discovered what he'd fallen prey to. That was the main reason they'd cast him out, destroying his tools and books; a mage brought so low as to use his skills for personal theft was no longer trustworthy. Especially not one that could summon demons. Demons were clever and had the

226

minds of sharp lawyers when it came to wriggling out of the bonds that had been set on them; that was why raising them was proscribed for any single mage of the Guild, and doubly proscribed for one who might have doubts as to his own mental competence at the time of the conjuration.

Of course, he was no longer bound by Guild laws since he was outcaste. And if this stranger could provide the wherewithal, the tools and the supplies, it could be easily done.

"Just tell me what you need, old man—I'll get it for you." The haggard, grimy face was avid, eager. "You bring me a demon to break this curse, and the bottle's yours."

Two days later, they stood in the cellar of the old, rotten mansion whose garret the mage called home. The cellar was in no better repair than the rest of the house; it was moldy and stank, and water-marks on the walls showed why no one cared to live there. Not only did the place flood every time it rained, but moisture was constantly seeping through the walls, and water trickled down from the roof-cisterns to drip from the beams overhead. Bright sparks of light glinted just beyond the circle of illumination cast by the lanthorn, the gleaming eyes of starveling rats and mice, perched curiously on the decaying shelves that clung to the walls. The scratching of their claws seemed to echo the scratching of the mage's chalks on the cracked slate floor.

The man-woman sat impatiently on the remains of a cask off to one side, careful not to disturb the work at hand. It had already cost him dearly—in gold and blood. Some of the things the mage had demanded had been bought, but most had been stolen. The former owners were often no longer in a condition to object to the disposition of their property.

From time to time the mage would glance searchingly up at him, make a tiny motion with his hand, frown with concentration, then return to his drawing.

After the fourth time this had happened, the stranger wet his lips with a nervous tongue, and asked, "Why do you keep doing that? Looking at me, I mean."

The mage blinked and stood up slowly, his back aching from the strain of staying bent over for so long. His red-rimmed, teary eyes focused to one side of the man, for he still found it difficult to look directly at him.

"It's the spell that's on you," he replied after a moment to collect his thoughts. "I don't know of a demon strong enough to break a spell that well made."

The man jumped to his feet, reaching for a sword he had left back in the mage's room because the old man had warned him against bearing cold steel into a demon's presence. "You old bastard!" he snarled. "You told me—"

"I told you I could call one—and I can. I just don't *know* one. Your best chance is if I can call a demon with a specific grudge against the maker of the spell—"

"What if there isn't one?"

"There will be," the mage shrugged. "Anyone who goes about laying curses like yours and leaving justice-glyphs behind to seal them is bound to have angered either a demon or someone who commands one. At any rate, since you want to know, I've been testing the edges of your curse to make the mage-rune appear. I'm working that into the summoning. Since I don't know *which* demon to call, the summoning will take longer than usual to bear fruit, but the results will be the same. The demon will appear, one with a reason to help you, and you'll bargain with it for the breaking of your curse."

"Me?" The stranger was briefly taken aback. "Why me? Why not you?"

"Because it isn't my curse. *I* don't give a damn whether it's broken or not. I told you I'd summon a demon—I didn't say I'd bind him. That takes more skill—and certainly more *will*—than I possess anymore. My bargain with you was simple—one demon, one bottle of Lethe. Once it's here, you can do your own haggling."

The man smiled; it was far more of a grimace than an expression of pleasure. "All right, old fraud. Work your spell. I'd sooner trust *my* wits than yours anyway."

The mage returned to his scribbling, filling the entire area lit by the lanthorn suspended overhead with odd little drawings and scrawls that first pulled, then repelled the eyes. Finally he seemed satisfied, gathered his stained, ragged robes about him with care, and picked a dainty path through the maze of chalk. He stood up straight just on the border of the inscriptions, raised his arms high, and intoned a peculiarly resonant chant.

At that moment, he bordered on the impressive—though the effect was somewhat spoiled by the water dripping off the beams of the ceiling, falling onto his balding head and running off the end of his long nose.

The last syllable echoed from the dank walls. The man-woman waited in anticipation.

Nothing happened.

"Well?" the stranger said with slipping patience, "Is that all there is to it?"

"I told you it would take time—perhaps as much as an hour. Don't fret yourself, you'll have your demon."

The mage cast longing glances at the shadow-shrouded bottle on the floor beside his visitor as he mopped his head with one begrimed, stained sleeve.

The woman-man noted the direction his attention was laid, thought for a moment, weighing the mage's efforts, and smiled mirthlessly. "All right, old fraud—I guess you've earned it. Come and get it."

The mage didn't wait for a second invitation, or

229

give the man-woman a chance to take the reluctant consent back. He scrambled forward, tripping over the tattered edges of his robes, and sagged to his knees as he snatched the bottle greedily.

He had it open in a trice, and began sucking at the neck like a calf at the udder, eyes closing and face slackening in mindless ecstacy. Within moments he was near-collapsing to the floor, half-empty bottle cradled in his arms, oblivion in his eyes.

His visitor walked over with a softly sinister tread and prodded him with a toe. "You'd better have worked this right, you old bastard," he muttered, "Or you won't be waking—"

His last words were swallowed in the sudden roar, like the howl of a tornado, that rose without warning behind him. As he spun to face the area of inscriptions, that whole section of floor burst into sickening blood-red and hellish green flame; flame that scorched his face, though it did nothing to harm the beams of the ceiling. He jumped back, frightened in spite of his bold resolutions to fear nothing.

But before he touched the ground again, a monstrous, clawed hand formed itself out of the flame and slapped him back against the rear wall of the cellar. A second hand, the color of molten bronze, reached for the oblivious mage.

A face worse than anything from the realm of nightmare materialized from the flame between the two hands. A neck, arms, and torso followed. The hands brought the mage within the fire—the visitor coughed on the stench of the old man's robes and beard scorching. There was no doubt that the fire was *real*, no matter that it left the ceiling intact. The mage woke from his drugged trance, screaming in mindless pain and terror. The smell of his flesh and garments burning was spreading through the cellar, and reached even to where the man-woman lay huddled against the dank wall; he choked and gagged at the horrible reek.

And the thing in the flames calmly bit the mage's head off, like a child with a gingerbread mannikin.

It was too much for even the man-woman to endure. He rolled to one side and puked up the entire contents of his stomach. When he looked up again, eyes watering and the taste of bile in his mouth, the thing was staring at him, licking the blood off its hands.

He swallowed as his gorge rose again, and waited for the thing to take him for dessert.

"You smell of magic." The thing's voice was like a dozen bells ringing; bells just slightly out-of-tune with one another. It made the man-woman nauseous and disoriented, but he swallowed again and tried to answer.

"I . . . have a curse."

"So I see. I assume that was why I was summoned here. Well, unless we enter into an agreement, I have no choice but to remain here or return to the Abyssal Planes. Talk to me, puny one; I do not desire the latter."

"How—why did you—the old man—"

"I dislike being coerced, and your friend made the mistake of remaining within reach of the circle. But I have, as yet, no quarrel with you. I take it you wish to be rid of what you bear. Will you bargain to have your curse broken? What can you offer me?"

"Gold?"

The demon laughed, molten-gold eyes slitted. "I have more than that in mind."

"Sacrifice? Death?"

"I can have those intangibles readily enough on my own—starting with yours. You are within my reach also."

The man-woman thought frantically. "The curse was cast by one you have reason to hate."

"This should make me love you?"

"It should make us allies, at least. I could offer revenge—"

"Now you interest me." The demon's eyes slitted. "Come closer, little man."

The man-woman clutched his rags about himself and ventured nearer, step by cautious step.

"A quaint curse. Why?"

"To make me a victim. It succeeded. It was not intended that I survive the experience."

"I can imagine." A cruel smile parted the demon's lips. "A pretty thing you are; didn't care for being raped, hmm?"

The man-woman's face flamed. He felt the demon inside of his mind, picking over all of his memories of the past year, lingering painfully over several he'd rather have died than seen revealed. Anger and shame almost replaced his fear.

The demon's smile grew wider. "Or did you begin to care for it after all?"

"Get out of my mind, you bastard!" He stifled whatever else he had been about to scream, wondering if he'd just written his own death-glyph.

"I think I like you, little man. How can you give me revenge?"

He took a deep breath, and tried to clear his mind. "I know where they are, the sorceress and her partner. I know how to lure them here—and I have a plan to take them when they come—"

"I have *many* such plans—but I did not know how to bring them within my grasp. Good." The demon nodded. "I think perhaps we have a bargain. I shall give you the form you need to make you powerful against them, and I shall let you bring them here. Come, and I will work the magic to change you, and free myself with the sealing of our bargain. I must touch you—"

The man-woman approached the very edge of the flames, cautious and apprehensive in spite of the demon's assurance that he would bargain. He still did not entirely trust this creature—and he more than certainly still feared its power. The demon reached out with one long, molten-bronze talon, and briefly caressed the side of his face.

The stranger screamed in agony, for it felt as if

232

that single touch had set every nerve afire. He wrapped his arms over his head and face, folded slowly at the waist and knees, still crying out; and finally collapsed to the floor, huddled in his rags, quivering. Had there been anything left in his stomach, he would have lost it then.

The demon waited, as patient as a snake, drinking in the tingles of power and the heady aura of agony that the man was exuding. He bent over the shaking pile of rags in avid curiosity, waiting for the moment when the pain of transformation would pass. His expression was oddly human—the same expression to be seen on the face of a cruel child watching the gyrations of a beetle from which it has pulled all the legs but one.

The huddled, trembling creature at the edge of his flames slowly regained control of itself. The quivering ceased; rags rose a little, then moved again with more purpose. Long, delicate arms appeared from the huddle, and pushed away from the floor. The rags fell away, and the rest of the stranger was revealed.

The visitor raised one hand to her face, then froze at the sight of that hand. She pushed herself into a more upright position, frowning and shaking her head; she examined the other hand and felt of her face as her expression changed to one of total disbelief. Frantic now, she tore away the rags that shrouded her chest and stared in horror at two lovely, lily-white—and very female —breasts.

"No—" she whispered, "—it's not possible—"

"Not for a human perhaps," the demon replied with faint irony, "But I am not subject to a human's limitations."

"What have you *done* to me?" she shrieked, even her voice having changed to a thin soprano.

"I told you, I would give you a form that would make you powerful against them. The sorceress' geas prevents her from allowing any harm to befall a woman—so I merely made you woman in reality,

233

to match the woman you were in illusion. They will be powerless against you now, your enemies and mine—"

"But I am *not* a woman! I *can't* be a woman!" She looked around her for something to throw at the demon's laughing face, and finding nothing, hurled curses instead. "Make me a man again, damn you! Make me a *man!*"

"Perhaps. Later, perhaps. When you have earned a boon from me. You still retain your strength and your weapon's expertise. Only the swordswoman could be any danger to you now, and the sorceress will be bound to see that she cannot touch you. *My* bargain now, bandit." The demon smiled still wider. "Serve me, and it may well be I shall make you a man again. But your new body serves me far better than your old would have. And meanwhile—"

He drew a swirl of flame about himself. When he emerged from it, he had assumed the shape of a handsome human man, quite naked; one whose beauty repulsed even as it attracted. He was still larger than a normal human in every regard, but he no longer filled a quarter of the cellar. He stepped confidently across the boundaries of the circle, reached forward and gathered the frozen woman to him. She struggled wildly; he delighted in her struggles.

"Oh, you make a charming wench, little toy; you play the part as if you had been born to it! A man would have sought to slay me, but you think only to flee. And I do not think a man would have guessed my intentions, but *you* have, haven't you, little one. I think I can teach you some of the pleasures of being a female, as well as the fears, hmm? Perhaps I can make you forget you ever were anything else—"

His laughter echoed through the entire house— but the rest of the inhabitants did no more than check the fastenings of their doors and return to the safety of their beds, hoping that whatever it was that was laughing would overlook *them*.

With another gesture, the demon transformed the bleak basement into a setting from a whore's nightmare; with his other hand he held his victim crushed against his chest while he reached into her mind with his.

She gasped in shock and dismay, feeling her will crumble before his, feeling him take over her senses, and feeling those senses rousing as he wished them to. He ran his hands over her body, stripping away the rags until she was as nude as he, and in the wake of his hands her skin burned with fever she could not repress.

As the last remains of her will fell to dust before his onslaught, her body, too, betrayed her; responding as the demon desired.

And at the end, she did, indeed, forget for that one moment what it had been like to be a man.

Kethry twined a lock of amber hair around her fingers, leaned over her cup and hid a smile. She found the side of herself that her swordswoman-partner was revealing disarming, and quite delightful—but she doubted Tarma would appreciate her amusement.

The common room of their inn was far from being crowded, and the atmosphere was relaxed and convivial. This was really the best such place they'd stayed in for months; it was well-lit, the food was excellent, the beds comfortable and free of vermin, the prices not outrageously extortionate. And Tarma was certainly enjoying the company.

As she had been every night for the past three, Tarma was embroiled in a religious discussion—a discussion, not an argument; although the two participants often waxed passionate, neither ever found offense or became angered during their disagreements.

Her fellow-scholar was a plump little priest of Anathei of the Purifying Flame. He was certainly a full priest, and might even (from his cultured accent) be a higher prelate, yet he wore only the same soft, dark brown, unornamented robes of the least of his order's acolytes. He was clean-shaven and quite bald, and his cheerful brown eyes seemed to regard everything and everyone with the open-hearted joy of an unspoiled child. No straitlaced ascetic, he—he and Tarma had been trading rounds of good wine; tonight reds, last night whites.

Tarma looked even more out of place seated across from him than she did with her sorceress-partner. She towered over him by a head, her every movement proclaiming she knew very well how to manage that sword slung on her back, her hawklike face and ice-blue eyes holding a controlled intensity that could easily have been frightening or intimidating to a stranger. With every article of her weaponry and earth-brown clothing so precisely arranged that what she wore might almost have been some kind of uniform, and her coarse black hair braided and coiled with militant neatness, she looked as much the priest or more than he—half-barbarian priest of some warlike order, that is. She hardly looked as if she could have anything in common with the scholarly little priest.

She hardly looked literate. Certainly no one would expect erudite philosophy from her lips, not with the warlike accoutrements she bore; yet she had been quoting fully as many learned tomes as the priest—to his evident delight and Kethry's mild surprise. It would appear that service as a Sworn One did not exclude knowledge as a possible arena of combat. Kethry had long known that Tarma *was* literate, and in more than one language, but she had never before guessed that her partner was so erudite.

Kethry herself was staying out of the conversation for the moment. This evening she and her partner had had an argument, the first serious disagreement of their association. She wanted to give Tarma a chance to cool down—and to mull over what she'd said.

Because while it had been unpleasant, it was also, unfortunately, nothing less than the truth.

"You're not going out there alone, are you?" Tarma had asked doubtfully, when Kethry had voiced her intention to prowl the rather dubious quarter that housed the gypsy-mages. Kethry had heard that one of her old classmates had taken up with the wanderers, and was looking for news of him.

"Why not?" she asked, a little more sharply than she had intended.

"Because it's no place for a woman alone."

"Dammit, Tarma, I'm *not* just any woman! I'm perfectly capable of taking care of myself!"

"Look—even *I* can get taken out by a gang of street toughs."

"In the name of the gods, Tarma, leave me alone for once! You're smothering me! I can't go anywhere or do anything without you rushing to wrap me in gauze, like a piece of china—"

She'd stopped then, appalled by the stricken look on her partner's face.

Then, like lightning, the expression changed. "You're imagining things," Tarma replied flatly.

"All right—have it your way." Kethry was too tired to fight with her. "You will anyway. Any time you hear something you don't like, you deny it and shut down on me—just like you're doing now."

And she had turned on her heel and led the way into the inn's common room, ignoring the fact that Tarma looked as if the sorceress had just slapped her.

The voice of the little priest penetrated her musing.

"Nay," he said. "Nay, I cannot agree. Our teaching is that evil is not a thing of itself; it is simply good that has not been brought to see the truth. We hold that even a demon can be redeemed—that even the most vile of such creatures could become a blessed spirit if someone with time and patience were to give him the proper redirection."

"Always supposing your proselytizer managed to keep from being devoured or ripped to shreds before he got a single word out," Tarma croaked wryly, draping herself more comfortably over the edge of the worn wooden table. "He'd better be either agile or one *damned* powerful mage! No, I can't agree with you, my friend. Aside from what Magister Tenavril has to say about them, I've dealt with a few demons up close and on a quite personal basis. I have to side with the Twin Suns school; the demonic beings must have been created purely of evil forces. It isn't just the Abyssal dwellers that are bad clear through, either; I've known a few humans who could pass for demons. Evil is real and a reality in and of itself. It *likes* being that way. It wouldn't choose to be anything else. And it has to be destroyed whenever a body gets the chance, or it'll spread. Evil is easier to follow than good, and we humans like the easy path."

"I cannot agree. Those who are evil simply don't know what good is."

"Oh, they know, all right; and they reject it to follow pure selfishness."

"I—" the little priest blinked in the candlelight.

"Can you give me even *one* instance of great evil turned to good once good has been pointed out to it?"

"Uh—" he thought hard for a moment, then smiled triumphantly. "The Great Demon-Wolf of Hastandell!"

"Oh, that's *too* easy. Warrl!"

A shadow in a corner of the hearth uncoiled itself, and proved to be no shadow at all, but the *kyree*, whose shoulder came nearly as high as Tarma's waist. Closer inspection would reveal that Warrl's body was more like that of one of the great hunting-cats of the plains than a lupine, built for climbing and short bursts of high speed, not the endurance of a true wolf. But the fur and head and tail were sufficiently wolflike that this was how Tarma generally thought of him.

He padded over to the table and benches shared by the ill-assorted trio. The conversation of all the other occupants of the inn died for a moment as he moved, but soon picked back up again. After three days, the patrons of the inn were growing a little more accustomed to the monster beast in their midst. Tarma had helped that along by coaxing him to demean himself with a few tricks to entertain them the first night of their stay. Now, while the sight of him still unsettled a few of them, they had come to regard him as harmless. They had no notion of his true nature; Tarma and Kethry had tactfully refrained from revealing that he was just as intelligent as any of them—and quite probably could beat any one of them at chess.

"Here's your Demon-Wolf—one of his kin, rather." Tarma cocked her head to one side, her eyes far away as if she was listening. "*Kyree* is what they call themselves; they come from the Pelagir Hills. Warrl says to tell you that he knows that story— that Ourra didn't know the sheep he'd been feeding on belonged to anyone; when he prowled the village at night he was just being curious. Warrl says Ourra had never seen humans before that lot moved in and settled; he thought they were just odd beasts and that the houses were some kind of dead growths—believe me, I have seen some of what grows naturally in the Pelagirs—it isn't stretching the imagination to think that huts could grow of themselves once you've seen some of the bushes and trees. Well, Warrl wants you to know that when the priestess went out and gave Ourra a royal tongue-lashing for eating the stock, Ourra was quite embarrassed. Without there being someone like me or Kethry, with the kind of mind that he could talk to, there wasn't much he could do by way of apology, but he did his best to make it up to the village.

239

His people have a very high sense of honor. Sorry, little man—Ourra is disqualified."

"He talks to you?" the little priest said, momentarily diverted. "That creature truly talks? I thought him just a well-trained beast!"

"Oh, after all our conversation, I figured you to be open-minded enough to let in on the 'secret.' *Kyree* have a lot of talents—they're as bright as you or me. Brighter, maybe—I have no doubt he could give you a good battle at taroc, and that's one game I have no gift for. As for talking—Warrior's Oath—sometimes I wish I could get him to stop! Oh, yes, he talks to me all right—gives me no few pieces of unsolicited advice and criticism, and usually with an 'I told you so' appended." She ruffled the great beast's fur affectionately as he grinned a toothy, tongue-lolling grin. Kethry tossed him one of the bones left from their dinner; he caught it neatly on the fly, and settled down beside her to enjoy it. Behind them, the hum of voices continued.

"Now I'll give *you* one—evil that served only itself. Thalhkarsh. We had firsthand experience of that one. He had plenty of opportunity to see good—it wasn't just the trollops he had stolen for his rites. Or are you not familiar with that tale?"

"Not the whole of it. Certainly not from one of the participants!"

"Right enough then—this is a long and thirsty story. Oskar?" Tarma signaled the host, a plump, shortsighted man who hurried to answer her summons. "Another round—no, make it a pitcher, this may take a while. Here—" she tossed him a coin, as it was her turn to pay; the innkeeper trotted off and returned with a brimming earthen vessel. Kethry was amused to see that he did not return to his station behind the counter after placing it on the table between Tarma and the priest. Instead he hovered just within earshot, polishing the tables next to them with studious care. Well, she didn't blame him, this was a tale Tarma didn't tell often, and it wasn't likely anyone in Oberdorn had ever heard a firsthand account of it. Oskar would be attracting folk to his tables for months after they'd gone with repetitions of the story.

"From all we could put together afterward, Thalhkarsh was a demon that had been summoned purely by mistake. It was a mistake the mage who called him paid for—well, that's usually the case when something like that happens. This time though, things were evidently a little different," she nodded at Kethry, who took up the thread of the story while Tarma took a sip of wine.

"Thalhkarsh had ambition. He didn't want to live in his own Abyssal Planes anymore, he wanted to escape them. More than that, he wanted far more power than he had already; he wanted to become a god, or a godling, at least. He knew that the quickest ways of gaining power are by worship, pain, and death. The second two he already had a taste of, and he craved more. The first—well, he calculated that he knew ways of gaining that, too. He transformed himself into a very potently sexual and pleasing shape, built himself a temple with a human pawn as his High Priest, and set up a religion."

"It was a religion tailored to his peculiar tastes. From what I know most of the demonic types wouldn't think of copulating with a human anymore than you or I would with a dog; Thalhkarsh thought otherwise." Tarma grimaced. "Of course a part of that is simply because of the amount of pain he could cause while engaging in his recreations—but it may be he also discovered that sex is another very potent way of raising power. Whatever the reason, that was what the whole religion was founded on. The rituals always culminated with Thalhkarsh taking a half-dozen women, torturing and killing them when he'd done with them, in the full view of his worshipers. There's a kind of mind that finds that stimulating; before too long, he had a full congregation and was well on his way to achieving his purpose. That was where *we* came in."

"You know our reputation for helping women?" Kethry put in.

"You have a geas?" ventured the little priest.

"Something like that. Well, since Thalhkarsh's chosen victims were almost exclusively female, we found ourselves involved. We slipped into the temple in disguise and went for the High Priest—figuring if he was the one in charge, that might solve the problem. We didn't know he was a puppet, though I had guessed he might be, and then dismissed the idea." Kethry sighed. "Then we found our troubles had only begun. He had used this as a kind of impromptu test of the mettle of his servant; when the servant failed, he offered *me* the position. I was tempted with anything I might want; nearly unlimited power, beauty, wealth—and him. He was incredibly seductive, I can't begin to tell you how much. To try and give you a notion of his power, every one of his victims *ran* to him willingly when he called her, even though they *knew* what their fate would be. Well, I guess I resisted him a little too long; he became impatient with me and knocked me into a wall—unconscious, or so he thought."

"Then he made me the same offer," Tarma continued. "Only with me he demonstrated his power rather than just promising things. He totally transformed me—when he was done kings would have paid money for the privilege of laying their crowns at my feet. He also came damned close to breaking my bond with the Star-Eyed; I swear to you, I was within inches of letting him seduce me—except that the more he roused my body, the more he roused my anger. That was his mistake; I pretended to give in when I saw Kethry sneaking up behind him. Then I broke his focus just as she stabbed him; he lost control over his form and his worshipers' minds. When they saw what he really was, they deserted him—that broke his power, and it was all over."

"*She' enedra,* you were in no danger of breaking; your will is too strong, he'd have needed either more time to work on you *or* power to equal the Warrior's."

"Maybe. It was a damn near thing; too near for my liking. Well he was absolute evil for the sake of it—and I should well know, I had that evil crawling around in my mind. Besides that, there were other things that came out afterward. We know he took a few innocent girls who just had the bad luck to be in the wrong place; we *think* some clerics went in to try and exorcise him. It's hard to say for certain since they were hedge-priests; wanderers with no set temple. We do know they disappeared between one night and the next; that they did not leave town by the gates, and that they had been talking about dealing with Thalhkarsh before they vanished."

She trailed off, the set of her mouth grim, her eyes bleak. "We can only assume they went the way of all of his victims, since they were never seen or heard from again. So Thalhkarsh had plenty of opportunity to see good and the Light—and he apparently saw it only as another thing to crush."

The little priest said nothing; there seemed nothing appropriate to say. Instead, he took a sip of his wine; from the distant look in his eyes he was evidently thinking hard.

"We of Anathei are not fools, Sworn One," he said finally, "Even though we may not deal with evil as if it were our deadly enemy. No, to throw one's life away in the foolish and prideful notion that one's own sanctity is enough to protect one from everything is something very like a sin. The arrow that strikes a friend in battle instead of a foe is no less deadly because it is misdirected. Let me tell you this; when dealing with the greater evils, we do nothing blindly. We study carefully, we take no chances; we know everything there is to be

243

known about an opponent before we face him to show him the Light. And we take very great care that he is unable to do us harm in his misguided state."

Tarma's eyes glinted with amusement in the shifting light. "Then it may well be your folk have the right of it—and in any case, you're going about your conversions in a practical manner, which is more than I can say for many. Once again we will have to agree to disagree."

"With that, lady, I rest content." He bowed to her a little, and the bench creaked under his moving weight. "But we still have not settled the point of contention. Even if I were willing to concede that you are right about Thalhkarsh—which I am not—he was still a demon. Not a man. And—"

"Well if you want irredeemable evil in a human, we can give you that, too! Kethry, remember that bastard Lastel Longknife?"

"Lady Bright! Now *there* was an unredeemable soul if ever there was one!"

Kethry saw out of the corner of her eye that Oskar had not moved since the tale-telling had begun, and was in a fair way to polish a hole right through the table. She wondered, as she smothered a smile, if *that* was the secret behind the scrupulously clean furniture of his inn.

"Lastel Longknife?" the priest said curiously.

"I doubt you'd have heard of that one. He was a bandit that had set up a band out in the waste between here and—"

"Wait—I think I *do* know that story!" the priest exclaimed. "Isn't there a song about it? One that goes 'Deep into the stony hills, miles from keep or hold'?"

"Lady's Blade, is that nonsense going to follow us *everywhere?*" Tarma grimaced in distaste while Kethry gave up on trying to control her giggles. "Damned impudent rhymester! I should never have agreed to talk to him, never! And if I *ever* get my

244

hands on Leslac again, I'll kill him *twice!* Bad enough
he got the tale all backward, but that manure about
'Three things never anger or you will not live for
long; a wolf with cubs, a man with power and a
woman's sense of wrong' came damn close to ruin-
ing business for a while! We weren't geas-pressed
that time, or being altruistic—we were in it for the
money, dammit! And—" she turned to scowl at
Kethry. "What are *you* laughing about?"

"Nothing—" One look at Tarma's face set her off
again.

"No respect; I don't get it from stupid minstrels,
I don't get it from my partner, I don't even get it
from *you*, Fur-face!"

Warrl put his head down on his paws and contrived to look innocent.

"Well, if my partner can contrive to control herself, this is what really happened. Longknife had
managed to unite all the little bandit groups into
one single band with the promise that they would
be able—under his leadership—to take even the
most heavily guarded packtrains. He made good on
his boast. Before a few months passed it wasn't
possible for a mouse to travel the Trade Road
unmolested."

"But surely they sent out decoy trains."

"Oh, they did; Longknife had an extra factor in
his favor," Kethry had managed to get herself back
into control again, and answered him. "He had a
talent for mind-magic, like they practice in Valdemar.
It wasn't terribly strong, but it was very specific.
Anyone who saw Longknife thought that he was
someone they had known for a long time *but* not
someone anywhere within riding distance. That way
he avoided the pitfall of having his 'double' show
up. He looked to be a different person to everyone,
but he always looked like someone they trusted, so
he managed to get himself included as a guard on
each and every genuine packtrain going out. When
the time was right, he'd signal his men and they'd

ambush the train. If it was too well guarded, he'd wait until it was his turn on night-watch and drive away the horses and packbeasts; there's no water in the waste, and the guards and traders would have to abandon their goods and make for home afoot.''

"That's almost diabolically clever.''

"You do well to use that word; he was diabolic, all right. One of the first trains he and his men took was also conveying a half-dozen or so young girls to fosterage—daughters of the traders in town—the idea being that they were more likely to find young men to their liking in a bigger city. Longknife and his men *could* have ransomed them unharmed; could even have sold them. He didn't. He took his pleasure of each of them in turn until he tired of them, then turned them over to his men to be gang-raped to death without a second thought.''

The priest thought that if the minstrel Leslac could have seen the expression in Tarma's eyes at this moment, he'd have used stronger words in his song than he had.

"The uncle of one of the girls found out we were in a town nearby and sent for us,'' Kethry picked up when Tarma seemed lost in her own grim thoughts. "We agreed to take the job, and disguised ourselves to go out with the next train. That's where the song is worst wrong—*I* was the lady, Tarma was the maidservant. When the bandits attacked, I broke the illusions; surprise gave us enough of an advantage that we managed to rout them.''

"We didn't kill them all, really didn't even get most of them, just the important ones, the leaders.'' Tarma came back to herself and resumed the tale. "And we got Longknife; the key to the whole business.''

"What—what was the 'thorough vengeance'?'' the priest asked. "I have been eaten up with curiosity ever since I heard the song, but I hardly know if I dare ask—''

Tarma's harsh laugh rang as she tossed back her

head. "We managed to keep *one* thing from that songster, anyway! All right, I'll let you in on the secret. Kethry put an all-senses illusion on him and bound it to his own mind-magic so that he couldn't be rid of it. She made him look like a very attractive, helpless woman. We made sure he was unconscious, then we tied him to his horse and sent him into the waste following the track of what was left of his band. I've no doubt he knew *exactly* what his victims had felt like before he finally died."

"Remind me never to anger you, Sworn One." The priest shook his head ruefully. "I'm not sure I care for your idea of justice."

"Turnabout is fair play—and it's no worse that what he'd have gotten at the hands of the relatives of the girls he murdered," Kethry pointed out. "Tarma's Lady does not teach that evildoers should remain unpunished; nor does mine. And Longknife is another bit of scum who had ample opportunity to do good—or at least no harm—and chose instead to deliberately inflict the most harm he could. I think he got his just desserts, personally."

"If you, too, are going to enter the affray, I fear I am outnumbered." The priest smiled. "But I shall retire with dignity, allowing the justice of your assertions, but not conceding you the victory. Though it is rather strange that you should mention the demon Thalhkarsh just now."

Both Tarma and Kethry came instantly alert; they changed their positions not so much as a hair (Tarma leaning on both arms that rested on the table, Kethry lounging a little against the wall) but now they both had dropped the veneer of careless ease they had worn, and beneath that thin skin the wary vigilance of the predator and hunter showed plain.

"Why?" Tarma asked carefully.

"Because I have heard rumors in the beggar's quarter that some ill-directed soul is trying to re-establish the worship of Thalhkarsh in the old Temple of Duross there. More than that, we have had reports of the same from a young woman who apparently dwells there."

"Have you?" Kethry pushed back the hood of her buff-colored robe. "Worshiping Thalhkarsh—that's a bit injudicious, considering what happened at Delton, isn't it?"

"Injudicious to say the least," the priest replied, "Since they must know what will happen to them if they are discovered. The Prince is not minded to have light women slaughtered on altars instead of paying his venery taxes. I heard that after Thalhkarsh's depredations, his income from Delton was halved for the better part of three years. He took care to alter or tighten the laws concerning religious practice after that. Human sacrifice in any form is punishable by enslavement; if the perpetrator has murdered taxpayers, he goes to the Prince's mages for their experiments."

Kethry lifted an eyebrow; Tarma took a largish mouthful of wine. They'd both heard about how Prince Lothar's mages produced his monstrous mindless bodyguards. They'd also heard that the process from normal man to twelve-foot-tall brute was far from pleasant—or painless. Lothar was sometimes called "the Looney"—but *never* to his face.

The little priest met blue and green eyes in turn, and nodded. "Besides that," he continued, "There are several sects, mine included, who would wish to deal with the demon on other levels. We all want him bound, at the least. But so far it's all rumor. The temple has been empty every time anyone's checked."

"So you *did* check?"

"In all conscience, yes—although the woman didn't seem terribly trustworthy or terribly bright. Pretty, yes—rather remarkably pretty under the dirt, but she seemed to be in a half-daze all the time. Brother Thoser was the one who questioned her, not I, or I could tell you more. My guess would be that she was of breeding, but had taken to the street to supply an addiction of some sort."

Tarma nodded thoughtfully.

"Where is this temple?"" Kethry's husky alto almost made the little priest regret his vow of chastity; and when she had moved into the light, and he saw that the sweet face beneath the hood matched the voice, he sighed a little for days long lost.

"Do you know the beggar's quarter? Well then, it's on the river, just downwind of the slaughterhouse and the tannery. It's been deserted since the last acolyte died of old age—oh, nearly fifteen years ago. It's beginning to fall apart a bit; the last time I looked at it, there didn't *seem* to be any signs that anyone had entered it in all that time."

"Is it kept locked up?"

"Oh, yes; not that there's anything to steal—mostly it's to keep children from playing where they might be hurt by falling masonry. The beggars used it for a bit as one of their meeting halls, before the acolyte died, but," he chuckled, "One-Eye Tham told me it was 'too perishin' cold and damp' and they moved to more comfortable surroundings."

Tarma exchanged a look with her partner; *We need to talk,* she hand-signed.

Kethry nodded, ever so slightly. *We could be in trouble,* she signed back.

Tarma's grimace evidenced agreement.

"Well, if you will allow me," the little priest finished the last of his wine, and shoved the bench back with a scrape, "I fear I have morning devotions to attend to. As always, Sworn One, the conversation and company have been delightful, if argumentative—"

Tarma managed a smile; it transformed her face, even if it didn't quite reach her eyes. "My friend, we have a saying—it translates something like 'there is room in the universe for every Way.' You travel yours; should you need it, my sword will protect you as I travel mine."

"That is all anyone could reasonably ask of one

249

who does not share his faith," he replied, "And so, good night."

The two mercenary women finished their own wine and headed for their room shortly after his departure. With Warrl padding after, Kethry took one of the candles from the little table standing by the entrance to the hall, lit it at the lantern above the table, and led the way down the corridor. The wooden walls were polished enough that their light was reflected; they'd been tended to recently and Tarma could still smell the ferris-oil that had been used. The sounds of snoring behind closed doors, the homelike scents of hot wax and ferris-oil, the buzz of conversation from the inn behind them—all contrasted vividly with the horror that had been resurrected in both their minds at the mention of Thalhkarsh.

Their room held two narrow beds, a rag rug, and a table; all worn, but scrupulously clean. They had specified a room with a window, so Warrl could come and go as he pleased; no one in his right mind would break into the room with any of the three of them in it, and their valuables were in the stable, well-guarded by their well-named warsteeds, Hellsbane and Ironheart.

When the door was closed and bolted behind them, Kethry put the candle in its wall sconce and turned to face her partner with a swish of robes.

"If he's there, if it's really Thalhkarsh, he'll be after us."

Tarma paced the narrow confines of the room. "Seems obvious. If I were a demon, I'd want revenge. Well, we knew this might happen someday. I take it that your sword hasn't given you any indication that there's anything wrong?"

"No. At least, nothing more than what you'd expect in a city this size. I wish Need would be a little more discriminating." Kethry sighed, and one hand caressed the hilt of the blade she wore at her side over her sorceress' robes in an unconscious gesture of habit. "I absolutely refuse to go sticking my nose into every lover's-quarrel in this town! And—"

"Warrior's Oath—remember the first time you tried?" Tarma's grim face lightened into a grin with the recollection.

"Oh, laugh, go ahead! *You* were no help!"

"Here you thought the shrew was in danger of her life—you went flying in the door and knocked her man out cold—and you expected her to throw herself at your feet in gratitude—" Tarma was taking full revenge for Kethry's earlier hilarity at her expense. "And what did she do? Began hurling crockery at you, shrieking you'd killed her beloved! Lady's Eyes, I thought I was going to die!"

"I wanted to take her over my knee and beat her with the flat of my blade."

"And to add insult to injury, Need wouldn't let you lay so much as a finger on her! I had to go in with a serving dish for a shield and rescue you before she tore you to shreds!"

"She could have done that with her tongue alone," Kethry grimaced. "Well, that's not solving our problem here. . . ."

"True," Tarma conceded, sobering. She threw herself down on her bed, Warrl jumping up next to her and pushing his head under her hand. "Back to the subject. Let's assume that the rumor is true; we can't afford not to. If somebody has brought that particular demon back, we know he's going to want our hides."

"Or worse."

"Or worse. Now he can't have gotten too powerful, or everybody in town would know about him. Remember Delton."

Kethry shifted restlessly from foot to foot, finally going over to the window to open the shutters with a creak of hinges and stare out into the night. "I remember. And I remember that we'd better do something about him *while* he's in that state."

"This isn't a job for us, *she'enedra*. It's a job for priests. *Powerful* priests. I remember what he almost did to me. He came perilously close to breaking my bond with the Star-Eyed. And he boasted he could snap your tie to Need just as easily. I think we ought to ride up to the capital as fast as Hellsbane and Ironheart can carry us, and fetch us some priests."

"And come back to an empty town and a demon transformed to a godling?" Kethry turned away from the window to shake her head at her partner, her amber hair like a sunset cloud around her face, and a shadow of anger in her eyes. "What if we're wrong? We'll have some very powerful people very angry at us for wasting their time. And if we're right—we have to act fast. We have to take him while he's still weak or we'll never send him back to the Abyssal Planes at all. He is no stupid imp—he's learned from what we did to him, you can bet on it. If he's not taken down now, we'll never be able to take him at all."

"That's *not* our job!"

"Whose is it then?" Kethry dug her fingers into the wood of the windowframe behind her, as tense and worried as she'd ever been. "We'd better make it our job if we're going to survive! And I told you earlier—I *don't* want you cosseting me! I *know* what I'm doing, and I can protect myself!"

Tarma sighed, and there was a shadow of guilt on her face as she rolled over to lie flat on her back, staring at the ceiling; her hands clasped under her head, one leg crossed over the other. "All right, then. I don't know a damn thing about magic, and all I care to know about demons outside of a book is that they scare me witless. I still would rather go for help, but if you don't think we'd have the time—and if you are sure you're not getting into more than you can handle—"

"I know we wouldn't have the time; he's not going to waste time building up a power base," Kethry replied, sitting down on the edge of Tarma's bed, making the frame creak.

"And he may not be there at all; it might just be a wild rumor."

"It might; I don't think I'd care to bet my life on waiting to see, though."

"So we need information; reliable information."

"The question is how to get it. Should I try scrying?"

"Absolutely *not!*" Tarma flipped back over onto her side, her hand chopping at the pillow for emphasis. Warrl winced away and looked at her reproachfully. "He caught that poor witch back in Delton that way, remember? That much even *I* know. If you scry, he'll have you on *his* ground. I promise I won't cosset you any more, but I *will not* allow you to put yourself in jeopardy when there are any other alternatives!"

"Well, how then?"

"Me." Tarma stabbed at her own chest with an emphatic thumb. "Granted, I'm not a thief—but I *am* a skilled scout. I can slip into and out of that temple without anyone knowing I've been there, and if it's being used for anything, I'll be able to tell."

"No."

"Yes. No choice, *she'enedra*."

"All right, then—but you won't be going without me. If he and any followers he may have gathered *are* there and they're using magic to mask their presence, you won't see anything, but I can invoke mage-sight and see through any illusions."

Tarma began to protest, but this time Kethry cut her short. "You haven't a choice either; you need my skill and I won't let you go in there without me. Dammit Tarma, I am your partner—your *full* partner. If I have to, I'll follow you on my own."

"You would, wouldn't you?"

"You can bet on it." Kethry scowled, then smiled as Tarma's resigned expression told her she'd won the argument. Warrl nudged Tarma's hand again, and she began scratching absentmindedly behind

253

his ears. A scowl creased her forehead, but her mouth, too, was quirked in an almost-smile.

"Warrior's Oath! I *would* tie myself to a headstrong, stubborn, foolish, reckless, crazed mage—"

"Who loves her bond-sister and won't allow her to throw her life away."

"—who is dearer to me than my own life."

Kethry reached out at almost the same moment as Tarma did. They touched hands briefly, crescent-scarred palm to crescent-scarred palm, and exchanged rueful smiles.

"Argument over?"

"It's over."

"All right then," Tarma said after poignant silence, "Let's get to it now, while we've still got the guts for it."

Ten

Tarma led the way, as soft- and sure-footed in these dark city streets as she would have been scouting a forest or creeping through grass on an open plain.

The *kyree* Warrl served as their scout and their eyes in the darkness. The uninformed would have thought it impossible to hide a lupine creature the size of Warrl in an open street—a creature whose shoulder nearly came as high as Tarma's waist; but Warrl, although somewhere close at hand, was presently invisible. Tarma could sense him, though—now behind them, now in front. From time to time he would speak a single word (or perhaps as many as three) in her mind, to tell her of the results of his scouting.

There was little moonlight; the moon was in her last quarter. This was one of the poorest streets in the city, and there were no cressets and no torches to spare to light the way by night—and if anyone put one up, it would be stolen within the hour. The buildings to either side were shut up tight; not with shutters, for they were in far too poor a state of repair to have working shutters, but with whatever bits of wood and cloth or rubbish came to hand. What little light there was leaked through the cracks in these makeshift curtainings. The street itself was rutted mud; no wasting of paving bricks on this side of the river. Both the mercenaries wore thin-soled boots, the better to feel their way in the darkness. Kethry had abandoned her usual buff-colored, calf-length robe; she wore a dark, sleeved tunic over her breeches. Kethry's ensorcelled blade Need was slung at her side; Tarma's nonmagical weapon carried in its usual spot on her back. They had left cloaks behind; cloaks had a tendency to get tangled at the most inopportune moments. Better to bear with the chill.

They had slipped out the window of their room at the inn, wanting no one to guess where they were going—or even that they were going out at all. They had made their way down back alleys with occasional detours through fenced yards or even across roofs. Although Kethry was no match for Tarma in strength and agility, she was quite capable of keeping up with her on a trek like this one.

Finally the fences had begun to boast more holes than entire boards; the houses leaned to one side or the other, almost as though they huddled together to support their sagging bones. The streets, when they had ventured out onto them, were either deserted or populated by one or two furtively scurrying shadows. *This* dubious quarter where the abandoned temple that their priestly friend had told them of stood—this was hardly a place either of them would have chosen to roam in daylight, much less darkness. Tarma was already beginning to regret the impulse that had led her here—the stubbornness that had forced her to prove that she was not trying to shelter her partner unduly. Except that ... maybe Kethry was right. Maybe she was putting a stranglehold on the mage. But Keth was all the Clan she had. ...

Tarma's nose told her where they were; downwind of the stockyards, the slaughterhouse, and the tannery. The reek of tannic acid, offal, half-tanned hides and manure was a little short of unbreathable. From far off there came the intermittent lowing and bleating of the miserable animals awaiting the doom that would come in the morning.

"Something just occurred to me," Kethry whispered as they waited, hidden in shadows, for a single passerby to clear the street.

256

"What?"

"This close to the stockyard and slaughterhouse, Thalhkarsh wouldn't necessarily *need* sacrifices to build a power base."

"You mean—he could use the deaths of the beasts?"

"Death-energy is the same for man and beast. Man just has more of it, and of higher quality."

"Like you can get just as drunk on cheap beer as on distilled spirits?"

"Something of the sort."

"Lady's Blade! *And* he feeds on fear and pain as well—"

"There's plenty of that at the slaughterhouse."

"Great. That's *just* what I needed to hear." Tarma brooded for a moment. "Tell me something; why's he taking on human shape if he wants to terrify? His own would be better for that purpose."

"Well—this is just a guess—you have to remember he wants worship and devotion as well, and he won't get that in his real shape. That might be one reason. A second would be because what *seems* to be familiar and proves to be otherwise is a lot more fear-inducing than the openly alien. Lastly is Thalhkarsh himself—most demons *like* the Abyssal Planes, and their anger at being summoned is because they've been taken from home. They look on us as a lower form of life, a species of animal. But Thalhkarsh is perverse; he wants to stay here, he wants to rule over people, and I suspect he enjoys physically coupling with humans. The Lady only knows why."

"I . . . don't suppose he can breed, can he?"

"Windborn! Thank your Lady, no. Thank *all* the gods that demons even in human form are sterile with humans, or we might have more than Thalhkarsh to worry about—he *might* be willing to produce a malleable infant. But the only way he can reproduce is to bud—and he's too jealous of his powers here to bud and create another on this Plane with like powers and a mind of its own. He won't go creating a rival, that much I'm sure of."

"Forgive me if I don't break out into carols of relief."

They peered down the dark, shadow-lined street in glum silence. The effluvium of the stockyards and tannery washed over them, causing Tarma to stifle a cough as an acrid breath seared the back of her throat a little.

The street is clear, a voice rang in Tarma's head.

"Warrl says it's safe to go," Tarma passed the word on, then, crouching low, crossed the street like one of the scudding shadows cast on the street by high clouds against the moon.

She moved so surely and so silently from the shadows of their own building to the shadows below the one across the street that even Kethry, who *knew* she was there, hardly saw her. Kethry was an instant behind her, not quite so sure or silent, but furtive enough. Warrl was already waiting for them, and snorted a greeting before slipping farther ahead of them in the direction of the temple.

Hugging the rough wood and stone of the walls, they inched their way down the street, trying not to wince when their feet encountered unidentifiable piles of something soft and mushy. The reek of tannery and stockyard overwhelmed any other taint. From within the buildings occasionally came sounds of revelry or conflict; hoarse, drunken singing, shouting, weeping, the splintering of wood, the crash of crockery. None of this was carried into the streets; only fools and the mad walked the streets of the beggar's quarter at night.

Fools, the mad, or the desperate. Right now Kethry had both of them figured for being all three.

Finally the walls of buildings gave way to a single stone wall, half again as tall as Tarma. This, by the descriptions she'd gotten, would be the wall of the temple. Beyond it, bulking black against the stars, Kethry could see the temple itself.

258

Tarma surveyed the wall, deciding it would be no great feat to scale it.

You go over first, Fur-face, she thought.

My pleasure, Warrl sent back to her, overtones of irony so strong Tarma could almost taste the metallic emotional flavoring. He backed up six or seven paces, then flung himself at the wall. His forepaws caught the top of it; caught, and held, and with a scrambling of hindclaws that sounded hideously loud to Tarma's nervous ears, he was over and leaping down on the other side.

Now it was her turn.

She backed up a little, then ran at the wall, leaping and catching the top effortlessly, pulling herself up onto the stones that were set into the top with ease. She crouched there for a moment, peering through the darkness into the courtyard beyond, identifying the odd-shaped shadows by what she'd been told to expect there.

In the middle there stood a dried-out fountain, its basin broken, its statuary mostly missing limbs and heads. To the right were three stone boxes containing earth and dead trees. To the left had been a shrine, now a heap of rubble, that had been meant for those faithful who felt unworthy to enter the temple proper. All was as it should be; nothing moved.

I'd tell you if anything was here, wouldn't I? Warrl grumbled at her lack of trust.

She felt one corner of her mouth twitch at his reply. *I can take it that all's well?*

Nothing out of the ordinary outside.

It's inside I'm worried about.

She saluted Kethry briefly, seeing the strained, anxious face peering whitely up at her in the moon-shadows, then slipped over the top to land on cat-quiet feet in the temple courtyard.

She slid carefully along the wall, left foot testing the ground at the base of it for loose pebbles that might slip underfoot or be kicked away by accident.

The moon was behind her; so her side of the wall was entirely in shadow so long as she stayed close to it. Five steps—twenty—fifty—her outstretched hand encountered a hinge, and wood. She'd come to the gate.

She felt for the bar and eased it along its sockets until one half of the gate was freed. That gave Kethry her way in; now she would scout ahead.

She waited for another of those scudding cloud-shadows; joining it as it raced across the courtyard. Cobblestones were hard and a trifle slippery beneath her thin-soled boots; she was glad that the first sole was of tough, abrasive sharkskin. Dew was already beginning to collect on the cold stones, making them slick, but the sharkskin leather gave her traction.

She reached the shelter of the temple entrance without incident; Warrl was waiting for her there, a slightly darker shadow in the shadows of the doorway.

Ready? she asked him. She felt his assent.

She reached for the door, prepared to find it locked, and was pleasantly surprised when it wasn't. She nudged it open a crack; when nothing happened, she opened it enough to peer carefully inside.

She saw nothing but a barren antechamber. Warrl stuck his nose inside, and sniffed cautiously.

Nothing here—but something on the other side of the door beyond; people for sure—and, I think, blood and incense. And magic, lots of magic.

Tarma sighed; it would have been nice if this had been a false alarm. *Sounds like we've come to the right place.*

Shouldn't we wait for Kethry?

You go after her; I want to make sure there isn't anyone on guard in there.

Not yet. I want to know you aren't biting off more than you can swallow. Warrl waited for her to move on, one shadow among many.

She slipped in through the crack in the door, Warrl a hairsbreadth behind her. Moonlight shone down through a skylight above. The door on the other side of the antechamber stood open; between it and the door she had entered through was nothing but untracked dust.

She hugged the wall, easing carefully around the doorpost. Once inside the sanctuary she could barely see her own hands; she continued to hug the wall, making her way by feel alone. She came to a corner, paused for a moment, and tried to see, but could only make out dim shapes in the small amount of light that came from various holes in the ceiling of the sanctuary. It was impossible to tell if those sources of light were more skylights, or the evidence of neglect. Dust filled the air, making her nose itch; other than that, lacking Warrl's senses, she could only smell damp and mildew. The stones beneath her hands were cold and slightly moist. Beneath the film of moisture they were smooth and felt a little like polished granite.

She went on, coming at last around behind the statue of the rain-god that stood at the far end of the room. The shadows were even deeper here; she slowed her pace to inch along the stuccoed wall, one hand feeling before her.

Then her hand encountered emptiness.

A door.

I can tell that! A door to where?

To where the blood-smell is.

Then we take it. I'm going on ahead; you go back and fetch Kethry.

Now she was alone in pitchy darkness, with only the rough brick wall of the corridor as a guide, and the faint sound of her footsteps bouncing off the walls to tell her that it *was* a corridor. She held back impatience and continued to feel her way with extreme caution—until once again her hand encountered open air.

She was suddenly awash with light, frozen by it, surrounded by it on all sides. She would have been prepared for any attack but this, which left her blind and helpless, with tears of pain blurring what

261

little vision she had. She went automatically into a defensive crouch, pulling her blade over her head with both hands from the sheath on her back; only to hear a laugh like a dozen brass bells from some point above her head.

"Little warrior," the voice said caressingly. "I have so longed for the day when we might meet again."

"I can't say I feel the same about you," Tarma replied after a bit, trying to locate the demon by sound alone. "I suppose it's too much to expect you to stand and fight me honorably?" She could see nothing but angry red light, like flame, but without the heat; perhaps the light was a little brighter above and just in front of her. She tried to will her eyes to work, but they remained dazzled, with lances of pain shooting into her skull every time she blinked. There was a smell of blood and sex and something more that she couldn't quite identify. Her heart was racing wildly with fear, but she was determined not to let *him* see how helpless she felt.

"Honor is for fools—and I may have been a fool in the past, but I am no longer quite so gullible. No, little warrior, I shall not stand and fight you. I shall not fight you at all. I shall simply—put you to sleep."

A sickly sweet aroma began to weave around her, and Tarma recognized it after a moment as black *tran*-dust; the most powerful narcotic she knew of. She had only that moment of recognition before she felt her control over herself suddenly melt away; her entire body went numb in a single breath, and she fell face down on the floor, mind and body alike paralyzed, sword falling from a hand that could no longer hold it.

And now that you cannot fight me, said a silky voice in her mind, *I shall make of you what I will . . . and somewhat more to my taste than the ice-creature you are now. And this time your Goddess shall not be able to help you. I am nearly a god now myself, and the gods are forbidden to war upon other gods.*

262

The last thing she heard was his laughter, like bronze bells slightly out of tune with one another.

Kethry fretted inwardly, counting down the moments until she was supposed to try the gate. This was the hardest part, for certain; the waiting. Anything else she could manage with equanimity. Waiting brought out the worst fears, roused her imagination to a fever pitch. The plan was for Tarma and Warrl to check the courtyard, then unlock the gates for her. They would precede her into the temple as well. They were to meet in the sanctuary, after Tarma had declared it free of physical hazards.

It was a plan Kethry found herself misliking more with every passing moment. They were a team; it went against the grain to work separately. Granted, Warrl was with Tarma; granted that she was something of a handicap in a skulk-and-hide situation like this—still, Kethry couldn't help thinking that *she'd* be able to detect dangers neither of the other two would notice. More than that—her place was *with* Tarma, not waiting in the wings. Now she began to wish she hadn't told the Shin'a'in that she intended to investigate this place. If she'd kept her mouth shut, she could have done this properly, by daylight, perhaps. Finally her impatience became too much; she felt her way along the wall to the wooden gates, and pushed very slightly on one of them.

It moved.

Tarma had succeeded in this much, anyway; the gates were now unbarred.

She pushed a little harder, slowly, carefully. The gate swung open just enough for her to squeeze herself through, scraping herself on the wooden bulwarks both fore and aft as she did so.

Before her lay the courtyard, mostly open ground.

Remembering all Tarma had taught her, she crouched as low as she could, waited until the moon passed behind a cloud, and sprinted for the shelter of the dried-up fountain.

Under the rim, in shadows, she looked around; watching not for objects, but for movement, any movement. But there was no movement, anomalous or otherwise. She crawled under the rim until she lay hidden on the side facing the temple doors.

She watched, but saw nothing; she listened, but heard only crickets and toads. She waited, aching from the strain of holding herself still in such an awkward position, until the moon again went behind a cloud.

She sprinted for the temple doors, flinging herself against the wall of the temple behind a pillar as soon as she reached them. It was then that she realized that there had been something very anomalous at the gate.

The aged gates, allegedly locked for fifteen years, had opened smoothly and without a sound—as if they had been oiled and put into working order within the past several days.

Something was very wrong.

A shadow bulked in front of her, and she started with alarm; she pulled the sword in a defensive move before she realized that her "enemy" was Warrl.

He reached for her arm and his teeth closed gently on her tunic; he tugged at her sleeve. That meant Tarma wanted her.

"You didn't meet with anything?" Kethry whispered.

Warrl snorted. *I think that they are all asleep or blind. A cub could have penetrated this place.*

This was too easy; all her instincts were in an uproar. Too easy by far. She suddenly realized what their easy access to this place meant. This was a trap!

And now Kethry felt a shrill alarm course through her every nerve—a double alarm. Need was alerting her to a woman in the deadliest danger, and very nearby—

264

—and the bond of *she'enedran* was resonating with soul-deep threat to her blood-sister. Tarma was in trouble.

As if to confirm her fears, Warrl threw up his head and voiced his battle-cry, and charged within, leaving Kethry behind.

And given the urgency of Need's pull, that could only mean one thing.

Thalhkarsh *was* here—and he had the Sworn One at his nonexistent mercy.

The time for subterfuge was over.

Kethry pulled her ensorcelled blade with her left hand, and caused a blue-green witchlight to dance before her with a gesture from her right; then kicked open the doors of the temple and flung herself frantically through them. She landed hard against the dingy white-plastered wall of a tiny, cobwebbed anteroom, bruising her shoulder; and found herself staring foolishly at an empty chamber.

Another door stood in the opposite wall, slightly ajar. She inched along the wall and eased it open with the tip of her blade. The witchlight showed nothing beyond it but a brick-walled tunnel that led deeper into the temple proper. Warrl must already have run down this way.

She moved stealthily through the door, and into the corridor, praying to find Tarma, and soon. The internal alerts of both her blade and her blood-bond were nigh-unbearable, and she hardly dared contemplate what that meant to Tarma's well-being.

But the corridor twisted and turned like a *kadessa*-run, seemingly without end. With every new corner she expected to find *something*—but every time she rounded a corner she saw only another long, dust-choked extension of the corridor behind her. The dust showed no tracks at all, not even Warrl's. Could she have somehow come the wrong way? But there were only two directions to choose—forward, or back the way she had come. Back she would never go; that left only forward. And forward was yard after yard of blank-walled corridor, with never a door or a break of any kind. She slunk on and on in a kind of nightmarish entrancement in which she lost all track of time; there was only the endlessly turning corridor before her and the cry for help within her. Nothing else seemed of any import at all. As the urgings of her geas-blade Need and the bond that tied her to Tarma grew more and more frantic, she was close to being driven nearly mad with fear and frustration. She was being distracted; so successfully in fact, that it wasn't until she'd wasted far too much precious time trying to thread the maze that she realized what it must be—

—a magical construct, meant to delay her, augmented by spells of befuddlement.

"You *bastard!*" she screamed at the invisible Thalhkarsh, enraged by his duplicity. He had made a serious mistake in doing something that caused her to become angry; that rage was useful, it fueled her power. She gathered it to her, made a force of it instead of allowing it to fade uselessly; sought and found the weak point of the spell. She sheathed Need, and spreading her arms wide over her head, palms facing each other, blasted with the white-heat of her anger.

Mage-energies formed a glowing blue-white arc between her upraised hands; a sorcerer's wind began to stir around her, forming a miniature whirlwind with herself as the eye. With a flick of her wrists she reversed her hands to hold them palm-outward and brought her arms down fully extended to shoulder height; the mage-light poured from them to form a wall around her, then the wall expanded outward. The brick corridor walls about her flared with scarlet as the glowing wall of energy touched them; they shivered beneath the wrath-fired mage-blast, wavered and warped like the mirages they were. There was a moment of resistance; then, soundlessly, they vanished.

She saw she was standing in what had been the outer, common sanctuary; an enormous room, supported by two rows of pillars whose tops were lost in the shadows of the ceiling. Tracks in the dust showed she had been tracing the same circling path all the time she had thought she was traversing the corridor. Her anger brightened the witchlight; the green-blue glow revealed the far end of the sanctuary —the forgotten god stood there, behind his altar. The statue of the gentle god of rains had a forlorn look; he and his altar were covered with a blanket of dust and cobwebs. Dust lay undisturbed nearly everywhere.

Nearly everywhere—she was not the expert tracker Tarma was, but it did not take an expert to read the trail that passed from the front doors to somewhere behind the god's statue. And in those dust tracks were paw prints.

Desperate to waste no more time, she pulled her blade again and broke into a run, her blue-green witchlight bobbing before her, intent on following that trail to wherever it led. She passed by the neglected altar with never a second glance, and found the priests' door at the end of the trace in the dust; it lay just behind and beneath the statue. It had never been intended to be concealed, and besides stood wide open. She sent the witchlight shooting ahead of her and sprinted inside, panting a little.

But the echoes of running feet ahead of her as she passed into another brick-walled corridor told her that her spell-breaking had not gone unnoticed.

Common sense and logic said she should find a corner to put her back against and make a stand.

Therefore she did nothing of the kind.

As the first of four armed mercenaries came pounding into view around a corner ahead, she took Need in both hands and charged him, shrieking at the top of her lungs. Her berserk attack took the demon-hireling by surprise; he stopped dead in his tracks, staring, and belatedly raised his own weapon. His hesitation sealed his doom. Kethry let the eldritch power of Need control her body, and the bespelled blade responded to the freedom by moving her in a lightning blow at his unprotected side. Screaming in pain, the fighter fell, arm sheared off at the shoulder.

The second hired thug was a little quicker to defend himself, but he, too, was no match for Need's spell-imparted skill. Kethry cracked his wooden shield in half with a strength far exceeding what she alone possessed, and swatted his blade out of his hands after only two exchanges, sending it clattering against the wall. She ran him through before he could flee her.

The third and fourth sought to take her while— they presumed—Kethry's blade was still held fast in the collapsing body. They presumed too much; Need freed itself and spun Kethry around to meet and counter both their strokes in a display of swordsmanship a master would envy. They saw death staring at them from the witchlight reflected on the blood-dripping blade, from the hate-filled green eyes.

It was more than they had the stomach to face— and their lives were worth far more to them than their pay. They turned and fled back down the way they had come, with Kethry in hot pursuit, too filled with berserk anger now to think that a charge into unknown danger might not be a wise notion.

There was light ahead, Kethry noticed absently, allowing her rage to speed her feet. That might mean there were others there—and perhaps the demon.

The hirelings ran to the light as to sanctuary; Kethry followed—

She stumbled to a halt, at first half-blinded by the light; then when her eyes adjusted, tripped on nothing and nearly fell to her knees, her mind and heart going numb at what she saw.

This had once been the inner temple; Thalhkarsh had transformed it into his own perverted place of unholiness. It had the red-lit look of a seraglio in hell. It had been decorated with the same sort of carvings that had ornamented the demon's temple back in Delton. The subject was sexual; every perversion possible was depicted, provided that it included pain and suffering.

The far end of the room had been made into a kind of platform, covered in silk and velvet cushions, plushly upholstered. It was a clichéd setting; an overdone backdrop for an orgy. The demon certainly enjoyed invoking pain, but it appeared that he himself preferred not to suffer the slightest discomfort while he was amusing himself. The platform was occupied by a clutch of writhing nude and partially clothed bodies. Only now were some of those on the platform beginning to disengage and take notice of the hirelings fleeing for the door on the opposite side. Evidently not even the demon foresaw that Kethry would be able to get this far on her own.

The demon and his followers had been interrupted by her entrance at the height of their pleasures. And it was the sight of the demon's partner that had stricken Kethry to the heart—for the one being used by the demon himself was Tarma.

But it was Tarma transformed; she wore the face and body the demon had given her when he had first tried to seduce her to his cause. Though smaller and far frailer, she was still recognizably herself—but with all her angularities softened, her harshness made silken, her flaws turned to beauty. Her clothing was in rags, and she had the bruises and the look of a woman who has been passed from one brutal rape to another. That was bad enough, but that was not what had struck Kethry like a dagger to the heart; it was the absence of any mind or sense in Tarma's blank blue eyes.

Tarma had survived rape before; were she still aware and in charge of herself, she would still be fighting. Mere brutal use would not have forced her mind from her, not when the slaughter of her entire Clan as well as her own abuse had failed to do that when she was a young woman and far more

269

innocent than she was now. No—this *had* to be the work of the demon. Knowing he would be unable to break her spirit, Thalhkarsh had stolen Tarma's mind; stolen her mind or somehow forced her soul out of her body.

The demon, wearing his form of a tall, beautiful human male, was the first to recover from surprise at the interruption.

"Amusing," he said, not appearing at all amused. "I had thought the skill of those I had paid would more than equal yours, even with that puny blade to augment it. It appears that I was mistaken."

Before Kethry could make a move, he had seized Tarma, and pulled her before him—not as a shield, but with evident threat.

"Put up your blade, sorceress," he purred brazenly, "or I tear her limb from limb."

Kethry knew he was not bluffing, and Need clattered to the floor from her nerveless hand.

He laughed, a hideous howl of triumph. "You disappoint me, my enemy! You have made my conquest too easy!" He stood up and tossed Tarma aside; she fell to the pile of cushions with the limpness of a lifeless doll, not even attempting to break her own fall. "Come forth, my little toy—" he continued, turning his back on his fallen victim and beckoning to someone lurking behind the platform.

From out of the shadows among the hangings came a woman, and when she stepped far enough into the light that Kethry was able to get a good look at her, the sorceress reeled as if she had been struck. It couldn't be—

The woman was the twin of an image she herself had once worn—and that she had placed on the unconscious form of the marauding bandit Lastel Longknife by way of appropriate punishment for the women and girls he had used and murdered. It was an image she had never expected to see again; she had assumed the bandit would have been treated with brutality equaling his own by what was left

270

of his fellows. By all rights, he should have been dead—long dead.

"I think the bitch recognizes me, *my lord*," the dulcet voice said, heavy irony in the title of subservience. Platinum hair was pushed back from amethyst eyes with a graceful but impatient hand.

"You never expected to see me again, did you?" Her eyes blazed with helpless anger. "May every god damn you for what you did to me, woman. Death would have been better than the misery this *shape* put me through! If it hadn't been for a forgotten sword and an untied horse—"

She came closer, hands crooked into claws. "I've dreamed of having you in my hands every night since, gods—but *not like this*." Her eyes betrayed that she was walking a very thin thread of sanity. "What you did to me was bad enough—but being trapped in this prison of a whore's carcass is more than I can bear—it's worse than Hell, it's—"

She turned away, clenching her hands so tightly that the knuckles popped. After a moment of internal struggle she regained control over herself, and turned to the demon. "Well, since it was my tales to the priests that lured them here, the time has come for you to keep *your* side of the bargain."

"You wish to lose your current form? A pity—I had thought you had come to enjoy my attentions."

The woman colored; Kethry was baffled. She had only placed the *illusion* of being female on the bandit, but this—this was a real woman! Mage-sight showed only exactly what stood before her in normal-sight, not the bandit of the desert hills!

"Damn you," she snarled. "Oh, gods, for a demon-slaying blade! Yes, you *bastard*, I enjoy it! As you very well know, squirming like a vile snake inside my head! You've made me your slave as well as your puppet; you've addicted me to you, and you revel in my misery—you cursed me far worse than ever she did. And now, damn you, I want free of it and you and all else besides! I've paid my part of the bargain. Now you live up to your side!"

271

Thalhkarsh smiled cruelly. "Very well, my pretty little toy—go and take her lovely throat in both your hands, and I shall free you of that body with her death."

One of the acolytes scuttled around behind Kethry and seized her arms, pinioning them behind her back. He needn't have bothered; she was so in shock she couldn't have moved if the ceiling had begun to fall in on them. The slender beauty approached, stark, bitter hatred in her eyes, and seized Kethry's throat.

A howl echoed from behind her; a hurtling black shape leaped over her straight at the demon. It was Warrl—who evidently had met the same kind of delaying tactics as Kethry had. Now he had broken free of them, and he was in a killing rage. *This* time Thalhkarsh took no chances with Warrl; from his upraised hands came double bolts of crimson lightning. Warrl was hit squarely in midair by both of them. He shrieked horribly, transfixed six feet above the floor, caught and held in midleap. He writhed once, shrieked again—then went limp. The aura of the demon's magic faded; the body of the *kyree* dropped to the ground like a shot bird, and did not move again.

Lastel was not in the least distracted by this; she tightened her hands around Kethry's neck. Kethry struggled belatedly to free herself, managing to bring her heel down on the foot of the acolyte behind her, catching him squarely in the instep so that he yowled and dropped to the floor, clutching his ruined foot.

But even when her arms were free, she was powerless against the bandit; she scratched at Lastel's hands and reached for her eyes with crooked fingers—uselessly. Her own hands would not respond; her lungs screamed for air, and she began to black out.

The demon laughed, and again raised his hands; Kethry felt as if she'd been plunged into the heart of a fire. Crackling energies surrounded both of them; her legs gave beneath her and it was only

272

when a new acolyte caught her arms and held her up that she remained erect. With narrowing vision she stared into Lastel's pale eyes, unable to look away—

And suddenly she found herself staring down into her own face, with her own neck between her hands! Kethry released her grip with a cry of disbelief; stared down at at her hands, at herself, horror written plain on her own face. Lastel stared up at her out of her own eyes, hatred and black despair making a twisted mask of her face.

The demon laughed at both of them, cruel enjoyment plain in his tone. He eased off the monstrous pile of silks and stalked proudly toward them, sweeping the bandit up onto her feet and into his arms as he came to stand over Kethry, who had sagged to her knees in shock.

"I promised to change your form, fool—I did *not* promise into what image!" he chortled. "And you, witch—I have your rightful body in my keeping now—and you will never, never reverse a spell to which I and I alone hold the key!"

He gestured at his acolyte, who dropped his hold on Kethry-now-Lastel and seized Lastel-now-Kethry's arms instead, hauling her roughly to her feet.

"My foolish sorceress, my equally foolish toy, how easy it is to manipulate you! Little toy, did you truly think that I would release you when you take such delight in my attentions? That I would allow such a potent source of misery out of my possession? As for you, dear enemy—I have only begun to take my revenge upon you. I shall leave you alive, and in full possession of your senses—unlike your sword-sister. No doubt you wonder what I have done with her? I have wiped her mind clean; in time I shall implant my teachings in her, so that I shall have an acolyte of complete obedience and complete devotion. It was a pity that I could not force her to suffer as you shall, but her will combined with her link to her chosen goddess was far too strong to trifle with. But now that her mind is gone, the link has gone with it, and she will be mine for so long as I care to keep her."

Kethry was overwhelmed with agony and despair; she stifled a moan with difficulty. She felt tears burning her eyes and coursing down her cheeks; her vision was blurred by them. The demon smiled at the sight.

"As for you, you will be as potent a source of pain as my little toy is; know that you will feed my power with your grief and anguish. Know that your blood-sister will be my plaything, willingly suffering because I order it. Know all this, and know that you are helpless to prevent any of it! As for this—"

He prodded the body of Warrl with one toe. His smile spread even wider as she tried involuntarily to reach out, only to have the acolytes hold her arms back.

"I think that I shall find something suitable to use it for. Shall I have it mounted, or—yes. The fur is quite good; quite soft and unusual. I think I shall have it tanned—and it shall be your only bed, my enemy!"

He laughed, as Kethry struggled in the arms of his acolytes, stomach twisted and mind torn nearly in shreds by her grief and hatred of him. She subsided only when they threatened to wrench her arms out of their sockets, and hung limply in their grasp, panting with frustrated rage and weeping soundlessly.

"Take her, and take her friend. Put them in the place I prepared for them," Thalhkarsh ordered with a lift of one eyebrow. "And take *that* and *that* as well," he indicated the body of Warrl and Kethry's sword Need. "Put them where she can see them until I decide what to do with them. Perhaps, little toy, I shall give the blade to you."

Lastel's hands clenched and unclenched as he attempted to control himself. "Do it, damn you! If you do, I'll use it on you, you *bastard!*"

"How kind of you to warn me, then. But come—

you wear a new body now, and I wish to see how it differs from the old—don't you?"

Kethry's last sight of the demon was as he swept Lastel up onto the platform, then she and Tarma were hustled down another brick-lined corridor, and shoved roughly into a makeshift cage that took up the back half of a stone-lined storage room. Warrl's carcass and Need were both dumped unceremoniously on the slate table in front of the cage door.

The room lacked windows entirely, and had only the one door now shut and (from the sounds that had come after her guards had shut it), locked. Light came from a single torch in a holder near the door. The cage was made of crudely-forged iron bars welded across the entire room, with an equally crude door of similar bars that had been padlocked closed. There was nothing whatsoever in the cage; she and Tarma had only what they were wearing, which in Tarma's case was little more than rags, and in hers, the simple shift and breeches Lastel had been wearing. Though she searched, she found no weapons at all.

Tarma sat blank-eyed in the corner of the cage where she'd been left, rocking back and forth and humming tunelessly to herself. The only thing that the demon hadn't changed was her voice; still the ruined parody of what it had been before the slaughter of her Clan.

Kethry went to her and knelt on the cold stone at her side. "Tarma?" she asked, taking her *she'enedra's* hand in hers and staring into those blank blue eyes.

She got no response for a moment, then the eyes seemed to see her. One hand crept up, and Tarma inserted the tip of her index finger into her mouth.

"Tarma?" the Shin'a'in echoed ingenuously. And that was all of intelligence that Kethry could coax from her; within moments her eyes had gone blank again, and she was back to her rocking and tuneless humming.

Kethry looked from the mindless Tarma to the

275

body of the *kyree* and back again, slow tears etching their way down her cheeks.

"My god, my god—" she wept, "Oh, Tarma, you were right! We should have gone for help."

She tried to take her oathkin in her arms, but it was like holding a stiff, wooden doll.

"If I hadn't been so *damned* sure of myself—if I hadn't been so determined to prove you were smothering me—it's all my fault, it's *all* my fault! What have I done? What has my pride done to you?"

And Tarma rocked and crooned, oblivious to everything around her, while she wept with absolute despair.

Eleven

You lied to me, you bastard!" Green eyes blazed passionately with anger.

"You didn't listen carefully enough," Thalhkarsh replied to the amber-haired hellion whom he had backed into a corner of his "couch." "I said I would change your form; I never said *what* I would change it into."

"You never had any intention of changing me back to a man!" Lastel choked, sagging to the padded platform, almost incoherent with rage.

"Quite right." The demon grinned maliciously as he sat himself cross-legged on the padded platform, carefully positioning himself so as to make escape impossible. "Your emotions are strong; you are a potent source of power for me, and an ever-renewable source. I had no intention of letting you free of me while I still need you." He arranged himself more comfortably with the aid of a cushion or two; he had Lastel neatly pinned, and his otherworldly strength and speed would enable him to counter any move the woman made.

"Then *when?*"

"When shall I release you? Fool, don't you *ever* think past the immediate moment?" For once the molten-bronze face lost its mocking expression; the glowing red-gold eyes looked frustrated. "Why should you *want* release? What would you do if I gave you back your previous form—where would you go? Back to your wastelands, back to misery, back to petty theft? Back to a life with every man's hand against you, having to hide like a desert rat? Is that what you *want?*"

"I—"

"Fool; blind, stupid fool! Your lust for power is nearly as great as my own, yet you could accomplish *nothing* by yourself and *everything* with my aid!" the demon rose to his feet, gesticulating. "Think—for one moment, think! You are in a mage-Talented body now; one in which the currents of arcane power flow strongly. You could have me as a patron. You could have all the advantages of being my own High Prelate when I am made a god! And you wish to throw this all away? Simply because you do not care for the responses of a perfectly healthy and attractive body?"

"But it isn't *mine!* It's a woman!" Lastel shrank back into the corner, wailing. "I don't *want* this body—"

"But I want you in it. I desire you, creature I have made; I want you in a form attractive to me." The demon came closer and placed his hands on the walls to either side of Lastel, effectively rendering her immobile. "Your emotions run so high, and taste so sweetly to me that I sometimes think I shall never release you."

"Why?" Lastel whispered. "Why me, why this? And why *here?* I thought all your kind hated this world."

"Not I." The demon's eyes smoldered as his expression turned thoughtful. "Your world is beautiful in my eyes; your people have aroused more than my hunger, they have aroused my desire. I want this world, and I want the people in it! And I *will* have it! Just as I shall have you."

"No—" Lastel whimpered.

"Then I ask in turn, why? Or why not? What have I done save rouse your own passions? You are well fed, well clothed, well housed—nor have I ever harmed you physically."

"You're *killing* me!" Lastel cried, his voice breaking. "You're destroying my identity! Every time you look at me, every time you touch me, I forget what it was ever like, being a man! All I want is to be *your* shadow, your servant; I want to exist only for you! I never come back to myself until after you've gone, and it takes longer to remember what I was afterward—longer every time you do this to me."

The demon smiled again with his former cruelty, and brought his lips in to brush her neck. "Then, little toy," he murmured, "perhaps it is something best forgotten?"

Tarma was lost; without sight, without hearing, without senses of any kind. Held there, and drained weak past any hope of fighting back. So tired—too tired to fight. Too tired to hope, or even care. Emptied of every passion—

Wake UP!

The thin voice in her mind was the first sign that there was any life at all in the vast emptiness where she abode, alone. She strained to hear it again, feeling . . . something. Something besides the apathy that had claimed her.

Mind-mate, wake!

It was familiar. If only she could remember, remember anything at all.

Wake, wake, wake!

The voice was stronger, and had the feel of teeth in it. As if something large and powerful was closing fangs on her and shaking her. Teeth—

In the name of the Star-Eyed! the voice said, frantically. *You MUST wake!*

Teeth. Star-Eyed. Those things had meant something, before she had become nothing. Had meant something, when she was—

Tarma.

She was Tarma. She *was* Tarma still, Sworn One, *kyree*-friend, *she'enedra*.

Every bit of her identity that she regained brought more tiny pieces back with it, and more strength. She fought off the gray fog that threatened to steal those bits away, fought and held them, and put more and more of herself together, fighting back inch by inch. She was Shin'a'in, of the free folk of the open plains—she would not be held and prisoned! She—would—not—be—held!

Now she felt pain, and welcomed it, for it was one more bridge to reality. Salvation lay in pain, not in the gray fog that sucked the pain and everything else away from her. She held the pain to her, cherished it, and reached for the voice in her mind.

She found that, too, and held to it, while it rejoiced fiercely that she had found it.

No—not *it*. *He*. The *kyree*, the mage-beast. Warrl. The friend of her soul, as Kethry was of her heart.

As if that recognition had broken the last strand of foul magic holding her in the gray place, she suddenly found herself possessed again of a body—a body that ached in a way that was only too familiar. A body stiff and chilled, and sitting—from the feel of the air on her skin—nearly naked and on a cold stone floor. She could hear nothing but the sound of someone crying softly—and cautiously cracked her eyes open the merest slit to see where she was.

She was in a cage; she could see the iron bars before her, but unless she changed position and moved, she couldn't see much else. She closed her eyes again in an attempt to remember what could have brought her to this pass. Her memories tumbled together, confused, as she tried with an aching skull to sort them out.

But after a moment, it all came back to her, and with it, a rush of anger and hatred.

Thalhkarsh!

The demon—he'd tricked her, trapped her—then overpowered her, changed her, and done—something to her to send her into that gray place. But if Thalhkarsh had taken her, then where were Warrl and Kethry?

I'm lying on the table, mind-mate, said the voice, *The demon thinks he killed me; he nearly did. His magic sent me into little-death, and I decided to con-*

tinue the trance until we were all alone; it seemed safer that way. There was nothing I could do for you. Your she'enedra is in the same cage as you. It would be nice to let her know the demon hasn't destroyed your mind after all. She thinks that you're worse than dead, and blames herself entirely for what was both your folly.

Tarma moved her head cautiously; her muscles all ached. There *was* someone in the cage with her, crumpled in a heap in the corner; by the shaking of her shoulders, the source of the weeping—but—

That's not Kethry!

Not her body, but her spirit. The demon gave her body to the bandit.

What bandit?

The *kyree* gave a mental growl. *It's too hard to explain; I'm going to break the trance. Tend to your she'enedra.*

Tarma licked lips that were swollen and bruised. She'd felt this badly used once before, a time she preferred not to think about.

There was something missing; something missing—

"No," she whispered, eyes opening wide with shock, all thought driven from her in that instant by her realization of *what* was missing. "Oh, *no!*"

The stranger's head snapped up; swollen and red-rimmed amethyst eyes turned toward her. "T-t-tarma?"

"It's gone," she choked, unable to comprehend her loss. "The *vysaka*—the Goddess-bond—it's *gone!*" She could feel her sanity slipping; feel herself going over the edge. Without the Goddess-bond—

Take hold of yourself! the voice in her mind snapped. *It's probably all that damn demon's fault; break his spells and it will come back! And anyway, you're alive and I'm alive and Kethry's alive; I want us all to STAY that way!*

Warrl's annoyance was like a slap in the face; it brought her back to a precarious sanity. And with his reminder that Kethry was still alive, she turned

281

back toward the stranger whose tear-streaked face peered through the gloom at her.

"Keth? Is that you?"

"You're back! Oh, Goddess bless, you're back!" The platinum-haired beauty flung herself into Tarma's arms, and clung there. "I thought he'd destroyed you, and it was all my fault for insisting that we do this ourselves instead of going for help like you wanted."

"Here, now." Tarma gulped back tears of her own, and pushed Kethry away with hands that shook. "We're not out of this yet."

"T-tarma—Warrl—he's—"

Very much alive, thank you. The great furry shape on the table outside their cage rose slowly to its four feet, and shook itself painfully. *I hurt. If you hurt like I hurt, we are all in very sad condition.*

Tarma sympathized with Kethry's bewilderment. "He pulled a *kyree* trick on us all, *she'enedra.* He told me that when the demon's magic hit him, it sent him into little-death—a kind of trance. He figured it was better to stay that way until we were alone." She examined the confused countenance before her. "He also said something about you trading bodies with a bandit . . . and don't I know that face?"

"Lastel Longknife," she replied shakily. "He lived; he's the one that had Thalhkarsh conjured up, and I guess he got more than he bargained for, because the demon turned him into a real woman. He was the one spreading the rumors to lure us in here, I'll bet. Now he's got *my* body—"

"I have the sinking feeling that you're going to tell me you can't work magic in this one."

"Not very well," she admitted. "Though I haven't tried any of the power magics that need more training than Talent."

"All right then; we can't magic our way out of this cage, let's see if we can think our way out."

Tarma did her best to ignore the aching void within her and took careful stock of the situation.

282

Their prison consisted of the back half of a stone-walled room; crude iron bars welded across the middle made their half into a cage. It had an equally crude door, padlocked shut. There was only one door to the room itself, in the front half, and there were no windows; the floor was of slate. In half of the room beyond their cage was a table on which Warrl—and something else—lay.

"Fur-face, is that Need next to you?"

The same.

"Then Thalhkarsh just made one big mistake," she said, narrowing her eyes with grim satisfaction. "Get your tail over here, and bring the blade with you."

Warrl snorted, picked up the hilt of the blade gingerly in his mouth, and jumped down off the table with it. He dragged it across the floor, complaining mentally to Tarma the entire time.

"All right, Keth. I saw that thing shear clean through armor and more than once. Have a crack at the latch. It'll have to be you, she won't answer physically to me."

"But—" Kethry looked doubtfully at the frail arms of her new body, then told herself sternly to remember that Need was a *magical* weapon, that it responded (as the runes on its blade said) to woman's need. And they certainly needed out of this prison—

She raised the sword high over her head, and brought it down on the latch-bar with all of her strength.

With a shriek like a dying thing, the metal sheared neatly in two, and the door swung open.

"You are bold, priest," the demon rumbled.

"I am curious; perhaps foolish—but never bold," responded the plump, balding priest of Anathei. "I was curious when I first heard the rumors of your return. I was even more curious when the two who were responsible for your defeat before were missing this morning. I will confess to being quite confused to find one of them here."

He cast a meaningful glance at the demon's companion, curled sullenly on the velvet beside him. The sorceress did not appear to be happy, but she also did not appear coerced in any way. Come to that, there was something oddly different about her. . . .

"I repeat, you are bold; but you amuse me. Why are you here?" Thalhkarsh settled back onto his cushions, and with a flicker of thought increased the intensity of the light coming from his crimson lanterns. The musky incense he favored wafted upward toward the ceiling from a brazier at the edge of the padded platform where he reclined. This priest had presented himself at the door and simply asked to be taken to the demon; Thalhkarsh's followers had been so nonplussed by his quiet air of authority that they had done as he asked. Now he stood before Thalhkarsh, an unimpressive figure in a plain brown cassock, plump and aging, with his hands tucked into the sleeves of his robe. And he, in his turn, did not seem the least afraid of the demon; nor did it appear that anything, from the obscene carvings to the orgy still in progress on the platform behind the demon, was bothering him the slightest bit.

And that had the demon thoroughly puzzled.

"I am here to try to convince you that what you are doing is wrong."

"Wrong? *Wrong?*" The demon laughed heartily. "I could break you with one finger, and you wish to tell me that I am guilty of doing wrong?"

"Since you seem to wish to live in this world, you must live by some of its rules—and one of those is that to cause harm or pain to another is wrong."

"And who will punish me, priest?" The demon's eyes glowed redly, his lips thinning in anger. "You?"

"You yourself will cause your own punishment," the priest replied earnestly. "For by your actions

284

you will drive away what even you must need—admiration, trust, friendship, love—"

He was interrupted by the sound of shouting and of clashing blades; he stared in surprise to see Tarma—a transformed Tarma—wearing an acolyte's tunic and nothing else, charging into the room driving several guards ahead of her. And with her was the platinum-haired child he had last seen at his own temple, telling his brothers of the rumors of Thalhkarsh.

But the blade in her hands was the one he had last seen in the sorceress' hands.

The woman at the demon's side made a tight little sound of smothered rage as the demon's guards moved to bar the exits or interpose themselves between the women and their target.

"Your anger is strong, little toy," Thalhkarsh laughed, looking down at her. "Use it, then. Become the instrument of my revenge. Kill her, and this time I promise you that I shall give you your man's body back." He plucked a sword from the hand of the guard next to him and handed it to his amber-tressed companion.

And the priest stared in complete bewilderment.

Given the weapon, the bandit needed no further urging, and flung himself at Kethry's throat.

Kethry, now no longer the tough, fit creature she had been, but a frail, delicate wraith, went down before him. Tarma tried to get to her, knowing that she was going to be too late—

But Warrl intervened, bursting from behind the crimson velvet hangings, flinging himself between the combatants long enough for Kethry to regain her footing and recover Need. She fumbled it up into a pathetic semblance of guard position; then stared at her own hands, wearing a stupified expression. After a moment Tarma realized why. Need was not responding to her—because Need could not act against a woman, not even *for* a woman.

285

And between Tarma and her *she'enedra* were a dozen or so followers of the demon.

But some of them were the ones who had so lately been sharing her own body with their master.

She let herself, for the first time since her awakening, truly *realize* what had been done to her—physically and mentally. Within an eyeblink she had roused herself to a killing battle-frenzy, a state in which all her senses were heightened, her reactions quickened, her strength nearly doubled. She would pay for this energized state later—if there *was* a later.

She gathered herself carefully, and sprang at the nearest, taking with her one of the heavy silken hangings that had been nearest her. She managed, despite the handicap of no longer having *her* rightful, battle-trained body, to catch him by surprise and tangle him in the folds of it. The only weapon the Shin'a'in had been able to find had been a heavy dagger; before the others had a chance to react to her first rush, she stabbed down at him, taking a fierce pleasure in plunging it into him again and again, until the silk was dyed scarlet with his blood—

Kethry was defending herself as best she could; only the fact that the bandit was once again not in a body that was his own was giving her any chance at all. Warrl's appearance had given her a brief moment of aid when she most needed it. Now Warrl was busy with one of the other acolytes. And it was apparent that Tarma, too, had her hands full, though she was showing a good portion of her old speed and skill. At least she wasn't in that shocked and bereft half-daze she'd fallen into when she first came back to herself.

But Kethry had enough to think about; she could only spare a scant second to rejoice at Tarma's recovery. She was doing more dodging than anything else; the bandit was plainly out for her death. As had occurred once before, the demon was merely

286

watching, content to let his pawns play out their moves before making any of his own.

Tarma had taken a torch and set the trapped acolyte aflame, laughing wildly when he tried to free himself of the entangling folds of the silk coverlet and succeeding only in getting in the way of those that remained. Warrl had disposed of one, and was heading off a second. Kethry was facing a terrible dilemma—Need *was* responding sluggishly now, but only in pure defense. She knew she dared not kill the former bandit. If she did, there would be no chance of ever getting her own body back. There was no way of telling what would happen if she killed what was, essentially, *her* body. She might survive, trapped in this helpless form that lacked the stamina and strength and mage-Talents of her own—or she might die along with her body.

Nor did she have any notion of what *Need* might do to her if she killed another woman. Possibly nothing—or the magical backlash of breaking the geas might well leave her a burned-out husk, a fate far worse than simply dying.

Now Tarma had laid hands on another sword— one lighter than the broadsword she was used to, and with an odd curve to it. She had never used a weapon quite like this before, but a blade was a blade. The rest of the acolytes made a rush for her, forgetting for the moment—if, indeed, they had ever known—that they were not dealing with an essentially helpless woman, given momentary strength by hysteria, but a highly trained martial artist. Tarma's anger and hysteria were as carefully channeled as a powerful stream diverted to turn a mill. As they rushed her, evidently intending to overpower her by sheer numbers, she took the hilt in both hands, rose and pivoted in one motion, and made a powerful, sweeping cut at waist level that literally sliced four of them in half.

Somewhere, far in the back of her mind, a normally calm, analytical part of her went wild with joy. This strange sword was better than any blade she'd ever used before; the curve kept it from lodging, the edge was as keen as the breath of the North Wind, and the grip, with a place for her to curl her forefinger around it, made it almost an extension of her hand. It was perfectly balanced for use by either one hand or two. Her eyes lit with a kind of fire, and it wasn't all the reflection of torch-flames.

Her remaining opponents stumbled over the bleeding, disemboweled bodies of their erstwhile comrades, shocked and numb by the turn in fortunes. Just last night this woman had been their plaything. Now she stood, blood-spattered and half-naked as she was, over the prone bodies of five of them. They hesitated, confused.

Warrl leapt on two from the rear, breaking the neck of one and driving the other onto Tarma's waiting blade.

Eight down, seven standing.

Seven? There were only six—

Tarma felt, more than saw, the approach of one from the rear. She pivoted, slashing behind her with the marvelously liquid blade as she did so, and caught him across the throat. Even as he went down, another, braver than the rest, lunged for her. Her kick caught him in the temple; his head snapped to one side and he fell, eyes glazing with more than unconsciousness; Warrl made sure of him with a single snap of his massive jaws, then dashed away again to vanish somewhere.

Five.

I come from behind you.

Tarma held her ground, and Warrl ran in from under the hangings. The man he jumped had both a short sword and shield, but failed to bring either up in time. Warrl tore his throat out and leapt away, leaving him to drown in his own blood.

Four.

Tarma charged between two of those remaining, slashing with a figure-eight motion, knowing they would hesitate to strike at her with the swords

288

they'd snatched from their sheaths for fear of striking each other. She caught the first across the eyes, the second across the gut. The one she'd blinded stumbled toward her with blood pouring between his fingers, and she finished him as she whirled around at the end of her rush.

Two.

Kethry tried to simply defend herself, but the bandit wasn't holding back.

So she did the only thing she could; she cast Need away from her, and backed off far enough to raise her hands over her head, preparatory to blasting the bandit with a bolt of arcane power.

Warrl leaped on the right-hand man; tore at his thigh and brought him down, then ripped out his gut. Tarma's final opponent was the first that showed any real ability or forethought; he was crouching where Warrl couldn't come at him from the rear, with a sword in one hand and a dagger in the other. His posture showed he was no stranger to the blade. She knew after a feint or two that he was very good, which was probably why he'd survived his other companions. Now she had a problem. There was no one to get in his way, and the unfamiliar feel of her transformed body was a distraction and a handicap. Then she saw his eyes narrow as she moved her new sword slightly—and knew she had a psychological weapon to use against him. This was *his* blade she held, and he wanted it back. Very badly.

She made her plan, and moved.

She pretended to make a short rush, then pretended to stumble, dropping the sword. When he grabbed for it, dropping his own blade, Tarma snatched a torch from the wall beside her and thrust it at his face, and when he winced away from it, grabbed a dagger from the litter of weapons on the floor and flung it straight for his throat, knowing that marksmanship was not a thing that depended on weight and balance, but on the coordination of hand and eye—things that wouldn't change even though her body had shifted form considerably. As he went down, gurgling and choking, to drown in his own blood like one of the men Warrl had taken out, she saw that Kethry was being forced to take the offensive—and saw the look of smug satisfaction on the demon's face as she did so.

And she realized with a sudden flash of insight that they had played right into his hands.

"Why do you do nothing?" the little priest asked in pure confusion.

"Because this is a test, human," the demon replied, watching with legs stretched out comfortably along the platform. "I have planned for this, though I shall admit candidly to you that I did not expect this moment to come quite so soon, nor did I expect that the beast should regain its life and the swordswoman her mind. But these are minor flaws in my plan; however it comes out, I shall win. As you may have guessed, it is the sorceress' spirit that inhabits my servant's body; should he slay her, I shall be well rid of her, and my servant in possession of a mage-Talented form. Should the swordswoman die, I shall be equally well rid of her; should she live, I shall simply deal with her as I did before. Should my servant die, I shall still have the sorceress, and her geas-blade will blast her for harming a woman, even though she does not hold it in her hand—for she has been soul-bonded to it. And that will render her useful to me. Or should it kill her, she may well be damned to *my* realm, for the breaking of the oaths she swore. So you see, no matter the outcome, I win—and *I* am in no danger, for only my own magics could touch me in any way."

"I . . . see," the priest replied, staring at the bloody combat before them, mesmerized by the sight.

Tarma realized that they were once again playing right into the demon's hands. For if Kethry killed the one wearing her form, she would damn herself irrevocably, once by committing a kind of suicide, and twice by breaking the geas and the vow her bond with Need had set upon her—never to raise her hand against a woman—three times by breaking her oath to her *she'enedra*.

And by such a betrayal she would probably die, for surely Thalhkarsh had warded his creature against magics. Or Need would blast her into death or mindlessness. Should she die, she could damn herself forever to Thalhkarsh's particular corner of the Abyssal Plane, putting herself eternally in his power. It was a good bet he had planned that she must slay the bandit by magic, since Need would not serve against a woman—and certainly he had woven a spell that would backlash all her unleashed power on the caster. Kethry would be worse than dead—for she would be his for the rest of time, to wreak revenge on until even he should grow weary of it.

Unless Tarma could stop her before she committed such self-damnation. And with time running out, there was only one way to save her.

With an aching heart she cried out in her mind to Warrl, and Warrl responded with the lightning-fast reactions of the *kyree* kind, born in magic and bred of it.

He leapt upon the unsuspecting Kethry from the rear, and with one crunch of his jaws, broke her neck and collapsed her windpipe.

Both Kethry and the bandit collapsed—

Tarma scrambled after the discarded mage-blade, conscious now only of a dim urge to keep Kethry's treasured weapon out of profane hands, and to use the thing against the creature that had forced her to kill the only human she cared for. Need had hurt the demon before—

But she had forgotten one thing.

She wasn't a mage, so Need's other gift came into play; the gift that protected a woman *warrior* from magic, no matter how powerful. No magic not cast

291

with the consent of the bearer could survive Need entering its field.

The spell binding Tarma was broken, and she found herself in a body that had regained its normal proportions.

This was just such a moment that the priest had been praying for. The spell-energy binding Kethry into Lastel's body was released explosively with the death-blow. The priest took full control of that energy, and snatched her spirit before death had truly occurred. Using the potent energies released, he sent Lastel's spirit and Kethry's back to their proper containers.

There were still other energies being released; those binding Lastel's form into a woman's shape, and those altering Tarma. Quicker than thought the priest gained hold of those as well. With half of his attention he erected a shield over the swordswoman and her partner; with the other he sent those demon-born magics hurtling back to their caster.

Kethry had been stunned by Warrl's apparent treachery; had actually felt herself dying—

—and now suddenly found herself very much alive, and back in her proper body. She sat up, blinking in surprise.

Beside her on the marble floor was a dead man, wearing the garments she herself had worn as Lastel. Warrl stood over him, growling, every hair on end. But her mage-sense for energy told her that the tale had not yet seen its end. As if to confirm this, a howl of anguish rose behind her

"Noooooooooooo. . . ."

The voice began a brazen bass, and spiraled up to a fragile soprano.

Kethry twisted around, staring in astonishment. Behind her was Thalhkarsh—

A demon no longer. A *male* no longer. Instead, from out of the amethystine eyes of the delicate mortal creature he had mockingly called his toy stared Thalhkarsh's hellspawn spirit—dumbfounded, glassy-eyed with shock, hardly able to comprehend what had happened to him. Powerless now—and as female and fragile as either of the two he had thought to take revenge upon—and a great deal more helpless.

"This—cannot—be—" she whispered, staring at her thin hands. "I cannot have failed—"

"My poor friend."

The little priest, whom Kethry had overlooked in the fight, having eyes only for the demon, his servants, and Lastel, reached for one of the demon's hands with true and courageous sympathy.

"I fear you have worked to wreak only your own downfall—as I warned you would happen."

"No—"

"And you have wrought far too well, I fear—for if I read this spell correctly, it was meant to be permanent unto death. And as a demon, except that you be slain by a specific blade, you cannot die. Am I not correct?"

The demon's only response was a whimper, as she sank into a heap of loose limbs among the cushions of what once had been her throne, her eyes fogging as she retreated from the reality she herself had unwittingly created.

Tarma let her long legs fold under her and sat where she had stood, trembling from head to toe, saying nothing at all, a look of glazed pain in her eyes.

Kethry dragged herself to Tarma's side, and sat down with a thump.

"Now what?" Tarma asked in a voice dulled by emotional and physical exhaustion, rubbing her eyes with one hand. "*Now* what are we going to do with him?"

"I—I don't know."

"I shall take charge of her," the priest said, "She is in no state to be a threat to us, and we can easily keep her in a place from which she shall find escape impossible until she has a true change of heart. My child," he addressed himself to Tarma, concern in his eyes, "what is amiss?"

"My bond—it's gone—" she looked up at the priest's round, anxious face, and the look in her eyes was of one completely lost.

"Would you fetch my fellows from the temple?" he asked Kethry. "*That* one is locked within herself, but I may have need of them."

"Gladly," Kethry replied, "but can you help *her*?"

"I will know better when you return."

She ran—or tried to—to fetch the little priest's fellow devotees. She all but forced herself past a skeptical novice left to guard the door by night; the noise she made when she finally was driven to lose her temper and shout at him brought the High Prelate of Anathei to the door himself. He was more than half asleep, wrapped in a blanket, but he came awake soon enough when she'd begun to relate the night's adventures. He snapped out a series of orders that were obeyed with such prompt alacrity that Kethry's suspicions as to their friend's true rankings were confirmed long before three novices brought her his robes—those of an arch-priest—and half the members of the order, new-roused from their beds.

Though simple, hardly more ornate than what he had worn to the inn, the robes radiated power that Kethry could feel even without invoking mage-senses.

A half-dozen other members of his order scurried away from the convocation at the cloister door and came back wearing ceremonial garments and carrying various arcane implements. Kethry led the procession of cowled, laden priest-mages through the predawn streets at a fast trot. The night-watch took one look at the parade and respectfully stepped aside, not even bothering with hailing them.

When she got them as far as the open door of the temple, her own strength gave out, and she stopped to rest, half-collapsed against the smiling image of the rain-god. By the time she reached the inner sanctum, they had the situation well in hand. The bodies had been carried off somewhere, the obscene carvings shrouded, a good deal of the blood cleaned up, and—most importantly—Thalhkarsh placed under such tight arcane bindings that not even a demigod could have escaped.

"I believe I can restore what was lost to your friend," the priest said when Kethry finally gathered up enough courage to approach him. "But I shall need the assistance of both yourself and the *kyree*."

"Certainly, anything—but why? It will help if I know what I'm supposed to be doing."

"You are familiar with her goddess, and as Shin'a'in adopted, She shall hear you where she might not hear me. You might think of yourself as the arrow, and myself as the bow. I can lend your wish the power to reach the Star-Eyed, but only *you* of all of us know Her well enough to pick Her aspect from all the other aspects of the Lady."

"Logical—what do I do? Warrl says—'whatever you want he'll do'—"

"Just try to tell her Warrior that the bond has been broken and needs to be restored—or Tarma may well—"

"Die. Or go mad, which is the same thing for a Shin'a'in."

Kethry knelt at the priest's feet on the cold marble of the desecrated temple floor, Warrl at her side. Tarma remained where she was, sunk in misery and loss so deep that she was as lost to the world around her as Thalhkarsh was.

Kethry concentrated with all her soul as the priest murmured three words and placed his hand on her head and Tarma's in blessing.

Please Lady—please hear me, she thought in despair, watching Tarma's dead eyes. *I've—I've been less understanding than I could have been. I forgot— because I wanted to—that I'm all the Clan she has left.*

295

I only thought of the freedom I thought I was losing. I don't know You, but maybe You know me—

There was no answer, and Kethry shut her eyes in mental agony. *Please, hear us! Even if You don't give a damn about us,* she pledged herself to You—

Foolish child.

The voice in her mind startled her; it was more like music than a voice.

I am nothing but another face of your own Lady Windborn—how could I not know you? Both of you have been wrong—but you have wrought your own punishment. Now forgive yourselves as you forgive each other—and truly be the two-made-one—

Kethry nearly fainted at the rush of pure power that passed through her; when it ebbed, she steadied herself and glanced up in surprise.

The little priest was just removing his hand from Tarma's bowed head; his brow was damp with sweat, but relief showed in the smiling line of his mouth. As Tarma looked up, Kethry saw her expression change from one of pathetic bereavement to the utter relief of one who has regained something thought gone forevermore.

A heavy burden of fear passed from Kethry's heart at the change. She closed her eyes and breathed her own prayer of thanks.

So profound was her relief that it was several moments before she realized Tarma was speaking to the priest.

"I don't know how to—"

"Then don't thank me," he interrupted. "I simply re-opened what the demon had closed; my pleasure and my duty. Just as tending to the demon as she is now is my duty."

"You're certain you people can keep him—or should I say her?—from any more trouble?" she asked doubtfully of her erstwhile debating partner as Kethry shook off her weariness and looked up at them. To the sorceress' profound gratitude, Tarma looked to be most of the way back to normal—a rapid recovery, but Kethry was used to rapid recov-

296

eries from the Shin'a'in. The face she turned to Kethry was calm and sane once again, with a hint of her old sense of humor. She reached out a hand, and Tarma caught it and squeezed it once, without taking her attention from the priest.

"Sworn One, we are placing every safeguard known to mortal man upon her and the place where we shall keep her," the little priest said soberly. "The being Thalhkarsh shall have no opportunity for escape. Her only chance will be to truly *change*, for the spells we shall use will not hold against an angelic spirit, only one of evil intent. Truly you have given us the opportunity we have long dreamed of."

"Well," Tarma actually grinned, though it was weakly. "After all, it isn't every day someone can present you with a captive demon to preach to. Not to put too fine a point on it, we're giving you folk a chance to prove yourselves." She managed a ghost of a chuckle. "Though I'll admit I had no notion you were capable of restraining demons so handily."

"As you yourself pointed out, Sworn One, when one goes to preach to demons, the preacher had best be either agile or a very fine magician." The balding priest's brown eyes vanished in smile wrinkles. "And as your partner has rightly told me, while Thalhkarsh seems helpless *now*, there is no guarantee that she will remain so. We prefer to take no chance. As you say, this is our unlooked-for opportunity to prove the truth of our way to the entire world, and as such, we are grateful to you beyond telling."

With that, the little priest bowed to both of them, and his train of underlings brought the once-demon to her feet, bound by spells that at the moment were scarcely needed. She was numbly submissive, and they guided her out the way they had come, bound for their own temple.

Kethry got to her feet and silently held out her hand to Tarma, who took it once again with no sign of resentment, and pulled herself to her feet by it.

They left the scene of slaughter without a backward glance, moving as quickly as their aching bodies would allow, eager to get out into the clean air.

"Warrior's Oath—how long have we been in there?" Tarma exclaimed on seeing the thin sliver of moon and the positions of the stars.

"About twenty-four candlemarks. It's tomorrow morning. Is—*that's* not your sword, is it?" Kethry, lagging a little behind, saw that the shape strapped to Tarma's back was all wrong.

" 'No disaster without some benefit,' *she'enedra,*" Tarma lifted a hand to caress the unfamiliar hilt. "I've never in my life had a weapon like this one. There's no magic to it beyond exquisite balance, fantastic design, and the finest steel I've ever seen, but it is without a doubt the best blade I've ever used. It acted like part of my arm—and you're going to have to cut off that arm to get it away from me!"

Briefly alarmed by her vehemence, Kethry stretched weary mage-senses one more time, fearing to find that the blade was some kind of ensorcelled trap, or bore a curse.

She found nothing, and sighed with relief. Tarma was right, there was no hint of magic about the blade, and her partner's reaction was nothing more than that of any warrior who has just discovered her ideal dreamed-of weapon.

They limped painfully back to their inn with Warrl trailing behind as guard against night-thugs, stopping now and then to rest against a handy wall or building. The night-watch recognized Kethry and waved them on. The cool, clean air was heavenly after the incense and perfume-laden choke of the temple. When they finally reached their inn, they used the latchstring on their window to let themselves back inside and felt their way into their room with only the banked embers of the hearth-fire for light. Kethry expended a last bit of mage-power and lit a candle, while Tarma dropped her weapons wearily. Beds had never looked so inviting before.

And yet, neither was quite ready to sleep.

"This time we've really done it, haven't we?" Tarma ventured, easing her "borrowed" boots off her feet and pitching them out the open window for whoever should find them in the morning to carry away. She stripped as quickly as her cuts and bruises would permit, and the clothing followed the boots as the Shin'a'in grimaced in distaste; Kethry handed her clean breeches and an undertunic from her pack and Tarma eased herself into them with a sigh and numerous winces.

"You mean, we've locked him up for good? I think so; at least insofar as I can ever be sure of anything. And we aren't going to make the mistake of forgetting about him again."

"Lady Bright, not bloody likely!" Tarma shuddered. "We'll be getting messages from the Temple every two months, like clockwork; that was part of the agreement I made with little Nemor. Huh, think of him as archpriest—seems logical now, but he sure doesn't look the part."

"Until he puts on the authority. I could almost feel sorry for old Thalhkarsh. I can't imagine a worse punishment for a demon than to have sweetness-and-light preached at him for as long as he lives—which might well be forever."

"And besides—" Tarma smiled, getting up with a muffled groan and another grimace, and walking over to the window. She leaned out, letting the breeze lift her hair and cool her face. "Who knows? They might succeed in redeeming him. . . ."

"Tarma—all this—we both nearly died. I would have died with a broken promise to you on my soul."

Kethry paused for a long moment, so long that Tarma was afraid she wasn't going to finish what she had begun to say.

She turned from looking out the window to regard her partner soberly, knowing that Kethry had something troubling her gravely. Even Warrl looked up from where he lay on Tarma's bed, ears pricked and eyes unfathomable. Finally Kethry sighed and continued.

"I guess what I want to ask you is this. Do you *want* me—us—to stop this wandering? To go back to the Plains? After all, it's me that's been keeping us on the road, not you. I—haven't found any man I'd care to spend more than a night or two with, but that really doesn't matter to my promise. It doesn't take liking to get children. Oh, hell, there's always Justin and Ikan, I *do* like them well enough to share a bed with them for a bit. And once we had some children, I could keep myself in practice easily enough. I could establish a White Winds school even without the cash—I'm getting close enough to Adept to do that now. I'd rather have better circumstances to do that than we have right now, but I could scrape along. We certainly have the reputation now to attract good pupils."

Tarma turned back to gaze up at the waning moon, troubled. It was true that the most important thing in the world to *her* was the re-founding of her slaughtered Clan—and they *had* nearly died without being any closer to that goal.

There were times when she longed for the tents of her people and the open Plains with all her soul. And there were other negatives to this life they were leading. There was no guarantee something like this couldn't happen again. Being gang-raped, or so she suspected, had been the least of the unspeakable things she'd suffered unaware in Thalhkarsh's hands.

Far worse was the absence of the Star-Eyed's presence in her soul when she'd returned to herself. And when her goddess had not returned to her with Thalhkarsh's transformation, she'd been afraid for a moment that the Warrior would not take her back with her celibacy violated.

That had turned out to be a foolish fear, as her

priest-friend had proved to her. No sooner had he cleansed her of the last of Thalhkarsh's magic-bindings, then she felt the Warrior's cool and supportive presence once again in her heart; the asexual psychic armor of the Sword Sworn closed around her again, and she could regard the whole experience as something to learn and benefit from. She was heart-whole and healed again—in spirit if not in body.

Still, none of this would have happened if they'd returned to the Plains; in the very home of the Goddess of the Four Winds the demon would have been powerless, no matter what he had claimed; the bandit would never have made his way past the Outer Clans. And—Warrior's Oath, how Tarma longed to see the Tale'sedrin banner flying above a full encampment, with bright-faced children within and fat herds without. Kethry's wandering feet had nearly caused their deaths this time, and Tale'sedrin had nearly died with them. And her Clan, as for any Shin'a'in, was the most important thing in Tarma's life.

But no, it *wasn't* the most important thing, not anymore. Not if Kethry was going to be made a captive to see that dream achieved. A willing captive she would be, perhaps, but still a captive.

Kethry had been right—she *had* been stifling her friend, and with the best of intentions. She had been putting invisible hobbles on her, or trying to.

Her Shin'a'in soul rebelled at the notion—"You do not hobble your hound, your horse, your hawk, your lover, or your *she'enedren,*" went the saying, "love must live free." A prisoner was a prisoner, no matter how willingly the bonds were taken. And how truly Shin'a'in could Kethry be, bound? And if she were not Shin'a'in in her heart, how could her children follow the Clan-ways with whole spirits?

And yet—and yet—there remained Kethry's oath, and her dream. If Kethry died . . .

She closed her eyes and emptied her heart, and hoped for an answer.

And miraculously, one came.

A tiny breath of chill wind wafted out of the north, and coiled around her body, enclosing her in silence. And in that silence, an ageless voice spoke deep in her soul.

What is your Clan but your sister? Trust in her as your left-hand blade, as she trusts in you, and you shall keep each other safe.

Tarma's heart lifted and she turned back to face her partner with a genuine smile.

"What, and turn you into 'another Shin'a'in brood mare'? Come now, *she'enedra*, we treat our stock better than that! A warsteed mates when *she* is ready, and not before. Surely you don't reckon yourself as less than Hellsbane!" Tarma's smile turned wicked. "Or should I start catching handsome young men and parading them before you to tempt your appetite. . . ?"

Kethry laughed with mingled chagrin and relief, blushing hotly.

"Perhaps I ought to begin a collection, hmm? That's what we do for our warsteeds, you know, present them with a whole line of stallions until one catches their fancy. Shall I start a picket line for you? Or would you rather I acquired a house of pleasure and stocked the rooms so that you could try their paces at your leisure before choosing?"

Kethry rolled up into the covers to hide her blushes, still laughing.

Tarma joined the laughter, and limped back to her own bed, blowing out their candle and falling into the eiderdowns to find a dreamless and healing sleep.

For there *were* going to be tomorrows, she was sure of that now—and they'd better be in shape to be ready for them.

DAW

A note from the publisher concerning:

QUEEN'S OWN

An organization of readers and fans of the works of Mercedes Lackey is now being formed. Presently called "Queen's Own," the new Mercedes Lackey appreciation society is loosely structured and has no formal dues.

"Queen's Own" functions as an information center about Mercedes Lackey's books and music, and provides a network of pen friends for those who wish to share their enjoyment of her work.

For more information, please send a self-addressed stamped envelope to:

"Queen's Own"
P.O. Box 43143
Upper Montclair, NJ 07043

(This notice is inserted gratis as a service to readers. DAW Books is in no way connected with this organization professionally or commercially.)

DAW

A New Superstar in the DAW Firmament!

Mercedes Lackey

THE VALDEMAR TRILOGY

☐ **ARROWS OF THE QUEEN: Book 1**   (UE2189—$2.95)

Growing up in a repressive, puritanical environment, young Talia dreams of serving as a Herald—one of the Queen's elite special guard, who act as lawgivers, peacekeepers, and even warleaders. Chosen by one of the mysterious and powerful Companions, Talia is awakened to her own unique mental powers and magical abilities, and assumes a vital role in the attempt to save the kindgom from disaster.

☐ **ARROW'S FLIGHT: Book 2**   (UE2222—$3.50)

Talia, a full Herald at last, must face new and greater challenges as she rides forth on Patrol, dispensing Herald's Justice throughout the land. But in this realm, beset by dangerous unrest, enforcing her rulings will require all the courage and skill Talia can command—for if she misuses her special powers, both she and Valdemar will pay the price!

☐ **ARROW'S FALL: Book 3**   (UE2255—$3.50)

As Talia, the Queen's own Herald, undertakes a dangerous diplomatic mission, she is plunged into a sorcerous trap . . . a trap which may keep her from ever warning Valdemar and the Queen of the marching armies and sorcerous destruction which are even now reaching out to engulf them.